PA

Eric Van Lustbader
Second Skin, The Kai
ing Nicholas Linnea
Dark Homecoming. He graduated from Columbia
University in 1969, spent fifteen years in the music
industry and has also been a teacher. He lives with
his wife in Southampton, New York.

Dark Homecoming

Nicholas Linnear novels

The Ninja
The Miko
White Ninja
The Kaisho
Floating City
Second Skin

China Maroc novels

Jian
Shan
Black Blade
Angel Eyes
French Kiss
Black Heart
Sirens
Zero

The Sunset Warrior cycle

The Sunset Warrior
Shallows of Night
Dai-San
Beneath an Opal Moon
Dragons on the Sea of Night

PALE SAINT

Eric Van Lustbader

HarperCollins*Publishers*

HarperCollins*Publishers*
77–85 Fulham Palace Road,
Hammersmith, London W6 8JB

www.fireandwater.com

This paperback edition 1999
1 3 5 7 9 8 6 4 2

First published in Great Britain by
HarperCollins*Publishers* 1999

ISBN 0 00 649954 6

Typeset in Meridien by
Palimpsest Book Production Limited,
Polmont, Stirlingshire

Printed and bound in Great Britain by
Clays Ltd, St Ives plc

This is dedicated to the one I love:
My wife, Victoria

ACKNOWLEDGMENTS

My sincere thanks and deepest appreciation to the following, who donated their time, ideas, and encouragement:

Dr Phyllis DellaLatta
Dr Bob Prosser
Dr Sonny Singh
Dr Alan Packer
at the Columbia-Presbyterian Hospital in-vitro and molecular biology labs for their invaluable help.

Manny Ovalle, United States Secret Service

Jim Perez, FBI
Rex Tomb, FBI
Neal Schiff, FBI
Steve Mardigian, FBI

Ken Dorff, for items Arabic

I am indebted to the book *Enter the Zone* by Barry Sears, Ph.D. for information on eicosanoids. However, any extrapolations concerning the interrelation of eicosanoids, serotonin and shamanistic practices are purely the invention of the author.

And, of course, to the extraordinary personal history *Seven Pillars of Wisdom* by T.E. Lawrence, a constant fount of inspiration.

AUTHOR'S NOTE

While this is a work of fiction, the medical procedures on cloning depicted herein are entirely accurate. Even the as yet theoretical protocol for rapid aging is extrapolated from the most recent science speculation.

*As for man, his days
are as grass; as a flower
of the field, so he flourisheth*

Psalms 103:15

PALE SAINT

Book One

BEAST

October 1 – October 17

This is his first punishment,
that by the verdict of his
own heart no guilty man
is acquitted.

JUVENAL

ONE

On the morning he was called to prosecute the country's most notorious serial killer Robert Austin was thinking of baseball. It was Friday, October 1 and the only thing that had been on his mind was taking his fifteen-year-old daughter, Sara, to the Yankees game tomorrow afternoon. The Orioles were in town for the AL Championship Series, and Andy Pettitte was pitching. Through one of his thousand-dollar-an-hour attorney acquaintances on Park Ave. Austin had gotten seats close enough so Sara could study the master hurler's form. Under Austin's tutelage, she was developing a better arm than most of the boys her age, and an even better eye. Since she had joined the NYC Inter-Borough League, he had watched her blossom as she had absorbed the tricks he had learned in his youth. Now, partly because of her expertise, her team was going to be playing for the city championship on October 21.

The call came at 5 a.m. Austin rose out of a shallow, restless sleep, grabbed the cell phone off the night table, rolled out of bed, and padded out of the darkened bedroom all without waking his wife, Cassandra.

'Bobby,' Jonathan Christopher said in Austin's ear, 'hold onto your hat, I've got a hot one for you.'

Austin could hear the barely suppressed excitement in his friend's voice. In the tiny Pullman kitchen of the TriBeCa apartment, he woke the computer terminal out of Sleep mode, accessed the icon for the automatic coffee maker that Cassandra had filled the night before. The timer had been set for 7.30 a.m., the time they usually got up, and he switched it to Manual. Cassandra, the computer nut, had automated most of the rooms.

'I don't wear a hat, and you always have a hot one for me,' he said into the phone. At the District Attorney's office Austin drew all the bloody meat – the most thorny cases, the ones on which they needed wins most badly. That was because Christopher requested him. Christopher was a Homicide lieutenant whose successes at tracking down serial killers and multiple-victim rapists had earned him a coveted relationship with the D.A. as well as with most of the NYPD. Christopher could call his shots with the D.A.'s staff, and he could raid the resources of any precinct to gather his team together. 'The D.A. must've gained fifty pounds since I came on board. All he does is go out to three-course lunches with politicos.'

'When he runs for mayor I'll bet he takes you with him,' Christopher laughed. He was in his late thirties, and yet when he spoke Austin at once felt face to face with the weight of experience. He did nothing but work. It seemed his lone salvation. 'You'd eat that crap up.'

'Like hell I would.'

'Bullshit. I see how you handle the High-Profiles I give you. You're the original Golden Boy.'

'Conviction's the name of the game.' The smell of coffee filled the small kitchen, and Austin reached for his favorite mug, the one that Sara had given him when she was seven. It had a big red heart and 'Daddy' printed on it. 'Jon, what's up? You've given me three cases over the last six months or so, but I know you. You've been into something secretive all this time. This has got to be it, right?'

'You bet.' Christopher did everything but whoop in delight. 'Your new case is cooling his heels in Chinatown. A blue-and-white should be downstairs in ten.'

Austin, gulping his coffee, almost burned his tongue. 'Official transport. That's something I don't get every day. *Now* you've got my attention.'

'God*damn*, Bobby, it's happened.' Christopher's voice finally exploded with pent-up excitement. 'We finally caught the Pale Saint.'

'Good Christ!' Austin almost dropped his mug, as he felt a quick grab of queasy excitement in his gut. '*That's* what you've been working on?'

'Yep. It gets better. We got a lock; caught him at the murder scene, over at Tompkins Square, covered in the victim's blood. Only thing missing is the murder weapon, but we'll find that eventually.'

Even at this late date, after twenty-one victims, no one knew the Pale Saint's motives or even his weapon of choice. Something very sharp and long. Like a straight-razor, but perhaps not that at all because it punctured flesh as well as slashed it. But an old-fashioned weapon, surely, when compared to guns and machine pistols.

Whatever else remained unknown about him, this much was clear: the Pale Saint liked to get up-close and personal with his victims, which had led to speculation that he might be a Special Forces vet. But since he left virtually no forensic evidence at the crime scenes, his identity had remained a complete mystery even to the battery of forensic psychologists who'd reportedly been called in to pore over the crime-scene photos like ancient seers seeking portents in the entrails of sacrificial goats. The Republic was being disfigured but no one knew why.

Now they had him.

Austin had little time for such reflection. His keen sense of anticipation and horror was mixed with regret and a guilt familiar as an old sweater. 'Oh, shit.'

'What the hell does that mean? I hand you the case of the decade – hell, no, probably of the century, and that's what you say, Oh shit?'

'I had plans to take Sara to the playoffs.'

'The Pettitte game, huh?' They knew each other so well they often spoke in the peculiar shorthand of couples. 'Tough.'

'You're telling me.' Austin gulped down more coffee. 'I haven't seen my daughter for an hour straight in I don't know how long.'

'Bobby, I'm not gonna twist your arm. Should I throw this back in the D.A.'s lap? He'll probably give the case to Jonas.'

'That bonehead? He'll screw it up for you for sure.'

'That's why I need you.' Christopher's voice came through loud and clear. 'Finished your coffee yet?'

Austin put the mug down on the counter just as Cassandra walked in. 'I'll just be a couple of minutes. Tell the uniforms to stay right where they are.'

'Sure.' Christopher laughed.

'But how come Chinatown? I'd assume a perp of this magnitude would be booked at Manhattan South.'

'We had to find a place to stash the Pale Saint far away from the media until the Commish gets his act together for the news conference.' The tone of Christopher's voice changed. 'Listen, Bobby, don't be pissed. Long after the hollering from this case dies down, Sara'll be there, throwing that wicked spitball you taught her.'

'What are you talking about? A spitter's illegal. She throws a split-fingered forkball, and you know it.'

'Sure, sure,' Christopher said. 'See you in Chinatown.'

'Hey,' Austin shouted into the phone, 'congratulations, buddy!'

Austin broke the connection and turned around.

'Tell me that wasn't Christopher.' Cassandra had taken up his mug and was sipping the hot coffee. No injudicious gulps for her.

Austin watched her calmly regarding him. 'I haven't seen you all week. What happened to "Hi, honey, how are you"?' Unlike him, Cassandra had the unnerving quality of being fully awake the moment she opened her eyes.

She gave him a mock-pout of regret and kissed him on the lips. 'Mmm. I did this last night when I got home. Pity you didn't respond.'

'I didn't get in until close to midnight. Then I turned off the light just to rest my eyes.'

'You were dead to the world.'

'A serious bout of court overload.'

Sometime this year, she'd cropped her blond hair short enough so she never needed to style it. Long and lean as a horsewoman, she had the bold face of an explorer, the cool, calculating eyes of the risk-taker. There was something deeply erotic in the way she moved her body without any trace of self-consciousness. As in the tomboy he had loved in his youth, her sexuality swam mysteriously beneath the surface, and was all the more desirable for that.

'I blame Christopher.'

'I thought we weren't going to get into that again.'

Cassandra burst into a smile. 'Well, hell, Bobby, I wanted to celebrate. Dillard and I finally did it! We've completed a successful trans-genic protocol.' She put the mug down and wrapped her arms around him. She smelled of citrus and sleep. 'We took the gene we mapped from the pineal gland and put it into a lab rat zygote. You know what a zygote is.'

'A non-divided fertilized egg. I could recite the definition in my sleep.'

'From embryo to fetus to new-born Minnie's growth rate is astonishing.'

'Minnie?'

'That's what I named the female lab rat. Minnie. And the best part is we will actually be able to control the growth rate by injections of Tetracycline. This proves my theory is right on the money. The pineal is the primary active regulator of aging!'

'Maybe Dr Dork finds this scientific gobbledygook romantic, Cass, but I don't.' It was times like this he wished Cassandra wasn't an M.D.-Ph.D. in molecular biology, genetics and embryology.

'What's that supposed to mean? And I wish you wouldn't call him that.'

'It means that he gets to spend long hours mooning over you while you two are at the lab.'

'Hutton is harmless. He's just protective of me, that's all.' She hugged Austin tightly to her and looked at him candidly. 'Don't be jealous, honey. These past few weeks have been a real bitch at the lab. But can't you be even a little happy for me? No? Then I'll be happy for the both of us.' She reached down between his legs. 'How about I work this gland –'

Austin pulled away from her. 'God, Cass, your timing's way off.' He was already hurrying down the hall.

'I know that tone of voice.' Cassandra followed him doggedly into the bedroom. The same relentless quality that made her such a great researcher could be infuriating at home. 'What about your plans for tomorrow?'

'I won't know for sure till later.'

'Oh, Bobby, we both know what that means. Your date with Sara's out.'

He stripped off the boxer shorts he slept in. 'You take her to the game then. She shouldn't miss Pettitte pitch.'

Cassandra groaned. 'I wish I could. Gerry scheduled me to be interviewed on Dean Koenig's cable TV show.' Gerry Costas was the head of the Vertex Institute – the money people who had funded the lab.

'That's easily taken care of. Get Dr Dork to do it. He and Costas are like two peas in a pod. Didn't they both graduate from Yale or something?'

'Harvard.'

'Upper crust is upper crust, my dear,' Austin cracked with a stiff upper lip.

'And I wish you wouldn't call him Dr Dork. His name's Dillard. Anyway, he's my colleague but I'm the head of the lab. I can't miss this interview, Bobby. It would look bad for Vertex. Dean Koenig is trying to close us down again, and this time he just might succeed. He's managed to get the backing of the Christian Convocation. Koenig and his goddamn self-righteous ethics.'

'It's just old-fashioned fire and brimstone.'

'I know, but he's an expert at trading on ignorance and fear, and in today's world there's so much to be frightened of. I can't let him damage us. Helix Technologies, our major competitor, is looking for

7

any advantage over us. They'd snatch away our clients in a heartbeat.' She took a breath. 'Just this once tell Christopher no. Please.'

'I don't like this any better than you do, but I can't.' He padded into the bathroom with Cassandra at his heels. 'This case is so high-profile I've got to take it. I owe it to Jon.'

'And what do you owe to our daughter?' Her face had gotten hard and steely. It was the formidable expression she used when she was forced to defend her controversial theories on DNA replication. 'It's bad enough we don't see each other much, but she – dammit, Bobby.'

With his hand on the shower taps, he turned around. 'Cass, you don't understand. They've caught the Pale Saint, and Jon has asked me to prosecute him. The bastard's a born killer. How can I say no?'

If he was expecting her to relent, he was wrong. 'I couldn't care less about the Pale Saint. Of course I'm grateful he's in custody, but he's not part of our world, thank God. And, by the way, whatever kind of monster the Pale Saint is he's not a "born killer".'

Hot water sent steam curling like a dragon's tongue upward toward the white enamel ceiling. 'Now I have to hear about Dr Dork's pet theories –'

'I happen to agree with Hutton on this. And I'm telling you for your own good. Bobby, you sound just plain ignorant when you say things like that. Lots of traits are hereditary – genetic predispositions for disease – your high blood pressure, for instance, or cancer and diabetes, obesity and alcoholism. In the believe-it-or-not category, there's even documented medical evidence that patients with transplanted livers or hearts begin to have the same tastes and cravings as their donors. But homicidal mania is definitely *not* an inherited trait. Human beings are born with certain personalities, that's clear enough. Hutton has spent a decade researching the subject; he's staked his entire professional reputation on the fact that environment, nurturing or the lack of it – the experiences of childhood – are the determining factors when it comes to extreme aberrations like homicidal mania.'

'But you two *wunderkinds* haven't proven it yet, have you?' Of course he knew they hadn't. 'It's still nothing more than a theory that you can't –'

'I refuse to get into a debate of trait theory when we could be making love,' Cassandra said.

'Sorry. I can't do either.'

'If Christopher chooses to work twenty-four hours a day because his personal life's a shambles, let him. But don't let him drag you into it.'

'Cass, that's unfair.'

'I don't care. Sara is counting on you. Dammit, Bobby, you made her and me a promise I expect you to keep. As it is, you spend more time with Christopher than you do with her – or me.'

'Give me a break, will you? You're the one who's playing spin the pipette with Dr Dork.'

'Bobby, stop it right now. I may spend lab time with Hutton but –'

He stepped into the shower and began to soap up but she wouldn't let him go. Holding onto the shower curtain, she leaned in. A fine spray coated her face, individual droplets standing out like tears on her lashes.

'I thought we had worked all this out when I was offered the grant. The opportunity of creating the first full-fledged DNA bioscience lab was just too good to pass up. We both decided while I got the lab up and running you'd spend time with Sara, remember?'

Austin rinsed off. 'Okay, but that was eighteen months ago, and frankly, I don't see any letup in your schedule.'

'I've told you, it's the research. And now that we've got our breakthrough we're that much closer to a solution for aging. That'll silence Koenig and make believers of everybody else. We're so close now I can almost feel it here in my hand –'

Austin stepped out of the shower and began to towel off. 'Honey, listen to yourself.'

'And look at you, running off at five in the morning to do Jon Christopher's bidding.'

'You make him sound like Simon Legree. It's not like that.' He threw the towel aside and padded back into the bedroom to dress.

'Isn't it? Every time he calls you go running off. Bobby, we can't go on like this. If we do, what's going to happen to Sara? She'll have no parents at all.'

Austin climbed into undershorts and trousers, went hunting for a clean shirt. 'Honey, let's just drop it, okay?' He told himself that he should have known better than to verbally mix it up with his wife at five thirty in the morning. He never had a prayer. He grabbed his tweed overcoat and battered attache case. 'This is the last time I disappoint her, I promise. I'll tell Jon he's got to cut me some serious slack the minute I finish this case.' He put his free arm around her as she walked him down the hall. 'Okay?'

Cassandra's gray eyes searched his face. 'It'll be your job to tell Sara she won't be going to the game.'

'The minute I get home.' Austin's mind was already on the first questions he was going to ask the Pale Saint. 'I'll think of something to soften the blow.'

'You'd better,' she said as she headed off toward the kitchen. 'By the way, you forgot to shave.'

He rubbed his stubbly jaw and groaned. He had no time now to shave. On his way out, he opened Sara's door a crack. She lay on her side, at the far end of her pale blue room. A night light in the form of a skull she'd gotten for Halloween delivered a faint halo about her head. Her breathing was slow and even. Pale hair like her mother's fanned out over the pillow like spun gold, but her dark eyes, now closed, were his.

Her right arm was curled in front of her face, the fingers as open and innocent as the expression on her face. She was in between those awkward ages when children's features seemed oversized and mismatched. She was so beautiful. To Austin, she looked just like the angel his mother had described from a fairy tale when he was a young boy.

For a long moment, he watched his daughter in sleep and wondered if there was anything in the world more precious than a child.

The first rays of sunlight on this glorious, perfect morning in October struck the tops of the World Trade Center towers as the squad car hurtled toward Chinatown. The rest of the buildings was still in shadow, the dark masses of glass pulling the eye inevitably downward to the ginkgo and plane trees. In less than an hour the autumn leaves would shine like burnished copper. By that time, Austin would have faced the unknown: the man known only as the Pale Saint.

This was a case to end all cases. As Christopher had said, it would make his career. He'd be quite famous. Not that being famous meant a damn to him. He was well-known and respected in his profession, and that was quite enough recognition for him. After all he hadn't become a lawyer for fame or fortune. Far from it. Austin fervently believed that finding one's place in the world was just about the only thing that really mattered. And Austin was sure of his place in the world, his role in the grand scheme of things. If he hadn't been, he'd never have been able to sleep at night.

Tires squealed as the squad car turned onto East Broadway. Over the years, both Italian and Jewish immigrants had given way to inexorable change as the Chinese pushed out the original borders of their ghetto.

The precinct was in a section of East Broadway that smelled like Kowloon; the strong and unmistakable smells of ginger and star anise crept out from behind steel-shuttered storefronts. The building was so decrepit it had been scheduled for demolition for years. The only reason it was still standing was the city's lack of money. But for this morning, at least, it had become the most important structure in the entire NYPD system.

As Austin trotted up the steps he squinted in the dimness at the pair of uniforms lurking in the shadows on either side of the doorway. The old glass light globes, shattered by street punks, had never been replaced. He saw Reuven Esquival, Christopher's behavioral psych.

'We expected you a half-hour ago.'

'You must've been here half the night,' Austin said.

'All of it, more like.'

'Shit.'

Esquival shrugged. 'Yeah, well, on the front lines you learn to live without sleep.'

'Tell me about it.'

Austin opened the precinct door and went inside. The interior was swampy with the old odors of Big Macs, sweat and fear. Overhead, bare bulbs disfigured the darkness. A balding plainclothes detective nodded to Austin and signaled for him to follow. His name, Walter Kowalchuck, appeared on a plastic ID tag clipped to his lapel.

'You ID this joker yet?'

Kowalchuck grunted. 'None on his person; no cooperation from the perp whatsoever. What else is new? All we can say for sure is he's a white man in his early thirties. We're running his prints now.'

That seemed to end the terse exchange.

The near-deserted halls echoed eerily. The endless rows of steel file cabinets seemed emblematic of the failed aspirations of the long parade of perps who had made the same trip down this hall to the interrogation rooms. Now the Pale Saint had joined that parade.

Their shoe soles abraded the old wood and linoleum floor with unpleasant sounds that reminded Austin of the descriptions he'd read of the Pale Saint's handiwork. Truly, it was the stuff of nightmares. Nevertheless, the reports were impossible to put down. Like passing a multi-car wreck on the Long Island Expressway. You slowed down despite yourself. The more blood, the more twisted wreckage the slower you went until you found you'd stopped altogether and were gawking, half-ashamed, like a hundred other mesmerized motorists.

Like a razor blade being stropped, that was what the sound was like. Was that the same sound the unknown weapon made when it pierced skin and flesh? Ask the Pale Saint. Austin wondered which category he'd fall into? Was he one of those so craving attention he'd spill each murder in gut-wrenching detail, or would he sit stony-faced and mute against all interrogation, a martyr to a cause that made sense only in his own terribly confused mind?

Some psychic had crawled out of the woodwork and, in an interview in the *Post*, had named the madman the Pale Saint, after a shamanic deity prophesied to emerge at the millennium. Crackpot idea or no, Pale Saint was just the kind of mediagenic name the press salivated over, and so the serial murderer had been christened, emerging from the public font a celebrity for whom late-twentieth-century America possessed a curious and unhealthy attraction.

Kowalchuck had stopped at the end of the hall. He handed over the official paperwork.

A couple of cops stood outside an unmarked door. Austin could see a stack of smeared paperboard cartons in a corner. The smell of congealed fast-food grease made his stomach seize up. Or maybe that was apprehension for what was waiting for him behind the closed door.

'I thought there'd be more,' he said, betraying his nervousness.

'More what?' Kowalchuck asked.

'Cops.'

'Pulled outta here 'bout twenty minutes ago,' Kowalchuck said. 'Some whacko holed up at the General Post Office on Fortieth. Got a sniper rifle; two civilians already down.'

Austin nodded mutely. The city stumbled on, filled with rage and frustration. He closed his eyes for a moment, imagined a baseball diamond, the ball being thrown around the infield, ending up in the pitcher's glove. He centered his mind on the game. The slow, almost ritualistic pace served to calm his nerves, cleanse his mind of extraneous thought. It was always like this. In law school, he'd take ten minutes before an exam to replay in his mind every detail of an inning of baseball. Nerves calmed, mind cleansed, he'd ace the test. Graduated Columbia Law with honors. This was why he'd bypassed so many offers of high-paying positions at prestigious law firms to become an ADA. He could still look at himself in the mirror. Those litigators at the posh Park Ave. firms all had war stories of eely defendants they'd gotten off. No matter what they said, they all had their price. Austin was different.

'Ready?'

Austin opened his eyes.

Kowalchuck was staring at him. Austin nodded, and the detective opened the door.

The individual sitting in the cell-like room did not look like much: a man of average height, muscular but not overly so. He was sitting at an old table of piss-yellow wood that was bolted to the floor, its top scarred with a nebula of cigarette burns and coffee stains caustic as acid. His chair was similarly bolted down, as was the second chair on the opposite side of the table. Apart from an old and peeling radiator, these were the only pieces of furniture in the room. The perp wore a checked flannel shirt, blue jeans and well-worn work boots. A denim jacket with a plaid lining was flung across the table. Austin noted his belt had been removed, also the laces of his boots. Then he saw the perp was in leg, wrist, and waist irons.

'What's this?'

'Christopher's orders.' Kowalchuck, laconic as ever, jammed two sticks of gum in his mouth.

'What about his civil rights? He's shackled like a mad dog.'

'Good analogy,' Kowalchuck said. 'In that regard, we prefer to think we're preserving the rights of the twenty one people he killed.'

'Not that I disagree, necessarily,' Austin said. 'But I don't want the P.D. assigned to him to start squawking to the ACLU.'

'Leave that to Christopher. We're talking evil here. *Real* evil they never heard of in the Public Defender's office.' Kowalchuck flicked a key back and forth between his fingers. 'The sonuvabitch has run rings around us for months. No freakin' way we're taking chances with him now.'

The perp seemed oblivious to this exchange, though it centered on him. He was staring fixedly at the backs of his square, capable-looking, deeply suntanned hands, which lay on the disfigured tabletop. Austin could see his scalp beneath hair white as milk. It was sun-dark and glowing faintly in the rude overhead light.

He looked up suddenly, aware of Austin's presence. His eyes goggled, starting like Mexican jumping beans. They were set deeply above a handsome, aquiline nose and a wide, almost voluptuous mouth. This was a man who, while not quite nondescript, could easily move through a crowd without being noticed. The kind of man whose home town neighbors would say on being interviewed: 'Why, he was such a normal

13

boy, generous and polite. Who would have thought he'd grow up to be a monster?'

'Who are you?' the perp asked. 'Nobody has answered my questions for hours. Will you?' His intonations possessed none of the angular dissonance of New York-ese; rather, there was a distinct softness to his vowels that spoke of a childhood in the nation's heartland or even further west.

As Austin slipped his briefcase onto the table, he noticed that Kowalchuck was still in the room. 'I need to be alone with the perp.'

'That wouldn't be my first choice.' Kowalchuck was chewing his gum furiously. Maybe he had a sweet tooth. On the other hand, maybe he was nervous. 'If I were you.'

Austin sat down. 'Then that makes two of us happy you're not me.'

Kowalchuck grunted and opened the door just enough to slip his body through sideways. 'Suit yourself. We'll be right outside. Just knock when you've had enough.' The door was locked behind him.

Was that the ghost of a smile on the perp's face? 'I like what you said to that man. Isn't he a piece of nasty business?'

A curiously old-fashioned phrase, Austin thought, just like his choice of mysterious murder weapon. 'My name's Robert Austin. I'm with the District Attorney's office. Who's defending you, someone from the Public Defender's office?'

'I don't know her name. I sent her away.'

'What? I can't take your statement unless –'

'I have no need of a lawyer.' The man offered a nervous smile. 'You see, I trust you, Mr Austin, though you may not yet trust me. Trust, I believe, is the most important human attribute in today's world.'

Austin did not have an answer for that. As he unfolded a notebook computer from his attache case, the perp gestured with his chin. 'All set to write the first draft.'

'We don't do drafts of statements.'

'That's not what I meant.'

Austin blinked. 'I beg your pardon?'

The perp's voice went through a sudden shift. 'The book, isn't that what you're thinking? You'll make a couple of million, and that's before film rights. Better agent up, get the best deal you can. In this day and age nothing captures the public's fancy for long.' His tone, which had been bitter with self-pity, returned to its previous softness. 'Pardon me, I'm not thinking clearly. I really don't know why I'm here.'

'You'll soon be charged with murder in the first degree. I have every expectation other charges will follow.' Austin glanced at his paperwork. 'You were found at a crime scene – in the northwest quadrant of Tompkins Square Park in the East Village – crouched over the victim. You refused to give your name or provide any identification to the officers on the scene or in subsequent interviews with Lt Christopher or –'

'It's Morris. Jack Morris,' the perp blurted out. 'And I don't know anything about that murdered man. I saw him lying there, crumpled like an empty cigarette pack, and I went over to help. Poor thing.'

'What time was that?'

Morris lifted his manacled hands to display his nails. Their beds were filthy. 'Mr Austin, look for yourself. I'm a simple working man – a mechanic. What I do is here for all to see. I make engines run, I don't make them stop.'

'Really?' Austin consulted his paperwork. 'At approximately two o'clock this morning you made William Cotton's heart stop.'

'Who?'

'The man you murdered, Mr Morris. His name was William Cotton.'

'I wouldn't know anything about that.'

'His blood, Mr Morris. Your hands were soaked in it up to your wrists –'

'No,' the man across from Austin frowned, 'I see this won't work with you.'

'– as if you were digging like a ferret inside his chest.'

Morris sat stiffly as if he'd taken serious offense. 'That would be a sacrilege. I promise you it wasn't anything like that.'

'No? Suppose you tell me what you did with his eyes. You gouged them out of their sockets and then did what with them?'

The perp's face grew gray with rage. 'I pity you. You're here at the behest of institutions so mammoth they've lost all reason for being.' He leaned forward intently, as men in a bar often do when the conversation gets into its meat. 'You see, unlike you, I value life. You destroyed yours the moment you went to work for them. Yoked like an ox to an authority that gives no more thought to your welfare than an elephant does to a flea. Ceding control to institutions is like giving a monkey a machine-gun. You never know what will happen, you just know it's going to be really bad.'

'Can we get back to the murder?'

15

'If you insist.' Morris sat back, relaxed and content. Austin had once owned a cat who'd looked just like that after he'd hawked up a particularly bothersome hairball. 'I killed him like I killed all the others.'

'How many others?'

'Twenty. But there will be more. This was just a prelude.'

Austin's eyes flickered. 'Reality check, Mr Morris. Do you know where you are?'

'I'm in Lt Christopher's custody.'

Austin gave him a pitying smile, thin as a razor's edge. 'For the moment, let's stick with William Cotton. Why did you murder him?'

'He was a senior vice-president for Advent On-Line, did you know that?'

'The Internet provider?' Austin flipped a page of his paperwork. 'So killing him wasn't random.'

'Nothing in the universe is random.' Morris folded his hands one atop the other. As he did so, the chain between the manacles made a sound akin to the jangle of a horse's hardware.

'None of the murders were random, is that what you're saying? They're all part of a plan?'

'Bravo, Mr Austin! Head of the class!'

Like lightning-play, a little thrill tap-danced along Austin's spine. 'Tell me more about the plan.'

'Do you play cards, Mr Austin?'

Austin looked at the other man skeptically.

'This is not an idle question, I assure you. Nor is it the maundering of a madman.'

'I have no time to play cards,' Austin said at last.

'But you have time for a computer, I see.'

'I need it for my job.'

'Do you? Whatever happened to a tablet and pencil?' He jerked his chin in the direction of Austin's notebook computer. 'How much did that cost you? A thousand dollars? Two thousand?'

'Mr Morris, this isn't the time –'

'You want an answer to your question – or don't you?'

Austin sighed. 'Somewhere in between.'

'For two dollars you could have bought a deck of cards and had a helluva lot more fun engaging your hands and mind in the real world than hooking into a network of virtual reality.'

Austin sat back. 'I get it. You're one of those – what do you call them?'

'Neo-Luddites.'

'Right. Like the Unabomber.'

Morris shrugged. 'If the analogy works for you, why not? We're in the midst of another cultural upheaval no less frightening than the Industrial Revolution. As then, millions of people are being kicked out of jobs. Whole industries are being plowed under a tidal wave of silicon chips and ether-nets. While these poor bastards are marginalized, at best, and, at worst, made obsolete, a new generation of robber-barons – the men who run the Leviathans like Microsoft, Intel and Disney – are making more money than it's possible to imagine. A wonderful and beneficial information-age future is upon us, the media tells us, but beneficial to whom? The media has been gobbled up, itself become a Leviathan, and cannot be trusted, if it ever could. Tell me, what will happen to the horde of rudely unemployed who can't find relevance for themselves in this brave new world?'

'So your answer is to kill the people responsible for this revolution?'

'One by one,' Morris said. 'It's the only way to combat the forces of chaos and evil, the decay of morality, the loss of the work ethic, the rise of a kind of fundamentalism that is twin to totalitarianism. Don't you see? I'm performing a ritual. It's a wake for the death of the American dream.'

Austin thought about this for some time. 'Let's be more specific. What's the significance of the marks you carve on the victims' foreheads?'

'The runes.'

Austin waggled a hand. 'Some kind of ancient writing nobody understands anymore, right?'

'Consult your software dictionary, Mr Austin.' The perp shifted uncomfortably in his bolted-down chair. 'Meanwhile, I'd like to get up and walk around a little.'

'I'm afraid I can't allow that.'

Morris shrugged, returning to the study of his wretched fingernails as Austin accessed the dictionary on his computer. In a moment, Austin looked up. 'It says here that a rune is "any of the characters in several alphabets used by the ancient Germanic peoples from the third to the thirteenth century."'

Morris smiled. 'Typical. That's one very limited definition. A broader one is that a rune is an incantation of magic power.'

'Give me an example.'

Morris shook his head. 'Runes may not be spoken, only written.'

Austin swiveled the computer around so the keyboard was facing toward the man across the table. 'Show me what you carved into the victim's forehead.'

'Not with that.' He gestured to the attache case. 'Do you have a pen and tablet in there?'

Austin pulled a yellow legal pad and a Bic pen out of his case, then paused as if undecided.

'You can trust me,' Morris said, 'to tell the truth to you and to no one else.'

As Austin handed the pad and pen over, sudden intuition led him to ask: 'Do you believe in God?'

'God,' the Pale Saint said as if he had expected the question, 'and the devil.' He lunged across the table with his entire body, thrusting out his left arm, oblivious to the manacle gouging cruelly into his left wrist. Chains rattled ominously as the metal point and plastic body of the pen pierced Austin's left eye so deeply it went straight through and entered his brain. He rocked back, wobbling crazily as if he were on a small boat in rough weather. He opened his mouth but no sound emerged.

'No blood, either,' the Pale Saint said, as if divining his thoughts. 'You're alive, after a fashion.'

Rooted to the chair, Austin could still make out with his undamaged eye the Pale Saint's face looming like an enormous moon in front of him. He seemed transformed. Eyes turned vulpine greedily drank in everything at once, as if to devour it wholesale. His wide mouth seemed a knife blade's slash, a weapon attached to powerful jaws, the front end of a new form of engine of destruction. Or one ancient as Time.

'You see, the brain is a wondrous organ. It can sustain a gunshot, a spike driven through it, any number of nasty physical insults without the entire organism being immediately destroyed. In fact, I imagine if you were taken at once to the hospital it's likely you would live. But such a thing is not possible. Your destiny lies elsewhere.'

This creature was examining his handiwork with uncommon care. If there was pain anywhere inside himself, Austin was unaware of it.

Abruptly, the Pale Saint smiled in the manner of someone remembering a good joke. 'I know all about you, Robert, where you were born, where you went to school, each girl you met, dated, then discarded.' He put a forefinger up to his lips. 'But if I were a betting man, how would I bet? That you'll stay with Cassandra or leave her? No, you'll stay. There's Sara to think of, isn't there? Yes.'

The Pale Saint blinked, as if suddenly remembering where he was. He waggled his fingertips and the chains chinked again. 'Were you fooled like everyone else? This is blood, Robert, not dirt. Dried in there so thoroughly I'd need lye and a wire brush to get it out. But there's no need. On the contrary. The blood is tangible evidence of my work, the old skin of creative effort pared off my soul. It is the vestige of the demon inside myself. It is the goad, the spur, the meaning of my life.' He smiled, showing the yellow teeth of a fox. 'Judging by appearances, it won't be long before you find evidence of the same demon inside yourself.'

Austin, who could not speak, could not even shake his head back and forth, was obliged to mutely observe this obscenity as if it were no more than a Las Vegas magic show.

'Oh, you'll like this one when I summon her,' the Pale Saint said. 'You'll look into her bitch face and you'll know her name. Without question, you saw her as a child.'

The Pale Saint pursed his lips. 'Childhood is where we're made, so I'm given to understand. That being the case, I imagine you're curious about mine. I'm afraid I can't tell you. To do so would involve memory, and memory is a false friend. Memory doesn't dredge up what happened; it re-creates the past in the version that will best suit our present needs. So forget memory; bury it in a trunk at the foot of your bed as if it never existed.' He cocked his head. 'You getting any of this, Robert? I pray you do, truly.'

The Pale Saint put his face into Austin's. 'As to my plea, of course it is Guilty. I take full responsibility for what I've done. And for what I am about to do. That's the point. My *self* is all I have. It's all I am or ever will be. My parents I renounced long ago. I burned a photograph of them, and they were gone.' He put his fingertips together. '*Poof!* Only tomorrow exists, like a lamp burning in the night. And what a terrible tomorrow it will be, I promise you. The end of the world as we know it, metaphysically speaking, of course. I know this with a certainty branded upon my soul, because I am the messenger, the anointed one, the Pale Saint.'

He paused for a moment, his gaze moving almost lovingly over Austin's face. 'Fate has provided you for my purpose – or I have provided Fate with the opportunity in which to thrive. You'll understand me when I tell you my secret, won't you, Robert? Yes, I do believe you'll get it, because, you see, you're so *intimately* involved.

19

'First, I'll tell you why I need Cotton's eyes.' He leaned over and began to whisper in Austin's left ear. He did that quite deliberately, knowing that Austin could no longer hear out of his right ear.

As he spoke, Austin's one good eye slowly closed. Beneath the lid, a single tear formed. It welled up, despite his best efforts to control it, and slowly slid down his cheek until it reached the apex, where it hung, trembling like a spider web in the breeze.

'Ah, yes.' The Pale Saint scooped the tear onto his fingertip. 'I knew you would understand.' He licked the drop, savoring its salty taste, before turning Austin's notebook computer around to face him. 'Now you know what I plan to do, and why. It's time to summon the demon.'

When Detective Kowalchuck heard the sharp knock on the door, he was furtively smoking a cigarette. It was against regs to light up inside a precinct, even a derelict like this one, but Kowalchuck was so pissed off he'd thought, *Fuck it*. He'd been pissed off even before that smart-ass ADA had flushed him from the perp room like he was a piece of shit in the toilet. Just because he and Christopher were asshole buddies.

Kowalchuck took another deep drag, shook his head disgustedly. Manpower shortage or no manpower shortage, he should've had more backup here. It was criminal what the Mayor was doing to the Department, squeezing the life out of it like a hard freeze in an orange grove. Already, this harsh life was making Kowalchuck dream of retirement in the Florida Keys: hot sun, beautiful pale blue water, standing in the front of a small boat, throwing the line at the nose of a bonefish . . .

The knocking on the door came again, more urgent this time. Golden Boy had wanted to be in there on his lonesome, now let him wait to get out. Kowalchuck sucked cigarette smoke into his lungs and slowly let it drift out his nostrils. Romero was halfway through one of his large-size Snickers bars so sweet they set Kowalchuck's teeth on edge. Borrows was off in the men's room, jerking off for all Kowalchuck knew. That was about all Borrows was good for, as far as Kowalchuck was concerned, and he had been assigned here. Another matter for Kowalchuck to be pissed off about. Were the bureaucrats in the Department nuts or just dim? Either way it was bad for people like him, just wanting to do their tour.

He took a last long drag on his ciggie, flung the filter to the filthy floor and, with one hand on the butt of his holstered service revolver, he unlocked the door.

The smoke escaped his half-open mouth as he saw the ADA slumped over the table. 'What the fuck –?'

'Heart attack,' the Pale Saint said. 'He just keeled over like –'

'Get the fuck back!' Kowalchuck, service pistol drawn and aimed at the man standing near him, advanced toward the table.

'I'm telling you, man –'

'Shut your freakin' face, you scumbag!' Kowalchuck bent over the unmoving form. With dread in his heart, he reached out and squeezed the shoulder. 'Hey,' he said. 'Hey!' *If this man has died on my watch, they're gonna burn my ass but good,* he thought.

Kowalchuck shouted wordlessly as he saw the pen thrust through Austin's eye. He grunted heavily as the Pale Saint's fist struck him in the side so hard two ribs caved in. He tried to swing the gun around, but another thunderous blow caught him square in the windpipe. He gagged and went down to his knees, eyes watering, bile burning his throat. Then the toe of the Pale Saint's work boot struck his left temple and he lost consciousness.

By this time, Romero had his gun out. The end of the Snickers bar still protruding from his mouth, he entered the room, and the Pale Saint shot him dead with Kowalchuck's gun. As he slumped to the floor, the Pale Saint was already rummaging through Kowalchuck's pockets. He found the key to his irons and freed himself.

Advancing into the hallway, the Pale Saint caught Borrows coming out of the men's room. He shot the astonished cop once in the forehead. Then, the hallway echoing with fast-approaching footsteps, he used the corner of Austin's attache case to break a wired-glass window. Doors burst open at the far end of the hall. He could see at least four uniforms, guns drawn. No time to hack away all the jagged shards clinging to the sill. One of the uniforms fired, and a bullet whined, chipping plaster and paint off a corner near the Pale Saint's head. He threw the attache down and levered himself through the broken window. By the time the uniforms took the measure of the disaster that had befallen their comrades, he had melted into the blue autumn shadows strewn like the homeless across the city's streets.

TWO

'Blood,' Jonathan Christopher said. 'It's all over the sill. You think it's just from the perp or also the cops? They both bled quite a bit after he shot them.' He was a large man, with the broad shoulders and long, sleek muscles of a swimmer. His hooded eyes above a hawk-like nose gave little away, but he was quick to smile, and when he did so he made you feel as if you'd known him all your life.

'Typing will tell us by process of elimination,' Emma D'Alassandro said as she carefully broke off bloody glass shards and bagged them with gloved hands. 'There are also one or two bits of what appear to be epithelial tissue.'

'His skin.'

D'Alassandro nodded. 'This is exciting, Jon: with this and the prints we took from Austin's computer, it'll be the first tangible evidence he's left at a crime scene. When we find him we've got the case sewn up. He's as good as on death row.' She was the forensic pathologist Christopher had chosen for his team. Petite, dark-haired and intense, with a small nose and sharp chin, she was passionate about her chosen profession, and more serious-minded than was healthy for any pathologist. She was an information junkie, to whom sleep and relaxation were equally insignificant. She was neat, precise – a health food addict who was appalled by the garbage the rest of the team ate.

'Speaking of those prints.'

'Esquival is running them through the modem himself. An answer is imminent.' She grinned. 'I've got a hunch the prints'll show up in the central database. We're up-linked with every federal, state and local agency from coast to coast.' She gave him a quick, concerned glance out of eyes glossy as black olives. 'Boss, can you keep your mind on this?'

'Don't, for God's sake, mother me.' The derelict precinct was over-run by police personnel working with the lock-jawed desperation that ensued after one of their own was murdered. This time, it was four, so God alone knew what was in their hearts. The crisis at the GPO had been defused, it was true, but only now, after the fact, had Chief Brockaw freed up personnel. It was always this way with bureaucracies. Christopher thought these thoughts in order not to think too hard about Bobby. He deliberately kept his attention fixed firmly on the sill. 'I was just thinking even if the blood's all his, there isn't very much. He wasn't hurt badly, maybe just a couple of cuts.'

'But the prints, Jon. Don't look so glum. If he was Special Services or anywhere in the armed services, he's ours now.'

'No, he *was* ours,' Christopher said bitterly. 'Now God alone knows where he is.'

'We have more of him now, Boss: his prints, his photo, his blood –' Emma paused as the Assistant Medical Examiner and a forensic photographer asked Christopher to direct them to the interrogation room, then hurried by. 'Sooner or later, we'll get him now.'

'Jon –!'

Christopher turned as Reuven Esquival hurried up, waving a sheaf of faxes. As the team's resident behavioral scientist, he had worked with Christopher before, on loan from the FBI in Arlington. Long and lanky, he was usually easygoing, but the bitter frustrations of this case had seriously frazzled his nerves. Lately, in order to keep sane, he'd taken to playing practical jokes on Emma that astonished Christopher with their inventiveness even as they drove the pathologist up a wall. He was as sloppy as she was neat. He gorged on all manner of junk food; grease was his god. Christopher thought of them privately as Oscar and Felix; it was often fascinating to watch them torture one another in tiny ways. Christopher was convinced it was their way of saying they cared.

'About the perp's prints,' Esquival said. 'No match at DMV, the city's public agencies or any branch of the Armed Services.'

'Let me see that.' D'Alassandro snatched the faxes from him, then gave a little shriek as his thumb came off in her hand.

'You bastard!' D'Alassandro shouted at him.

Esquival guffawed as he picked the latex thumb off the floor, but he quickly sobered as he continued the bad news. 'We can't get a match, period. The computer came up with *nada*. It's like the man doesn't exist.'

'Impossible.' Christopher moved down the hall in his characteristic elongated strides. He never appeared in a hurry, but his gait ate up so much real estate those not up to it had to hustle uncomfortably in his wake. 'He exists, all right. Maybe we'll get lucky; maybe he was printed for some minor infraction in some backwater town. We need to widen the circle. Emma get on it as soon as you've finished bagging evidence.' He was a born commander: he knew what to delegate, and when. 'Reuven, go back to the interrogation room and get me some answers. I want to know what the hell happened in there.'

'Hey, wait a minute, I thought Reuven was going to help me,' D'Alassandro protested. 'I'm up to my elbows in forensic evidence that has to be bagged pronto, and I can't do it all myself.'

'I'll get a uniform from out front to give you a hand.'

D'Alassandro mumbled something nasty under her breath that Christopher contrived to ignore. 'This guy carves symbols on his victims' foreheads,' he continued. 'He didn't do that with Bobby; instead, he wrote in Bobby's computer. That could be significant – get me a hard copy of everything on the hard drive, pronto. Emma, keep me up to date on this fingerprint angle.'

'There's another thing,' Esquival said. 'A real looker of a woman is making all kinds of trouble outside. Claims she's the wife of one of the victims. She's demanding to see her husband.'

'Short blond hair, gray eyes, curses like a teamster,' Christopher said.

Esquival nodded. 'That's her.'

'Sounds like Cassandra Austin's here.' Like a force of nature, Christopher was sweeping them all toward the precinct's entrance. 'We're not even through going over the bodies yet,' he said to Esquival. 'I told her to stay away when I gave her the news. I don't want her to see him, not like this.'

'From what I've seen, it won't make any difference to her what you want,' Esquival said, puffing to keep up.

'I'll see you guys as soon as I can,' Christopher said, as he opened the front door. 'We've already got uniforms canvassing the area. It's teeming with homeless. Someone must've seen our perp escape.' He went through the door. 'Meanwhile, I've got to deal with an unstoppable force by the name of Cassandra Austin. If she's still around when the media show up they'll make her the sideshow *du jour*.'

Christopher picked Cassandra out of the swarm of blue uniforms on

East Broadway and his stomach did a somersault. She wore an olive ankle-length overcoat with epaulets, black suede boots and a black-and-yellow scarf. Her short blond hair accentuated her features, making her appear both more forceful and more sexy. Even through the expression of anxiety and pain her face was beautiful. He remembered how, in the face of adversity, her already formidable presence projected itself almost like a physical blow. This had been true even when they had been running wild as teenagers, troubled kids from troubled homes, exhilarated by their own daring exploits. They were thirteen when they had met upstate, where his father and her mother went for the summer. And they had continued their friendship during each succeeding summer, thrown together and bonded, as it were, by their mutual desire for escape.

With a renewed pang in his heart that should not have been there, Christopher went down the steps toward her. Two patrolmen had been assigned to her, and it wasn't nearly enough. She had made some headway toward the precinct's cracked stoop, and when she saw him she made an end run around the unfortunate young patrolman on the left. He whirled as she brushed past him, reached out to make a grab and was astonished she had the strength and agility to throw him off.

'Hey, wait a sec, miss, you can't –!'

'I can and I am,' Cassandra said in a voice so steely the patrolman hesitated.

'That's all right, Ramirez.' Christopher waved the cop off. 'She's in my charge now.' He turned to her. 'Cass, I'm so sorry –'

Sunlight fired off the diamonds around her wrist as she struck him an open-handed blow across the face. 'Damn you, Jon. You killed Bobby, you and your god*damn* high-profile cases.'

Christopher, his cheek red and stinging, held his ground. 'Believe me, Cass, I'm as sorry as you are that Bobby's dead.'

'You tell me you're sorry, but what does that really mean? You two spent countless hours together – days, nights, weekends, any time at all, it didn't matter to you. You'd call and he'd always come.' She took a step toward the precinct and he blocked her. 'Let me see him. It's the very least you can do.'

Christopher began to steer her away from the entrance, but she bridled, snatching her elbow out of his grasp. 'Don't.' Her voice was almost a sob. 'Just let me pass.'

'Try to understand, Cass.' Christopher took a step closer to her so he could lower his voice amid the growing tumult. 'The good news is we have the Pale Saint's prints, and traces of his blood and skin on the window frame when he made his escape. But we're still sifting the whole place for clues.'

'Give me a little credit. I'm a scientist, for Christ's sake. I know how to keep sites pristine.'

For a moment, the pain left her eyes and her gaze seemed far away. He remembered how she could get like that; when they were younger he always imagined that she was dreaming of a perfect world where parents loved one another and never considered splitting up.

'I'm just trying to spare you.'

'Like you used to in the old days. You didn't have to protect me then, and you sure don't have to now.'

He nodded. 'Right, I know. You could always take care of yourself, I knew that, but I couldn't help it. But this is different. I've seen Bobby. Trust me. You don't want to. In an hour, maybe, but not right now. Dammit, Cass –'

Without warning, she'd flown up the steps and, before he could stop her, had pulled open the precinct door and had rushed inside.

Cursing under his breath, Christopher lunged after her. He grabbed hold of her before she could get too far down the hallway. As he spun her around, she looked at him and said: 'I'm begging you.' Her voice was breathless with a combination of emotion and exertion. 'In an hour it'll be too late. How can I face Sara, otherwise? How can I tell her I didn't see him, that I wasn't able to say goodbye for both of us.'

Christopher hesitated, and in that moment, the front door burst open and Chief of Police Anthony Brockaw strode through.

'Christopher!' He beckoned in the manner of a Roman Caesar. 'A word with you, if you please.'

'Shit,' Christopher said. He gave Cassandra a quick glance. 'I gotta do this.' He looked over at the Chief. Brockaw already had a door open and, as he met Christopher's glance, he gestured for him to follow him inside. 'Wait right here for me,' Christopher said. 'I'm warning you, Cass, don't make a move without me.'

Brockaw closed the door behind him as soon as Christopher entered. 'This is a mess, Jon.'

Christopher, facing him, said nothing. They were in the men's locker room. It stank of mold and old socks. Water dripped fitfully in a sink whose porcelain had worn away in patches to a lurid blue-green. The narrow doors of rusting metal lockers lay open, as if to reveal the ghosts of the men who'd once patrolled these streets. Behind them, you could see through one or two narrow gaps rodents had made in the rotting plaster, what remained of the women's locker room.

Despite the now shabby atmosphere of the workaday past, the room was charged with the Chief's presence. He was not a tall man; rather, he was wide without being fat. His blue jowls and black caterpillar eyebrows made it appear as if his face was set in a perpetual scowl. His dark eyes, set off by his coffee-colored skin, darted here and there as he spoke, giving the impression either of vigilance or of paranoia, depending on one's point of view.

'This is a *helluva* mess, Jon.'

'It was a helluva mess the moment I was ordered to stash the perp with insufficient personnel.'

'See?' Brockaw's stubby finger stabbed out. 'That's just the kind of comment I don't need from you right now. I just came from the Mayor's office, and we gotta get some positive spin going on this, otherwise the media's gonna have my butt for lunch.'

'Four of our own are dead and you're talking spin control.'

'Some poor bastard has to.' Brockaw grunted. 'That's the difference between our jobs, Jon. You're on the line with perps. I'm on the line with the media.'

'Ringmasters of a deadline-driven circus. I don't give a damn for the media.'

'Jesus, don't I know that. You're passionate about two things: your job and your team. That's the way it should be.'

'I was also passionate about my son.'

'Quite right, sorry.' Brockaw seemed momentarily at a loss for words. Silence, punctuated by the doleful drip of water against the sink bottom. 'Look,' Brockaw hurried on, 'this case is already threatening to get out of control. Let's not have any illusions here – before it's over it's going to get a lot bigger and a lot nastier.' The Chief's brows furrowed until the two caterpillars over his eyes seemed to meet. 'Take some friendly advice. Find this perp and bring him to justice ASAP. You did it before –'

'I didn't do a damn thing.' Christopher's voice was anguished. 'He turned himself in.'

'What? I thought you got a phone tip from one of your snitches.'

'A phone tip, yes; from a snitch, I'm not so sure. I spoke with the perp for more than an hour, and then I went back to listen to the tape

27

of the call. That's what I was doing when he broke out. I'm convinced he made the call.'

'But that's nuts. Why would he deliberately get caught if he wanted to escape?'

'I've been thinking about that,' Christopher said. 'I think it was to show us he could do it. I'm convinced that's why we haven't been able to find the murder weapon. He stashed it somewhere before he made the call. And what did he do with the eyes he carved out of the victim?' Christopher shook his head. 'We ran his prints and so far have come up with zilch. He might as well not exist. In more than six months on the case I have nothing to show for our hours of work but a bunch of leads that like a Chinese puzzle lead nowhere and everywhere. Do you get it now? All those leads were set for us like traps in a maze. From day one, he's been making monkeys out of us.'

The Chief made a cutting gesture with the edge of his hand. 'I don't want to hear that. The case has been politicized, and you know what that means. After we're finished here I want you to give a statement to my spin doctors so they can incorporate a quote from you in the press statement. You're out of the closet, Jon. Publicitywise, the Mayor wants a point man on this case, and you're it. You can kiss any semblance of morality goodbye. The gloves are off and blood's sure to flow.'

'Christ, Chief, this perp has sent me a river of blood. I fucked up on this. I had him and –'

'You did what you thought was right, Jon. There was a vet detective and two uniforms on him at all times. He was locked down and collared. What else could you have done?'

'I should have been in the room with the perp every minute. Instead, I went off to listen to the phone tape.'

'And came up with some interesting evidence. You did right, Jon. Besides, how d'you know you would have had any more success with him than the other men did? It could have been your dead eyes I looked into this morning.'

Brockaw sighed. 'I know you too well to say don't agonize over it, Jon. You're a perfectionist. In addition, I know what Austin meant to you.' He passed a hand across his face. 'We were all dealt a shitty hand on this one, but how could we know what this man was truly capable of?'

Reaching for the doorknob, Brockaw paused. 'A last word of advice. With three of our own and an assistant D.A. murdered you're going to be under a lot of pressure. Friends and comrades of the deceased will no doubt come to you to ask – well, you know what they'll ask of you. People are taking what happened here today personally; there's already talk around of blood vengeance. I won't have it, not in my Department. What we need to pull our fannies out of the pit is a squeaky clean apprehension. No dangling ends or technicalities that'll hit us in the ass at trial. The D.A. has already made this request of me on a personal level and we go way back.' There was something in Brockaw's expression Christopher didn't like.

'Are you intimating my friendship with Bobby will cause me to put the muzzle of my service revolver against this sonuvabitch's head and pull the trigger?'

Brockaw's gaze held Christopher's long enough for Christopher to cool down. 'We're both in the crucible, no shit. My point: from the moment we hold the press conference, the media's going to rehash and analyze every move we make.' He paused, about to open the door and let in the maelstrom of the outside world. 'It comes down to a question of whose blood is going to flow next, Jon. Do yourself a favor and make damn sure it's not yours.'

'He might as well not exist . . . From day one he's been making monkeys out of us.'

Cassandra, arms wrapped around herself, leaned against the stained wall of the precinct hallway, and tried to think about nothing. She was unsuccessful. Maybe she hadn't really meant to eavesdrop on Jon; maybe she simply needed to relieve herself. Maybe that was the only reason she'd wandered into the women's locker room. But she hadn't walked away when she'd heard Christopher's voice seeping through the crumbling wall. On the contrary, she'd put her ear into the echoey interior of an open locker and had listened as if to voices from the past. Who could blame her, her husband newly murdered, and desperate to know what was going on. But, oh Christ, she hadn't counted on hearing *this*. If Jon felt he had no hope of catching this demon, then she knew the Pale Saint would never be caught.

Heart racing, breath coming hot and fast in her throat, Cassandra retreated down the hallway and tried to stave off the panic that was setting in. She had always believed in the rightness of things, but this was all wrong. Part of her could not believe Bobby was dead; part of her *would* not believe it. This was the great anomaly about her, something she could never bring herself to tell Bobby, had never dared tell Christopher. Cassandra, the great scientist, who daily analyzed reams of mathematical and biological data was, at heart, a mystic. Like the seer whose name she bore, Cassandra possessed a disconcerting belief in the nature of things unseen and unheard by all but a very few. Perhaps it had been this belief that had driven her toward science, in an effort to explain what she knew, in her heart, could never be explained. That suspicion alone could not stop her; in fact, it drove her with a fierceness that none of the men in her life could ever understand.

She shifted her position now as one of the medical examiner's people brushed by her. He left, in his wake, a strong scent of aftershave, and she was instantly cast back to early this morning when she and Bobby were in the bathroom. She smelled him again just as if he were beside her, whispering in her ear, and her heart broke. She could not breathe; tears welled up behind her eyes so that she was forced to turn her face to the wall and count slowly to twenty while she pressed her forehead against the cool cracked plaster. *My God,* she thought, *how can I go on knowing that the last time Bobby and I were together, we were fighting like enemies? I can't do this,* she thought. *I can't. I want to be home, I want to cradle Sara in my arms, I long to rock us both to sleep so that when we wake up Bobby is standing over us, alive and well.*

But that wasn't going to happen. Not ever. Bobby was dead. She began to cry, silently and privately. As she did so, she realized she was weeping not only for Bobby but for Sara and for herself, because she knew she could not yet face Sara, could not tell her what had happened to her father. She'd need all her strength for that, and right now she did not feel strong.

She wept and wanted to go on weeping forever – which was not like her. She felt like giving up – which was *definitely* not like her. She shivered. What was happening to her? She felt so damn helpless, as if nothing she could do or say now would make the slightest difference. And she was so full of rage against a universe she had all her life cherished but which now seemed to have cruelly turned against her. Bobby was dead. In the blink of an eye, in the beat of a heart, and now what was the use of it all? She had believed them all charmed – she, Bobby, Sara – special in the eye of the universe, destined for greatness. How foolish that notion seemed now.

She felt hot tears sliding down her cheeks. Hot as blood, freshly flowing. She remembered what Christopher had said just now about how the Pale Saint had left his blood on the window glass.

An idea was forming in her mind. Dimly, she knew she must still be in shock, but another part of her, the mystic who had always believed

30

in the rightness of things, would not be stilled. *If I can get a blood sample,* she thought, *there are tests I can run, tests the police lab never even heard of. I can see right down into the chain of his DNA. Who knows? Maybe he's got some kind of disorder or disease that can help Jon find him.*

She knew this was more than possible. She was a scientist who was known to be a revolutionist rather than an evolutionist. She took risks in the pursuit of her almost uncanny instincts. And her proven ability to leapfrog over the plodding steps of other researchers had quickly become her greatest asset. It was that same part of her that would not let her reconsider what might be a reckless decision.

Completely ignoring Christopher's admonition to stay put, she walked down the shabby precinct hallway. No one challenged her; they were all too busy. She was searching for a certain window, the one the Pale Saint broke through when he escaped. She saw it and Emma D'Alassandro at the same time. D'Alassandro was standing in front of the broken window, a case full of her equipment by her side, impatiently instructing a young, pimply-faced uniform cop on how to assist her. Cassandra stopped in her tracks. She had met D'Alassandro only a few times, but she knew her well enough to be certain she wouldn't let her near the window.

From the look on D'Alassandro's exasperated face, she wasn't making much headway briefing the pimply uniform on proper forensic procedure, and Cassandra felt for her. She watched D'Alassandro shake her head, then head off down the hallway.

With a quickly beating heart, she watched the pimply uniform kneeling beside the forensic kit, sorting the blood samples from the broken window D'Alassandro had given him. Cassandra gathered herself. She walked swiftly and purposefully toward Pimple-face, all the while keeping an eye out for D'Alassandro.

'Hi! I work with Emma D'Alassandro. Need some help?'

Bobby had always said her smile could light up Times Square in a power outage and, as Pimple-face glanced up, she knew he had been right.

'Do I ever,' he said eagerly. 'I can hit a bullseye at twenty yards with my service revolver but I'm all thumbs with this stuff.'

As Cassandra knelt down beside him she could see the sweat running down his neck into a collar already wet. She took the samples from him and deftly slid them into the kit's slots. 'You've got to do it from straight above, like so,' she said, 'otherwise if the sample scrapes against the sides of the case it'll become contaminated.'

31

Pimple-face bobbed his head gratefully. 'You know, this isn't the kind of job I envisioned when I graduated the academy.'

'I understand. No problem,' Cassandra said, fitting more samples into the case. 'Got any more?'

As Pimple-face turned around to look, she palmed one of the samples that contained blood and epithelial tissue, slipping it into the pocket of her overcoat.

'Nope.' He let out a breath, obviously relieved. 'I guess that's it for the moment.'

'Great.' She rose, and he followed suit. Cassandra looked around. 'I'll go find D'Alassandro. You sit tight.'

'Sure.' Pimple-face grinned as she began to walk off. 'Hey, thanks again!'

She was right where she was supposed to be when Christopher returned from his disturbing meeting with the Chief.

'Jon –'

'C'mon.' Christopher took her elbow, leading her around a corner and down the hall toward the room where Bobby Austin still sat, the Bic pen through his left eye and brain. 'I'll take you to see him.' He escorted her inside, where D'Alassandro and Esquival were wrapping things up with the M.E.'s photographer. 'Cassandra Austin,' he announced softly as the photographer left.

Esquival stood. 'We're sorry for your loss, Mrs Austin.'

D'Alassandro nodded in Cassandra's direction but otherwise was as rigid as a sentry on duty.

'This way,' Christopher said, as he led Cassandra around the side of the chair in which Bobby Austin's body still sat. 'Careful.' The two members of his team regained their wits long enough to remove themselves from the room with a few further murmured words of condolence.

Cassandra did not hear them; her gaze was riveted on her husband's corpse. It sat straight and tall in the chair. His good eye was open, as if still staring at the face of his murderer.

'There's no blood.' Cassandra said this automatically; while the rest of her was on hold, her scientist's trained eye continued its relentless examination.

'No.' Christopher shifted nervously from one foot to another. 'That's one of the mysteries we've been trying to solve.'

'How the hell did he stitch Bobby's lips together?'

'He used the corkscrew from Bobby's pocket knife and the thread from one of his overcoat buttons.'

Cassandra continued to stare at her husband's waxen face. 'Why did he do that?'

'I have no idea. I wish I did.'

'What did the M.E. say about the lack of exsanguination?'

'Cass, I don't really think this is the time or place to discuss –'

'Just tell me, Jon! I want to know a physician's professional opinion of this.'

She said this with great determination, but the slight quaver in her voice gave away the intensity of her underlying emotional distress. He sighed. 'Right now, he hasn't a clue. But he's hopeful the autopsy will give him a better idea.'

Cassandra nodded. Then, she did an odd thing: she bent over Austin and sniffed his neck. 'I can't smell him.' She stood bolt upright as the tears came. 'Jon, I can't smell him anymore.'

In an instant, she had fled, and was lost within the rush of bodies clogging the hallway.

Christopher, torn between his duty to go after her and his desire to remain with his friend until the M.E.'s people came to take him to the morgue, could only look on with anguish and fervently wish this day had never dawned.

Lying on a mattress no thicker than his forearm, the Pale Saint closes his eyes. He knows it is the wrong thing to do, but he cannot help himself. The thunder of the garbage truck outside makes his teeth grind and his eyes water. His heart is pounding. It is dark there behind his eyelids, dark as the inside of the trunk that squatted at the foot of his parents' bed.

Through this darkness swims an image, slick as oil rising to the water's surface. It shines, too, with a peculiar phosphorescent light: a female face, electric blue and white, haloed in the same colors, the features smearing into one another as if they were finger-painted by a three-year-old child. The image blazes with an ice-blue light so dazzling it is positively hallucinogenic.

The mouth on Mama's image begins to move: 'Lord, sonny, you are a sore trial to me. You're such a willful boy, willful from the moment your head appeared like a red wrinkled wad of felt between my legs.'

To block out his mama, he conjures up Faith. She is beautiful like sunlight through treetops, like a sudden heavy downpour after a drought, or the rising of the pale moon on a cold, clear night. As beautiful as the perfect skeleton of the prairie dog, baking in the sun, as beautiful as its skin cured and stretched so thin Faith can see through it patterns of shadow and light thrown by the moonlight.

Moonlight reminds him of the copper moon sitting low in the sky, flickering on and off as the thick twists of black smoke rose from the blaze. By that time, there is nothing left for him on the Great Plains. The electric blue eye has been snuffed out. Everything dead. But not buried. For that, the fire is needed.

As he watches the kerosene-accelerated flames consuming the dark and cavernous house of his youth, he looks beyond to the darkness of the great prairie along which scrolls of dust skitter and dance. He is aware of the nocturnal animals skulking and pawing around the edges of the brightness, drawn by its heat and its holy energy.

Into this living darkness, he recites aloud the lines from the Bible Mama had once used as a cudgel against him: ' "And he looked toward Sodom and Gomorrah, and toward all the land of the plain, and beheld, and lo, the smoke of the country went up as the smoke of a furnace." '

The Pale Saint's eyes fly open. He lies on his bare mattress, chest heaving, lips drawn back from clenched teeth, licking off the sweat that rolls down the sides of his nose. He snatches up a Hershey's chocolate bar from a pile near his thin mattress and eats half, no more, no less.

Slowly, savoring the slightly chalky chocolate taste, he returns to his world. He looks around his apartment at his hairy sofa; his wooden chairs, hard as church pews; his threadbare rug, someone else's stained castoff; his mattress at the foot of which carefully, almost reverently, folded was a handmade tribal-patterned blanket; his desk piled high with folders, newspaper clippings, papers, textbooks and manuals; his gunmetal gray lamp that reminds him of a stingray; his bookcase he made himself from white pine boards, meticulously fashioned, with pre-cisely mitered corners and weighty adjustable shelves, a bookcase filled with texts on anatomy, neurology, psychology, pathology, comparative religion, acupuncture, metaphysics and unexplained phenomena, the spines of these learned books dust-free and perfectly aligned; his ancient American stereo with a turntable rather than a CD player; his Bob Dylan album collection, the pristine cardboard slipcases in chronological order as neatly aligned as his books; an old stone mortar and pestle he'd found in Mexico; his beloved photographic and video equipment; a blue glass bottle, old and once shattered, now glued back together; his stained beige work boots with their brand-new laces; the eyes of his latest sacrifice, lying on a sheet of newspaper.

The Pale Saint squiggles his toes through the rough pile of the thread-bare rug. Then he rises and goes over to the desk, and without sitting down, turns on the gunmetal gray lamp. Fluorescent light blooms, giving stacks of white paper violet haloes.

He opens a folder with his right hand as he turns on the stereo. Bob Dylan begins to wail, 'Most likely you go your way and I'll go mine,' as the Pale Saint stares down at the photo affixed to the top sheet in the file.

It is Jon Christopher's photo he is staring at. Grainy and slightly out-of-focus because, although he was using very fast film, he was moving and so was Christopher when he snapped the shutter. He chews his chocolate slowly, meditatively, making each bite last. When he is finished with the first half, he carefully puts the other half along-side the other uneaten halves. Some of them are so old beneath the brown wrapper the chocolate has become pale and chalky as the soil of Oklahoma.

With his fingertips touching the photo, the Pale Saint thinks of his most recent sacrifice, William Cotton. No murder he commits is without logic and necessity. In this regard, he understands Christopher perfectly, for the Pale Saint, too, would hunt down anyone killing purposelessly – for thrill or for sport. These are heinous, despicable acts he could never condone. No, he would track such a disrespectful offender to the ends of the earth and kill him. Like Christopher. Or perhaps not. It has yet to be determined just what Christopher is capable of doing, or how far he will go in the pursuit of that elusive state he calls justice.

Thinking these thoughts he stands before the open newspaper which holds the eyeballs of the sacrifice. Reverently he carries them over to the desk, where violet-tinged light darts and sparks off their convex surfaces. He places them onto the photograph of Jon Christopher. 'Now I see you.' He stares fixedly down at the grainy, slightly fuzzy two-dimensional face. 'I see all the way through you.'

THREE

On his way to the Austins' apartment, Christopher spotted Sara. She was walking her silver-colored Weimaraner named Hound. He honked his horn and pulled into a No Parking spot, flipping down his car's Police ID. Sara was listening to her Walkman so he leaned on the horn.

She turned as he got out of the car, and took off her earphones. 'Uncle Jon!'

Hound barked and, tail wagging, buried his head in Christopher's cupped hands.

'How you doing, boy?' Christopher said before he took Sara in his arms, lifted her off her feet and spun her around. As he did so, he was astonished all over again to feel the quick beat of life inside her. It was funny, he thought, how memories long buried could flare and spark in the blink of an eye, so that the past seemed as vivid as yesterday. He recalled the moment when he had introduced Bobby to Cassandra. It was as if he'd heard an echo like a rifle shot along a ridge, or a door being slammed shut in a prison of his own making. In that moment, his life had slid sideways onto another track which, up until that moment, he could not have known existed. He had watched Cassandra walk away from him, knowing in that deepest place inside himself that she would never come back.

'Hi, honey,' he said as he set her down. 'You seen Mom today? I was looking for her.'

She shook her head. 'She called me from the lab just as I got home from school. She said she wouldn't be more than an hour.' She grinned. 'God, it seems like I haven't seen you for ages.'

As they walked toward the loft, she reached up, laughing, and slipped the earphones on him. Rock'n'roll filled his head with raucous sound.

'Alice in Chains?'

Sara bobbed her head. 'You always get it right. My Dad, he's impossible. He wouldn't know Alice in Chains from Smashing Pumpkins.' She took the earphones back while Christopher, reminded all over again of Bobby, felt the breath go out of him.

As they went into the building, he wondered what the hell Cassandra was up to. It was obvious she hadn't yet told Sara about her father. The news conference was due to begin in time to make the evening news and then the whole world would know that Bobby Austin was dead. What could Cass be thinking, running off to her lab at a time like this? It made no sense to him.

Christopher wandered through the loft while Sara checked the phone messages. In Sara's bedroom, there were a group of photos on her night table. He picked one up, a little shock going all the way through him. The photo was fifteen years old: Christopher and Mercedes as they appeared leaving their wedding reception. She was in the red suit she had worn on their honeymoon flight to the Bahamas, but she still wore her bridal hat and veil, apparently reluctant to remove it. She was staring into the camera, a look of pure delight transfiguring her beautiful face. Christopher's hair was longer then. He had changed out of his tux into a sports jacket and casual slacks. His head was turned slightly, and it was clear he was looking at something or someone just out of the frame, maybe, who knows, the shadow of Mercedes' premature death?

Christopher picked up the photo to get a better look. Beneath the jacket, he noticed now with a start, he wore a knitted polo shirt given to him by Cassandra.

He put down the photo, picked up the one of Andy. Christopher's son had been caught unawares. He was with Sara, she in her baseball uniform, he with a team cap she had given him. Had this been taken just two years ago?

'There's this kid, Ben, in class,' Sara said, mercifully interrupting his train of thought. She stood in the doorway, watching him as he replaced Andy's photo. 'He's in a wheelchair, but that's better than the way he was, in critical condition at St Vincent's. A stupid boy, half-blind on boilermakers, plowed his father's Buick right into him. Ben was standing on the curb, you know, not doing anything. Just about to step off.' Christopher, looking back at her from across the room, was startled to see Bobby's dark intelligent eyes staring at him. 'I mean, it was different with Andy, I know. He didn't just fall.'

No, Christopher thought, *he didn't.*

'But there's something about Ben that's so like Andy. There's this big sadness, like his whole life is sitting on his shoulders. When I'm around him I want to cry. It makes me wonder whether he wanted to walk in front of that car just like Andy wanted to jump.'

'I don't know, honey.' The pain of his son's fall from life was like a dull ache behind Christopher's eyes, something he might claw and claw at but never get rid of.

'People want that sometimes, I think.'

'How do you mean?' Christopher felt the pull of the photo, which seemed to glare accusingly at him. *You didn't do enough,* Andy seemed to be saying. *Why did you let me jump into that empty pool?*

Sara came and took Christopher's hand, leading him back to the living room. 'I think all Andy wanted was what Ben wants,' she was saying, 'what everyone wants, really, to be happy.' She cocked her head. 'Only, some people, you know, don't know how.'

Christopher squeezed her hand. 'If only I'd known how to get through to him.'

'I know you did your best, Uncle Jon.'

Christopher was racked by guilt. But it wasn't just the guilt he felt over Andy's death. Because Bobby's death had somehow broken the lock at Christopher's core, the place where he'd hidden away the truth: that he would never love another human being as deeply, as completely as he loved Cassandra.

Hound began to bark, and Sara took him into the kitchen to feed him. Christopher picked up a book that had Sara's cramped scribbles all over the flyleaf. It was *Seven Pillars of Wisdom* by T.E. Lawrence. Heady reading for a fifteen-year-old, but then Sara had always been precocious. He began to read the opening chapter. Lawrence's style was poetic, idiosyncratic, but for all that something about it seemed immediately familiar. He continued on, as if impelled by a mysterious force. Then he reached a passage that made the hair on the backs of his hands stir. *Easily was a man made an infidel, but hardly might be converted to another faith,* Christopher read. *I had dropped one form and not taken on the other, and was become like Mohammed's coffin in our legend, with a resultant feeling of intense loneliness in life, and a contempt, not for other men, but for all they do.*

His heart beating fast, he flipped through his notebook and re-read what the Pale Saint had written in Bobby Austin's computer just after he had killed him: 'Easily am I made an infidel, but hardly might be converted to another faith. Like a coffin awaiting its burden, I have shed one form and not yet taken on the other . . .' Was the Pale Saint's paraphrasing of Lawrence deliberate or unconscious?

Sara came back into the room. She gave him a disconcertingly direct look. 'Uncle Jon, as long as you're here . . . I mean, can I talk to you?'

Christopher moved closer to her. 'You know you can.' He reached over and drew her toward him, more or less quoting from the end of every episode of *Hawaii 5-0*: 'Okay, Danno. Book 'er. Murder one. Aloha.'

His Steve McGarrett accent was so exaggerated and so bad that Sara immediately began to giggle. Christopher rocked her gently, and said in a very soft voice, 'What's up, honey?'

She put her head back against his chest and closed her eyes. After a very long time, she said, 'There's this big scary thing inside me. Sometimes it gets so huge I'm afraid there won't be room for anything else.'

'What d'you think the big scary thing comes from?'

Sara shrugged.

'But you know, don't you?'

'My parents are both so wrapped up in their work . . . When they fight, it seems like that's all there is – an anger that keeps churning but that also somehow keeps them together. Why are they so angry, Uncle Jon?'

'Probably because they're so wrapped up in their jobs. It must be scary for them, too.'

Sara squirmed around, looked up at him. 'You think?'

He nodded. 'It sure was for me when Andy was alive. I think about that a lot now. The time I didn't spend with him.' His heart broke; the knowledge of Bobby's death was sitting in the back of his throat like a fishhook just ready to snag Sara, if he wasn't careful, and pull her under. He knew he had to speak to her as if Bobby was still alive. 'But you can't just sit with the fear, Sara. Your mother would be so upset if she knew –'

'You won't tell her,' Sara said with some anxiety.

'Of course not,' he assured her. 'I'm like a priest in confession.' He turned her around so he could look into her eyes. 'Anyway, I won't have to, will I? Because you'll do it yourself.'

'Oh, I can't. They're not like you, Uncle Jon. Mom's totally clueless, and Dad, well, he expects me to be strong. That's the only way he says I'll become a winning pitcher.'

Christopher's cell phone rang. He held up a forefinger while he flipped the phone open.

D'Alassandro's voice rang in his ear. 'We've got a problem.'

Christopher walked away from Sara. 'Go.'

He could hear the hesitation in D'Alassandro's voice. 'Are you with Mrs Austin now?'

'No.' Christopher watched Sara go back to her book. 'What's on your mind?'

He could hear D'Alassandro take a deep breath. 'Okay, there's a blood sample missing from my case. From the broken window the perp went through. I checked three times so I'm sure. At first, I thought it was Esquival playing one of his damned practical jokes, but then I spoke to Lang, the uniform who was helping me with the collating. He says while I was in the interrogation room, a woman showed up who said she worked with me. She specifically used my name.'

'Was she wearing an ID tag?'

'He doesn't recall.' She cleared her throat. 'The thing is, he remembered *her* really well – because she was so good-looking, he said, and so helpful with the collating. Tall, short blond hair, gray eyes, dressed in an olive overcoat with epaulets, a diamond bracelet on her right wrist, and I won't repeat what he said about her figure.'

'Oh, hell.' Christopher saw Sara glance across at him and he smiled for her benefit.

'Why would Cassandra Austin do that, steal a blood sample?' D'Alassandro said. 'I mean, what possible use could she have for it?'

'No idea,' Christopher said. Now he really wondered what Cassandra was doing at her lab that was important enough to keep her away from Sara at a time like this. 'But I sure as hell am going to find out. How's it going otherwise?'

'One good thing. I'm betting all the blood on the window fragments belongs to the perp,' D'Alassandro said. 'So far, prelims show it doesn't match anyone else who was in the precinct at the time. On the down side, the computer's finished its search. This guy doesn't exist, at least not officially.'

'Back to square one, damn.' Christopher thought a moment. 'I want you to pick up a copy of *Seven Pillars of Wisdom* by T.E. Lawrence.'

'Wow. Seems a little deep for detective work.'

'Not for this case.'

D'Alassandro's breath quickened. 'Hey, does this mean you've got a lead?'

'Maybe,' Christopher said thoughtfully, then he slid the phone into his pocket and went back to Sara.

'Everything okay?'

'Sure,' he lied, and swiftly switched back to their former topic. 'I want you to talk to your mom.'

'Oh, Uncle Jon –'

'Just try, okay?' He ruffled her hair and laughed. 'It'll be good for your mental toughness.'

She laughed, too. 'Okay, but I'm telling you we're just gonna piss each other off.'

'Maybe she'll surprise you,' he said, then gestured. 'How'd you get interested in that book?'

'I saw *Lawrence of Arabia* and fell in love with Peter O'Toole.' She scrunched up her face. 'Well, not so much Peter O'Toole, although he was pretty yummy in the flick. I thought I'd find out what the real T.E. Lawrence was really into.'

'And what do you think now?'

'I think this war in the desert, this war of independence, changed him.' She met Christopher's gaze with her father's unwavering look before she glanced down at the text. '"Our aim was to seek the enemy's weakest material link and bear only on that till time made their whole length fail."' She looked up. 'See, he knew that about the Arabs, that their will was stronger than the Turks', that in the end he could break them. But along the way something else happened, something unexpected and terrible. The war made him . . .' She paused, searching for the right word, then ran her finger down the page. '"By our own act,"' she read, '"we were drained of morality, of volition, of responsibility, like dead leaves in the wind."' She looked up. '*That's* what happened to him: he became a dead leaf in the wind of the war he was fighting.'

Something happened to Christopher as she said this, a mysterious connection, a tremor of recognition deep inside the marrow of his bones, as if he'd heard those words spoken before, or would hear them spoken in some moment yet to be born.

Shaking himself loose from this eerie sensation, Christopher leaned over and kissed her on the forehead. 'You be sure to keep me updated on your opinion of Mr Lawrence. Right now, I've got to go.'

She looked at him. 'I think Andy would have liked Lawrence as much as I do.'

Christopher paused. 'I'm sure he would have, honey.'

'When she gets home, I'll tell Mom you were looking for her.'

He gave her a small smile. 'Don't grow up so fast, okay?'

She nodded. 'Uncle Jon,' she said suddenly, 'everything's all right, isn't it?'

Sara looked at him for a very long time, then, impulsively, she drew her arms around him so tightly he knew she didn't want to let go. 'Come see me again as quickly as you can.'

'You bet,' he said. As he kissed her tenderly on each cheek, he tried not to see Bobby's face with the Bic pen driven through his eye.

The Vertex Institute had purchased for Cassandra a four-story brownstone on Grove St, west of Seventh Ave. The institute's directors decided on a brownstone, rather than a larger loft building in Soho for reasons of privacy, they said. For privacy, read security. Vertex was a high-profile biosciences company, one of the two major private resources for HARP, the federal government's Healthcare Antiaging Research Program. The other was Helix Technologies. The two companies were rivals, bitter enemies that were continually jockeying for prominence. Because both Vertex and Helix were vulnerable to Congressional review and public opinion, there was a great deal of infighting that Cassandra, thankfully, wasn't privy to. Gerry Costas kept her well insulated from the highly politicized side of the business.

A previous owner must have been something of an arborist because the brownstone had a small, square garden in the rear with an arching horse chestnut that bloomed pink in the spring, and a dwarf Japanese maple whose leaves turned flame-color in the fall. At the rear of the garden was a short stone path that led to a smaller back building.

Vertex had completely gutted the inside of both buildings and redesigned them according to Cassandra's specifications. The result was a series of self-contained labs where all work could be done in absolute isolation.

Christopher had visited Cass at work just once, and then he had accompanied Bobby when his friend had wanted to surprise her. It was three days before Thanksgiving; her birthday. She had been working at NYU Medical Center on First Ave. Christopher had carried the three-tiered strawberry shortcake he had had made up specially for the occasion, while Bobby cradled in his hands the engagement present he'd selected for her, a diamond bracelet he couldn't afford but which, after that night, to Christopher's knowledge, she never took off.

For many years afterward he'd fooled himself into believing that they'd all been so happy that night.

Now, as he confronted the quartet of armed guards who screened all visitors to the Vertex lab, Christopher was in an altogether different mood. He was assailed by emotions which threatened the professional detachment necessary for his work. They were good, these guards, checking his credentials against a computer readout; they would not let him pass until they had verified his shield number. It seemed absurd, almost comical, four armed guards to protect a scientific laboratory, until Christopher remembered the threats made against the lab by Dean Koenig. A guard handed him a plastic pass with his digital computer-generated photo on it. It was just like the one you got when you went to have your driver's license renewed. He was given directions to Cassandra's lab, where he found her hunched over her notes. But before he could get to her, a handsome man with eyes bright behind colored contact lenses intervened.

'May I help you?' He had the slightly exaggerated Boston accent that Christopher found grating because it almost always was an affectation.

He opened his badge and watched the look on the handsome man's face. 'Remember me, Doc?'

This was Dr Hutton Dillard, Cass's associate and self-appointed watchdog. Though he was from a terribly upper-crust Main Line Philadelphia family, he was as protective of her as if he were her Latino husband. He was the kind of guy who added Mister or your professional title to your surname; if he knew you well, he dropped the title. Graduated Harvard Med, researched at Walter Reed before Cass hired him. Christopher had met him at a medical fund raiser Bobby and Cass had dragged him to; plus, he'd heard plenty from Bobby. He didn't like the man, but then no one did, possibly not even Cass. But, according to her, he was a helluva researcher.

'Here on *police* business, Lt Christopher?' With his clipped and measured cadences and emphases he managed to make the word sound like an Orthodox rabbi uttering the word *traife*.

'Just a little chat with your boss.'

'She's not my boss,' Dr Dillard said as Christopher went past him. 'Dr Austin is my associate.'

To Dillard's right, an assistant turned on a miniature ceramic oven. The sound seemed muffled, as if it had been absorbed by the vast array of complex equipment that filled the lab. Far across the room, past a phalanx of gleaming stainless-steel tubes, pipes attached to compressors and ventilators, was a window through which he glimpsed copper-colored leaves being whipped off tree branches by the brisk October wind. Cassandra looked up at his approach. By the look in her eyes he was sure she had been expecting him.

'I'm sorry I ran out like that, but I . . .'

'Are you okay?'

'My glacial exterior is still intact, if that's what you mean. Sheridan called.' Dan Sheridan was the D.A., Bobby's boss. 'He was very nice. He insisted on taking care of the finances of the funeral. I didn't know what to say.'

'I think you should say yes.'

'That part still seems so unreal, putting Bobby in the ground.' She paused a moment, while she looked away at nothing or, in her mind, everything. Then, in that disconcerting manner of hers, she abruptly refocused on him. 'I can see you're angry, Jon.'

'Maybe confused is a better word for it,' he said. 'I know you're in shock. Why else would you deliberately disobey my order, impersonate a detective, and steal an official piece of evidence from the crime scene?'

'You told me to stay put,' she said. 'I didn't think it was an order.'

'Well, it was.'

'I don't take orders,' she said, 'from anyone.'

She seemed unnaturally calm. Was she in shock or just being pigheaded? Once, Christopher realized, he would have known. Now he did not. Already, he felt the interview slipping away from him. This was not a common experience for him. He could intimidate the cross-section of criminal minds that crawled through the city's streets; but Cassandra was different. With effort, he pulled himself together. 'I saw Sara.'

'I know. She called right after you left. You scared her, showing up like that.'

'Yeah, well, I was looking for you. You should have been there, Cass. You've got to tell her –'

'Jon, stop it. She's *my* daughter; this is *my* family, not yours. Funny, that's something you never could get through your head.'

Not funny at all, Christopher thought. He could see Dillard watching them out of the corner of his unnaturally blue eyes. 'Dammit, think of Sara. Do you want her to hear about her father from the five o'clock news?'

Cassandra's eyes blazed, but she did not raise her voice. 'Don't you assume anything, okay? I appreciate you telling me yourself, but from the moment you gave me the news I felt incredibly helpless, filled with a black rage, but instead of falling to pieces I've decided to do something *now* so I won't have to be like that when I do tell Sara.' There were tears standing in the corners of her eyes, but her expression was one of pure defiance. 'I'll tell her in my own time, in my own way.'

She's like a general with her troops, he thought: *hard, peremptory, direct.* He decided to try another tactic 'Cass, you'd better tell me what the hell is going on here. Why did you steal that blood sample?'

'That old precinct . . . I happened to overhear your conversation with Brockaw, Jon, about not being able to catch this . . . murderer.'

'Oh, Jesus.'

'That's when I got the idea. I can help. This lab is the perfect place to –'

'Goddammit, Cass, I don't give a rat's ass about your ideas.'

'But, Jon –!'

The flat of his hand seemed to cut across her words. 'No buts!' he shouted.

There was a brief pause in the well-coordinated hum of activity in the lab as the assistants looked up and Dr Dillard took a couple of irate steps in their direction.

'Lt Christopher, I must insist –'

'Stay right where you are, Doc,' Christopher warned.

Dillard looked at Cassandra, who shook her head curtly. The iron discipline that she had implemented among her staff reasserted itself, and the hum of scientific activity slowly returned. Dillard, however, was smoldering, in that well-mannered way they must have taught him at Harvard.

'Cass, take it from someone who knows, you're in shock. You're not thinking clearly. Whatever you had in mind, I want you to forget it. Leave this investigation to the professionals.'

'You are so thick-headed. Will you just let me tell you –'

'Give me your word right now that you won't use that stolen blood sample, Cass. This minute. Otherwise I'm going to have to take you in.'

'You wouldn't.'

'Try me. You're already in enough trouble as it is. Theft of police property and impersonating a police officer are serious offenses.'

She was wearing a lab coat identical to the one she had on when he and Bobby had come in with the cake and the diamond bracelet to celebrate her birthday. Her hair had been long then, pulled back in a thick French braid. Christopher remembered how it burned like pale fire. He had never thought of overhead lab lights as being particularly romantic before.

'Damn you,' she whispered.

He didn't have to be a detective to know that their current clash of wills had less to do with the present than it did the past. But this self-knowledge was of little use. Bobby's death had ripped open a wound that had never truly healed. In fact, he saw now, it had festered beneath the surface he'd so carefully laid over it on the night of the wedding, when he'd stood beside his best friend and watched Cass walk down the aisle toward them, away from him forever. Now, watching the hurt flooding her face all over again, he felt sick to his stomach. He hated himself, and yet it was this very self-loathing that incited him onward.

Cassandra watched him for some time out of the corner of her eye. 'When I stand too close to you, like now, I feel a chill all the way to my bones, do you know that?'

Christopher died a little inside, but maybe that was okay, maybe that was what he'd wanted all along, to be punished for his sin against her and Bobby. Cassandra may have stolen police property and impersonated an officer, but it was he who had committed the more serious crime.

'Why do you say nothing? I'm angry with you, and I know you're angry with me – how angry? Say it, Jon.'

Christopher did not want to get into this at all now – perhaps not ever. It cut too close to the bone. Bad enough when he was with her he walked a delicate emotional tightrope.

'Are you going to stop? I want your answer.'

'Okay,' she said, 'but in return I want you to tell me whether D'Alassandro needs the one sample I appropriated out of all the samples she gathered.'

'What D'Alassandro needs or doesn't need is irrelevant.'

'Not to me, it isn't. I would never have taken anything vital to her investigation. Do you understand me, Jon?'

Christopher could see that if she was going to lose this particular battle of wills, she was going to make damn sure she'd won back some of her pride.

'How could you possibly know –'

'It's my job to know.' She'd been ready for him. 'D'Alassandro knows and so do you. All those samples are from one man – the man who murdered Bobby.' She gazed at him from her beautiful gray eyes. 'You know I'm right, Jon.'

'Still –'

'My taking one isn't going to jeopardize your investigation. In fact, it's not going to make a damn bit of difference to you.' Her gray eyes drew him into their orbit of light as if he had no more control than a moth to a flame. 'But it means everything to me.' She searched his face, as if remembering every moment of their friendship. 'I know if you take a minute, Jon, you can understand this. I *know* it.'

He looked around the lab: at the miniature city of equipment, at the diminutive engines quietly humming, at Dillard, ostensibly at work but covertly watching them, at the assistants at their stations, busy with their mysterious procedures, at the window and its tiny fragments of autumn.

'Dammit, Cass, why must you be like this? No one can be hard as nails all the time.'

'We can't help it. About this thing, we're the same,' she said without any trace of irony in her voice.

'Yeah, right,' he said after a time. 'So what's it going to be?'

'Jesus Christ, Jon, what went wrong between us?'

'Everything.'

She let out a long pent-up breath. 'You really mean that, don't you?' When he didn't answer her, she said: 'Tell me something, Jon. Honestly.'

'If I can.'

'How typical.' A vein pulsed in her forehead. At last, she said, 'Do you have any lead – anything at all – on this man, this Pale Saint?'

Christopher decided it wouldn't help to lie or even to stretch the truth. 'Too early to tell.'

'When are you going to stop lying to me? I know you won't find him easily – if at all. I heard you say as much to Brockaw, remember?' Then she pointed to a test tube spinning in the centrifuge. 'He's in there – what do you call him, the perp? Right. The perp's DNA, his very essence is right in my hands. You see, Jon, I got to thinking. I can do tests here so sophisticated your lab tekkies would be lost in a matter of seconds. See, I can be of help. I can maybe find something within his DNA structure that can –'

Why did he suddenly feel a ripple of cold premonition down his spine? 'Christ, Cass, the last thing I need right now is for you to get

47

involved. You were married to the latest victim, for Christ's sake. Besides being against I don't know how many regulations, it's just plain wrong.'

'Is it?' she said. 'Now that you've heard why I needed the blood sample aren't you going to change your mind and let me continue?'

'Absolutely not. This is finished, here and now, do you understand me?'

'What kind of a detective are you, anyway?' Seeing his reaction, she mocked him: 'Go wherever the case leads you. What happened to the great Christopher's first law?'

'There are exceptions to any rule. You promised you'd terminate this, whatever you call it, this experiment and you will. Is that clear?'

She stared at him coldly.

He unsnapped a pair of stainless steel manacles, rattled them in front of her. 'Or do you want to be booked downtown?'

She abruptly turned away. 'I'm getting the hell out of here,' she told Dillard as she grabbed her coat and purse, 'now that there's no pressing reason to stay.'

Dillard shot Christopher a venomous look as Christopher held the door open for her.

Christopher drove Cassandra home. Not a word passed between them. On the way, he took her to the CME's office and stood beside her in the viewing room while she made the formal ID. He watched her carefully – clinically almost – to see if she would falter, but her glacial calm did not flicker. She signed some papers and that was it. While they were at the CME's they continued their glacial silence; they might have been in separate universes. At her doorstep he made her promise to talk to Sara ASAP. She did not invite him inside, but he found himself imagining what it would be like. No good. Anyway, he was required to make an appearance at the Chief's press conference. The first public showing of the point man on the Pale Saint case. For point man read scape goat. If he failed to bring the Pale Saint in, the Mayor sure wasn't going to take the heat. Christopher would be dismissed from the case, and another detective brought in. That would more or less be the end of Christopher's career in Homicide. He could expect to shuffle papers at some fly-bitten desk far away from the media spotlight until his retirement or his death, whichever came first.

Cassandra did not turn around as Christopher sped off down the street, but she felt an unsettling hollowness inside her now that he was gone. Guilt and a kind of helpless rage flared inside her that she should feel this for him – feel anything at all – with Bobby just dead.

'Sara?' She put the key in the lock and pushed open the door. 'Honey, I'm home.'

Sara appeared in makeup, looking startlingly adult, yet vulnerable, like a model in a Calvin Klein ad, and Cassandra caught her breath.

'Just practicing,' Sara said, misinterpreting her mother's expression. 'I'll go wipe it off.'

'No.' Cassandra reached out for her and held her. 'No need.' It seemed unnaturally hot in the apartment, or perhaps just close as she walked with her daughter into the living room. Blue shadows dusted the street outside, and the tops of the plebald plane trees danced in the autumn wind. 'I have something to tell you.' She was filled with sudden irrational fear that if she let go Sara would vanish. 'There's been a terrible accident. Your father has been killed.' She was weeping as she said this, though she had promised herself she would not. Some promises held no weight against tragedy, which often brings surprise as well as shock and sorrow.

Sara sagged in Cassandra's arms as if she had been felled by a bolt from a crossbow. 'Daddy,' she said as she had when she was very young and ill with the high fever that accompanies ear infections. Abruptly, she pulled away from Cassandra. 'No!' she shouted. 'Daddy's taking me to the ALCS tomorrow. He got these great seats right over the Yankees' dugout so we can watch Andy Pettitte pitch.'

Cassandra's heart was filled with her daughter's disbelief as well as her own sorrow. 'Honey –'

'It can't be true. He was taking time off work; he was going to show me Pettitte's slider up-close.'

'Sara, Sara . . .'

'Daddy, Daddy, Daddy.' It became a harsh and keening cry, and she turned her face into her mother's breasts and was a child again as Cassandra rocked her, stroked her gently as they both knelt upon the hardwood floor.

That tiny pool of calm didn't last. Sara soon pushed Cassandra away from her and rose, half-running to the bathroom. Cassandra followed her. She stood in the doorway, watching as her daughter stared at herself in the mirror. Her tear-streaked image reared above the miniature skyline of creams and lotions lined along the counter top. With a savage sweep of her forearm, Sara swept away all the pretty glass jars and bottles. The sound of their smashing was like the wave of thunderclaps of a storm reaching its zenith.

Cassandra, weeping, took Sara up in her arms, but she was beyond solace.

'There wasn't time!' Sara cried. 'It isn't fair! There wasn't time!'

'I know, I know, sweetheart.'

Her own grief, coupled with seeing Sara so distraught, made Cassandra inarticulate. She longed to say the words that would soothe her daughter, that would make things right, but they remained a mystery to her. In the face of Bobby's shocking death all words seemed smothered in a black and airless vortex. It would be easy to give in to this despair, Cassandra knew. She had seen it overwhelm Christopher when his wife had died, and then when Andy had killed himself two years ago. For Sara's sake, if not for her own, she needed to struggle past this dreadful, electric silence.

'Sara,' she said softly through her tears, 'nothing will bring him back the way he was, but memory is powerful, you'll see. More powerful even than death.' She stroked strands of stray hair off Sara's damp, fevered forehead. 'If we talk about Bobby, if we continue to remember him, he will remain close to us. And that's the point now, isn't it? To keep him close, so that he won't fade away.'

Sara, curled in a ball and shivering slightly, nodded. 'I'll never forget him,' she whispered. 'Never.'

Later, in the semi-darkness of the city, Cassandra peered out the window, down through the Bradford pear trees. Seeing the remote TV trucks parked several blocks away she was grateful for the police cordon around their building.

Cassandra ordered dinner from a neighborhood restaurant, but she discovered she had no appetite. Sara, for her part, did not emerge from her room, even when Cassandra begged her to come out. She went back to the window. Across the street, tables were set on the sidewalk in front of the restaurant from which she had ordered the uneaten food. Since this was New York, there were a few hardy souls in leather jackets, sitting out there. At one table, a handsome young man sat, smoking one cigarette after another, apparently waiting for someone who never appeared. Couples walked by. The soft murmur of life cradled them as Cassandra, set apart by the invisible wall of her grief, observed from a lonely distance. She forced up memories of Bobby: how on their first date she had burned his fingers handing him a hot fondue skewer; how he had been late for their wedding, caught in Center St traffic, and had run all the way to the church, sweating through his tux; how Christopher found the ring he had misplaced; how he had talked her out of naming Sara Jordan because he wanted his daughter to have a soft name; how he always sent her two dozen white roses on their anniversary, the date of which he always got wrong. *Is that all there is,* she asked herself, *all that's left of our years together?*

Suddenly, she could not bear to be alone with her thoughts a moment longer. On impulse she gathered up her dinner and, shoving it into a plastic bag, went out of the house. Up the block, on the corner of Houston St, a homeless man had set up a kind of postmodern lean-to made of rotten plywood and cardboard. During the warm months, he hung out on a bench in the nearby park, but when it began to get cold he built his lean-to over subway grates.

Bobby had been in the habit of giving him food or old clothes, or just stopping on his way home from work, to talk to the man. On occasion, she'd find him at the window, leaning out to make sure the homeless man was all right.

The lean-to possessed the stench of a charnel house, which had always put Cassandra off. Also, the homeless man's small head made him seem to her like someone from a circus sideshow: the Amazing Pinhead! But now, somehow, she was drawn here. She knew she had to make some physical act, something symbolically tied to Bobby, in order to bring herself out of a grief that was threatening to make her implode.

The homeless man, who had apparently shed his name along with all his other worldly possessions, accepted her offering with a laconic word of thanks. Then he looked up at her from his wild man's crouch, and she could see the canniness in his beady, black crow eyes. 'You're Bobby's wife, ain't cha?' His breath stank of the alcohol he somehow ingested without killing himself.

She nodded, a lump in her throat.

The homeless man sniffed. 'Haven't seen him for a while.'

'He's dead.' The horrific words slipped out of her mouth like unctuous oil. She began to gag.

'Dead.' The homeless man opened the plastic bag, took instant inventory of the food. When he raised his head, his eyes caught her on twin spikes. 'Can't eat; can't sleep, that it?'

She looked helplessly at him.

'Go home,' he said. 'Be thankful you have one to go to.'

Cassandra returned slowly to the loft. Haloes wreathed the street lights and the heels of passersby clicked rhythmically against the cement. Folk music drifted like woodsmoke out of the restaurant across the street. The handsome young man had gone, presumably alone. Cassandra saw a pair of young lovers strolling toward her. Their lean bodies emitted an urgency discernible even at a distance. As she watched their ardent kiss, she was possessed by the strongest desire to call Christopher.

She started awake in the middle of the night, feeling as if she had never fallen asleep. Her hair was plastered by sweat to her forehead and the nape of her neck. Automatically, still on the verge of her bad dream, she reached out for Bobby, and when instead she found the cool sheet she ran to the bathroom with the dry heaves. She flushed the toilet several times, even though it wasn't necessary. The minty sting of mouthwash cleared the sour taste of her own stomach acid. She spit into the sink and watched the blue-green liquid swirl down the drain.

She could not return to bed, could not in fact imagine ever sleeping in it again. Instead, she prowled the apartment, enveloped by a darkness that seemed utterly appropriate.

She listened listlessly to the message Gerry Costas had left on her answering machine, expressing condolences, telling her to not to worry about skipping tomorrow's interview on Dean Koenig's cable TV show, he'd take care of it. He offered her instead a vacation on the company, all she had to do was contact Vertex' travel department and they'd take care of the arrangements. It was the third such message he'd left, and it somehow depressed her.

At last, she turned on the TV as if it were a light, and watched soundless music videos with the distracted, almost manic, inattention of an autistic child. She wanted to return to her lab but she could not – would not – abandon Sara to the darkness that followed such a terrible and intimate death.

Rapt within the darkness and her peculiar solitude, Cassandra stared sightlessly at the flickering TV screen. What she saw was the sliver of the Pale Saint's skin she had extracted from the blood sample. She saw, in her mind's eye, the chain of his DNA as if it were a flag unfurling on a charnel field of war. And it was at that moment the idea came into focus. She believed now that it had been there from the moment Christopher had told her about the Pale Saint's blood because she had been preparing for this moment ever since Vertex had set up her lab. It somehow surprised her that she had had no compunction at all about lying to Christopher. Of course she had had no intention of terminating her experiment. On the contrary, she was about to take it to another level that was altogether unprecedented.

She rose, her pulse pounding in her throat, and went to the window. She looked out onto the nighttime street and it seemed as if the street lights were chains of DNA molecules. Sleep was out of the question now, she was too excited to pay attention to any doubts she might feel. What she had in mind would have to be done in absolute isolation, in total secrecy, which meant she'd have to lie to Gerry Costas. She hated to do that but experience had taught her that at one time or another expediency made liars of us all. It was the right thing to do, she was certain. Gerry would never understand what she really had in mind, let alone condone it. As head of Vertex he was a businessman; at the end of the day, the bottom line was all he cared about. Later, she'd have time to compile the anti-aging data that would cement her career and make Vertex a fortune, but business had become secondary; she had a personal agenda. Bobby's death had made it so. Her desperation to see justice done, her desire to make some kind of sense out of the chaos, was overwhelming, but she knew the path she had chosen was terribly difficult and perilous.

She realized she was standing by the phone. She had no memory of getting from the window here. It was as if she'd been sleepwalking. She snatched the phone off its cradle and dialed Hutton Dillard's number.

He answered after the sixth ring. 'Cassandra? Are you all right?'

Somehow his staid formality served to calm her wildly beating heart.

'I want you to meet me at the lab at six a.m.'

'That's in . . . a little over three hours. Cassandra –?'

'We're about to enter the history books, Hutton. We're going to launch Construct.'

'Perhaps I didn't hear you correctly.'

'Nothing wrong with your hearing.'

'Surely you can't be serious.'

Cassandra's voice lowered. 'I need your help. You're the only one I can turn to. Not even Gerry can know about this. Please.'

'Ethical concerns aside, we don't even have the DNA to –'

'We do now.'

'Wait a minute!' She heard the edge of panic in his voice. 'Dear God, Cassandra, tell me this has nothing to do with Mr Austin. You're not planning to resurrect your husband.'

'Certainly not.' She would never tell him that in her desperation and grief the notion had momentarily crossed her mind. 'The implications are too terrible to contemplate. I couldn't bear it if we tried the protocol and it failed. And if we did succeed, he wouldn't be Bobby. He'd have none of Bobby's memories – all of our shared life would be gone. The thought of confronting a Bobby who was not Bobby is . . .' She was unable to go on.

'Well, that's an enormous relief.' Dillard hesitated. 'Cassandra, are you all right?'

She tried to take a couple of deep breaths.

'Yes, yes, I'm okay. Look, I'll explain everything tomorrow at the lab. You know the one I mean.'

'I do.'

'Then you'll do it?' Silence. 'Hutton,' she whispered, 'I need to know you're with me on this. I can't launch Construct alone.'

'You know I'd do anything for you.'

'God, I love you.'

'But Cassandra, I . . .' For a moment he almost seemed tongue-tied, but that was impossible, she told herself. Hutton Dillard was *never* at a loss for words. 'I have grave reservations which I need to talk to you about at length.'

'Tomorrow morning, Hutton. See you at six sharp.'

After she cradled the phone she felt as if she had thrown off a drugged stupor. Turning off the TV, she padded into the kitchen and made herself an enormous peanut butter-and-jelly sandwich on that squooshy white bread she and Christopher always took with them on their sojourns into the woods of upstate New York.

Christopher dreamt he was a stag alone in the forest. Only this was a forest not of trees but of modern buildings. As Christopher turned his antlered head this way and that all that existed as far as the eye could see were buildings and more buildings reaching up into the sky. All at once, he became aware that the sidewalks were slick with blood. He stamped his forelegs in agitation, and moved on, but the blood was everywhere. A derelict in a doorway with Bobby Austin's face made him cry out in an animal voice he did not recognize.

He began to run on his four powerful legs, and as he did so, as the buildings blurred, as his flanks became sheened with sweat he felt the fear welling up inside him. By a trick of memory he heard the rustle of the wind through green leaves, he scented sharp pine resin, the musk of small mammals, he saw golden sunlight dappled with shadow across a vast carpet of pine needles. He experienced these things with utter clarity but also with deep sadness because he knew these were only memories dimly realized from a distant past he could only dredge up in fragments that flickered away from him like flames guttered in a draft.

Christopher, the stag, ran and ran through bloody streets and avenues and back alleyways until his lungs labored and his heart fairly burst, and still all that could be seen were buildings and more buildings, and the blood. Nevertheless, he ran on, not knowing what else he could do. He ran until he awoke with a start and a gasp. He stared at the stars burning the night through the skylight of his top floor apartment. Then, his chest heaving just as if he himself had run and run until his heart had fairly burst, he drew his knees up, locked his arms around them. Resting his sweating forehead against his knees he thought of the Pale Saint out there in *his* city, making the blood run in the forest he'd sworn to protect.

FOUR

'How's Minnie?' Dillard asked, peering into the cage.

'Fine.' Cassandra held Minnie, the female lab rat with the mutated pineal. 'She's already an adolescent.'

'Incredible.'

'Time for another shot of Tetracycline. We want to maintain her aging at a normal rate now.' She injected the lab rat with the antibiotic while it squealed and squirmed. 'That's okay, honey,' she crooned to the animal. 'It's all over now.' She gave the furry back a few strokes before placing Minnie onto the cage floor.

It was 6.15 in the morning, and the two researchers were in a separate section of the Vertex labs off-limits to all personnel but them.

Dillard watched her as she stripped off latex gloves. 'You and I have gone over the theory behind Construct a thousand times; we know it's sound. Look at Minnie. The hyper-aging protocol works, and because of the adjustments we've made it will work every time. We can start the human phase right away. It will only take –'

'Stop right there. You've seen how controversial our work with animal DNA manipulation has been. It has caused a firestorm of debate within the Institute of Bio-Ethics, sharp criticism from some of our more conservative colleagues, and has infuriated and terrified Dean Koenig and his reactionaries, the Christian Convocation, the Right to Lifers and any number of radical fundamentalists all too ready to use violence as a means to their ends. Now you want to jump to a human model? Vertex has turned you down twice already. I was here when Costas ordered you to put Construct in mothballs. Construct is just the kind of ethically irresponsible project Koenig keeps accusing us of doing. The response from the IBE would be bad enough, but if Koenig got wind of it he'd demonize us so thoroughly Vertex would be out of business within a month.'

'The blockheads at the IBE have been a thorn in my side for years,' Cassandra said. 'They're not researchers, they're whiners and hand-wringers. What do they know about us, anyway? We're out here on the cutting edge of history, the ones in the trenches putting our theories and our reputations on the line. The simple truth is they can't do what we can. Their criticism is nothing more than professional jealousy. If we left DNA technology up to them we'd all be sitting on our hands.' She shook her head. 'And as for Dean Koenig and his thugs, they can go straight to hell.'

'Personally, I have no affinity for Mr Koenig, but what about Costas? He pays our salaries.'

'Just the point,' Cassandra said. 'Costas is an administrator. He reports to the Vertex board. His god is the bottom line. Whether or not we make scientifically significant breakthroughs is secondary to his mind-set.' She shook her head. 'How long have you and I been searching for a way to delay the onset of aging? It's the very essence of our work here.'

'True, but must I point out that we've barely gotten through the one animal protocol. We really must do more. Minnie has to be monitored, studied, all our calculations checked over and over before we do another. I mean, my God, you don't even know what this one mutated lab rat will be like a month from now, let alone a year. And you want to jump straight from this into a *human* experiment? But all that aside, there's a larger issue: how do we choose whose DNA will be used?'

'That's the beauty of all this, Hutton. Fate dropped a perfect subject into my lap.' She told him how she had come upon the blood and epithelial tissue of the Pale Saint.

'You stole a sample from the New York City Police? Lord, Cassandra, that's why this detective was up to see you yesterday, wasn't it?'

She patted the back of his hand. 'Don't look so worried, Hutton, I've taken care of it.'

'But why would you want this . . . beast's DNA? He seems like the last person on earth you'd want to clone.'

'On the contrary, he's perfect for Construct. Here's my thinking. First, because the subject is a serial murderer only the ACLU would be likely to bring up the ethics issue, and maybe not even them. *Nobody* wants to be on this sonuvabitch's side. Anyway, they're not going to find out.

'Second, this one's special. I've done a complete DNA mapping on the sample. There's already something going on with his pineal. I don't know what it is yet, but I can tell you this: he's a perfect subject for us.' She took a breath before rushing on, oblivious to the effect her proximity was having on her colleague. 'This is the opportunity we've been praying for. It's like a sign from God.'

Dillard winced. 'Please don't invoke His name that way. It's sacrilegious.'

'Sorry.' Cassandra had to continually remind herself of his strict religious upbringing. 'But, listen, Hutton, we can't let it slip through our fingers. We'll learn *volumes* about how the pineal affects aging.'

He sat for a moment, lost in thought. 'You realize that we are aware in only the most rudimentary way of the dangers inherent in Construct. We're in such uncharted territory there are bound to be surprises, perhaps very nasty ones.'

'They could just as easily be pleasant surprises. But without question, they'll be ground-breaking ones. Revolutionary. Trust me, you've just got opening night jitters.'

'Is that what this is?' He lifted his hands. 'Look, they're shaking. It's as if we're diving into the Marianas Trench without a lifeline.'

'And as a researcher isn't that just where you want to be, in the deepest water? That's where all the great discoveries are made.' Cassandra left her stool to pace around the lab. 'Logical step-by-step analysis certainly has its place, but it's only part of the research story, you know that. Coincidence, happenstance, luck, fate, and at times, leaps of faith are all requirements for discovery.'

'The problem with that argument, Cassandra, is that you are looking at only one side of the coin. The other side is this: if you aren't careful, you'll surely be drowned by your own zeal. Like it or not, you're on ethically shaky ground.'

'All leaps of faith have at their core great risk.'

'You see what even the idea of this kind of risk does to me. I've been trained to do things by the book.'

She gripped his shoulders. 'That's on the outside, Hutton, but I know you. On the inside, there's a bit of the rebel. No, no, don't waste energy denying it. You've been working on your theory of environmentally acquired traits in humans for a decade. You've published nine brilliant articles on the subject.' She looked him in the eye. 'Tell me, how stiff has the debate been against you?'

He sighed, then nodded. 'Very stiff, indeed, but that's just politics.'

'Bull. You have reams of computer-generated statistics, but you'll never be taken seriously until you have actual clinical proof to offer.' Cassandra's eyes were alight. 'You've taken on the establishment this far, why not go all the way? We now have the means to get you your proof. We will clone this serial murderer. I trust your theories enough to bet the clone will have no homicidal tendencies. Tell me, do you trust them as much as I do?'

'Yes, of course. But –'

'Then prove it – to me and to yourself.' She gripped him. 'God, Hutton, *this* is why we do what we do – to open wide the door into the unknown when auspicious fate gives us the privilege.' She squeezed his shoulders. 'The chance we have been given happens maybe once in a lifetime – to most researchers it never happens at all.'

Dillard smiled. 'You know, I always said that your boundless enthusiasm made you an exceptionally beautiful –'

'Watch it, Doctor!'

'– researcher.' He nodded. 'All right. Let's go.'

Cassandra gave him the thumbs up sign, turning her mind fully to creating the trans-gene that would cause the rapid aging in her clone of the Pale Saint. She was struck by the absurdity of the situation. Here she was about to advance the furthest boundaries of known science, and the procedure she was going to use was about as simple as using a home pregnancy test.

She took a test tube filled one-third with a combination of distilled water and EDTA, a buffer that would prevent crucial enzymes from degrading, and took up a micro-pipette. Some years ago molecular biologists had discovered that certain diseases such as diabetes and some forms of cancer were hereditary. Even though members of the same family might carry the gene for those diseases, they could go their whole life without contracting the disease because the gene was never activated – or as Cassandra and her molecular biologists would say, it was never expressed.

When Cassandra gave her lectures she used the analogy of a gate opening and closing. If the gene 'gate' was closed nothing happened. But if the gene was activated, if the gate was opened, the DNA in the gene would undergo a two-step chemical process. In the first, called transcription, the DNA would replicate itself as a simpler molecule called RNA. In the second, called translation, the RNA acting as a kind of molecular field general would give orders to the cell to manufacture an even simpler protein. It was this unique protein that would cause

59

the change in the human body – a hereditary cancer, diabetes or in the case of the clone hyper-aging.

Using the micro-pipette, Cassandra placed three genes in the test tube. The first was the gene she had discovered in the human pineal gland that when activated accelerated the speed of aging. The second gene would create Actin, a protein that would open the gene gate. The third gene contained a receptor site for Tetracycline. At some point, the aging rate would need to be controlled, slowed down to normal or the clone would die of old age a few weeks after it attained adulthood. When an introduced Tetracycline molecule attached itself to the mutated gene's receptor site the hyper-aging protein would cease to be made, the gene gate would be closed and aging would become normal.

Cassandra held the test tube up to the light. All three genes were in the liquid. Now she needed to bind them together. This was astonishingly simple. She added a pre-manufactured enzyme called DNA ligase which is the foundation of all DNA technology and ATP, a triphosphate energy source that was the catalyst for the binding. This particular ATP was a version Cassandra herself had made. Usually the DNA binding process took overnight. With her ATP it was accomplished in a matter of minutes.

'How does it look?' Dillard asked.

'We'll soon find out,' she said.

She needed to separate the ligated gene – the three genes fused into the one trans-gene – from the other stray bits of DNA matter floating in the liquid. This was a fairly straightforward procedure because the newly formed trans-gene was larger than the others. Hutton had set up a standard amount of agarose gel for her. The gel had a weak electrical current running through it, positive on top, negative on the bottom. Cassandra poured the contents of the test tube onto the gel. DNA, like all acids, was negatively charged so the smaller pieces were pulled very quickly through the gel, while the larger ligated piece – the trans-gene – remained in the gel itself.

Cassandra now transferred the square of gel into a Petri dish filled with ethidium bromide. She turned on a UV light and saw the outline of the trans-gene fluorescing like a neon sign.

'Beautiful as a summer's day,' she said.

She cut that piece of gel with a razor blade and placed it into a syringe with a special filter at the end where the needle would be. Depressing the plunger, she ejected the trans-gene in its water and EDTA base into another test tube while leaving the gel behind. She now had her trans-gene, but the most crucial step was to come. It needed to be purified before it could be injected into the egg. Stray proteins were the single most aggressive danger to the trans-genic process – any one of them left over from the ligation protocol could kill the egg. So she added five micro-liters of phenol chloroform, which dissolved all the proteins while leaving the DNA material untouched.

She held in her hand the purified trans-gene.

'All set,' she said to Dillard.

He had readied the micro-manipulator. This machine, an essential tool in all in-vitro fertilization labs, was essentially a powerful micro-scope attached to mechanical arms at the ends of which were micro-syringes, micro-pipettes and other miniature implements. Cassandra put her eye to the lens. Observing the cells from the Pale Saint's epithelial tissue, she thought it must be divine providence that had caused the Pale Saint to leave skin as well as blood behind in his escape from the precinct house. Adult human skin was the perfect medium for cloning. Blood was no good because its DNA isn't surrounded by a nuclear membrane; semen is composed of haploid cells, meaning that only half of the body's genetic material is contained within it. On the other hand, skin is perfect because, though the cells are adult, already differentiated – meaning they are epithelial cells, as opposed to blood cells or organ cells, for instance – their nuclei are not. The nuclei of skin cells are toti-potent: they still have the potential to grow into any and every kind of cell in the human body.

Cassandra remembered the classic DNA experiments in the 1960s. Researchers removed the nucleus from a frog's egg and replaced it with the nucleus from the cell of another adult frog. The result was the birth of an entirely new frog. How many light-years was she now from those first tentative steps? She wished those pioneers were here with her to see the fruits of their labors. In a sense, she knew they were.

Now she took a deep breath and carefully pierced the cell's wall and extracted the nucleus. Beside her, Dillard prepared a glass slide with the immature unfertilized human egg cell. They needed an immature cell because until maturity the cell retained its ability to divide on its own. Human egg cells were another staple of all in-vitro labs; it had not proved difficult to procure immature ones.

'Ready?' Cassandra asked without taking her eye off the nucleus she had extracted.

'All set,' Dillard confirmed. He rose from his stool and transferred the glass slide to Cassandra's micro-manipulator. A moment later, she had it in her field of vision, she extracted the immature nucleus and inserted the nucleus from the cell of the Pale Saint's skin tissue. In effect, she was replacing the host egg's twenty-three strands of DNA with the full forty-six of the Pale Saint's DNA. There was of course still host DNA in the cytoplasm – the material of the egg cell that surrounded the nucleus – but this was non-migratory and made up only about one percent of a human's DNA. It would not interfere or bind with the Pale Saint's DNA that was now dominant in the egg. The very pricking of the egg with the injection had the effect of fooling it into thinking it was being fertilized. Soon it would begin to divide on its own in a process known as parthenogenic activation.

This cell was now a complete toti-potent cell: it had the ability to grow as a sperm-impregnated egg will in the mother's uterus into a complete human being – in this case a clone of the serial murderer, the Pale Saint.

While she had been doing this, Dillard had been busy triple-checking the seven-foot vertical Plexiglass vat filled with synthetic blood and amniotic fluid. It sat on a wheeled gantry that ran back to a huge computer-driven double-walled chamber into which one could look through a window with glass three inches thick. Next, he checked the gauges and readouts on the two apparatus attached to the vat via thick, snaking hoses: the heart-lung machine, which would oxygenate the fetus, and the dialysis unit, which would flush impurities from the fluid.

'Backup generator engaged. Green lights across the board,' he told her.

Cassandra nodded. With a heavily thumping heart, she said, 'Here it comes.'

Dillard loaded the purified hyper-aging trans-gene into a micro-pipette of the micro-manipulator. This new life was contained in such an infinitesimal amount, about a pico-gram in weight, one-quadrillionth of a gram, Cassandra never ceased to be filled with the wonder of her profession. Including the surrounding fluid, she was going to inject perhaps a micro-liter into the prepared egg cell. It had to be done quickly before the egg divided because this new hyper-aging gene needed to be part of the DNA of every cell.

Cassandra glanced up, saw Dillard watching her intently. He seemed to be holding his breath, or was that what she was doing? She was aware of her heart pounding in her chest. Perhaps he was aware of this too, because he nodded encouragingly. She looked through the eyepiece of the micro-manipulator and injected the egg with the trans-gene.

With a catheter, she extracted the egg and placed it in a sac made of a semi-permeable polymer. This was the artificial womb in which the egg would very rapidly develop into an embryo and then into a fetus. Like the vat into which it would be placed, the sac had been manufactured by Vertex to Cassandra's precise specifications. Cassandra lowered the sac into the vat, where it hung, suspended.

'Now there's no turning back,' Dillard said. 'I feel a bit like Dr Frankenstein in his lab.'

'There's an unfortunate analogy, Hutton.'

He gave a small laugh that betrayed his nervousness. 'Sorry, but the parallel is inevitable.'

'But not the parable, let's hope.'

Cassandra rolled her stool to the chrome task bar attached to the front of the chamber and hit the square on the computerized touchpad that retracted the vat into the chamber. With a soft rumble, the vat moved smoothly away from them, until it reached the far end of its length of track, in the center of the chamber. She pressed another square and the chamber's thick door swung shut with a deep sigh of hydraulics. She activated one of four flatscreens. It was immediately lighted by a video image of the sac, and data began to flow into her taskstation – the computer-directed sensory array that would monitor and maintain through the software program she developed every critical element of the environment. It would even warn her of impending problems, as well as suggesting possible solutions.

'Computer on-line,' Cassandra said. 'Fire the puppy up.'

'What?'

'Begin recording, Hutton.'

From this moment on, everything that occurred inside the birth chamber would be digitally recorded, downloaded directly into the computer's optical disc drive. Inside the chamber, four armored video cameras allowed her to choose her angle of view as well as to zoom in to her subject. A set of Feather-Lite earphones would let her hear the fetus's heartbeat when the time came. Cables composed of fiber optic filaments bundled inside a Kevlar skin ran like arteries between the double walls of the birth chamber, connecting it like an umbilicus to the outer world of the lab. From their taskstations at the perimeter of the chamber, the two scientists could monitor every aspect of the fetus's development. They could also test and manipulate the environment whenever they pleased using a complex system of robotic arms, hands and tools all controlled from their taskstations.

It was done.

While Cassandra had been at work she had not had time to think about the implications of her actions. Only now was it beginning to sink in. She was mesmerized by the enormity of what was contained inside that polymer sac.

To Dillard, she seemed so far away it was physically painful to him. He was compelled to pull his stool up next to hers. 'How are you doing? The tragedy – you shouldn't even be here now.'

'No, I absolutely *have* to be here.' She gestured again. 'Honestly, Hutton, if I didn't have this to engage me I don't know what I'd do.' She looked into the birth chamber where the object of her intense professional desire hung, growing minute by minute. 'I'm not prepared . . .'

'I know.' Dillard touched the back of her hand briefly. 'I was brought up by my grandmother. She lived to be ninety-two but I knew for more than a year that she was dying. It didn't matter. No one is prepared for death, no matter when it comes.'

'That's so true, but –' Her head swung around to face him. 'You see, I can't stand being helpless,' she blurted out. 'Everyone has something – some irrational fear that gets under their skin and into their bones. This is mine. This project, it's saving me right now. I have to do it, otherwise I'll come undone, do you understand?'

'Of course I do. I'm merely trying to be the voice of reason.'

She smiled faintly. 'And I appreciate that, Hutton. That's why we make a good team. We may not always agree on methodology, but I always felt I could trust you implicitly to understand my point of view.'

'And I'll do everything now to insure that trust is not misplaced.' He squeezed her hand reassuringly.

Cassandra watched the readouts from her taskstation. 'My God –' She switched cameras, giving them a first-rate closeup of the sac. 'Hutton, look at this!'

Dillard, bending down over her shoulder to peer at the flatscreen monitor, whistled low in his throat. 'The zygote has already become an embryo.' He checked his logs, then came back. 'The hyper-aging is almost five times as fast as it was with Minnie.'

'It's working.' Cassandra was ecstatic. 'Hutton, it's working!' She jumped up, embracing him quickly and kissing him on the cheek. Her eyes were shining as she looked deep into his eyes. 'Do you realize our place in history?'

Just as quickly she was back on her stool. 'I'm recalibrating my figures,' she said as her fingers danced over the taskstation keyboard. 'This baby will be born in eight days. It will reach maturity in nineteen days. After that, we'll begin the daily Tetracycline therapy to decelerate his aging rate down to normal.'

Absorbed by the study of her dials and readouts, she failed to recognize the flicker of naked longing on Dillard's face or mark the slight unbending of his very proper demeanor in the wake of her spontaneous outpouring of emotion.

Christopher ate breakfast very early every morning at the same tiny hole-in-the wall joint on Mercer St. It was called, appropriately enough, No-Name.

The joint, painted an indeterminate light color, consisted of three postage-stamp-sized tables and a pink-and-gray patterned Formica counter with chrome trim, a relic from the Fifties. Facing the counter, one step up, were eight stools of chrome and lipstick red Naugahyde. Behind the counter and a narrow space for the server was a pass-through to the cramped kitchen on which rested a brass bell which the cook hit with the flat of his hand when an order was ready to be picked up. An old-fashioned juke box was playing Los Lobos and Roseanne Cash, unfashionable low-key stuff that appealed to Christopher. Only one other stool was occupied. A regular, a gorilla of a man whose hips and rump overflowed the stool like tapioca, was slurping up an enormous breakfast as if it were liquid.

Kenny, one of Christopher's snitches, was a man with a pot belly, a tattoo of a naked woman, and dirty blond hair pulled back in a ponytail. He also had a keen eye and a nose for troublemakers. He was an interesting case. Up until about a year ago he designed audio components for a manufacturer across the Hudson in Hoboken. When he was falsely accused of sexual harassment by a female co-worker, he was bounced without even a hearing. Now here he was serving food from 6 a.m. to 2 p.m., then programming music as DJ Kendo at The A List from midnight till 5 a.m.

As he munched on his toast, Christopher turned around to look out onto the street. He watched the doorway across the street for some time.

'She there?' Kenny asked.

'She's always there,' Christopher said, 'this time of day.' He turned back to Kenny. 'Get me a container of soup, a buttered roll and some coffee with lots of milk and sugar to go.' As Kenny went to fill the order, Christopher added: 'Make that Half and Half.'

'You got it.'

When Kenny handed Christopher the paper bag, he said, 'Thanks.' He hurried across the street to where the young girl lounged in the doorway. In another time, another place she might have been pretty, but her long brown hair was matted with grease and her skin was bad. Her nose was red and runny, from a cold or drugs Christopher couldn't say. Her face was pierced in a couple of unappetizing places, and Christopher's detective's eye said she was about five-six and a very thin hundred-fifteen pounds.

She was a runaway who gave quickie blowjobs at night and hung around shivering in the mornings. Christopher often worked with Missing Persons on his own time, where he'd gotten a certain rep for getting kids like this out of the cold.

This one was tough, though, Christopher had to admit as he watched her wolf down the meal he'd brought her. She was venal; there was a callus around her soul that so far at least he'd been unable to pierce. He spoke to her as he always did, but she said nothing. He'd just have to keep trying.

Back inside No-Name, Kenny refilled Christopher's coffee cup.

'She doesn't look so good, the kid.'

'No,' Christopher said, 'that she doesn't.'

'Crying shame,' Kenny said.

Christopher nodded. 'That's what it is.' He turned back to Kenny. 'About the perp we're after – this Pale Saint, I've got to find him – and quickly. Otherwise, God knows how many more people are going to die.'

Kenny nodded. 'Already on the network. You got anything?'

'He thinks he's smarter than the rest of us.'

'Well, hell, they all think that.'

'Yeah, but with this one,' Christopher said, 'it just might be the truth.'

The Chief Medical Examiner for the City of New York was named Shankar Natarajan, but everyone called him Stick. Dr Natarajan encouraged it; he liked the all-American moniker. He was not an Indian who burned incense and ate vegetarian. He liked Sherlock Holmes, Bach and strong black tea, in that order. Also the smell of formaldehyde, which reminded him of the impermanence of life.

He was a tall, cadaverous man, with skin the rich color of stained teak. He had large, almost luminous eyes one could imagine glowing in the dark, and hair so black it gave off blue highlights in the fluorescent lights of the cold room.

The cold room, in the basement of the CME's building on 31st St and First Ave, was where the cadavers were autopsied and stored. Stick loved it in the cold room because that's where all of life's mysteries were solved. To Stick's mind, forensics was basically detective work of the highest order, just like Bach was music of the highest order; in this city finding out how people died was often a difficult and demanding business.

Not surprisingly, Stick was so busy that it invariably took a couple of days to get in to see him. It was rare to get an immediate interview, even rarer when one got summoned to see him.

'I asked you down this morning,' Stick said to Christopher, 'because I'm greatly disturbed by this situation with Bobby Austin.'

'What situation?' Christopher held the cup of excellent French roast coffee Stick had given him, but now he was in no mood to drink it. To Christopher's knowledge nothing greatly disturbed Stick. Now he stood corrected.

'Here's the gist of it,' Stick said. He looked around his office, which was filled to overflowing with all manner of reference material and medical arcana: books, magazines, thesis papers, medical journals as well as the latest updates on retro-viruses and rare tropical diseases. 'The main trauma occurred before death. That is unequivocal. There are several aspects of the wound that fascinate and disturb me. First, this trauma was done with the precision of a neurosurgeon.'

'How do you mean?'

'The Bic pen – this particular surgeon's scalpel – was inserted through the eyeball, along the optic nerve to the *Thalamus opticus* and thence through the *corpus callosum* until it reached the pineal gland. This gland, you should know, is very small – perhaps the size of a miniature pine cone for which it is named. It's not an easy target. When he reached it, he extracted it whole.'

'What would he want with the pineal?'

'What do homicidal maniacs want, period?' Stick shrugged. 'For me, however, there's a mystery far more vexing. With a wound of this nature the victim should have bled like a stuck pig – excuse the analogy.'

'It's okay.'

'That Austin *didn't* exsanguinate – I mean not a single drop – is medically indefensible.'

'In other words you can't explain it.'

'That's about the size of it.'

Christopher remembered Cassandra asking him about the medical opinion on this when he'd taken her in to see Bobby *in situ*. Why had she been so insistent about knowing the findings?

'In short,' Stick went on, 'this is a mystery of profound proportions.'

'Is there an answer?'

'There's *always* an answer to a mystery,' Stick said. 'It's just that we may not be able to accept it.'

'What the hell does that mean?'

Stick shrugged his narrow shoulders. He wore a suit a size too big for him. The collar of his white shirt was frayed. 'In the absence of traditional answers, we must turn to . . . other possibilities. The example I should like to give you occurred when I was a child, before I came to this country. I saw a rather curious and frightening demonstration in a dusty square on La Figue. Do you know where that is? It's one of the Seychelles Islands.'

Stick wrapped his long-fingered hands behind his head as he stared up at the ceiling. 'That area of the Indian Ocean is odd inasmuch as the poisonous animals and fish that inhabit it are the most lethal in the world. For instance, stingrays, whose venom would merely inflame your foot and ankle if you stepped on their tail anywhere else in the world, here will paralyze you so you drown within minutes. Curious. No one knows why. Anyway, in this little square, I saw a man push an iron spike clear through his eye without a drop of blood being spilled. He appeared to feel no pain, either. He smiled at us and chattered away in a sing-song voice during this bizarre ceremony just as if he were at a social tea.'

'It wasn't a scam – for the tourists, I mean.'

'No, indeed.' Stick pursed his thick lips. 'I remember it was some kind of holy day, not Buddhist or Muslim. I can't say which religion, really. Perhaps my father knew but he's long dead. In any event, the man passed before us and urged us to touch the spike. It would purify us, he said. I was terrified but I could not help myself. I touched the place where it pierced his eyeball and entered his skull. There was no doubt what had happened.'

Stick sat up abruptly, his large liquid eyes focused fully at Christopher.

'Fascinating how certain childhood memories are often the most vivid.'
He shrugged again. 'There's another thing you should know. Based
on my memories of that day, but certainly not my years of medical
knowledge, I am willing to wager that Austin did not immediately
die. No, sir. He sat there, possibly without any pain at all, aware of
everything that was going on around him.'

'Christ, Stick, that can't have happened.'

'What you mean is that you can't imagine it happening. But it most
assuredly did.' The CME slowly shook his head. 'What I have told
you today proves that what happened to Bobby Austin is not without
precedent, but as a Western physician I am at a loss to explain it.'

'And as an Eastern man?'

Stick gave Christopher a small smile. 'As an Eastern man I know
without being able to explain it that Bobby Austin was no victim of
murder. He became a sacrifice in some kind of very primitive ritual.'

In the bottom of the eighth inning the Orioles scored their first run
off Andy Pettitte. Sara groaned. Until then he'd held them hitless and
everyone, even Cassandra, was holding their breath. There was capacity
crowd this Saturday afternoon, and the electric buzz of thousands
of people, the smells of hotdogs, beer and peanuts filled Cassandra
with nostalgia. She and Bobby and Christopher used to go to ball
games on Sundays. Sometimes Christopher's wife Mercedes would
come, but she didn't care for the game much, and then she got
sick and died. Cassandra felt a little shiver run through her. She
remembered Christopher's face at the funeral, white and pinched.
She remembered standing between him and Bobby at the grave side
in a rain so fine it was mist. She could smell fresh flowers like naked
flesh and the rich scent of newly turned earth. The priest spoke in
Spanish and when she slipped her fingers through Christopher's she
saw he was looking at her with an expression that pierced her to
her soul. She'd flushed and looked away and, so inappropriately,
had thought of the long ago afternoon when she'd been with him
in the sunlight and the shadows of the upstate locust trees. At that
moment, Christopher's fingers had tightened in hers, and her heart
had skipped a beat just as if he'd shared that intimate memory with
her. Suddenly terrified, she'd pulled away from him to stand head down
with her hands clasped demurely in front of her for the remainder of
the service.

Between innings, Sara turned to her. 'Mom, do you feel him here?'

Cassandra started, sure for a disorienting moment that her daughter had meant Christopher.

'I can feel Daddy here, watching Andy Pettitte with us.'

Cassandra smiled. 'I'm sure he is.' But her scientist's trained mind saw unbidden his body, down in the cold room of the CME's office, being dismantled piece by piece like an engine that had ceased to function.

She drew tendrils of Sara's hair back behind her ear.

Sara flinched away. 'Mom, don't.'

'Honey, are you sure you still want to play in the championships?'

Sara, who had been absorbed in watching Pettitte take his warmup tosses, threw her mother a barbed look.

'I mean, no one would think less of you if, after what's happened, you wanted to sit out –'

'God, you're so clueless,' Sara said. 'That's the *last* thing I'd do. Dad would *kill* me. I mean, me pitching in the championship game is what he wanted for me.'

'Yes, but is it what you want for yourself?'

'See what I mean? How can you even ask that?'

An arctic silence rose between them for the span of several innings. Cassandra was so upset, she couldn't think of anything to say to her daughter or even follow the rudiments of the game she'd picked up from Bobby.

She was so relieved when Sara turned to her at last and said: 'Will Uncle Jon be visiting us more now?' that she blurted out: 'When he has the time. Why do you ask?'

'Because he said he would, and because I'd like to see more of him.' Sara cocked her head. 'Wouldn't you?'

'You know I . . .' Cassandra felt her cheeks flushing, then she smiled uncertainly. 'I'd like that.'

'Because you know he needs us every bit as much as we need him. Is it okay if I ask him to come by more?'

'Of course it is.' Cassandra hesitated. The previous flare-up was still vivid in her mind. What had she done? 'Sara?'

'What?'

Cassandra, watching her daughter hunched forward, following every minute motion of Andy Pettitte's pitching motion, felt defeated. 'Nothing.'

FIVE

'Let's all update with the latest data,' Christopher said. 'We're including Sgt Lewis today because he's been in charge of finding the Tompkins Square Park murder weapon.'

Jerry Lewis was a tall man, with dark hair and the eyes of a tailor. Christopher liked those eyes; they were the eyes of a kind man who saw every detail. 'No luck so far retrieving the weapon, unfortunately,' he said.

'No surprise there,' D'Alassandro said. 'We haven't been able to pull a one from any of the murder scenes.'

'Emma, you're up,' Christopher said. He and his team were in what he liked to call the Case Room, an 18-foot by 18-foot square dead center of the team's decidedly non-regulation quarters in a storefront on the Lower East Side. The huge stainless steel commercial refrigerator and gargantuan Vulcan gas range in the back room came in handy when the team members were spending long hours here. The Case Room was painted in black enamel – thick plaster walls, pressed tin ceiling, old wood parquet floor that Christopher himself had scraped of sixty years of accumulated dirt and wax before he had painted it. Everything in the Case Room was black – desks, chairs, antique wood file cabinets, phones, faxes. Only the plastic computer terminals glowed white as bleached bones in the eerie atmosphere. The place took some getting used to; pallid reflections from the high-gloss paint provided the curious illusion of a space without limits. It was disorienting and it understandably gave outsiders the heebie-jeebies, which was the point. Christopher, who had his way of doing everything, was intent on discouraging visits from Departmental brass or their odious emissaries from One Police Plaza.

He and his team sat at a round black table that could accommodate six comfortably, eight with a squeeze. The offices outside were crawling with uniform staff the chief had assigned to the case, support staff Christopher had assigned to keep track of the neighborhood canvassing and the futile search for further evidence in the vicinity of the Tompkins Square Park murder.

Emma D'Alassandro peered at the flatscreen of her notebook computer. 'Okay. As my prelim suggested, William Cotton, the Tompkins Square Park victim, showed no defensive marks whatsoever.'

'That fits the Pale Saint's signature,' Christopher said. 'No defensive marks means there was no struggle. Logical conclusions: one, he knew the Pale Saint.'

'That would go for all the other twenty-one other victims, not counting our guys who went down in the precinct,' Esquival said. 'Not probable.'

'I agree,' Christopher said. 'Which leaves us with the other conclusion. Would you recap that one for us, Reuven.'

'Glad to.' Esquival opened a dog-eared manila folder, whose cover was tattooed with all manner of scribbled notes and doodles. 'I believe that what we're dealing with here is a genocidal murderer. What differentiates him from your everyday homicidal flavor, for instance, is that in a very real way the genocidal murderer is already dead. Psychically dead, I mean. How does this happen? Typically, a trauma – or a chain of traumas – in his childhood destroys a vital part of him. He is incapable of feeling remorse or compassion. He inhabits a world of shadows and death; alone in a way it is virtually impossible for us to imagine. He is, for all intents and purposes, permanently cut off from his fellow man. In fact, his mission in life – his very reason for remaining alive – is to kill as many people as he can, to bring them over, as it were, to join him in his blasted landscape of psychic death. That's what makes him so frightening: he seems to pop out of thin air, murder at random, and then disappear back into his unknown twilight world.'

'So this perp kills and will keep on killing,' Lewis said.

'Until physical death do him part, that's right,' Esquival said. 'And he's got his reasons, believe me. Besides the one I already mentioned, which is the most common, he could be morbidly obsessed in the process of death itself, he could be killing himself over and over, or even someone else.'

'Which is why,' Christopher said, 'we need to get a line on this bastard. Once we know why he's killing, we have at least a shot at predicting where he'll strike next.' He pointed at Esquival. 'Full profile, Reuven, one more time.'

'Right.' Esquival wet a finger and turned a page. 'He's highly intelligent, a loner, possessed of an outsized ego, interacts with people only when absolutely necessary. He doesn't engage in sexual acts with his victims nor does he attack them, nor does he mutilate them post-mortem.'

'What do you call sticking a Bic pen through Bobby Austin's eye?' Lewis said.

'We'll get to that in a minute,' Christopher interrupted. 'But for now, Jerry, we don't think that's equivalent to the kinds of post-mortem mutilations we normally find.' He nodded for Esquival to go on.

'He brings his murder weapon with him, he uses it – whatever it is – expertly, and up until the incident in Chinatown he has been meticulous in cleaning up after himself at the murder site.' Esquival turned another page. 'As for background, he almost certainly comes from a broken home; he almost certainly is an only child, but in any event not from a large family. He exhibits firm knowledge of anatomy, psychology, philosophy, metaphysics and shamanism. By his accent and diction we can safely assume he was raised somewhere in the Mid-west; by his vocabulary that he's a graduate of at least college, possibly a couple of years of grad school as well or even a med school dropout. But, again, we've had no luck with that angle. Clearly, he's not psychotic; you've got to be extremely clear-headed to execute the number of murders he's committed over this long a time span. You can be sure a true psychopath would have been caught by now. Like many serial killers, he may initially offer help or even succor to his victims; he may even feel as if he's helping them. Certainly, they must feel that from him – a trust that, when broken – swiftly, shockingly, cruelly – they are so paralyzed they cannot respond in time to even try to fight back. So, in summary, he possesses high degrees of intelligence, strength and animal cunning. At home outdoors. Also, he has a helluva sense of humor.'

'Sense of humor?' D'Alassandro said. 'Oh, c'mon.'

'What else would you call it?' Esquival said. 'The man commits murder, then turns himself in to Christopher solely so he can show us how easy it is to escape.'

'It wasn't easy,' D'Alassandro said, unamused. 'He had to kill four people to do it.'

'Right,' Esquival said, scribbling in his file. 'Exhibits zero degree of remorse.'

'God, you're evil.' She shook her head while Esquival laughed.

'Hand me that paper bag, would you?' he said as he scanned down the page in his folder. D'Alassandro swivelled to her right, reaching out. 'What is this, your lunch?' She let out a yelp as a bloody head dropped out of the wet bottom of the bag and rolled toward her.

Esquival was laughing hysterically as she kicked the rubber replica away from her. There was real blood on it and the thing had the meticulous detail of a high-end movie prop.

'Jesus Christ, Reuven!'

'Oh, c'mon, Em.' He scrambled to fetch the fake head. 'I'm only rendering a community service.'

'Really?' D'Alassandro fought to calm the hammering of her heart. 'What might that be?'

'Developing your sense of humor.' He gestured. 'Look. Even our estimable Jerry Lewis was amused.'

D'Alassandro shook her head, more in control now. 'I swear, one day I'm going to come up with a practical joke that's going to bite you in the butt.'

'That'll be the day.'

'Okay, children, recess is over,' Christopher said briskly. 'Jerry, about the pen through the eye, and now we must include the excision of William Cotton's eyes. We think it's a kind of ritual, and rituals don't belong in the same category as mutilation. Right, Reuven?'

'You betcha.'

'You guys don't believe all that hocus pocus about primitive rituals, do you?' Lewis asked.

'It doesn't matter what we believe,' Christopher said. 'But it appears our perp believes it. I think this angle has real potential. The Pale Saint sees his victims as sacrifices. To make matters even more interesting I happened to come across something written by T.E. Lawrence that says more or less the same thing.'

'*Seven Pillars of Wisdom*,' D'Alassandro said.

Christopher nodded. 'Also, I just came from the M.E. The real kicker is that he can give me no legit medical explanation for the complete lack of exsanguination in Bobby Austin's corpse. In Stick's words, with a wound like that he should've bled like a stuck pig.' Christopher looked pointedly at D'Alassandro. 'D'you have any theories as to why he didn't?'

D'Alassandro thought a moment. 'Maybe I do, but I'm afraid it's going to sound a little far-fetched, Boss.'

'Not after what we've seen,' Christopher said. 'Shoot.'

D'Alassandro nodded. She'd recovered from Esquival's little prank and was all business. 'While it's too early for all the toxicological tests, I can tell you definitively that all the blood and epithelial tissue I took from the precinct window belongs to one man.'

'Our boy,' Esquival said. D'Alassandro grimaced when he said this.

'I can also tell you that my own prelims show a fair degree of alcohol in the perp's blood.'

'Wait a minute,' Esquival said, 'if you're saying he was drunk when he murdered William Cotton and Austin, I'd bet my butt you're wrong.'

'You'd be right,' D'Alassandro said. 'These are not your everyday run-of-the-mill alcohol molecules. In fact, I'm only guessing that's what they are because of certain structural similarities. Beyond that, the blood also had abnormally high levels of the hormone serotonin.'

'Which is?' Christopher asked.

'The medical community is still out on that one. It seems to be manufactured in the pineal gland, it might or might not be related to heightened health and immune system, aging; all manner of theories regarding its function or functions have emerged in the last several years without there being the slightest shred of credible evidence to back them up. In short, it's another one of the body's mystery hormones.' She shrugged. 'What I can tell you for certain is that the perp is used to a high level of these substances in his system. It's how he functions day to day. I'd say there's no sensory or motor or cognitive impairment whatsoever. In fact, it's possible the opposite is true.'

'Explain,' Christopher said.

'Last night I pulled off the Web a couple of little-known studies dealing with Native American shamans that purport to show that a high level of serotonin as well as a certain degree of alcohol or alcohol-related complex molecules are necessary to reach the shamans' semi-ecstatic state. These complex molecules have yet to be studied in any detail, but it is known that in these semi-ecstatic states senses are actually heightened to an almost painful intensity so that semi-consciousness – what laymen would call dream state – merges with consciousness, producing a kind of alternate reality on which, it is supposed, shamans operate.'

'At first we thought he might be Special Forces, a battle-hardened vet of some kind,' Lewis said. 'Now you're theorizing he's some kind of primitive sorcerer?'

'It's looking more and more likely,' D'Alassandro admitted. 'I mean, the Special Forces thing was pure blue-sky theory; this is based on hard forensic evidence.'

Lewis shrugged. 'Maybe he's just a lush.'

'Maybe I'm Margaret Thatcher,' Esquival said, and D'Alassandro snickered. Lewis looked like he didn't know what to make of either of them.

'There's more,' Christopher said, bringing them back to the topic at hand. 'The title *Seven Pillars of Wisdom* is taken from a quote from the Bible – the Book of Proverbs, to be exact: "Wisdom hath builded her house; she hath hewn out her seven pillars."'

'That's right.' D'Alassandro referred to her notebook computer. 'Surfing the Web, I also came across some fascinating theories concerning T.E. Lawrence. One was that he was the first of what have come to be called neo-Luddites.'

'The original Luddites,' Esquival continued, 'were weavers in Nottinghamshire in 1811 England who rebelled against the life changes dictated by the Industrial Revolution: namely automation. They took their name from their purely fictional hero, General Ned Ludd. There was some violence, a manufacturer was killed, and the Luddites were more or less persecuted into extinction. Now, with the Computer Revolution upon us, neo-Luddites have surfaced. They've been labeled technophobes, but that does them an injustice. Basically they're against the absolute reliance on technology to the exclusion of anything else.'

'Examples,' Christopher said.

'They're against computers, which they claim provide messages without meaning; they're against the Net, which, they claim, reduces all information to the same level so that the mathematical, the moral, the sexual, the banal, the sacred and the profane are undifferentiated, given the same weight, and therefore become meaningless, especially to children who use the Web as a classroom or a research source.' Esquival consulted his notepad. 'I came across something the Unabomber wrote, "If you had any brains, you would have realized that there are a lot of people who resent bitterly the way techno-nerds like you are changing the world."' He looked up. 'Neo-Luddites see a world controlled by a kind of cult of information and it terrifies them. Many people at first took them for crackpots – you know, just another fringe element. But a lot of what they've been warning about has already happened and now some of them look downright prescient. To give you just two for instances, companies now routinely rely on CD-ROM programs to train their personnel, and fifteen-year-old boys who are proficient at Mortal

Kombat but still don't know how to approach a girl are being hired by corporate America to create Web sites.'

Esquival took up a sheaf of papers. 'I've analyzed what the Pale Saint wrote in Bobby Austin's computer and I believe it's more or less in line with neo-Luddite philosophy.' He glanced briefly at his notes. 'He makes references to the proliferation of giant conglomerates, corporate buyouts – his word is, let's see, *coups* – of the media, the sense of truth getting lost in corporate priorities, the demeaning and victimization of people by these new, vastly enlarged entities. He likens the march of Disney, GE, IBM, Microsoft and Time-Warner, among other super-conglomerates to armies on a field of battle, whose avowed goal is both the amassing of territory and the dissemination of carefully created pop culture.'

'Whew!' Lewis said. 'It reads like a condensed version of *1984*.'

'William Cotton was –' Christopher consulted his notepad '– VP of Advent On-Line, an Internet provider.'

'About that,' Esquival said. 'I've told you before that serial killers fall more or less into three categories: the thrill-seeker, who gets physically aroused by his acts; the opportunist, who goes on a killing spree in order to cover up an embedded crime; and the crusader, who sees himself on a noble or even holy mission to rid the world of what he considers evil. I've said before and I'll say it again now, the Pale Saint is from this last category. His writings confirm that.'

'Reuven, do you have the files of the previous victims?' Christopher asked.

'Re-evaluated them this morning in the light of this new evidence,' he said. 'All of them were in one way or another involved in media, computer, computer-services or Net-provider businesses. The scope was so wide, however, that before this new info we couldn't figure any pattern.'

'Now we're getting somewhere,' Christopher said. 'I want to hear more about this T.E. Lawrence connection, Emma.'

'Right. Again, I'm not saying I believe any of this stuff. I mean you know the kind of crackpots who crawl the Web, it's like techno-nerd Ricki Lake time. But, okay, according to some of these theories, the reason Lawrence "went native" after he was assigned to the Arabs was that he was a secret neo-Luddite. He was never less than loyal to his homeland, but he came to deeply identify with the Arabs – primitive men who lived simple lives close to nature. Lawrence wrote: "Bedouin ways were hard even for those brought up to them, and for strangers terrible: a death in life." Yet he adored their way of life.' D'Alassandro turned a page. 'This phrase "death in life" repeats itself in his writing over and over. For instance: "Blood was always on our hands: we were licensed to it. Wounding and killing seemed ephemeral pains, so very brief and sore was life with us. With the sorrow of living so great, the sorrow of punishment had to be pitiless. We lived for the day and died for it."'

'A curious thing,' Esquival went on. 'These same references to death in life repeat themselves in the rituals of primitive shamans, whether it be Native Americans or Northern Asians. They're also echoed in what the Pale Saint wrote in Austin's computer.'

'So we're back to the working theory that our serial killer is a shaman,' Lewis said. He seemed to have been convinced by the mounting evidence.

'One other thing,' Christopher said, telling them about the ritual Stick had seen performed in the Seychelles.

'That seals it in my book,' Esquival said.

'I agree,' D'Alassandro added.

'But why was the Pale Saint drawn to Lawrence in the first place?' Lewis asked.

'Maybe our perp is homosexual like Lawrence,' Esquival said. 'It would fit the profile of his kind of serial killer.'

Christopher was remembering the eerie tremor of recognition he'd felt when Sara had read him the quote: *He became a dead leaf in the wind of the war he was fighting.* 'The Pale Saint may or may not be homosexual, but I'm willing to bet he's not just another neo-Luddite,' he told them. 'One thing I *do* know: he's a soldier fighting a war. *That's* his connection with T.E. Lawrence; he was attracted to him even before he read *Seven Pillars of Wisdom.*'

'I think you're onto something, Loo,' Esquival said. 'Lawrence was fighting a war in a desert. It was a physical desert, of course. But I think our perp's desert is of another kind – it's a desert of the soul, the black, blasted place he's been left to wander. It's no wonder he identifies so strongly with Lawrence.'

'This is good work.' Christopher paused for a moment. 'About us not seeing a pattern before. William Cotton's death seems to be some kind of watershed in the Pale Saint's career. It signals a change in his signature. The perp took the time in Tompkins Square Park to excise the eyes from William Cotton's skull. Why? He didn't do that with any of his other victims. He punctured Bobby's eye then wrote what amounts to a diatribe in Bobby's computer. Why? According to Stick, Bobby took some time in dying. That seems deliberate on the perp's part. Why?

'Here's what I want to know: what's changed to make the Pale Saint suddenly alter his signature? Before Bobby's death, we knew next to nothing about him; now we seem to know a great deal – or at least we can make some fairly accurate guesses. Why? What's our "X" factor?'

'William Cotton,' Esquival said. 'The signature changed with him.'

'He's the most recent of the neo-Luddite targets,' Lewis said. 'Nothing new there. Unless the perp knew Cotton.'

'His signature changed again with Bobby Austin,' D'Alassandro pointed out.

'But he was in custody at the time,' Christopher pointed out. 'He killed three other people in the same incident. Something before that had to have provoked him.'

'I agree with the Loo,' Esquival said. 'His signature changed at the Tompkins Square Park murder. And by the evidence at hand, I'd have to say he's escalated to a new level.'

'What do you mean?' Lewis asked.

'I don't think the excisions are random – and I'd stake my rep they're not mutilations.'

'You don't have a reputation,' D'Alassandro said, 'so that's not much of a stretch.'

Esquival grinned toothily at her. 'What I'm saying is I'd bet the farm these eyes somehow figure in his rituals.'

'You mean he's *using* them?' D'Alassandro said.

Esquival pointed to her and said in his best barker's nasal twang: 'Bingo. Give the little lady a prize!'

'Right now, William Cotton's our starting point,' Christopher said, breaking up the meeting. 'I want to know everything there is to know about him.'

'You're heading for a migraine,' Hutton Dillard said.

Cassandra pressed fingers into the corners of her eyes until she saw red stars. She had been at this for sixteen hours straight and she knew Dillard was right. There was a deep ache between her shoulder blades and her neck suddenly seemed made of stainless steel.

'All the readings are perfect,' Dillard said. 'Just as you predicted. The fetus is developing normally. Look, you designed the software running this computer. Let it do its work. Why don't you take this opportunity to –'

'No!' Cassandra could not allow herself to rest. 'I want to keep monitoring. The moment the fetus is whole I want to start bombarding it with delta-wave radiation. The Japanese have proved the deep sleep will accelerate the growth.'

'The computer will perform that task automatically,' Dillard pointed out.

'You don't understand. I want to be there when it happens. I *need* –'

'Cassandra, enthusiasm is an admirable trait, but even by your standards this is excessive. I am constrained to point out you are pushing the limits of your endurance. Considering what's happened to you in the last several days, do you think that's wise?'

'Wise or not, I've got to do it.' Cassandra winced as the first bright aura of the migraine pulsed behind her eyes. She steadied herself with a hand against the thick chrome task bar that ran across the front of the birth chamber. She took a couple of deep breaths while she dug in the pocket of her lab coat. If she took two Extra Strength Excedrin early enough in the cycle the 250 mg of Aspirin and 65 mg of caffeine in each tablet were usually enough to knock out the headache. She gulped a couple down with a third of a cup of cold coffee.

'At least let me take over for a while. Close your eyes for a half-hour and rest.'

She shook her head doggedly. 'The fetus's growth rate is so fast I'll miss too much.'

'The video will catch you up. You can replay every frame you slept through.' He smiled. 'Come on. Rest just a little. Besides, it'll give me some time to work on something. I'd meant to surprise you, but –'

'What? Tell me.'

'Will you take that cat-nap?'

She laughed. 'Okay. I promise. But a half-hour, that's it.'

Dillard nodded. 'All right. I've been thinking about how we have to administer a shot of Tetracycline to Minnie every day. It's cumbersome enough with a lab rat, let alone a human subject. So I've been working on a subcutaneous capsule that would time-release the proper dosage for a week at a time.'

'Hutton, that's wonderful!'

His smile widened. 'And the best part is, it'll be ready by the time we need to decelerate our clone's hyper-aging.'

'Okay, I'm sold.' She went across the lab to her desk, plopped herself in the swivel chair and put her feet up on the desktop. Settling her head back against the vinyl, she put on a pair of odd-looking earphones. She toggled the switch that released a soft sonic frequency of less than six cycles per second, which matched the human brain's delta waves, thus inducing almost immediate deep sleep. 'Just for a half-hour.' Her tone held a warning note. 'Remember.'

'Sweet dreams, Cassandra.'

Bobby's funeral was on a fog-bound Friday. That night, Cassandra came to see Christopher. She arrived at his door after midnight, but he had yet to retire. He had, in fact, been re-reading the odd, disjointed message the Pale Saint had left on Bobby's computer, which he had come to think of as a manifesto.

'Am I disturbing you?'

'Not at all.' He was grateful for the distraction. He made way for her to come in, and closed the door behind her.

In a single, fluid motion, she shucked her coat. 'There's something I need to ask you.'

'Would you like something to drink?'

They stood, not close, but not far apart either, looking at one another. After a moment, Cassandra ran a hand through her hair and her eyes flickered. 'Some water.' She dug in her pocketbook. 'I need to take some more Excedrin.'

Christopher got her a glass of ice water and she drank it all down with a couple of the pills. 'It seems like I've had this same migraine for five days and it just isn't giving any ground,' she said as she handed him back the glass.

'Sit down.' He indicated an ocher corduroy sofa into which she plopped with a deep sigh. She pushed off her shoes, tucked her legs under her, put her head against the back and closed her eyes. While he had the chance, Christopher put away the Pale Saint's manifesto. It wouldn't do to let her see it.

'It would be normal,' he said, 'not sleeping.'

'That's the odd thing. I'm sure I'm never going to get to sleep, then all of a sudden I'm dreaming, and it feels like I'm dreaming the whole time I'm asleep.' Her eyes opened and she moved her head to look at him. 'I dream of one place, Jon, of the woods. *Our* woods. *Our* time.'

'That's not surprising,' he said. 'Dreaming of another time, another place when life was simpler.'

'Was it simpler then?' Her gray eyes were unwavering. 'I used to

81

think so, but now I'm not so sure. It seems to me they were very complicated times indeed.'

'How do you mean?'

She stirred on the sofa. 'Why are you standing, Jon? Why don't you sit? You're making me nervous.'

He dropped into a deep, upholstered chair, stretched his legs out in front of him. They were very close to hers. He felt very heavy, as if weighed down by the secrets he was carrying.

Cassandra sighed. 'In these dreams, Jon, I'm running. My heart is booming, I can hear the blood thundering through me, my breath is hot in my throat. At first I wondered what I was running from. Those woods were always so peaceful, so welcoming and trustworthy. It was as if we belonged there; that we would be taken care of there, always. I thought about that when I woke, and then, tonight I had it again – this strange dream of running through the woods – and I realized I'm not running *away* from something, I'm running *toward* it.'

After a long time, Christopher said: 'Do you know what you're running toward?'

'I thought you could tell me.'

'Me, but how would I know?'

'Somehow I thought you would.'

He leaned forward. The urge to tell her he loved her was so strong he was choking on it. 'Cass, I –'

'Never mind.' She waved his words away. 'I'm exhausted. I don't know what the hell I'm saying or feeling anymore.'

'I'm sorry, but I think that's exactly the case.'

She nodded, and closed her eyes again. 'I need to ask you something.'

'Shoot.'

Cassandra rose and got herself more water. Even with her back turned she was aware of Christopher's eyes on her. When she came back, she said: 'What did the CME say about the wound through Bobby's eye?'

'Are you sure you're up to this, Cass?'

She cocked her head. 'You're doing it again.'

'What?'

'Trying to protect me. There's no need.'

'Even you –' He stopped abruptly, aware of how angry her response had made him. 'There are times when everyone needs to be protected.'

'Except you, right, Jon? Yes, of course. Because it's your job to protect

82

everyone around you.' She put her glass down on the coffee table. 'One day you're going to have to tell me who gave you that job, and why it's the only one you think you know how to do.'

'I hate it when you get flip.'

'Is that what you think, that I'm being *flip*? Christ, Jon, even you can't be that dense.'

And just like that they were back at each other's throats. How had it happened? Christopher asked himself. So he did the only thing he could do: he turned his mind to the business at hand and repeated what Stick had told him about the precision of the thrust through the eyeball and into the pineal, which had then been extracted.

For a long time Cassandra said nothing, and he thought with her eyes closed she might have fallen asleep. Then, she said: 'I knew it.'

'What did you know?'

'That the pineal gland was involved.'

He sat forward, his interest suddenly piqued. 'Jesus, Cass, how *could* you know?'

'"Know" is an interesting word, so fraught with meanings. I had a hunch. Bobby died without any exsanguination. The CME has no rational explanation for that, but I do. See, even to me, the pineal is something of a mystery. But one thing we *do* know for sure is that the gland regulates the biological clock. It secretes serotonin during the day and melatonin at night. These substances regulate both the cyclic bodily processes and, on a more specific level, the tempo of impulses between nerves. As we age the amount of these substances the pineal secretes decreases, so the debate rages: is the pineal merely a passive monitor of aging or is it active, causing the aging process? My most recent experiment has proved my theory that the pineal's role is active. You see, an organ that can control the pace of aging and regulate synaptic response throughout the body could also, theoretically, control blood flow.'

She dipped a forefinger in her water, used it to draw the image of an eye at the end of a stalk on the tabletop. 'The human pineal is the same in structure and evolution as something in lizards called the pineal eye. See here –' she drew a surrounding image '– it emerges via this stalk from the brain and lies just above and between the eyes right beneath the skin.'

'What is it?' Christopher asked.

'Good question. No one knows for sure. When examined microscopically, we've discovered a network very similar to that found in the human eyeball.'

'But it's under the skin. What could it see?'

'Jon, do you know the legend of the Third Eye? It's not so much legend, really, because many people – almost all primitive cultures, in fact – believe in its existence. It resides here –' She touched the tip of her finger to the center of his forehead. '– in the pineal. It's the place where your higher powers reside, all your instincts, your connections to the natural world.'

Cassandra paused for a moment to gather her thoughts. 'My theory is that the pineal gland is the seat of higher learning, that it is in fact the Third Eye. But it's been exceptionally difficult to prove. You know how the entire function of the appendix has been lost over time? Well, something similar has happened to the pineal: its fundamental purpose has altered. Once, I'm positive it was a major organ, as essential to life as the heart or the lungs or the liver.

'Over the centuries, as man has bred himself away from the forests and the land, as he has built guns and cities and cars and planes to house himself, he has lost the ability to use the pineal because he no longer needed those primitive instincts in order to survive. But in primitive cultures where shamanism flourishes studies have shown that herbal potions and preparations used by shamans the world over affect the pineal. This phenomenon is little understood in the modern world even by researchers who profess to have a passing interest in phytopharmacology.'

'How does all this affect my investigation?' Christopher had a sudden image of Stick describing the bizarre religious rite on La Figue. 'Do you know why the Pale Saint wants the pineal glands of his victims?'

Cassandra pursed her lips and he knew she was up to something. 'I thought you told me to stay out of your investigation.'

'That was before Emma came up with some intriguing forensics. It seems possible – even probable – that our boy is a shaman.'

'Interesting.' Cassandra sat back, tapping her forefinger against her lips.

'Okay, spill it,' Christopher said. 'I know you're dying to tell me.'

'You've got it wrong,' Cassandra said quietly. 'It's you who are dying for me to tell you.'

Christopher stood up; his heart was pounding. 'Maybe, just maybe, we're both right.'

Cassandra gave him a long, steady look. When he sat down again, she said: 'Again, it's a hunch. The pineal is sacred to shamans. It's the godhood of mankind – the place where, in effect, the shamanistic gods have touched mortals. For shamanistic societies, it is pure magic. On a more prosaic level, I believe that shamans can control the secretions of the pineal to such a degree they can perform what look to modern man like miracles.'

'Such as stopping blood from flowing out of a wound.'

'Yes, exactly. To answer your question in the simplest way possible, the Pale Saint is attempting to take this magic from his victims at the moment of their deaths or very shortly thereafter.'

Christopher was abruptly tense. 'This sounds like much more than a guess.'

Her gray eyes met his, but she said nothing.

'Jesus, Cassandra, you've been going on with that experiment.'

'Lucky for you.'

'You promised me – We had a deal.'

'I lied, Jon. I had to, don't you see. I told you I could perform more sophisticated tests than Emma could. Now do you want to hear about my findings or not?'

'I won't forget this, Cass.'

'Then don't forget to thank me when I'm done.' She waited a beat while he digested the sudden turn of events. 'The Pale Saint has massively high levels of serotonin in his blood, also other more complex substances that I know from my research are manufactured by the pineal gland, substances conventional serologists would not know how to categorize.'

'D'Alassandro also found serotonin.' He told her of Emma's latest report on the perp's serology – the amount of mysterious molecules in his blood he thrived on that were alcohol-related yet not alcohol at all. 'I was looking for hard proof that the Pale Saint is in fact a shaman; now I have it. I do owe you a vote of thanks, Cass.'

Cassandra stood, and he could see the excitement flooding through her. 'There's more, Jon. Much more.'

'I know that tone of voice, Cass,' he said as he rose. 'I'm wondering how much more I can take.'

She smiled. 'Let's just say my work has taken an historic turn.' She reached for her coat. 'I think it's time you came with me.'

Twenty minutes later, she was leading him through the Vertex lab, and out a side door that had been closed when he had visited just days before. They were in a small room lined with books. A burnished wood desk, executive's swivel chair, desktop PC all faced a window looking out over the horse chestnut and Japanese maple trees, lit by small spotlights. They were so artfully placed, they could have been looking into a moonlit glade, though the night sky was leaden.

Cassandra stood staring through the glass. 'I'll share a secret with you, Jon. One of many to come. I love looking out here. Most people I allow in here, like it, too, this view. They like it for the garden – that's what they see. Do you know what I see when I look out here? I see the small building that's almost hidden by the trees. Even in winter it's difficult to see because of the forest of branches.' She pointed. 'But that's the place – *my* place, Jon. And no one knows about what goes on there except a very few people at the very highest level at Vertex. The work we do here in human DNA replication and cloning –' she gestured back through the closed door to the lab they had been in '– is controversial enough to cause people like Dean Koenig and the Christian Convocation to lobby like hell to shut us down. But if they knew about what went on inside that little building –'

She broke off abruptly and went to the wall of books. Pressing a hidden stud on a shelf, she caused a section to slide open, revealing the brushed chrome interior of a small elevator. They stepped inside and, as she pushed a button, the door slid soundlessly shut. When the door opened, he found they were in an underground passageway of pressed concrete. The smells of machine oil and dampness thickened the atmosphere.

'As you have no doubt guessed, we're directly underneath that lovely garden,' she said as she led him down the passageway. Small bulbs inside wire cages lit their way, and the soles of their shoes scraped against the raw concrete. 'I suppose I should start at the beginning. A couple of years ago, I came across an obscure thesis paper. It was written by Hutton Dillard. It was his contention that environment, not genetics, made the individual. They both had a role to play, but in a shoot-out how a person was brought up would win every time. Scientists and academicians don't like to believe in a theory like that; it's not considered scientific. Well, the sociologists believe it, but they're hardly considered scientists.' They were coming to the end of the passageway. 'Anyway, I sought Dillard out and hired him on the spot for my genetics work at Vertex. I know what Bobby thought of Hutton, and I suspect you're no different, but the fact is no one else could have helped me do what I've just done.'

There was a short flight of gritty concrete steps at the far end of the passageway which they mounted. From the pocket of her lab coat, Cassandra produced a key ring. She fit a key into a lock, pushed down on a brushed steel handle, and they were inside the small building on the far side of the garden. He noted that she was careful to lock the door behind them.

He followed Cassandra into another laboratory, where the hum of complex machinery and generators throbbed like the heart of something huge and faceless. Christopher did not care for labs or surgical theaters, which he found indistinguishable because they managed to extinguish the humanity from the human equation.

Cassandra stopped directly in front of the gigantic hulk of the birth chamber. Through the thick glass panel he glimpsed something that seemed to swim in a field of reddish liquid.

'Cass, what in the name of Christ is that?' he said in a hoarse whisper.

'It's history in the making,' she said, switching on the flatscreens at her taskstation. 'We're growing a clone of your perp, the man who murdered Bobby: behold the Pale Saint.'

Christopher stared from her to the fetus and back again.

'We're using a new animal protocol on him. Tomorrow, he'll be a newborn infant. Nineteen days after that, he'll be nineteen years old. Then, we'll begin chemotherapy designed to slow the aging back to its normal rate.' She shook her head. 'Don't look at me like that.'

'What the hell do you think you're doing? How did you talk Vertex into okaying this?'

'To be frank, they don't know. They wouldn't allow it if they did.'

'And what about Dillard?'

'He's got his own agenda, his own theories to prove. That's his stake in this.'

Christopher took a deep breath. 'I need to understand this clearly, Cass. You brought me here for a reason, what is it?'

Cassandra moved closer to him; she smelled like spring rain. 'Jon, look what's happened: the Pale Saint allows himself to be captured solely so he can prove to you he can escape. The killing isn't going to stop with Bobby and those poor police officers, you know that. I think it's just a prelude. Think! If you can't stop him he's going to go on killing innocent people just like Bobby.'

'Don't you think I know that? We'll find him, Cass. I promise.'

She was in a fever now. 'No, you won't. What's more, you know it. This guy can do things you haven't even thought of. He's already proved as much.' She pointed. 'Take a good look at what's growing in the artificial womb. Who better to catch this madman than his clone?

He'll know what the Pale Saint knows: his habits, his preferences – everything. He –'

'You're playing at God, Cass. You can't know that.'

'But I do. God has nothing to do with what's going on here. This is the scientific process at work; it's knowledge, information, progress, and it can't be stopped. I've broken the age-regulation barrier – that's a fact. Dillard has done the work: while some human traits are encoded within his or her genes, others are not – they're a product of his environment, of how he was brought up. He believes that homicidal tendencies are acquired.'

'Bully for Dillard. So he's a whiz at theories, he can dazzle scientific symposia and medical journals. But now it's put up or shut up time and what if he's wrong? We already have one brilliant madman out there. What if you spawn another? How can you take that chance?'

'Because I believe in Hutton's theories,' she said. 'And because I've got a foolproof backup.'

'Really? And what might that be?'

'You.'

Christopher looked at her as if she had started to speak Mandarin Chinese. 'Come again?'

'You'll train him, Jon.'

'What? Are you nuts?'

Cassandra was already plowing on: 'You'll teach him all he needs to know. You'll give him a strong sense of ethics, of right and wrong. Who better than you, Jon? And it will work because he'll imprint on you, just like injured animals from the wild imprint on the people who save them and raise them. He'll want to be just like you. He'll make the best pupil imaginable because he's an empty vessel eager to be filled. And you'll do it. You'll make him into the best detective –'

'Oh, no.'

'I'm telling you you've run out of options. You'll never get this bastard without me. You can't not take the chance that I'm right.'

'The hell I can't. No, Cass. Uh uh.' He made a curt, cutting gesture as he headed for the door. 'Count me out.'

'Jon, I need you to make this work. The clone needs –'

'Stop it, Cass. That *thing* in there doesn't need anything from me, and neither do you. I won't be a party to this monstrous experiment, and that's final.'

'You're being a flat-out idiot.'

'Dammit, Cass, there are other points of view in the world besides yours. You've never really been able to recognize that fact.'

'Just because I fight for what I think is right?'

'Believe it or not, there's a difference between standing up for your beliefs and just running roughshod over everyone else's.'

'You've never gotten over that I out-pointed you with the longbow,' she snapped despite herself because now she was angry.

'*You've* never gotten over the fact that if I hadn't dragged you out of the rapids you would have drowned.'

'Wait a minute.' She pulled him back to her as he was about to leave. 'This isn't about my experiment, is it, Jon? It's about you and me. It's always been about you and me.'

'Cass, I –'

'No, no. I'm tired of doing battle with you. Every time we see one another it's the same thing – this, I don't know, hellish animosity – tears at us.' She looked at him with her luminous gray eyes. 'Jon, do you realize what's happened? We've somehow become enemies.'

'There's no somehow about it.'

'What does that mean? Do you know what's going on here? If you do, tell me. Please. Because I can't stand –' She turned her head away for a moment. Then she took a deep breath. 'Saturday I took Sara to the ball game, just as Bobby wanted. And do you know what she said to me?' When she turned back to him there was a glitter in her eyes from the tears she was holding back with a valiant effort. 'She wanted to know if you'd be seeing us more now. Why would she say that, Jon?'

'I don't know.' He moved away, but she pursued him.

'She said that's what you told her. Did you?'

'I might have, but –'

She took hold of him. 'Look at me, Jon.' She waited until their eyes met. 'Sara knows. When I looked in her eyes –' She stopped, bit her lip. 'She feels the pain you carry around inside you, Jon. She wants to make it go away but she knows she's not the one who can. The mistake she's made is in thinking your pain is only your guilt over Andy.'

'That's what it is.'

'Oh, yes, I know, only too well. But I also know Andy's only part of it.'

'I don't know what you mean.'

Despair washed over her. 'Oh, dear God, Jon, what am I going to do with you?'

Silence, save for the hissing of the machines in which the clone of the Pale Saint was minute by minute growing.

'All right,' she said, 'I'm going to tell you something I swore I never would. But I don't care now. Ever since Bobby was killed, I –' She stopped, momentarily at a loss. 'Jon, the night before I got married I sat alone in my apartment and cried.' She shook him hard. 'I thought only of you and I *cried*, do you understand me?' Her beautiful gray eyes searched his face. 'I hoped, stupidly, that the phone would ring, that you'd call and – All I wanted – all I needed – was a word from you. Some sign that this wasn't what you wanted.'

'It was none of my business, Cass.'

She slapped him then, a stinging blow to his cheek. 'It was every bit your business.' Then she placed her hand gently over the red area. 'Darling enemy, don't you get it yet? Is it so hard to tell me how you feel?'

'It was never easy for me, and then when you met Bobby – it became impossible.'

'Why?'

'Because.' He looked away, then back into her face. 'Because I never understood what it was . . . that went on between us until it was too late.'

Cassandra lowered her head slowly until her forehead rested against his chest. 'Jon, what really happened that summer afternoon, after we were finished swimming? We were lying naked, innocent teenagers. You were asleep. I rolled onto my stomach . . .'

It took a long time for Christopher to answer her. 'I wasn't asleep; I only pretended to be. I watched you open your body and touch yourself. I watched you come.' His voice was a whisper. 'It was so amazing seeing you so abandoned, so – there was nothing but your naked body and the sunlight and the wind rustling through the trees and that yellow and white butterfly passing from flower to flower. You seemed . . . so powerful, and so untouchable, so unlike the Cassandra I knew, and yet at the same time so very much her. At that moment I wanted –' His voice was so strained he could barely speak. 'I wanted everything: you, the sunlight, the wind through the locusts, even that butterfly, which was gone so very quickly. And –' He stopped, suddenly unable to go on.

'And –?' She prompted.

'Don't make me say this, Cass. Bobby –'

'Bobby's dead, Jon.'

'But that's just it. He –'

'I loved him, in my own way. But after he died it was you I found myself thinking of. I was so racked by guilt that I pushed it all down, but it won't go away. So now you tell me what you were going to say because if there's one thing I understand when it comes to you and me and Bobby, it's guilt.'

'Cass –'

'I won't let you go until you do.'

'Oh, God,' he said, as he buried his face in her neck, 'you and the sunlight and the wind through the locusts and that damn butterfly in whatever heaven it's in now, I still want it all.'

He felt her sobbing, at last, Cass, the iron woman who always wanted to best him at everything.

'Do you know,' she whispered as she held him close, 'how long I've been waiting to hear you say that?'

T.E. Lawrence had written: 'Our excuse for over-running expediency was War.' To the Pale Saint, who stands in front of an electronics store, staring into the great blue flickering eye of a TV set, it seems that his life is this War that so fascinated Lawrence. 'Blood was always on our hands: we were licensed to it. With the sorrow of living so great, the sorrow of punishment had to be pitiless. When there was reason and desire to punish we wrote our lesson with gun or whip immediately in the sullen flesh of the sufferer, and the case was beyond appeal.'

He has thrown himself with desperation into the idea of War because, like Lawrence, he longs to be changed. He wants to be set free from the prison of the dark and cavernous house overseen by the great blue eye that flickers and glows like a beacon beckoning aircraft in the night; he wants to escape the dustbowl of the great prairie where everything travels – wind, rain, sun, moon, storms, even the billowing dust he despises so thoroughly – except him. He wants to return to a time Before. And he knows with a certainty, as Lawrence must have known, that only War has sufficient power to change him.

Onto the dark plate glass of the window is etched the pale reflection of a young girl who stands in a doorway across the street. The Pale Saint watches her for some time as the hawk, flying high in a sky white with heat, surveys the territory below that belongs only to him.

The phosphors given off by the TV image flicker all around her, throwing her image into shadow, as if burning her to carbon bits. The Pale Saint sees this, and more. To him the flickering re-enacts the War between flame and shadow, day and night, good and evil. And now, out of the carbon bits another face forms.

Mama.

'Mama,' he whispers to her, 'you have more strength than most any man I know. Including Pappy.'

'Your pappy. Don't make his kind no more,' she says, with a hatred so strong and pure it borders on reverence. 'Wicked, wicked man. Jesus wept, he surely deserved his end.'

What kind of relationship she had with Pappy it's impossible to say. She was of course away most of the time, long in the night screaming at the top of her lungs. Pappy held no truck with that; he treated her life's work as if it didn't exist at all. That truculence must have maddened her considerably. What in the world had caused them to put up with each other?

Of course in the end she hadn't put up with him. Eventually Pappy crossed the line. He put a torch to their lives and became anathema.

So how come on the infrequent occasions Mama was home for more than a day, they coupled incessantly? The Pale Saint knew that because he could hear their frightful noises from upstairs and became afraid. He imagined Pappy taking her like the tomcat takes his bitches in heat because the sounds were so similar. He couldn't understand why they did it, it must hurt so much.

One day, he made the mistake of asking Mama about it. She took him by the ear and dragged him under the shower, washing his mouth out with soap. In doing so, she got almost as soaking wet as he did. Her undyed muslin frock stuck to her body and everything was outlined. His gaze was drawn to her breasts which, crowned by large, dark nipples, swelled beneath the homely fabric.

Mama, seeing the nature of his attention, narrowed her eyes and gave him a powerful backhand slap across his face. He sat down hard on the slippery porcelain.

'Wicked, wicked child!'

Water rained down upon his open mouth, making him swallow convulsively. He remembered from that moment an aching heat, along with the alkaloid taste of soap and the smell of sweet candle wax which emanated from Mama each time she returned home. It was the kind of smell that clings like a cat to a chair leg, the kind of smell you never forget.

'Mama, you're back. I've seen you on the TV, doing what you've always done. As if nothing ever happened. How could they let you go?'

And when in a frenzy he opens his eyes from this waking dream, he sees in the eye of the TV Dean Koenig ranting and raving about God and the devil, fire and brimstone, the damnation of America, and the Shining Light of his ministry. The Pale Saint knows this man. He has seen him many times. But even if he hadn't, even if this was the first time he had laid eyes on him, he'd know him inside and out. They are all the same, these righteous tent-pole preachers. They have told lies so often that they cannot now tell them apart from the truth. In their hearts is a darkness visible to only a privileged few.

He makes little snuffling noises as he chews until his mouth is full of foam. His back arches, his loins quiver with evanescent heat, and a stain spreads across the front of his trousers.

The clone emerged from the polymer uterus on schedule and perfect: pink and healthy and squalling. Cassandra held his head and his rear as Dillard slapped him gently to get his lungs working in oxygen instead of the synthetic amniotic fluid they had concocted for him.

Dillard was bug-eyed with excitement. Cassandra could imagine him already composing his Nobel Prize speech.

Christopher looked darkly upon the clone, conjuring up like a seer the inevitable future of the two identical humans confronting each other. But he was imagining not only the means to an end. In the realm of inevitabilities, he found himself fearful that the twisted evil in the one would present itself in the other.

Neither of the men's reactions was surprising. But for Cassandra, the reality of the clone was stunning. She found herself wholly unprepared for the emotions that washed over her as she held the baby. The fierce hatred she had held close to her heart, hardening it against anything that stood in her way, began to melt like ice in summer. She recalled with absolute clarity the tiny weight of Sara on her stomach as she was placed there by the OBGYN surgeon, seeing in her daughter's cloudy eyes all the innocence that she had assumed had been trampled underfoot by the modern world. Now she saw that same innocence in this child and, considering the source, she was both astonished and fearful.

Christopher sensed this change in her and he called her on it, which started a heated argument over not merely proper scientific protocol, but the ability of women versus men to nurture new life.

Dillard, standing a little apart as he monitored the instruments, could not resist making the most of the blowup. 'Like it or not, Christopher, the clone will see Cassandra as its mother.'

'That'll be the day,' Christopher snorted in disgust. 'This is a god-damn laboratory experiment, like bacteria in agar.' He turned abruptly away.

'My advice is you'd better get used to her new role,' Dillard called after him.

'Is that so? My mommy told me never to take advice from a preppie.' Christopher slammed the door on his way out.

'Damned infidel,' Dillard muttered under his breath.

'Look, Hutton,' Cassandra said, rapt by the infant in her arms. 'Look at this miracle.'

'Indeed.' Dillard raised an eyebrow. The fact was he was besotted with the thought of the fame and riches this infant would lay at his feet. 'Minnie the rat has nothing on *this*.'

'*Him*,' Cassandra snapped. 'He's a male human being.'

Was it his imagination or was she holding the infant more tightly to her breast? His fear that a personal involvement with the subject would lead her to violate standard laboratory procedure overrode his burning desire to take her side against Christopher. 'To be honest, Cassandra, we don't yet know *what* it is.'

She stared at him, rocking a little.

He moved a little closer, lowering his voice. 'It is not my intention to be harsh, Cassandra. But you must be realistic. It pains me to admit it, but Christopher is right on this point. It won't do for you to get attached to the subject. What if the experiment must be prematurely terminated?' He reached out toward the infant and Cassandra instinctively swung him away. 'Before Minnie how many failures did we have? How many rats did we have to kill?'

'That was different.'

'No,' he said, 'it's not. This is still an experiment and all the parameters we assigned to our previous work with rats *must* be continued here. Surely you see that, Cassandra. Otherwise, we have no scientific protocol, no defense of our procedures, and even if we are successful our findings will be judged invalid.'

He watched the clone over the crook of her arm. 'This is your chance for glory – my chance for vindication for decades of work that has been dismissed.' Intending only to soothe her and stroke the infant, he reached out clumsily and poked him hard in the ribs.

The baby began to scream and Cassandra whirled on him. 'You've got to be more careful, Hutton,' she flared. 'He's a helpless infant.' She began to rock the child. 'See how he's calmed down?'

Dillard felt a grinding in his stomach. First it was Christopher who took her attention away from him. Now it was this infernal *thing*. He'd been so certain that this experiment would be the catalyst to bring them together, but to his rage it was so far turning out quite differently.

They named him Lawrence. Christopher thought that appropriate, given the Pale Saint's predilection for the writings of T.E. Lawrence. Cassandra, unaware of the irony, liked the name; Dillard didn't give a damn one way or the other – as far as he was concerned an experiment by any other name was still an experiment.

Because none of the usual Vertex assistants could be recruited, he and Cassandra worked out a specific schedule to be in the lab. They broke the day up into three eight-hour shifts, making sure to give themselves time to sleep, also several shifts a week when they would be in the lab together. Mostly, though, they worked solo in shifts.

The clone's learning curve was nothing short of extraordinary. He had discarded his diapers himself after two days, and was toilet-trained in a half-hour. His grasp of the English language was astonishing. Cassandra was witness to words becoming phrases, phrases becoming sentences, these sentences spilling out faster and faster until they became a torrent, as if he could not progress fast enough. He outgrew his clothes four times a day. Thirty hours after he was born, he was already absorbing the children's shows she had procured on cassettes from PBS and Nickelodeon, as well as old sit-coms from Nick at Nite. But then he was already a year-and-a-half old. Cassandra had been reading to him almost from the moment he had been born, but now he sat in front of the large-screen TV-computer monitor and watched hour after hour. It was far from an ideal way to bring up a child, she knew, but it was expedient.

Lawrence's steady diet of video cassettes made for countless oddities. For instance, Cassandra caught him humming the theme songs from *The Mary Tyler Moore Show* and *I Dream of Jeannie*. He could say 'Big Bird,' 'Oh, Mr Grant!' and 'Yes, Master,' before he said far more basic words. Conspicuously missing from his vocabulary was the word 'Daddy'.

As his teeth grew in, his tastes in food changed. She was obliged to teach him to use his teeth simply for eating, otherwise he tended to bite and tear at things like an animal. Also troubling was what he drew as soon as Cassandra provided him with crayons, which had been in the afternoon of the second day: long horizontal lines at the ends of which were jagged triangles. He kept at this with a kind of excessive zeal that was downright frightening.

By contrast, he resisted all efforts to wean him from the quasi-artificial dreamland of the delta wave-enhanced sleep. The one time she had tried to put him to bed without it he had lain awake for so long that Cassandra, concerned, had run a sequential EEG and found that his brain was totally lacking in the delta-wave emanations necessary for deep sleep. She mentioned this to Dillard, who showed her his chemical readouts on Lawrence's brain which were characterized by abnormally high levels of serotonin and consequentially low levels of melatonin.

Also, Lawrence insisted on sleeping inside the cavity of the birth chamber, even though Cassandra had prepared a bed for him in the lab itself. Dillard had been relieved, pointing out with his usual sang-froid that it was easier to monitor the clone when he was inside the chamber. Cassandra, on the other hand, was concerned that he was already showing signs of having the Pale Saint's reclusive tendencies. When Christopher pointed out that she should be elated at the thought because it meant the experiment was working, she only grew angry, and privately began to consider ways to bring him out of his antisocial shell.

They all found themselves struggling with the rapidity of his growth. Each time they dropped off to sleep, his peculiar biology would reinvent his body and mind, so that when they saw him again he would be another year older, his bones stretched, his features evolved, his skin gleaming with newly released hormones and neuropeptides, his mind grown exponentially. Since there was no suitable analog in human experience against which to judge these vaults of growth, they took on a shadowy, dreadful, almost supernatural presence, even for the scientists who had evolved their genesis. 'It's like observing some monstrous predator growing into God alone knows what,' Dillard said, manning his array of monitors and probes, until Cassandra shushed him lest Lawrence overhear.

Consequently, and without their being aware of it, the clone took them over. It was odd, since he was the one who was under constant scrutiny, that to them the tables seemed turned. Like an unstoppable army on the march, he embedded himself in their waking hours and haunted their dreams with the ceaselessness of swarming bees. For Dillard, he became a kind of road show attraction he dreamed of taking on a triumphal international tour of universities and teaching hospitals following his Nobel Prize. For Christopher, he became a nightmare shadow of the Pale Saint, escaping from the lab, lost to them in the vast labyrinth of the city, where he would join with the original in an unprecedented orgy of bloodletting. For Cassandra, he was nothing that simple. He was an object of curiosity, fear and loathing, yes; but he was also a child, helpless and lost and alone, at the mercy of terrible and, she had no doubt, terrifying biological forces that each hour of every day ripped his body and mind asunder.

He read with a voraciousness none of them could fathom. Cassandra could not get him books fast enough. He read anything and everything: history, arts, science, philosophy, the Bible. But what he understood of it all was anyone's guess.

As he grew in these prodigious, appallingly non-human leaps, the problems of his accelerated development manifested themselves like weeds sprouting too furiously to be pulled up. Though the clone's grasp of grammar and vocabulary was nothing short of astounding, he had developed a pronounced stutter. He also seemed to have an almost instant antipathy toward Dillard. It wasn't long before he was devising fiendishly clever tricks to play upon the researcher. For his part, Christopher seemed to encourage this behavior, though Cassandra begged him to try to control Lawrence.

Christopher was, in the end, the only one who could control the clone. Though Lawrence was prone to tantrums, moody silences, even outbursts of verbal abuse against Dillard, he never failed to be ready and waiting for Christopher's lessons. And when Christopher left the lab, Lawrence's face would go frighteningly slack as he sank back inside himself. Cassandra pleaded with Christopher to spend more time with the clone, but the investigation ground on and Christopher was often needed elsewhere. The William Cotton lead, which had once seemed so promising, looked more and more like a dead end as they compiled their data on the victim. He'd been born and raised in the San Fernando Valley of California. Went to school there, then to Stanford for two years before dropping out and starting his own Internet business. If there was any prior connection to the Pale Saint, none of Christopher's team could find it.

The dead end was a kind of blessing for Lawrence, Cassandra had to admit, because Christopher gradually began to spend more time with him. Step by step, he taught the clone the basics of morality and ethics – the differences between lying, stealing and killing, and love, respect and compassion. To do this, Christopher drew on his intimate knowledge of human nature as defined by life on the street. He showed the clone how desperation could drive a man down the wrong path, how a thirst for revenge could warp even the strongest mind. But what he emphasized most was the rule of law. Man's distinction over the beasts of the world, Christopher told the clone, was his creation of law, his sense of right and wrong. The clone's mind was like a sponge, absorbing every lesson, so that Christopher never had to repeat a demonstration or an explanation.

As the lessons progressed, Christopher discovered that the clone had mastered a way of gaining permission to do and say things without quite asking for it. This was an adult trait that Christopher admired in him, though he'd never tell the clone so. In fact, Cassandra observed that the more the clone hung on Christopher's words, the more Christopher seemed to pull back. It was as if, in Christopher's mind, Lawrence had already been irredeemably polluted by the sick soul of the Pale Saint, as if he were a patient with a contagious and incurable disease. At those times, especially, Cassandra's heart ached for Lawrence, who was already too much like a specimen under a microscope. She was able to see that, despite his hyper-aging, his bizarre and often frightening behavior, he needed what every young boy needed: attention, love, a sense of stability and order. She saw what Christopher could not or would not see: that Christopher by dint of his profession and his morality was the perfect paradigm of order and stability.

By the second week, Cassandra had no choice but to acknowledge that the disturbing signs of Lawrence's accelerated development were proliferating. He spent even more hours compulsively drawing those jagged triangles. His stutter waxed and waned with his moods, becoming markedly worse when he was upset. Perhaps as a consequence, he spoke very little. He began to have nightmares – no mere amorphous night terrors, but specific dreams that terrified him. In all of them a skeleton appeared; a skeleton who walked and spoke to the clone as if they were intimates. Their attempts to query Lawrence about the dreams led to screams so piercing Cassandra instantly terminated the interrogation. Dillard would have continued in the name of science, but even Christopher didn't have the heart.

And then there was the clone's reaction to Sara. Despite Christopher's strenuous objections, Cassandra knew she was right to give Lawrence a playmate. He was in desperate need of interaction with someone who was not yet an adult. Who could they recruit but Sara? And yet, as the days progressed, Sara tried every way she knew how to play with Lawrence without success. She even asked him, as Christopher had suggested, what the triangles meant without getting an answer. She felt he really didn't know.

Dillard was ecstatic. 'Most of our colleagues operate under the assumption that DNA carries no memories,' he said, 'despite numerous documented evidence that specific tendencies do survive at the cellular level. These are what I call preference imprints. Actually, we have no precedent. As I said to you at the beginning, we're in uncharted territory. The fact is we don't really know how much "memory" or of what kind is contained in these imprints.'

'What are you saying, that in some way, whatever he's trying to draw comes from the Pale Saint's memories?'

'Perhaps the word *memory* is too specific.' Dillard hesitated. 'The brain, you know, works like a complex filter, trying to put into perspective the great jumble coming in from our five senses. Here, I suspect another kind of sense is at work, one that emanates from the DNA level. The triangles are symbols that the clone is attempting to decipher.'

'Just like the skeleton,' Christopher said.

'Perhaps,' Dillard said with the imperiousness with which he always addressed Christopher. 'But let's not get carried away. We must be careful not to attribute *everything* that goes on inside his head to the Pale Saint. That's no way to build an unassailable scientific model.'

Cassandra fretted over Lawrence's refusal to enter into a dialog with Sara, knowing that cooperative play was a normal behavioral stage of growing up. For her part, Sara seemed unconcerned with Lawrence's anomie, and spent her time doing homework while beside her the clone, seemingly oblivious, drew his enigmatic triangles or watched episodes of his TV shows over and over again. Even Christopher, watching the two of them like a hawk, seemed to relax a bit.

Unlike the three adults, Sara appeared totally unfazed by both Lawrence's existence and his hyper-aging; in fact, she thought he was way cool. Christopher said he wasn't particularly surprised. Sara was already used to entertainment, computers and ether-nets that deliver information at dizzying speeds. Why should a creature born to velocity seem anything but way cool? In a way, he was a metaphor for her way of life, a living symbol of the future toward which she was hurtling at Pentium-based speed.

When Sara unexpectedly said she wanted to cook for him, Cassandra had admonished 'No junk food. He's already developed an insatiable craving for Hershey's chocolate bars.' She needn't have worried. Sara brought the electronic bread maker from the loft, and the delicious scent of baking whole wheat or rye bread permeated the lab. She brought in huge paper shopping bags bulging with pots and pans and food, clearing a space for herself in one corner of the lab, resourcefully using a Bunsen burner for heat. Lawrence, never keen on formula or jarred baby food in the first few hours of his accelerated life, ate whatever she made for him: hot buttered bread, blueberry or apple muffins she baked at home, steamed vegetables, omelets filled with colorful surprises like zucchini, red peppers or orange marmalade.

Cassandra watched all this activity with the astonishment of a child on Christmas morning. But her happiness and pride were marred by Lawrence's reaction or, rather, his lack of one. He never thanked Sara, or in any way acknowledged the attention she lavished on him. But one day when he was six, she appeared at the lab with a hardball, scuffed as a result of her corkscrew pitches, which she gave to him. She showed him how to throw it, and tried to play catch with him. Instead, he cupped the ball in his hands and tried to bite clean through its hide. Sara seemed disappointed, but after she had left for the day, he kept it with him when he went to sleep.

The next day, Sara brought Hound into the lab. Lawrence stopped his obsessive drawing and stared at the Weimaraner for a long time. Then, quite calmly, he got up, walked over, and spoke to it.

'You've cuh-come back,' he said in a voice that gave Cassandra the oddest feeling. When Christopher questioned him about the dog, the clone merely shrugged and said, 'I've seen him before. In my duh-dreams.'

Hound put its snout in the palm of Lawrence's hand and made a whining sound in the back of its throat. From that moment on, whenever Sara brought the Weimaraner to the lab, Lawrence and the dog were inseparable.

Meanwhile, Christopher continued working with him in their daily sessions.

'I want you to tell me what you've learned about trust,' Christopher said to the clone on the ninth day.

The clone thought for a moment. 'People want to be helped. Cuh-confidence, hope, trust attracts them. The world is basically good. But there are people – evil people – who use that trust against others. They violate that trust, turn it to their own ends. For that they must be puh-punished.'

Cassandra, listening as she worked on the trans-gene protocol, noticed that Lawrence's stutter seemed less pronounced when he spoke with

Christopher, just as she was acutely aware that Christopher never rewarded Lawrence with even a single word of praise for his quick reads of the lessons. She tried to compensate by telling Lawrence how well he was doing, but he seemed indifferent to her. In fact, every effort she made to draw him out seemed to push him further inside himself. Just as troubling, he had lately begun to shy away from her with the same kind of tenacity with which he'd clung to her during the first week.

'Are all the criminals you catch punished?' the clone was asking Christopher.

Christopher nodded. 'If they're proven guilty. This is one of the cornerstones of civilization. If they break the law, they're punished.'

'The skel-skeleton should be punished,' the clone said.

This gave Christopher pause. Up until now, the clone had refused to talk about the skeleton. 'How do you know the skeleton is evil?'

'Buh-because he wants me to trust him. He lies down next to me and puts his bony fingers on my heart. Tap-tap, tap-tap. I luh-look at him and he grins. "Trust me," he says with his teeth clacking. "I know your heart. I'm the only one."'

'It doesn't matter what he says or does,' Christopher told the clone. 'The skeleton isn't real. He's just part of your dream.'

'No, he's real. Like Duh-Dillard.'

'Why are you afraid of him?'

'I duh-don't want Duh-Dillard near me.'

Christopher had meant the skeleton, a figment of the clone's imagination he was determined to find out more about, but he was intrigued by the clone's misunderstanding of his question. 'Why? Has Dr Dork hurt you?'

'No, but he will,' the clone said with eerie certitude.

'I don't know where you got that idea. Dillard is a putz, but he wouldn't hurt a fly.'

'"Perhaps the word *memory* is too specific. The brain, you know, works like a complex filter, trying to put into perspective the great jumble coming in from our five senses."' The clone mimicked Dillard's voice with such eerie perfection that Cassandra felt the hairs at the back of her neck stir. 'He hates me,' Lawrence said in his normal voice, 'I can feel it like an itch under my skin.'

On the same day, Christopher suggested he take the clone out of the lab. By this time, the clone was interacting with Sara. They drew together and listened to music. But what he appeared to like best was when she read to him from Shakespeare's plays. In no time, he was joining in, and the reading almost magically metamorphosed into acting as they each took to their parts with an abandon Cassandra had never before seen in either of them.

Lawrence's almost overnight bonding with Sara was what convinced her Christopher was right in suggesting he take the clone out of the lab. They didn't dare tell Dillard, who would have been apoplectic at the thought. Cassandra picked out his clothes, but Lawrence pushed her away. He dressed himself in blue jeans, a tee-shirt and cotton sweater, sneakers. He was by this time a long-muscled, willowy young man. The straight, light-brown hair of his childhood was already beginning to turn platinum, and in his face the seeds of the Pale Saint's physiognomy was almost at full flower. It wasn't until he pulled on the baseball jacket Sara had left behind that Cassandra realized he had dressed himself just like her. She was ashamed at feeling a shiver of apprehension crawl down her spine.

Christopher took the clone on a tour of Greenwich Village. They strolled slowly down MacDougal St. It was Christopher's intention to expose the clone to kids more or less his age. The smells of coffee, spices, felafel and incense wove a mosaic that gave the air a distinctly Middle Eastern edge. Not that the clone could appreciate the reference, Christopher thought. He'd been bundled like a beetle in formaldehyde behind the walls Cassandra and Dillard had made for him. Maybe Dillard thought it was okay for someone to learn on the computer and from books, but then Dr Dork didn't look like he'd had much street education himself. Christopher knew better; to understand the nature of good and evil, the clone needed to feel that he was part of something larger, to see that he looked like all these other kids, to do the things they did.

They crossed lower Sixth Avenue to Bleeker St, then to Christopher St. Clearly he liked the espresso Christopher got for him at Cafe Figaro because he asked for another one while he eavesdropped on a girl with spiky, lavender hair and a much-pierced right eyebrow tell her boyfriend that if he didn't get his tongue pierced she was quits with him.

'A piece of metal in my mouth. What's the big fucking deal?' he asked her.

'The word is *commitment*,' she said, 'to me, to us, to this relationship. If you're not fully committed, if you're not ready to go all the way for what you believe then you picked the wrong woman to be with.'

'I luh-like her,' the clone said. 'She reminds me of Sara.'

But he was less happy on West 4th St. In front of the 'Jack the Ripper Pub,' he told Christopher he felt as if he was suffocating. Christopher tried to get more out of him but he became mute as a rock, and so abruptly pale that Christopher began to worry. In the end, he took the clone back east to Tompkins Square Park, where they sat amid the trees, sunlight and open space.

The clone appeared calmer, but Christopher watched him carefully.

'Feeling better?'

The clone nodded. 'Uh huh.' He sat, swinging his feet and bouncing the heels of his sneakers against the pavement like any other fifteen-year-old. Which only brought home to Christopher all over again, how unlike any other teenager this creature was. 'I felt –' He looked at Christopher with the Pale Saint's eyes. 'The wuh-world outside, here, it's like chaos. So many people all at once.'

'I'm sorry if it was too much for you,' Christopher said. 'But I want you to get a sense of the real world. It's more than that lab.'

'Yeah, so I see.'

Christopher was wondering if he might pick up some hint of the Pale Saint who had so recently committed murder here. It was the reason he had chosen to take the clone into Tompkins Square.

'I want you to tell me if you feel anything out of the ordinary,' he said.

'Okay.' The clone continued to swing his legs back and forth. He watched a teenage girl pedal past them on a bike. When she came abreast of them, she gave him a smile.

'I wuh-wish everyone was like Sara,' the clone said at length. 'Sara is smart.'

'What do you think makes her smart?' Christopher asked.

'She knows things.'

'What kinds of things?'

'All kinds,' the clone said.

'Give me an example.'

'Well, she knows how to throw a spit ball, and how to cuh-cook meatballs and spaghetti.'

'I like her meatballs and spaghetti.'

'I know,' the clone said. 'That's why she muh-makes it.' He pursed his lips. 'I thought you were her father.'

'I'd like to be, now that her real father's dead.'

The clone gave Christopher a canny, sideways look. 'Cuh-can I have a chocolate?'

Christopher went to a nearby newsstand, brought back a Hershey bar, which was the only thing the clone would eat when he wanted chocolate.

'I w-want to go to her baseball game,' the clone said, happily stuffing the chocolate bar into his mouth. 'It's the championships and she's pitching. I wuh-want to see her play; if she wuh-wins it means she's the best, right?'

'Right.'

'It's important to wuh-win, isn't it?'

'Often, yes. But life is much more complex than that.'

'Tell me.'

Christopher thought a moment. 'Suppose you were Sara and you were all set to pitch in the championships. But at the last minute, Cassandra had an accident. You could either play in the championships or help her. What would you do?'

The clone screwed up his face. 'Is this a trick question?'

'No,' Christopher said.

'I wuh-want to win,' the clone said, trying to reason it out. 'But . . .' He looked up at Christopher. 'How bad is Mom hurt?'

'You won't know that until you see her,' Christopher said. 'But that's the wrong question to ask . . .'

'It doesn't m-uh-matter how buh-bad she's hurt,' the clone said, getting it now. 'It only muh-matters that she's hurt and nuh-needs help.'

'That's right.' Christopher nodded. 'There will be times in your life when you'll have to make these kinds of decisions. And sometimes the choice won't be nearly so clear-cut. How you respond – what choice you make – goes a long way toward showing what kind of person you are.'

The clone took his time finishing his chocolate bar. As he chewed, he said: 'Wuh-will you and Mom take me to see Sara play?'

'I think it'll be okay, but that's Cassandra's decision to make.'

The clone shook his head, swinging his legs back and forth, back and forth. He smacked his lips, licking all the chocolate off them. 'I duh-don't see why I have to stay in the luh-lab when no one else has to.'

Christopher, knowing that they had arrived at a crucial moment, was careful what he said next. 'You already have some idea that you're different – from Sara, say, or me. But now is the time for you to understand just what that difference is.' When the clone's eyes met his, Christopher went on. 'You have the DNA of someone else. That was deliberate. Cassandra and I . . . we're trying an experiment.'

'I'm the experiment, right?'

'Yes. We want to see if you can find someone.'

'But how? I duh-don't know very many people, and the wuh-world is so buh-big. Anyway, I'm stuck in the luh-lab all the time.'

'That will change. The man is here, somewhere in the city.' Christopher smiled. 'We believe – because you share the same DNA – that there will be some kind of connection.'

'Connection?'

Christopher nodded. 'Think of Hound. When Sara brings him to the lab he's on a leash. Cassandra and I think you and this man may be tied to either end of a kind of leash that links you.'

'Who is he?'

'He's an evil man, you see. He kills people.'

'He takes their trust and violates it.'

Christopher considered this for a moment. 'Perhaps, in a way he does. In any case, he doesn't care one bit about his victims as individuals. There's a hollow core inside him; it pushes him so that he can't stop. He just kills, and he's going to keep on killing unless we can stop him. To be honest, we haven't had much luck so far. That's where you come in. Cassandra and I think with your special knowledge and makeup you can find him for us. This is very important, but I won't lie to you – it's very likely to be dangerous.'

'Like in *Mission: Impossible*.'

'Except this isn't a TV show; it's real life.'

'You duh-don't believe me, but the skeleton's real life.'

'I think he's real to you.'

The clone dropped his gaze to his swinging legs for a moment. 'This muh-man has killed a lot of puh-people, hasn't he?'

'Yes, he has. He has absolutely no regard for human life.'

The clone looked thoughtful for a moment. 'I can understand why you nuh-need to find him; I mean, morally,' he said with unerring logic. 'Plus, it's your job to buh-bring order out of chaos. But I think it's also in here, your nuh-need to find him.' He touched Christopher's heart with his fingertip, tap-tap, tap-tap, just as he'd described the skeleton touching his. 'But what got Mom so hot on his tail?'

Christopher was somewhat startled, not only by the slang the clone so effortlessly picked up. It seemed he already had a clue that there was a personal aspect to this particular hunt. There was no point lying to him; on the contrary. 'This man whose DNA you share most recently murdered Cassandra's husband, Bobby Austin. Bobby was also my best friend.'

The clone looked up into Christopher's face. 'Then there's nuh-no question. I have to find him, don't I? I just *have* to, even if it kills me.'

Book Two

ENGAGEMENT

October 18 – October 22

*We are all prisoners
of cell biology.*

H.B. PEARL

SIX

Christopher was reviewing with Esquival the fruitless results of his daily search of VCAP. The Violent Criminal Apprehension Program was a nationwide database the FBI started up in 1984. It purported to list all crimes of a violent nature anywhere in the country. At least, that was the theory. The reality was another matter entirely. The paperwork required to make the database current was formidable, and even the most diligent of law enforcement officials were hard-pressed to complete their own paperwork, let alone the forms required by the FBI. So the system remained voluntary, and therefore patchy. Yet what data was in the VCAP was absolutely reliable, and it was being filled in more and more each day, so it had its uses. Esquival had been accessing the VCAP daily, searching for murders with similar signatures to those committed by the Pale Saint in hopes of finding a trail that would lead them to the perp's real identity.

'Nothing,' he said.

'Just like all our yesterdays.'

Christopher could hear the frustration in the FBI man's voice, and clapped him on the back. 'He's got to have a past, Reuven. We all do.'

'Yeah? Jesus, I can tell you this guy's not like any of us.'

'And I refuse to believe that this spate of killings is his first.' Christopher looked at the pulsing computer screen. 'We've got to keep digging, Reuven. Digging as fast as we can.'

'What's the point? This perp is like a gust of wind. He's everywhere and nowhere all at once.'

The phone rang and Christopher grabbed the receiver.

'Jon, you'd better come over to the lab,' Cassandra said when he answered.

'Can't right now. I'm right in the middle –'

'I think you'd better come now. It's about Lawrence.'

Listening more closely, Christopher could hear the breathlessness in her voice. 'What's happened?'

'I'm not sure,' she said, 'but I think it might have something to do with the Pale Saint.'

'I'm on my way,' Christopher said. He was halfway out the door, when he shouted over his shoulder to Esquival. 'Beep me when you hit something.'

'*If* I hit something,' Esquival said morosely, but Christopher was already gone.

Cassandra looked up from her endless readouts when Christopher came into the lab. 'Lawrence had a vision.'

'What d'you mean "a vision"?'

'He "saw" someone; in his mind.'

'You mean he dreamed it.'

'He wasn't sleeping,' she said. 'The video log and the status stream confirm he was awake and functioning.'

'Then what –?'

'I told you. He had a vision. And look.' She pointed to the readouts she had been studying when he came in. 'This is the digital log just before, during, and after Lawrence's vision. D'you see? His temperature rose dramatically. And there were quantitative changes in his brain chemicals.' Her fingertip moved over the flatscreen. 'Here, his serotonin level spiked, and remained elevated for the duration of the vision. Once it was over, the level plummeted, and he began to manufacture melatonin at an astonishing rate.'

Christopher looked through the armored glass at the clone inside the birth chamber. 'Is that unusual?'

'Are you kidding? If it wasn't documented here I'd say it was impossible.'

'Interesting. D'Alassandro was sure the peculiar hormone levels in the Pale Saint's blood came from ingesting God knows what kind of chemical cocktail. The clone hasn't been eating anything but good old-fashioned American food, has he?'

'Of course not. Nevertheless, my scientific findings indicate his brain chemistry is not what we would consider normal for a human being.' She looked at him steadily. 'Jon, do you see the implications? I'd say it's a sure shot that the Pale Saint also has the power to manufacture these substances at will.'

110

'Meaning?'

Cassandra shrugged. 'We don't know enough about the properties of either of them to say, but I've got a hunch. I'd be thrown out of the AMA for saying this but I believe it has to do with that Third Eye we discussed. As I told you, serotonin and melatonin are manufactured in the pineal. That's the gland the Pale Saint seems fixated on: the Third Eye. Perhaps Lawrence is seeing . . .'

'What?'

'The past, the future, what's inside the Pale Saint's head. I don't know.'

'Jesus God,' Christopher said. 'This is just the kind of break we were praying for. But is that what's really going on or is this just a case of desperate wishful thinking?'

Cassandra got up and went to stand at the chamber's window. Lawrence was lying on a tilt-table hooked up to an array of monitors that Dillard was adjusting. The clone's eyes flicked from Cassandra to Christopher and back again. 'I don't know, Jon.'

Christopher looked at the clone, saw building like a beast the hateful image of the Pale Saint.

'I need to speak with him.'

'In a minute. He's being tested.'

'I can see that. What did he say?'

She turned to face him. 'He saw someone in a dark place, cold and dank. Underground.'

'The skeleton?'

'I don't know . . . I don't think so.' Cassandra swept a hand through her short hair. 'Anyway, he said there was a terrible danger . . . and death.'

'Whose death?'

'Jon, I –'

'I need to talk with him. Now.'

'But Hutton –'

'The hell with Dr Dork,' he said as he brushed past her. He opened the door to the birth chamber. A thousand machines seemed to be humming at once, as if Christopher had entered a gigantic beehive.

'I need to talk to your subject, Doc.'

Dillard jumped up. 'Christopher, how dare you come in here. Laboratory protocol dictates –'

'Out!' Christopher thundered.

Dillard glared at him.

'Don't get into a pissing match with me, Doc.'

Dillard made a disgusted sound as he sidled out of the birth chamber.

Christopher looked at the clone, whose eyes did not waver or blink. Christopher remembered those eyes from the Pale Saint's interrogation in Chinatown that ended up so wrong. It was difficult not to be intimidated by them. There was a kind of strength or resolve there that Christopher found terribly familiar. And then it hit him. He'd been standing with Chief Brockaw at a press conference three years ago after he had successfully brought to justice a serial murderer who raped his victims before and after he'd killed them. *'There's that look in your eye,'* Brockaw had said. *'What look?'* Christopher had asked him. *'The one,'* Brockaw replied, *'that was there when I met you, right after the first time you killed a perp.'* He must be mistaken. The clone was only two weeks old; what could he know of death?

'Dad, I'm so glad you cuh-came.'

Christopher started. 'What did you say?'

'I said I was glad to see you, Dad.'

'Jesus, let's nip this in the bud,' Christopher snapped. 'I'm not your father.' He peered down at the clone, who said nothing in reply. 'Cassandra tells me you had a vision of some kind. I'm here so you can tell me what it is you saw. It's important if we're going to find the Pale Saint.'

'I saw tuh-two people,' the clone said. 'The skeleton and someone who looked just like me. One who lived under the guh-ground, one who didn't. One was already dead.'

'Which one was dead,' Christopher said as he approached the clone. 'The skeleton or the one who looked like you?'

The clone looked at him in a peculiar manner as he cocked his head. 'The skeleton, of course.'

His heart beating fast, Christopher thought of Esquival saying that the Pale Saint was already dead. He said to the clone: 'What happened then?'

'Then the two of them merged. Like cuh-colors. Red and buh-blue makes green.'

'So the skeleton is the Pale Saint.' *Or is it,* Christopher wondered, *that the clone was the Pale Saint?*

The clone licked his lips; his skin seemed pale and waxy. Remembering the visions was dreadfully hard on him, Christopher could see. Like pulling knives out of his own flesh. Still, he needed more. 'What happened next?'

'The skull?'

'What skull.'

'There's a skull, under the guh-ground.'

'Whose skull, someone the skeleton murdered?'

'It's buh-big, this skull. Buh-big as the world.'

'That makes no sense.'

'I've seen it before. In my duh-dreams.'

'Then it's nothing.'

Lawrence began to fidget. 'Can I guh-get up now?'

Christopher unplugged him. As the readouts went nil one by one, he could see Dillard getting up a good head of steam outside in the lab.

'Duh-Dr Dork looks like his eyes are guh-going to pop like corks,' the clone said.

Christopher could see Cassandra trying to mollify him. He cranked the table out of its horizontal position. 'Dr Dork has got to learn to roll with the punches,' he said.

As the clone gained his feet, Cassandra came in and closed the door carefully behind her. Outside, Dillard had all but steam blowing out of his ears.

'Jon, what are you doing messing with Hutton's protocol? He's gone ballistic out there and right now I can't say I blame him.'

'Your hunch was right.' Christopher indicated the clone. 'He's made a kind of psychic connection with the Pale Saint.'

'Oh, my God.' Cassandra stood rooted to the spot.

Christopher turned his attention back to the clone. 'Now tell me exactly what happened after the two images merged.'

'There were two people again.'

'The skeleton and the Pale Saint?'

'No.' The clone licked his lips again. His pallor seemed more pronounced, as if he were losing blood. 'It wuh-was you. You wuh-were there with the skeleton. In the underground place. The place of death.'

'And then?' Christopher asked. Much to his dismay, his skin had begun to crawl.

'He was creeping . . . in the darkness underground. And I could see the muh-mountains, and under them wuh-was the skull.'

'What mountains?' Christopher asked.

Lawrence rummaged through a stack of shelves. He pulled out several of the hundreds of drawings he'd made of the triangles. 'Here,' he said, 'the mountains in his mind.'

Christopher took the drawings from Lawrence and studied them. 'Which mountains are these?'

'The Rockies.'

Christopher let out a breath. 'So that's where he'll go next. The Rocky Mountains.'

'No,' Lawrence said. 'That's where he cuh-came from.'

Christopher felt a bolt of electricity climb his spine. 'Lawrence, do you know where in the mountains he was born? What town or area?'

The clone shook his head. 'Just the mountains.'

'But what about this underground place?' Cassandra asked. 'Is it real, Lawrence, or is it something in the skeleton's mind?'

'It's both.'

Christopher saw Cassandra give him a quick, searching look.

'He luh-likes the underground, the duh-dark, the smell of earth.'

They could see how terrified the clone was of this vision.

'That has nothing to do with you, Lawrence,' Cassandra said. 'You know that, don't you?'

The clone seemed to ignore her. He looked directly at Christopher. 'Wuh-while he was creeping I saw something . . . something in his muh-mind.'

'What was it?' Christopher asked.

'A thing. This luh-long.' The clone lifted his hands so that they were approximately a foot apart, Christopher estimated. 'Muh-made out of metal.' Into Christopher's mind leaped the image of the Bic pen stuck through Bobby's eye. The clone's eyes shone large and over bright in his waxen face. 'It was an instrument – that's *his* wuh-word. An instrument of duh-death.'

A deep and impenetrable silence seemed to settle over the birth chamber. At length, Christopher said: 'Did you see this . . . instrument? Did he kill with it?'

'Yes,' the clone said. 'After he . . . killed the man in the park, he put the instrument into a guh-garbage can.'

'A garbage can in the park.'

'On a street cuh-corner just outside.'

'What corner?' Christopher pressed.

The strain was showing on the clone's face, and Cassandra said: 'For God's sake, Jon –'

But he hushed her with a flick of his hand. 'What corner?' he repeated.

'There was a . . . telephone on the cuh-corner,' the clone said at last. 'A telephone that duh-doesn't work.'

'Christ,' Christopher said under his breath as he pulled out his cell phone. He called D'Alassandro and gave her the particulars – everything but where the information had come from.

'Drop everything and get on it,' he concluded, 'now.' Then he turned back to the clone. 'You said the skeleton killed the man in the park. No one here told you about that murder.'

'No.'

'Then how did you know?'

A kind of helpless look came over the clone. 'Did I duh do something buh-bad?'

Cassandra's eyes gave Christopher a warning flick and she put her arm around him. 'Jon wasn't scolding you, Lawrence. He sometimes forgets you're only really two weeks old.' As she said this she was glaring at Christopher. 'But tell us how you knew about the man in the park.'

'I duh-don't know,' the clone said, shrugging. 'He juh-just popped into my head like the skeleton.'

'And this place,' Christopher asked, 'this underground place?'

'Duh-don't go, Dad,' the clone pleaded. 'If you do, I'm afraid you'll duh-die.'

'I'm not going anywhere,' Christopher said even as he wondered what strange, forbidden place Lawrence had seen.

'Lights, Camera, Action! Ah-ha-ha-ha!' Paul Layton threw wide his arms as the lights came up on the interior of a brand-new television studio, the heart of a concrete building so modern it looked like a bunker. What was incongruous was that it was nestled in among the elms and sycamores just south of Kingston, in upstate New York. 'I can assure you no expense was spared,' Layton said to the man with him. 'Yessir, it's state of the art, right down to the digital uplink to the satellite feed. No more of those vexing audio or video dropouts at vital moments, guaranteed!'

Layton brayed his laugh as he was programmed to do. As station manager, he'd been told in no uncertain terms by the owners of the Evangelical Nations Network to give this man the deluxe treatment. But then again this man was so highly regarded, Layton hardly needed honchos telling him anything about him. It was like meeting the Pope or something, he thought nervously.

'And what about this set?' He slapped one of the balsa wood pillars. 'Some brainstorm, eh? Making you look like you're sitting on the porch of a big ol' ante bellum house was my idea. Very folksy, very comfy, very down home.'

'That's me to a "T".' Dean Koenig smacked his lips as he craned his neck. 'The pillars, the wicker furniture, the house backdrop with the warm lights coming through the paper window shades. Heck, son, this whole kit-and-kaboodle is as fine as my first going-to-church suit.'

Dean Koenig might come on with the aw-shucks syntax of your beloved uncle, but his body had the vaguely disquieting shape of a torpedo. As he sat himself down in the wicker chair of power in the ENN television studio, the *Mighty Marching Christian Hour* banner showed plainly behind him. The studio's three television cameras zoomed in on him as a technician fitted him with a miniature microphone and earpiece. Layton washed his hands and nodded his head in anxiety. It would be his head if anything went wrong with tonight's broadcast from ENN's new around-the-clock television center because this new satellite feed delivered the network to an audience far larger than anyone at the network had previously imagined. And this man, Dean Koenig, with his enormous popularity, was in no small part responsible for the flood of money that allowed this facility to be built.

'Anything I can get you before magic time?' Layton asked.

Dean Koenig shook his head in that manner that only great men achieved. The thick silver hair swept back off his wide forehead was fixed in place with the panache only a professional hairdresser could achieve. His nails were as highly polished as his wingtip shoes, and his cheeks glowed with robust health, but after a while you could see that the twinkle in his bright blue eyes flourished with the sight of blood. Figurative blood, that is. As seen on television, which he often was, Koenig possessed that most vital asset of the successful politician: he looked like a man with vision. A man who took situations by the throat and shook them until they re-arranged themselves to his complete satisfaction.

He gave innumerable interviews, was beloved by talk-show hosts for repartee that was often as amusing as it was outrageous, had ghost-written two best-selling books, and had lately been given a daily forum on the *Mighty Marching Christian Hour*. This cable television show, just about to commence, had been a moribund entity until Koenig had stepped on board. Now it was ENN's flagship show. Tonight it went coast-to-coast.

At the stroke of midnight, the red light on Camera One lighted up and Dean Koenig was launched upon the late-night airwaves to compete with the likes of David Letterman, Ted Koppel, Larry King, music videos, tired seventies re-runs, and infomercials hosted by celebrities resurrected from the graveyard of obscurity.

'My dear friends,' Dean Koenig began, 'procreation, the creation of life – any life – is a sacred act, a solemn act, a loving act. It is all these things because it is a kind of compact between you and God.' Dean Koenig spoke plainly and directly to the hearts and souls of the *Mighty Marching Christian Hour* faithful so that each and every one of them was certain he was sitting in their living room, chatting just to them. 'But without that Divine spark it becomes a travesty of life, and therefore an abomination in the eyes of our Lord, Jesus Christ.'

Dean Koenig smiled benignly. His china blue eyes were twinkling to beat the band, which meant of course that he smelled blood. 'As I have told you time and again there are agents of the devil – people as godless as they are heartless and unfeeling – who want nothing more than to carry out the will of Satan. Theirs is heinous, hideous work –' Here he made a horrified face as of a priest who had come upon an unspeakable sex act. 'In fact, my dear friends, it pains me even to speak of it.' His jaw thrust forward in a heroic manner. 'And yet I must, though it puts me in jeopardy from these very people, though they have already spent untold thousands of dollars, exerted untold pressure to get me off the air. I will prevail. I will not keep silent because I have a responsibility to you, my dear friends, to tell you of their immoral work, to warn you that right now, AT THIS MOMENT AS I SPEAK TO YOU, they are planning ways to steal from you your children and your children's children. That's right. *Your* flesh and blood. And what do I mean by *steal*? Why, my dear friends, they want to reach down into the wombs of the righteous, of the Godfearing. They want to cut your children open. They want to manipulate your children's genes, the very *essence* of life, the God-given gift that makes every person individual. They want to take what God himself put into your children and replace it with material they have made in their godless laboratories. Now you may ask, Can such an unspeakable evil truly exist? Can men be foolish enough and blasphemous enough to think they can usurp the province of God? Yes, yes! Believe it or not, THEY WANT NOTHING LESS THAN TO APPROPRIATE GOD'S SACRED WORK. Truly, this is madness, truly, this is Chaos, truly, this makes a mockery of God's sacred Word, His promised Apocalypse, where, my dear friends, the righteous will be lifted up by our Lord, Jesus Christ and saved from the flames that will engulf the unbelievers and the sinners alike.

'Satan has many minions, but none more heinous, more devious, more deeply sinful than these people who call themselves *scientists* – researchers who suck blood money from you and from me for their hideous projects – money that could – and should – be spent better educating our children so that they, too, can stand up to these darlings of the devil and cry ENOUGH! I drive you OUT, infidel, OUT into the desert of your own making, OUT into the bitter, godless place where you will wither and die. You will NEVER steal my birthright, you will never steal the birthright of my children, you will never steal the birthright of the children of my children!'

Dean Koenig's eyes were sparking like diamonds in sunlight now as his voice thundered out through the airwaves to grip his millions of rapt listeners. Even the technicians who worked the show were caught up in his peroration.

'These *scientists* – these minions of evil have a name. They toil in the harness of a company called the Vertex Institute. Quite possibly they are carrying out their misdeeds in the very city where you live, where you worship, where you raise your innocent children. Yes, my dear friends, you heard me right: if you reside in the great city of New York as I do, or in our nation's capital, these godless sinners are your neighbors. THEY ARE IN YOUR MIDST AND THEY MUST BE STOPPED.

'And to add insult to injury, Vertex receives funding every six months from the Federal government. Yes, yes, this is the gospel. Congress – made up of the very same men and women who you voted for to represent your interests – has fallen under the spell of these sinners. Your government has betrayed you. The very people to whom you have entrusted your welfare have been turning over your hard-earned money to Vertex to further its godless projects. Gerald Costas is responsible for the unprincipled direction of Vertex's research. And the chief researcher, who coldly, cruelly oversees the creation and manipulation of genes – the material they want to implant inside your children – in Satan's laboratory is Cassandra Austin. I urge you now – EACH AND EVERY ONE OF YOU WATCHING THE *MIGHTY MARCHING CHRISTIAN HOUR* – to contact your congressman and representative in Washington – phone them, write to them, fax them, e-mail them – and demand they cut off all appropriations to Vertex. YOUR VOICE – THE VOICE OF THE RIGHTEOUS – MUST BE AND SHALL BE HEARD.'

He clasped his hands together as if in prayer. 'And now that I have cast the scales from your eyes, my dear friends, now that you have seen the light, there is one last matter that demands your attention. As many of you know, a few weeks ago we were scheduled to have on as our special guest Cassandra Austin, the head of gene research for Vertex. We offered her ample time to explain her views, and to defend them here on this forum, under the eyes of our Lord, Jesus Christ. She refused at the last hour, and has repeatedly refused our patient requests to reschedule her appearance. Which leads us to the inescapable conclusion that she *cannot* defend her godless, soulless work before you, my dear friends, and before God. His light has struck her dumb. BY HER FAILURE TO RESPOND, SHE HAS CONDEMNED HERSELF. We who are moved by the goodness of the Divine will of Jesus Christ have a duty to Him as well as to our families and to our Godfearing neighbors. I beg you to call Gerald Costas at Vertex – you see the phone and fax numbers, as well as the e-mail address written across the bottom of your screen – and demand that he immediately terminate Cassandra Austin's contract. Let him know in no uncertain terms that without that immediate termination we will throw our entire weight into severing Vertex's affiliation with the United States Government.' He briefly lowered his head. 'In the name of Jesus Christ, we need responsible and Godfearing people to stand up against the reckless abandonment of this most sacred compact between mankind and our Lord and savior, Jesus Christ! His will be done, in all things, amen.'

Dean Koenig beamed his telegenic smile out over the cable airwaves. 'And now, my dear friends, until tomorrow at this time, in His name I wish you a peaceful night filled with all His sacred grace and loving kindness.'

Late at night, Christopher came into the lab to work with the clone. Dillard was with him running another battery of his seemingly interminable tests.

The clone grinned when he saw Christopher. 'You're juh-just in time,' he said.

'For what?'

'I have something I wuh-want to show you. Something I've muh-made.'

Dillard took the leads off the clone, who came over to Christopher. When he was very close, he dug into the pocket of his jeans, then held out his hand. It was cupped around the hardball Sara had given him. It was scuffed, with a greenish tinge where it had bounced through grass.

Slowly, with that peculiar look on his face, the clone manipulated his fingers so that the ball slowly revolved until a hollow bored into it was revealed. How he had done this Christopher had no idea. It was a rather large hole and, as the clone continued to rotate the ball, Christopher could see what was inside the hole: a baby mouse, the dry fur flaking slowly from its tiny desiccated carcass. The muzzle of the skull protruded slightly from the hole, as startlingly white as a bridal veil.

'What the hell is that?' Dillard said, startled.

'This is where he guh-goes,' the clone said, his eyes never leaving Christopher's face. 'This is where he duh-dreams.'

'Who?' Christopher said. 'The skeleton?'

The clone nodded.

'Listen, you,' Dillard said sternly, 'give that to me.'

Lawrence moved away from Dillard's outstretched hand.

'Now see here!'

Christopher got between Dillard and the clone. 'Let him keep it.'

Through clenched jaws, Dillard hissed, 'You're undermining my authority, Christopher.'

'What authority, Doc? As far as I can see, you have none.'

Dillard made a sound of contempt. 'It's disgusting. He shouldn't be allowed –'

Christopher turned his back on Dillard, said to the clone: 'I'd be very interested in how you managed this.'

With a brief glance at Dillard, the clone said: 'I made the buh-bowl at night, wuh-when everyone thought I was asleep. The duh-dog got me the mouse.'

'Insidious devil's mind,' Dillard muttered.

'It's a good thing you didn't try to take it away from him,' Christopher told him. 'I believe he will fight tooth and nail to hold onto it. It's become an object of reverence.'

'Black, evil reverence.' Dillard shuddered visibly. 'I want no more part of this. I have more work to do on the transdermal patch.' He stormed out of the chamber and across to the other side of the lab.

Christopher stayed where he was. He was intrigued by what the clone had made of the baseball. He'd seen variations on that kind of vessel. He'd caught a case a couple of years ago. A serial murderer who sort of communed with the bodies of his victims. He kept them around, especially the skulls and brains. He ground them up and placed them in a hollowed out gourd. When caught, he claimed the souls of all his victims were in there, still existing, though in what way Christopher couldn't imagine. He'd asked Esquival about it, and the psychologist said the custom came from Africa by way of the West Indies. It was a kind of shamanistic magic. The idea seemed to be that you could keep the soul of a dead person alive inside this vessel. It seemed clear to Christopher now that the Pale Saint did something similar. Perhaps he'd placed William Cotton's eyes into a similar container.

Christopher regarded the clone who, hour by hour, was being transformed into the living image of the Pale Saint. Inside, it appeared, the same thing was happening. How far would the similarities go? Christopher asked himself. That was the question around which everything revolved.

'Now that we've gotten rid of Dr Dork,' he said, shaking off his dark thoughts, 'are you ready to get to work?'

'You buh-bet,' the clone said eagerly as he stuffed the eerie vessel back into his pocket.

Christopher had already added the fundamentals of police work: how to get information out of people, how to defend yourself against physical assault, how to get in and out of places; in short, how to handle yourself on the street. But because he was required to keep the clone in the lab he could not use the kind of direct examples that could put a point across better than a thousand word lecture. This disturbed Christopher, who believed there was no real substitute for hands-on training. Nevertheless, he began to teach the clone the essentials of the con game because they so vividly illustrated the fundamentals of human emotion and response.

'Con is short for confidence,' Christopher said.

'The other person gives you his cuh-confidence, right?' the clone said at once.

'Eventually, yes,' Christopher said. 'But before that he has to feel that *you* have given *him* your confidence. That's the true secret of all cons; it's why they work every time. Once the other person trusts you, he'll give you just about anything, even if you tell him not to.'

'Really?' This seeming anomaly clearly intrigued the clone.

Christopher nodded. 'He'll want to because he feels a kinship with you, a closeness, a certain bond that separates both you and him from the rest of the world, that makes you worthy of his trust.'

'People wuh-want that closeness,' the clone said with unnerving accuracy. 'It's real important to them.'

'Yes, it is,' Christopher said. 'Maybe the most important thing a human being has. It's also something that the skeleton lacks. It's no

121

wonder these visions frighten you. He has no one. The darkness in his mind has cut him off from everyone and everything human.'

'Except me,' the clone said.

Christopher had no answer for that. Instead, he began to explain a 'tell' to the clone. 'I want you to watch Dr Dork and describe to me his "tell".'

It took Lawrence three minutes, an astonishingly short time. 'Wuh-when he's f-f-frustrated or angry,' the clone said, 'he puh-pulls at his left earlobe.'

'Yes,' Christopher said. 'Everyone you will meet has some kind of "tell", a physical habit they're not even aware of, that gives away what they're thinking.'

'Is that important?'

'It often is,' Christopher said. 'People may lie to you but the "tell" never will. It will show you what they're really thinking.'

'Show me.'

Christopher looked around. 'Dr Dork will go ballistic.'

'I duh-don't care.'

Christopher looked at the clone for a minute. 'Yes, well you know what? I don't either.'

He waited until Dillard was drowsing over his work, then took a digital photo of the interior of the chamber out of his pocket and taped it to a bracket he'd brought. He taped the bracket to the bottom of the video camera. As he did so, he heard the camera's autofocus adjust to the distance of the photo. 'There,' he whispered. 'Now we can get out without Dr Dork knowing anything about it.' Before they left the chamber, he showed the clone how to roll up the spare blanket to make it appear as if he was still in bed. 'Just in case the Dork comes back,' he said.

Shadows, born beneath the streetlights, aimed themselves ominously at the two figures. As they headed uptown in Christopher's car, the clone dutifully recited whatever he could remember from his visions, but unlike the specific images that Christopher hoped would lead his team to the Tompkins Square Park murder weapon, Christopher could make no sense of these: jumbled snippets of violent death, ceaseless ranting in the stifling darkness, and a raging fire, gobbling up all the stars in the night sky.

On Broadway and 44th, Christopher stopped in front of a game of Three Card Monte. The man working the con, a coffee-colored Latino with a scar beneath his left nostril, was at the eye of a crowd of people, bent over and sweaty with greedy anticipation. It was like watching a whirlpool forming. 'The fleecers and the fleeced,' Christopher said, pointing out the shills from the tourists. 'You see how the game works,' he said to the clone, who shook his head. 'Then look at the man with the cards. Find his "tell". When you do, you'll understand the game.'

As he had done with Dillard, he discovered the 'tell' almost immediately. 'He taps the table five times with his knuckle – three times, then two – when he's changed the card.'

'Right,' Christopher said, feeling like a man who has just loaded a new gun for the first time. 'Here's five dollars. Don't lose it.'

Not only didn't the clone lose the money, he made it back ten times over in the space of ten minutes. It happened so fast it made the con man's head spin. He lifted his chin in the time-honored signal and the shills began to close in on the clone. That's when Christopher stepped in and showed them his badge, then the butt of his holstered gun.

Later, eating a Hershey bar he'd bought with his winnings, the clone said: 'That was fun.'

'That's the first mistake you made all night,' Christopher admonished. 'None of this is fun. It's hard work. And for some people, like the guys I just rousted, it's their living. Never forget that. People think you're depriving them of their living, they're going to get mean and they're going to get violent. That should be the first thing you think of before you ever step into their circle. Okay?'

The clone took another bite of chocolate. 'Okay.' Multi-colored neon from the monolithic signs suspended overhead fell across his face like schools of fish rushing headlong into deeper water.

In the place where he sleeps, there is a full-length mirror he has bought. He installed it himself in a spot just beneath the fluorescent light on the inside of the bathroom door. The bathroom itself is small as a coffin. It suits him like a tuxedo at a wedding.

He swallows the contents of a small glass beaker into which he had poured a filthy-looking mixture of ground herbs and powdered essences.

He stands before the mirror, quite naked, and mouths a single word: 'Osteology.' The smells of herbs, acrid and musky, do not disguise the odor of human ash. It rises from a gray pigment he has mixed himself. Dipping two fingers into the pigment, he begins to paint long lines down his body. These lines intersect where, beneath, his joints are. He traces the humerus, the largest bone on his arms, then the ulna, and the radius. He traces the phalanges of his hands. He traces the shield of his sternum, the flare of his ribs, the bones of his pelvis, then his legs. Lastly, he daubs his face, outlining his orbital sockets, the parietals, the occipital, the temporal, sphenoid, maxillary, malar, all the bones of the cranium and the face standing out in stark relief.

He stares with terrifying concentration at the image forming in the mirror. A death's head sits atop the reconstruction of his own skeleton. This is how he has learned to build his power, ingesting the herbs and the powders while his bones emerge through muscles, sinew and flesh.

He sighs and, in one fluid movement, he is standing before her, a god looking down upon his subject. He examines her carefully, as he had in the moment just before he leapt at her, in the last instant of her consciousness, before he took her life and held its incandescent flame in the center of his cupped palm. Her eyes are open, staring at nothing. They are brown eyes, large and cow-like, as vacant now as they had been in life.

She had been slouched in the shadows of the East Village tenement doorway where she always hung out in the mornings and evenings, hands stuffed in her pockets, her nose running, looking like she was waiting for him. Which, of course, she had been. He had bought her a steaming cup of coffee, which she consumed like an animal.

As with all his sacrifices, he knew her type, if not yet her soul. Young, alone, body-pierced, drifting aimlessly through life, a creature in torment. She had proved to be brainless as the audience of a TV show, who laugh and applaud when they're told to, and otherwise remain still and docile as lambs. She had been willing to follow him down to her own death. Stupid as sin.

Yes, he thinks, stupid as sin. Unlike Christopher.

But without doubt she has her purpose. Not *the* purpose, for she, like all the others he has encountered, is not the one. Early on, he knew it, as if at her skin's first compression beneath his touch it gave up all its secrets like the stink of a dead flower. None belonged to him. Or, more accurately, none interested him, though they were at the moment of her demise all at his mercy. The hollowness, the vast black void continues unabated at his core.

Now the Pale Saint leaves the blue-white pool of fluorescent light to kneel before his latest sacrifice. Using a Polaroid camera he squeezes off shot after shot, the flashes like tiny lightning bolts ricocheting off the corners of the room. He pins one up on his wall, then he takes up an iron implement and, using a single sharp movement, pierces the end through her left eye. Not a drop of blood spills forth. Using a long thin stainless-steel implement, he probes deeply and expertly behind the orbital socket. He knows when he reaches the sacred spot because he feels the contact like a mild electric current, and a tiny moan escapes his lips. He makes a small, precise circle with the tip of the implement, and extracts the tiny, acorn-shaped gland.

Dark-red in the palm of his hand, lying against his life-line, the pineal seems to pulse with inner life. He puts his palm against his lips and feels the weight of it like a fledgling wren on his tongue. He swallows convulsively, his mouth thick with saliva.

Soon it will be time to rid himself of the corpse; but even that will serve a purpose. He looks down at the young girl, who is now truly dead, in all the ways that humans can be dead.

He feels deep inside him a certain stirring. 'She's not the one, Faith, not the one,' he whispers. 'Sleep now. Have patience.'

SEVEN

Emma D'Alassandro's nostrils were filled with the stench of a decaying city. All around her, piles of garbage rose greenish-white in the early morning light like the mountains of the moon. That she and her fellow scavengers – Esquival and a Dept of Sanitation guide – were clothed in special overalls, boots, and gloves to protect them only added to the illusion.

'Are you sure *this* is the correct quadrant?' She had to scream at Offenbach, the D.S. guide, over the incessant screeching of the seagulls. There were so many of them, like clouds they sometimes obscured the sun.

Offenbach consulted a clipboard, tapped his forefinger against it and nodded. 'That's what my paperwork says.'

'Yeah, well, two days ago that frigging paperwork said we should look in Quadrant B-Eleven, yesterday it said Quadrant D-Fourteen, and today it's F-Eight.'

'The cans in those four square blocks on the southeast side of Tompkins Square Park are picked up once a week. For some reason, this particular load you're interested in was brought here. Someone forgot to file the buff copy.'

'The *buff* copy?' D'Alassandro said somewhat incredulously.

'Yah. Whaddaya want, an affidavit?'

'At this point, an affidavit would definitely help,' D'Alassandro snapped.

'Heh, heh, yeah,' Offenbach drawled. 'New Yawk, ya gotta love it.'

D'Alassandro gritted her teeth. She could not abide bureaucrats because inevitably their expertise at pushing papers made them think that in the same way they could push people around.

Esquival had shown up an hour ago with an Egg McMuffin in his mouth and another one for her. She was sure he'd brought it because he knew she hated fast food of any sort. She'd swallowed the vile thing while they'd shared a cup of indifferent coffee. D'Alassandro, offal-stained shovel in hand, signaled to him. 'How you doing?'

'How do you think I'm doing?' Esquival shouted. 'I'm hip-deep in shit.'

She saw him stiffen. 'Hey, wait a minute. What's this?' He dug down into the muck.

D'Alassandro paused. 'Got something?'

'Yeah. I think so.' Esquival slogged over to her, depositing the contents of his shovel at her feet.

D'Alassandro looked down at something that glinted metallic in the sunlight, and her heart raced. 'My God, that's it!' she cried. She bent down and moved the sludge away with her gloved hand. 'Oh, shit!' She picked the thing up. It was an obscenely huge chrome-plated dildo. 'Goddammit, Reuven!' She heard him laughing and threw the thing at him. 'Would you stop clowning around and get back to work!'

He saluted smartly. 'Aye, aye, *mi capitan!*' And still laughing, he returned to the place where he had been digging.

D'Alassandro gripped her shovel and bent to continue her nasty excavation work, then looked up at Offenbach. 'What are you laughing at? We could use another hand here.'

'Nah, that's all right,' he said blandly. 'It's not in my contract.'

'Pardon?' D'Alassandro stood up.

'I'm a supervisor, see. Management.' He lifted the clipboard as if he was Moses come down from the mountaintop. 'I graduated out of the rank and file. I don't do grunt work no more.'

'Is that so? Listen, buster, I don't take that kind of crap from anyone.' D'Alassandro threw him a shovel. 'Management just got down and dirty like everyone else on this detail. Or would you rather I call your supervisor and tell him you're obstructing the most important police investigation of the decade?'

Scowling, Offenbach put his clipboard under his arm and pushed the spade blade into the garbage. 'Cripes,' he muttered, 'this city sure ain't what it used t'be.'

'Heh, heh, yeah,' D'Alassandro said, imitating him. 'New Yawk, love it or leave it.'

Three hours later, they found what Lawrence had described to Christopher.

*   *   *

127

When D'Alassandro and Esquival came into the Case Room, Christopher was going over the day's leads and sightings with Sgt Lewis. These were the tedious parts of the case, the ones that, thankfully, were run down by the added uniforms Brockaw had assigned to the team. In Christopher's experience, they almost never went anywhere, but they needed to be explored nonetheless.

Christopher looked up and said, 'What the hell is that smell?'

'Guess where we were, Loo?' Esquival said. They hadn't bothered to strip off the special outfit they had been wearing.

'I don't have to. Any luck at the garbage dump?'

'Yup!' D'Alassandro dropped an evidence bag onto his desk.

Christopher turned over the item inside the plastic bag, examining it intently. The blood was rushing through his temples with such force that he could scarcely hear himself think. The clone's intuition or 'vision', or 'sight', whatever the hell you wanted to call it, had been right on target, he thought.

'I'd sure like to know the source of this tip, Loo,' Esquival said.

'All in good time.' Christopher turned over the object.

'We had to run the load down in the armpit of Brooklyn,' D'Alassandro said, 'don't ask me where, because I don't ever want to go there again. And, Boss, please don't ever make me work with Sanitation again. They're such deadheads they don't even know how to take orders.'

'If you carried a gun like the rest of us, if you'd let me use mine,' Esquival said, 'we'd have gotten cooperation a helluva lot sooner.'

'Not to mention a lawsuit, you Neanderthal,' D'Alassandro said. 'Besides, I don't want anything to do with a gun; I spend my life seeing what they can do to people,' she said. 'Christ, Boss, I never saw so many seagulls in my entire life! Did you know they scream?'

'Laugh,' Christopher said.

'Huh?'

'That's what they call them: laughing gulls.'

'Well, it's no joke out there.'

'It's no joke in here, either,' Esquival said, holding his nose. With a professional comedian's flourish, he thrust at her a giant-size plastic bottle of Lysol. D'Alassandro grabbed it and promptly squeezed off a mighty shpritz at his face.

'Good one,' Esquival laughed, as he ducked away.

Christopher handed over the evidence bag. As the two of them looked on, Esquival pulled on a pair of rubber gloves, and drew out the contents. It was a metal item about a foot in length and maybe an inch-and-a-half at its widest. One end was flat, the other tapered down.

'What the hell is this?' he asked.

'Except for the fact that it's square,' Esquival said, 'it looks like a nail the Jolly Green Giant would use to keep his pole beans off the ground.'

He moved it more directly into the pool of light from his desk lamp, and immediately saw what had excited D'Alassandro on the way back to the Case Room. 'There's blood on the metal, fairly new. Also, from the patina on the surface, I'd say this nail's old.'

'How old?' Christopher asked.

'Older than either of us.' Putting it down on the plastic bag, Esquival swiveled around and called up like a genie the massive on-line electronic encyclopedia to which D'Alassandro had insisted they subscribe. It took him some time to find what he was looking for because he had to surf a number of databases. 'Got something. Here it is in American History. Oh, yeah, come to papa.' He signaled them to come around to the terminal.

'This thing is nineteenth-century stuff. It was used out west exclusively because of the particularly hard composition of the road bed through the Rockies.'

The Rockies, Christopher thought. He felt a little shiver go through him. *So far the clone is batting a thousand.* He snapped on a pair of disposable rubber gloves and took up the object and compared it to the drawing on the screen. 'They're identical,' he said.

'Right.' Esquival swiveled around to look at D'Alassandro and Christopher. 'Odd as it may seem, the Pale Saint is using an antique railroad spike to kill his victims. And a rare one to boot.' He hit a key and the screen now showed two spikes, one shorter than the other. 'See, our spike's different, about two inches longer and more tapered than this other, more common one.'

'No wonder he can use it to excise the pineal gland.' D'Alassandro laid out a series of forensic photos of William Cotton, extreme closeups. 'The shape conforms to the entry wound that killed William Cotton,' she said. 'When I get the results of the tests back, I'll lay odds that blood's Cotton's. It's definitely the murder weapon.'

'I'd have to agree.' Christopher hefted the spike. 'Reuven, as soon as Emma's done with this send it off to the FBI lab in Washington. Maybe your pals can give us a little more info on it. And dragoon more uniforms to canvass antique dealers. You said these were kind of rare. I want to get an idea if these Western railroad spikes are collectible, and if so whether there's some kind of buy and sell network.' He turned to go. 'D'Alassandro,' he said over his shoulder, 'in your spare time –'

'What spare time?' she mumbled.

'In your spare time,' he went on, 'check the Internet for a collector's website. It's a long shot, but you never know, we might get lucky.'

'Your tip about this spike sure panned out, Boss.' She eyed him in that canny way of hers. 'Any chance there's more good vibrations from the same mysterious source?'

'Let's get on this new information, boys and girls,' Christopher said, nipping off any more speculation on that topic.

Cassandra was logging in Lawrence's latest readouts, when Dillard appeared from the other side of the lab. His face was pinched and drawn.

'Cassandra, there you are,' he said. 'I didn't see you come in.'

'Hutton, you look awful. When was the last time you slept?'

'We have a serious problem.' His tone leaked impatience with her. 'I've been trying to address it all night.'

Cassandra was instantly on alert. 'With the subdermal delivery system?'

'No, I'm well on my way to perfecting that. Within the week we'll be able to use the subdermal patch. It will time-release the drug and arrest the hyper-aging for a full month before it needs to be replaced.' He took a breath. 'Assuming, that is, we get a chance to use it.'

Cassandra felt a clutch at her heart. 'What do you mean?'

'It's Minnie.' He meant the rat that was the subject of the trans-genic hyper-aging protocol. 'She's dying, and the data says it's of old age.'

'But it's not time yet.' Cassandra switched readouts on her flatscreen, frantically began to check the computer data Dillard had been poring over all night long.

'Indeed, it's not. But the fact remains the rate of aging has increased dramatically.'

'Why didn't you call me?'

'You were so spent when you left here yesterday I thought I'd give you a break.'

'Well, you thought wrong,' Cassandra snapped.

'I'm sorry, but this thing has me rattled. I mean to say, the hyper-aging slowed down after I upped the dosage of Tetracycline, but it didn't shut off as it was supposed to. It is continuing at the same rate.'

Cassandra gave him another quick glance. 'That's impossible.'

Dillard nodded. 'I would have agreed with you last night, but look for yourself.'

Her fingers were flying over the computer keyboard as she cross-referenced Dillard's findings with those of their previous experiments.

'Clearly, it's happened. The computer models never gave us this as a possibility. The trans-gene simply isn't expressing itself the way our theoretical studies predicted it would.'

Cassandra looked up from the flatscreen terminal. 'What are the implications for Lawrence?'

'You know what they are, Cassandra. Ominous. Chances are this anomaly in the trans-gene will kick in and he'll age so rapidly he'll die within two weeks. If not before.'

Cassandra was back scanning data. 'All the more reason we've got to find a way to re-establish control over the trans-gene.'

'In a minute,' Dillard said, 'first let me pull a rabbit out of a hat.'

Cassandra brushed aside his words; Hutton was at his worst when stymied. 'Let's agree to be professional adults, okay?' She had no time to deal with his anger. 'Somewhere in our computer model is the answer to the problem. Together, we'll find it, I'm certain.'

Dillard crossed his arms over his chest in his best I-told-you-so manner. 'Face facts, Cassandra. The subject's a timebomb. The trans-gene could go critical at any time. We just don't know. And there goes my Nobel Prize.' He shook his head. 'Damn you, and damn me for letting you talk me into this particular piece of insanity.'

That night Cassandra awoke calling Bobby's name. Christopher, passing outside her bedroom on his way to the bathroom, paused. Today, at Sara's insistence, he had moved into the guest room in the Austins' loft. Though she would not tell Sara this, Cassandra had had vague misgivings; when she came near Christopher she felt pulled by the conflicting currents of desire and propriety. She found herself wanting him so badly she was as aware of his presence as if he was an arrow that had pierced her breast. And yet Bobby's face, hovering close, iced her with guilt.

Before he could turn away, she said, 'Did I wake you?'

He stood, suspended, in the open doorway. 'Too busy thinking. The clone's vision led us right to the murder weapon.'

Cassandra's eyes opened wide. 'My God, Jon –'

'Yes, I know. It's happening . . . happening so fast it almost seems to be out of our control.'

She stared into space for what seemed a long while. 'Will you sit next to me?'

'Cass, I –'

'Just for a little while.'

He sat rather tentatively on the bed, she noticed, as if waiting at the edge of a forest for a rare and reclusive creature. She reached for the glass of water on the night table. Passing close to his bare flesh, she fancied she felt a streak of heat on her skin. 'My throat feels raw, as if I'd been screaming for hours at the top of my lungs.' The digital clock said it was just after three in the morning. She hadn't gotten back to the loft until after one – twelve hours straight trying to find a cure for Minnie and for Lawrence without success, then a stop at the lean-to of the neighborhood homeless man Bobby had befriended to bring him a pizza and a thermos of tea, which she implored him to drink instead of that vile alcohol. Still, part of her wished that she was at the lab with Lawrence; the other part thanked God that she was here at this moment.

'You had a nightmare,' Christopher said.

'I wish I could remember it.' She made a face at the water's chlorine taste. When had city water gotten so bad? she wondered. She felt a pang of longing for the clear, sweet water they drank during their summers together. 'As it is, I'm left with this awful feeling of unease.'

'That makes two of us.' Naked to the waist, he looked enormous and powerful, as unstoppable as the freight train that used to barrel through the upstate wilderness outside Kingston.

She reached out for him, needing his solidity. 'I called Bobby's name, I know that.' Words – and emotions – came tumbling. 'I'm going to be doing that for some time. I'm going to burst out crying and –'

'It's okay.' He twined his fingers with hers. 'It would be odd if you didn't.'

She sighed. 'I loved him, you know. In a whole different way than I love you. Less complete, less . . .' She felt herself abruptly lost in thought, and wondered why she was trying to distract herself. Christopher's presence burned through as if he was a great thrumming engine. 'Sometimes I wished I could love him in the way in which he loved you – as a friend, as someone he could be completely relaxed with.'

'Bobby loved you. There was no question of that.'

'You're such a loyal friend.' She smiled ruefully in the darkness. 'But, you see, we were never truly a family, just three people inhabiting more or less the same space. His time with Sara was spent teaching her how to pitch. His time with me was spent making fierce love or fighting over – well, anything at all, really. That was it, all he knew how to give us. And maybe that was all I knew how to give in return.'

'That's no reason to blame yourself.'

'I don't blame myself for failing, I blame myself for not trying harder.' She lay under a thin sheet, limned in ribbons of wan light. She was aware of Christopher's gaze tracing the swell of her breasts. As if in direct response, her nipples rose. She bit her lower lip, excited and ashamed all at once. She felt as wanton as a teenager, as if her entire body had become a sexual instrument, as if through a flood of hormones, pheromones and endorphins it was of its own accord attuning itself to him. These feelings, so long kept hidden away, frightened her enough to make her keep talking: 'Poor Bobby. He meant well, I have no doubt, but he had other agendas. He was so hell-bent on saving the world. I always thought that was because the old bastard was such a mean-spirited sonuvabitch.'

'Bobby once told me it wasn't the old man's fault. A long time ago, his father had had a major falling out with his older brother and had been cut off from the family inheritance.' Christopher's eyes continued to drink Cassandra in. 'It seems the grandfather had been a nasty piece of work himself, one of those storied land barons at the turn of the century.'

'Who cares?' Cassandra said angrily. 'That was no excuse to treat your son like crap. Remember the old bastard's funeral?'

'How could I forget? No one but us showed up. The older brother was dead by then, but none of his children even called.'

'Served the old bastard right. I wanted to spit on his coffin for all the pain he had caused Bobby, but Bobby was crying. Later, he said it was because he was remembering the times the old bastard taught him how to pitch. What nonsense!'

'Maybe not, Cass. After the old man was cut off, baseball became his life, and he wanted to live it through Bobby. He pushed and bullied, and went into a prolonged depression when Bobby chose the law instead of professional baseball.'

'Bobby was that good? He never spoke about it.'

'I don't think he ever told anyone but me.'

Cassandra sighed. 'I suppose that was his obsession with teaching Sara to pitch. That was another thing I seem to have missed the boat on. At least, according to my daughter.'

'So the two of you spoke.'

'She did what you asked, Jon,' she said. 'She always does.'

'The Austin women have far too many secrets from each other.'

'Well, we have fewer now. We've had a couple of talks that made me see I misjudged her and Bobby both.' She was surprised to hear her voice trembling with so much emotion. 'It was hard hearing what she had to say.'

'Better this than nothing,' he said. 'I know from hard experience.'

'I was angry at you for what you did. Then angry at myself for being angry at you.' She looked at him. 'Does that make any sense?'

'Yes, it does.'

'I have a long way to go with her.'

'Maybe all the two of you need is the time to get to know one another.'

'And I so want to get to know her.'

She was having trouble breathing, as if in Christopher's presence the air lacked sufficient oxygen. She wondered whether he might be feeling the same thing. She tried to intuit something from his expression, but he was very still, as if the slightest movement would shatter something precious.

'What is it?' she whispered, finding that she could not take her hands off him.

'When I'm with you like this I can almost forget how much I want to destroy the Pale Saint.'

'Jon, don't –'

But he shook off her admonition. 'It's too late. I can't help it, that's the kind of man I am.' He laughed harshly. 'Maybe Dillard has a theory to explain it.' He paused, perhaps considering whether to go on. 'MacAffee, a detective at the One-Six came by to see me the other day. He's the fourth, and I'm sure there'll be more. He worked with Romero, one of the cops who was killed at the Chinatown precinct. He wants blood. Literally. He begged me, when we bring the Pale Saint in, to let him have twenty minutes alone with him. You can imagine why.'

Cassandra's breath caught in her throat. She felt abruptly terrified for him and for herself. It was as if her unremembered nightmare had come into cruel focus. 'What did you say?'

'Don't look at me like that, of course I told him no. I was careful, reasoned, almost detached, but that was for MacAffee and all the others. For myself, it's something entirely different. I feel this pulse inside me, this rage at what he did to Bobby, and then I know nothing is going to stop me when I finally bring him in.'

She gripped him. 'You *must* stop yourself, Jon. Bobby would want you to bring him in unharmed so he can stand trial, you know that. Bobby believed in the American justice system above all else. It was what he lived for.'

'I know that better than anyone,' Christopher said.

'You know *me* better than anyone.'

She trembled when Christopher pulled her up to him. Head back, neck arched, she seemed to rise from the foam of sheets. Her bare skin was lightly sheened. He said nothing. She felt his heart beating wildly beneath his chest, his secret scent rising to her, and it seemed as if she had been mysteriously and magically transported back to that moment in the summer's dappled sunlight when he watched her bring herself to shuddering climax. Her pulse quickened.

When he kissed her, she closed her eyes and sighed into his mouth. They stayed like that for a long time, as if neither wished the moment would end. When at length she broke away, she knew she had one last thing she needed to say before she would abandon herself to what was to come.

'Jon,' she began, 'about Lawrence, please don't hate him.'

She saw Christopher look away at the artificial light seeping like poison through the blinds. It was without color or texture, as if existing without real purpose. 'I think about Andy all the time, about how miserably I must have failed him for him to do . . .' He choked, and her heart went out to him. 'To kill himself.'

'You did the best you could.'

'Well, that's a sad commentary on my life.' He was very still.

'Jon,' she said softly, 'can't you see how your guilt is eating you inside. It won't even let you respond naturally to Lawrence.'

Because he had no answer for her he started to get up. But she stayed him with her voice. 'Don't go,' she whispered.

'Cass, this isn't the time –'

'We just found out that the trans-gene we put into Lawrence has the potential to go out of control.'

'Meaning?'

'If it does, and we can't find a way to reverse it, he'll die. Simple as that.' She stared bleakly at him. 'Please, Jon.'

He stretched out beside her, but she did not relax, and she did not fall back to sleep.

He gathered her into his arms so that she could feel his warmth flowing into her. She felt as cold as if he had dragged her out of an ice field.

'How long?' he asked.

'Oh, God, don't ask me that.'

'You know I have to.'

She put her head down. 'A matter of weeks, maybe less.' She moved again, closer to him. 'What did I do, Jon? Was it the right thing?' she whispered into his ear as if afraid the room might be listening and rendering a judgement.

'There is no right thing.' Christopher traced a line along the hollow between her breasts. 'We're in a whole new world where ethical theory is being rewritten hour by hour.'

'That's just talk. The truth is here, staring us in the face. Yes, he's the Pale Saint's clone. But, surely, that's not all he is. Are we only DNA, programmed to do as our forebears did before us? Don't we learn as we grow, don't we grow as we age? Jon, what else is life about?'

'Cass, I have no answers –'

'None of us does,' she breathed. 'But it's too late to find them out, isn't it? No matter what we do now it's too late for poor Lawrence.'

She turned then, and climbed swiftly on top of him, spreading her thighs. Their insides were warm and soft as melting butter. She reached down for him and pressed him against her belly. Christopher kept his gaze on her. She could not put a number to the times she had imagined this moment, only to wipe it away in disgust, profoundly ashamed that she should covet her best friend with a desire that transcended even her iron will to keep it fully suppressed. Instead of giving in, she had begun to think of him as the enemy, the intruder, the one who had poisoned her marriage with Bobby. The truth was simple: the marriage had been a mistake from the start.

She stroked him with her fingertips until he moaned and arched up against her. Her obvious urgency mirrored his own. She slipped him inside her and hunched forward, expelling all her breath, all her emotion in one steaming motion. She mouthed his name as if it were an incantation that could wipe away all the years of guilt, sorrow, the terrible yearning.

She was like a cauldron inside. She thrilled to see that he had no power to resist her. Her desire for him was like a second heart, frantically pumping in her lower belly. It fluttered like a butterfly until his cheeks were wet with her tears, until her thigh muscles bunched and rippled against him, until she groaned with each stroke into her, with each brush of her hardened nipples against him, until her whole pelvis clenched and spasmed.

As he exploded inside her, her head came down beside his, and he held her tightly, kissing her as she wept all over again. Long afterward, after they had made love again, slowly and sweetly and languorously, getting to know each other's body, as light from a new day crept across their twined forms, Cassandra awoke from a dream she could not remember and began to cry. She felt Christopher's arm around her, pulling her close, and she said: 'Jon, I just feel like the stars are about to go out.'

Cassandra and Dillard continued to run their batteries of tests on Lawrence. As yet, he showed none of the trans-genic problems encountered in Minnie. As for the rat, she continued to deteriorate at a rate that appalled them. After the boosted levels of Tetracycline failed, Dillard suggested they go back to other antibiotics in an attempt to turn off the rogue trans-gene. Nothing worked, however, and soon they both agreed they had to find another means of attacking the problem. The difficulty was neither knew in which direction to look.

Often, they were interrupted in their fruitless work by Lawrence, whose serotonin spiked visions were coming more and more frequently. The problem was he often did not remember nor could articulate what he had 'seen'.

'Look at the levels of serotonin he's putting out,' Dillard said, after the latest of these episodes. 'If we could only find a way to harness such production even a businessman like Costas would turn us into heroes.'

Cassandra, studying yet another set of complex calculations for a cure on her computer imaging program, nodded distractedly. Her personal voice mail was clogged, as it had been for the past few days, with calls from Gerry Costas. When she was in this secret lab, she was unreachable through normal channels. The messages had an increasingly urgent tone. That was not unusual; he was always hounding her for quarterly reports, expense updates, forecasts, and the like. Since she avoided paperwork like the plague, she was always behind Costas' schedule. Usually, he foamed at the mouth until he got what he needed from her. Not this time, she had decided. She had more important things to deal with than a growing mountain of – She snapped her fingers. 'Wait a minute!' Her head whipped around. 'Serotonin! Why didn't

I see it before!' She pushed herself free and went over to another flatscreen.

Dillard, caught in the undertow of her sudden excitement, followed her over. 'What are you doing?'

'Lawrence has so far shown none of the warning signs we saw in Minnie, right?'

'Right,' he acknowledged, 'but –'

There was a look of triumph on Cassandra's face. 'I'm betting his body's abnormally high serotonin level is keeping the trans-gene under control.'

She was working as fast as she could, checking data, referencing the clone's readout against Minnie's. 'See –' her forefinger stabbed out. 'Minnie's serotonin level is well within normal.' She did some quick calculations with percentages and body weight between the clone and the rat. 'So . . .' She drew out a vial and a micro-syringe, plunged the needle into the vial and drew out a liquid. Then she moved over to Minnie's cage. 'Let's see what happens when I inject Minnie with booster shots to bring her serotonin up to Lawrence's level.'

She opened the cage and took Minnie out. The rat, gray and haggard, lay quiescent in her hand. 'It's okay, sweetie,' Cassandra crooned as she prepared her. 'We're going to get you well.' She injected the serotonin, then, returning Minnie to her cage, hooked her up to her leads and switched on the readouts.

'Damn, damn, damn.'

There was no change in Minnie's blood chemistry, nor was there after a half-hour or an hour. The trans-gene was still on a runaway course.

Her face was a mask of frustration and fear. 'I was so sure I'd found the answer.'

Dillard looked away, knowing there was nothing he could say.

EIGHT

Dillard was on the verge of hysteria when Cassandra entered the lab the next morning.

'You're not going to believe this,' he nearly shrieked, 'but Christopher has been taking the subject out for little moonlight strolls.'

Cassandra had to think fast. 'How do you know that?'

Dillard gave her a bitter smile. 'I caught a glimpse of them last night as I was leaving the lab. I had turned back to retrieve the last batch of formulas we'd run through and I saw them skulking out of the back door.' His smile turned brittle and hard-edged. 'I tried to follow them but they lost me.'

Oh, God, Cassandra thought. 'Well, actually, Hutton, I already knew. Jon told me.'

'You're insane,' he shouted. 'One hundred percent certifiable.'

'Hutton, please calm down.'

'I'll do nothing of the kind. You allowed the subject out of the laboratory. How irresponsible can you possibly be?'

Cassandra had seen Dillard like this when his paper on learned traits had been rejected by *Cell* magazine.

'For God's sake,' she said with some exasperation, 'don't make a Federal case out of it.'

'Why not? You and Christopher have put the entire project in jeopardy. How long has the subject been unmonitored? Who knows what kinds of chemical, endocrinologic or hormonal changes occurred while he was out of the lab? Now it doesn't matter, because we'll never know. We've missed critical data that links one stage of hyper-aging to the next. *What* were you thinking?'

'Okay, it was wrong, I see that now,' Cassandra said, abruptly switching tactics. 'But I thought it was best for his development. Can we please go on from here?'

'Certainly not. Now you can see Christopher's true colors.'

'You're overlooking something. Jon is our own private security force,' she said trying desperately to soothe him. 'He's making sure no one inside or outside the lab finds out what we're up to. Our reputations – not to say our careers – rest on his expertise, Hutton. Think about what would happen if Dean Koenig, the IBE or even Costas got wind of what we're doing. We're under Jon's protection now so be a love and try to remember he's on our side, okay?'

'Nonsense, Cassandra, you're allowing personal feelings to get in the way of scientific observation. Your precious Jon Christopher couldn't care an iota about scientific discovery. All he wants is to use our subject in his own investigation. And in the process, he's going to take as gospel incomplete findings, manipulate them, use them out of context, make wild extrapolations so he can exploit them for all they're worth. That's one slippery slope I intend to avoid at all costs. Mark my words, if we don't end his meddling here and now he'll wind up compromising the scientific integrity of our study, and then we'll have embarked on this hazardous undertaking for nothing.'

'And what if Jon finds something here that can help him track down the Pale Saint? Don't you think Bobby deserves that?'

'Now you're trying to cajole me into compromising our work? I might as well defect to Helix Technologies. No, I won't accept it. What has gotten into you? The digital logs are all here. How on earth are we going to explain this missing period of time? A first-year lab assistant would see through the hole in our data.'

'Don't overdramatize, Hutton. You're talking as if Jon just opened the door to the lab and let Lawrence stroll out for an unsupervised period. Nothing could be further from the truth. He was continuing his education.'

'Listen to yourself. Has Christopher corrupted you so thoroughly that you can dissemble to me?' Dillard's face was red with rage. 'My God, I've seen enough to understand what's happening. You and Christopher have so thoroughly contaminated the project at this moment we can no longer tell whether his behavior is a product of the abnormal urgency of his genes or whether it stems from his environment. Don't you see? You're squandering what chance we've been given to prove our theories. But perhaps it's not too late. We still have a chance, but we must work quickly. We must clear everyone extraneous out of the lab. Christopher, your daughter. It's gotten out of control. We must re-establish strict scientific procedure, keep the subject under constant scrutiny inside the lab. That's where he belongs and that's where he must stay.'

'You talk about Lawrence as if he's nothing more than Minnie.'

'Yes, Cassandra that's precisely my point. This is an experiment. A subject is a subject, period.'

'We're talking about a human being, Hutton.'

'Is that what he is, Cassandra? I'll leave that question to the bio-ethics committee, and quite happily too. He's a vehicle to experiment on to prove our theories. Beyond this of what use is he? None.'

'I am alive; I think; I am.'

Dillard started as he turned to see Lawrence standing beside him.

'Get back in your chamber.' Dillard's face had gone red again. 'This is none of your affair.'

'Buh-but it is my affair,' Lawrence said. 'You can't keep me luh-locked up like some kuh-kind of animal.'

Dillard wheeled on Cassandra. 'Do you see what you and Christopher have wrought?'

'I applaud the fact that Lawrence has independent thoughts. Why don't you?' Cassandra shook her head. 'You can't blame him for not growing up the way you imagined he would.'

'I imagined a clean experiment that none of our colleagues, no one on the bio-ethics committee could refute. Not to mention the egg on the faces of everyone at Helix. Now that you and Christopher have shattered that dream I am compelled to do whatever needs to be done to salvage this fiasco. That includes ridding this lab of everyone but essential personnel.'

'My father *is* essential,' Lawrence said. 'And so is Sara.'

'I'm afraid you have no say in this,' Dillard said in his most officious manner. 'And Christopher isn't your father. It's high time you understood that.'

'Hutton,' Cassandra said, 'there's got to be a better way to handle this.'

'By your own hand, those options are now out of reach,' Dillard said. 'No contamination. If that means the subject must be kept locked inside the birth chamber, then so be it.'

'I wuh-want to see Sara pitch in the championships,' Lawrence said.

'You'll do nothing of the kind,' Dillard said stiffly.

'I will too, Dr Dork.'

'What did I tell you about calling me that?' Dillard snapped.

'Lawrence, you know better than to be disrespectful to other people,' Cassandra said.

'What about when people are duh-disrespectful to me?'

'Be still, you.' Dillard turned on Cassandra. 'Listen to me. If he so much as sets foot out of the lab again I'm going straight to Costas and shut this project down.'

'Hutton, I can't be bluffed. You want this project to succeed as much as I do.'

'Oh, I'm not bluffing. You've already seriously compromised what we've done here. I won't stand idly by and watch you destroy what's left of its integrity.'

Cassandra turned to Lawrence: 'Perhaps it will be best if you stay in the lab.'

The look on the clone's face nearly broke her heart.

When Christopher went into No-Name for breakfast, he noticed that the doorway across the street was empty. Kenny looked up. Setting down a plate of steak and eggs, he hurried from behind the counter, said as he approached Christopher: 'I think I got something for you.'

He pointed to the doorway across the street. 'When the kid never showed a couple of days ago I started asking around.' When Kenny squinted it made him look like an Airedale. He led Christopher over to a stool inhabited by a man huge and hairy enough to be a gorilla. He had dark unkept hair, a beetling brow and a definite odor both alien and unwelcome to the diner.

'This is the gent I mentioned,' Kenny said by way of introduction.

'You interested in that girl lurked across the street?' The man had a yap as big as Queens.

'That's right.' Christopher took a step toward him and immediately regretted it. 'What about her?'

'I seen her a few nights back. I come here alla time for a little pick-me-up before dinner. The wife has me on a diet when I'm home.' The gorilla chuckled as he patted his prodigious belly. A waft of foul odor hovered about him like a bad headache.

Christopher flipped open his notebook. 'You remember what time this was you saw her?'

'Gee, about seven, seven-thirty, definitely not later because it was still quiet in there; the Deadhead dinner crowd doesn't start staggering in till eight, the earliest.'

'Uh huh.'

'I could see her wiping her nose from time to time as she shuffled from one foot to the other, but then my food came, and when I looked back up I saw her take the paper cup he offered.'

Christopher felt the breath go out of him. 'Who was that?'

The gorilla frowned. 'Didn't see his face, but I guess there was nothing special about him. Average size, not big, not small. Wearing jeans, denim jacket, work boots. Basic stuff, not that designer crap you see all over. Couldn't see what kind of shirt he was wearing.'

'That's okay.' The gorilla had just jump-started Christopher's pulse. 'Keep going.'

'Everything he wore was well broken in. Could have been a construction dude, that would be my guess because now I think of it he was very tan, like he worked outdoors all the time – you know, rough, Marlboro Man type, not like a city slicker at all.' He snapped his fingers. 'And one other thing: his hair, it was white as milk, you know, sort of like the description of that Pale Saint dude.'

Across the street only shadows inhabited the doorway that had been her shabby home for weeks on end. The darkness of last night still cloaked the street, though high above the rooftops the sky was turning a deep October blue. The chill in the air, so welcome after the relentless heat and humidity of the summer, was like the tang of fresh yoghurt.

'You see what happened after he gave her the coffee?'

'He took her away, arm across her shoulders like they was lovers or sumthin'. Last I saw, he was whisperin' in her ear.' The gorilla's heavy body odor was making Christopher's eyes water. He pointed. 'They went east. That's all I seen.'

Christopher nodded. 'That's a good start.'

'Hey, you think it was this Pale Saint guy?'

'Do you?'

'Maybe.'

'Then you should've reported it to the police.'

'I would've, you know –' The gorilla's huge shoulders lifted and fell. '– but the cops an' I, we sort of don't get along, if you catch my drift.'

Christopher said he did. Kenny pushed a donut and a cup of steaming coffee on him as he went out the door.

*   *   *

Cassandra's stomach tightened as she saw the increased security around the front of the Vertex lab. She peered through the blinds in order to get a better view of the crowd of people. What the hell was this? she wondered. Then she saw the banners and hand-painted signs with quotes from the Bible proclaiming the sanctity of God's will, protesting 'The Work of the Devil', the evil experiments funded by Vertex. It was like an anti-abortion rally – a couple of hundred people ranged in a rough semi-circle around a portable podium from which the all too familiar figure of Dean Koenig was denouncing Vertex in general and Cassandra in particular. Hearing him shout her name through the amplified bullhorn made her wish she had gone on his show, so his flock could hear the truth for themselves. She even toyed with the idea of shouldering her way through the throng, crashing Koenig's pathetic display, to seize the moment and tell these people right now that they had nothing to fear from her or from Vertex.

In the end, though, she decided to do nothing. She could see that Koenig had already whipped these people up into a froth of righteous anger. People in that kind of fervor did not want to be confused by the truth.

The sight of Dean Koenig and all he represented camping out on her doorstep was enough to make her want to reappraise her liberal philosophy of life. While she might understand Koenig's innate fear of her experiments, she resented him spewing his bile, ludicrous though it might be, in her face.

She checked on Lawrence. Minute by minute, his features were maturing, as if when she wasn't looking, the very bones in his face were rearranging themselves. When she looked into Minnie's cage, the rat seemed so close to death now, her blood ran cold and she could not stop herself from picturing Lawrence, an old man, gasping out the end of his life, maybe only a week from now unless she found a way to turn off the rogue trans-gene.

The old windows, though firmly closed against the autumn chill, not only leaked frigid air but Dean Koenig's amplified voice as well. '"The light of the body is the eye,"' he declaimed, quoting from Matthew. '"If therefore thine eye be single, thy whole body shall be full of light. But if thine eye be evil, thy whole body shall be full of darkness. If therefore the light that is in thee be darkness, how great is that darkness!"'

She found it ironic that Koenig and men like him quoted freely from the Bible, using passages that served their needs, ignoring all the others.

While her parents were going through the most bitter phase of their divorce, she had stayed with her aunt Emily, her mother's sister, a woman already widowed and alone. To fend off her loneliness, Aunt Em had turned to the Bible. Every night when Cassandra climbed into bed, Aunt Em read to her from it in a clear, fluid contralto. Cassandra had found many of the readings a great comfort while she lay scared in an unfamiliar bed. So much so that she remembered most of them. Matthew had written about the darkness of evil, but he had also written: 'For if ye forgive men their trespasses, your heavenly Father will also forgive you: but if ye forgive not men their trespasses, neither will your Father forgive your trespasses.' But it was not in men like Dean Koenig to forgive those he saw as his mortal enemies; that was the irony of their Christian message.

'And how great is the darkness that holds forth on these premises!' Dean Koenig's stentorian voice resounded from the sidewalk outside. 'How great is the evil that twists the divine gift of God into the will of man? My dear friends, ask Gerry Costas, the head of this laboratory of Satan. Ask Cassandra Austin, the chief architect of Satan's blasphemous work. Ask her to tell you how she manipulates the very fabric of God's great scheme for mankind, how she distorts that which is natural, God-sent, and therefore sacred. Ask her how she plans to take your children from your wombs and change them forever. For the better, she says. But we see through Satan's honeyed words. We see the basic flaw: how can God's work be improved upon? How can a human being even contemplate such an unthinkable transgression against our Father without the will of Satan to guide her? My dear friends, against all odds, against all adversaries no matter how powerful, we champion the will of God. Cassandra Austin and Gerry Costas cannot be allowed to make profane that which is sacred. We must not allow it. And I pledge to you, my dear friends, that we *will not* allow it!'

She closed her ears to the continuing torrent, gritted her teeth, and concentrated on trying to find the key that would slow the hyper-aging of the rogue trans-gene. It was some time before she realized that Lawrence was staring at her. She got up, and went into the chamber where he was watching TV. The sound was off, however.

'What have you been doing?' she asked him.

'Mom, have you seen Guh-God?'

By which she knew he had been listening to Koenig's lies.

'No,' she said, 'no one has. God is invisible.'

'But He exists.'

'If you believe He does, then I suppose He does.'

'He muh-made all things.'

She nodded. 'Some people believe that.'

'But not me,' he said. 'You muh-made me.'

Cassandra found she had no answer to that.

Lawrence shifted. 'Do you think Guh-God hates me?'

She was startled. 'Why would he hate you?'

'Buh-because I'm duh-different, buh-because I'm duh-dying.'

'Oh, Lawrence.' Cassandra put her arms around him, held him tight. His arms stayed limp at his sides. 'You're not going to die. I promise you.' She pulled away far enough so that she could look into his eyes. 'And as for God, He exists inside everyone. Even you. God cannot hate.' She lifted her chin. 'That man outside is a liar. He spends his life twisting words around to suit his purpose. It would be foolish to listen to him.'

'Okay.'

When Cassandra let him go, he went over to the TV and turned up the sound. An episode of *The Honeymooners* was on. Lawrence began to laugh as Ralph Kramden's eyes started to bug out at some offense Ed Norton had committed. Cassandra, watching him, wondered that he could laugh at simple slapstick humor but fail to respond to the comfort she had offered him.

Christopher, in Alphabet City, was nearing the East River. The gorilla had said the Pale Saint had taken the runaway east, but Christopher was fast running out of real estate. He was familiar with this area, having in the past come into conflict with certain neighborhood residents who lived easily on the nether side of the law. These were made men who thought nothing of spilling blood in the night against the cornerstones of tenements like the urine of drunkards or animals. In fact, if Christopher remembered correctly, the dogs and cats in this neighborhood were treated better than the victims of the petty mobsters. There was a weed-choked empty lot which the residents jealously guarded against the constant threat of the homeless camping out, fouling the place they had chosen as a pet cemetery. Over the years, it had taken on a weird kind of hallowed quality so that when, in the early eighties, the city had tried to bulldoze the lot, the ferocity of the resulting demonstrations had dissuaded City Hall from further reclamation efforts.

Christopher hung on the chain-link fence the citizens had erected around the lot, peering in at the smattering of fresh and dried flowers that here and there criss-crossed the tiny graves. It seemed odd and refreshing to see so much natural ground in the city.

Nearly half the cemetery was still rank with thigh-high weeds, unlovely yellowish flowers with viney stems, and grotesquely curling vegetation recognizable, Christopher suspected, only by a botanist specializing in mutations. Then there was the bit of white, at the far side of the lot, in among the thickest and most virulent of the foliage. It was blue-white, really, because of the veins.

Christopher got down on his hands and knees, clawed his way through a gap in the fence that had been recently closed off with cheap baling wire. He scrambled across the cemetery, his shoes sending clods of dirt rolling and skidding. He disturbed a couple of the flower arrangements. He could smell the earth, along with urine and the sickly-sweet scent of meat that has been left out of the refrigerator too long.

His pulse beat fast because that last smell was all too familiar to him. It brought back the image of blood spattering against tenement cornerstones and eyes filmed in death.

'Ah, shit.' He knelt in the underbrush and stared at the profile of the dead girl. This was his girl, the runaway who kept herself alive by selling rude sex in the doorway across the street from No-Name; the one who was ever so slowly learning to trust him. Like William Cotton, her eyes were missing. Like Bobby Austin, her corpse was bloodless. He'd be willing to bet Stick would find her pineal gland missing, and he knew with a certainty that reached into the marrow of his bones who had murdered her.

When he stood up clumps of dirt clung to his trousers. He brought over some of the flowers he'd scattered in his haste, and laid them by her side. Then he craned his neck, peering upward at the tenement windows that overlooked the pet cemetery. He called the Case Room, asked for a squad car on silent approach. He had begun canvassing the buildings bordering the lot when the blue-and-white pulled up and Jerry Lewis and another uniform piled out. Christopher brought them up to date, and gave them their assignments to cover the neighboring tenements.

There was no reply to knocks on the doors of the first three apartments Christopher visited. The man in the fourth had just returned from a week in Atlantic City and had no idea what he was talking about. Lewis came and got him. An old woman hanging out on the stoop of his building claimed she had seen the Pale Saint skulking around, but her breath stank of gin and he was unsure whether to believe her. On the other hand, she was this building's unofficial busybody. She appeared to know everyone's business – which tenants brought girls home with them (or boys), at what time, and for how long. She described accurately the Pale Saint and pointed out the doorway into which she had seen him disappear after he had done his grisly bit with the runaway. Christopher instructed Lewis to collect the other uniform, call the M.E.'s office, then, check out the doorway down the basement, to see if there were any other exits out of there. 'Make sure they're all covered,' he said to Lewis.

'Loo, at least let me come in with you.'

'I need you out here,' Christopher said. 'I want an airtight perimeter, so that even if I miss him down there you won't. Clear?' When Lewis nodded, Christopher put his hand on the other man's shoulder. 'Call for more backup. When you've briefed them, take a team and come in after me.'

'I wish you'd wait for us, Loo. I got a bad feeling –'

'Can't afford the time,' Christopher said. 'I'm going in.'

Cassandra was immersed in her equations when Sara raced out of the birth chamber and said, 'Mom, Lawrence is starting to freak out.'

'What happened?' Cassandra asked as she and Sara ran toward the chamber.

'I don't know. One minute I was teaching him about baseball, and the next – blooie! His eyes got glassy and he wouldn't respond.'

Inside the chamber, Lawrence was sitting rigidly, staring off into space.

'Mom, is he going to be okay?'

Cassandra heard the anxiety in her daughter's voice. Over the last week, Lawrence had begun to spend more and more time with Sara. It was a relief to see him picking up normal teenage behavior and idioms from her. Though Dillard disapproved, Cassandra knew she had done the right thing in exposing Lawrence to someone his own chronological age. It did her heart good to see them laugh together, do normal teenage things. Though Lawrence never spoke of it, she knew that the sense of dislocation caused by the hyper-aging must be harrowing for him.

Cassandra passed a hand in front of his face. He didn't blink. She crouched down so that her eyes were on a level with his.

'Dad!' Lawrence said in a very loud voice, startling her. 'Dad.'

Dillard looked up, alarmed, from the sanctuary of his taskstation.

'Lawrence,' Cassandra said softly, carefully, 'what's happening?'

'Nonono!' yelled Lawrence.

'What do you see?'

He brushed off Cassandra's comforting touch and began flinging things off the shelves.

Cassandra pushed Sara roughly through the chamber door. Her daughter's eyes were wide and staring; she'd never seen him in this state before.

'Mom, I want to help him.'

'You can do that by keeping out of harm's way.'

'He's going to hurt himself, I know it.'

'Just stay there,' Cassandra ordered. 'I'll take care of it.'

'Cassandra, stop him!' Dillard shouted. 'It's finally happened, he's gone berserk.'

Ignoring him, Cassandra kept her attention on the clone. 'Lawrence, what is it? Jon isn't here right now.'

Lawrence's head snapped around and looked at her as if she'd gone mad. 'I know that,' he said with a disturbing measure of impatience. He pounded the side of his head. 'But Dad is *here*.'

'What *is* he going on about?' Dillard asked. 'He's making no sense.'

Lawrence stared at Dillard, as he had so many times before, stopping him in his tracks. At first, Cassandra had assumed Lawrence did this simply to make Dillard uncomfortable, as children sometimes do with adults to test out the nature and scope of their power, but over the days she had come to believe it was something altogether different than willfulness.

Lawrence whirled, went back to throwing things off the shelves until he found what he was looking for. He opened the tops of two small glass jars and began to daub his face with lines of red and black paint. He drew horizontal lines across his forehead, then vertical ones down his cheeks. Closing his eyes, he traced a red line from just above each eyebrow, over the eyelids, to a spot just beneath the eye sockets.

Only then did he turn and stare at her. 'I *see* him.'

A cold chill ran down Cassandra's spine.

'Good Lord, look at him,' Dillard shouted, coming to the other side of the thick glass. 'He's become some kind of savage.'

'What is it, Lawrence?' Cassandra was aware that her voice had dropped to a whisper. 'Tell me.'

'I have to guh-go.'

'Go where?' Cassandra said, her voice tight and painful in her throat.

'He's not going anywhere,' Dillard said as he slammed and bolted the chamber door, 'this I promise you.'

'Dad nuh-needs me.' Lawrence stared eerily into Cassandra's face with the Pale Saint's eyes. 'He's in the duh-dark place, it's duh-dangerous, cuh-crawling with *things* and –'

'And what?'

'He's nuh-not alone.'

A profound terror gripped Cassandra's heart. 'Lawrence, what do you see. Who's with Jon?'

'Please,' he whispered. 'Luh-let me go.'

'Is Jon in danger?'

The clone's eyes opened wide. 'Daddydaddy*daddy* –!' The last word rising to a shriek, he threw himself again and again at the locked door.

She tried to stop him, to calm him, even to speak to him, but he was far beyond her reach, off in the depths of the terrifying and unknowable territory to which she consigned him. Seeing him now as the trapped animal he had become, she felt only a rising despair at what she had been arrogant enough to attempt. She could not bear to see his pain, naked and glistening like organs stripped of their covering skin and flesh.

In a sudden frenzy, she snatched up the phone, speed-dialing Christopher's office. When she heard Esquival's voice, she said, 'Where is he?'

'Lieutenant Christopher? I don't know. Hold on.'

Cassandra waited breathlessly.

'I only just came in and there's nobody here at the moment to ask,' he said in a voice she didn't quite believe.

'Listen, I –'

'Sorry, Doctor, I don't have a lot of time right now. Do you want to leave a message?'

'I think something's –' She choked off the rest of her words, knowing she was sounding foolish. *Don't panic,* she told herself sternly. 'No. No message.' She hung up and dialed Christopher's cell phone, but got no answer.

I'm an idiot, she thought, hanging up. *Stay calm. Don't be paranoid about what Esquival said. There's nothing wrong.* But as she watched Lawrence frantically trying to get out a curious dread returned, so primordial the pale hairs on her forearms stirred. She was experiencing first-hand what she had assumed was merely a melodramatic phrase: in the thrumming silence of her high-tech lab she felt as if someone had walked over her grave.

NINE

Silence was what greeted Christopher down in the tenement basement. He had followed the route the old woman said the Pale Saint had taken. He was within the last row of brownstone tenements before the city gave way to the massive public housing projects built in the 1950s right up against the East River Drive. He turned off his cell phone, thumbed off the safety of his gun.

The basement was overrun with a rank animal smell that drew rats the size of kittens. He moved with a minimum of noise, setting his feet down and lifting them precisely so that the grit underfoot would not reveal his presence.

In the grimy, stinking darkness of the basement, he felt like a sleep-walker in the city of the dead. He was not about to take needless risks, but he could not hang back and be defensive. Too much had happened; the blood was running too high. He could not deny it. He'd been itching for this confrontation ever since he saw Bobby dead in the precinct house.

The basement was a warren of small, cluttered cubicles, holding the accumulated junk of tenants and janitor alike. With the toe of his shoe he checked out corners, the bottom of piles of plastic bags filled to bursting with God only knew what crap. The bare bulbs screwed into old-fashioned porcelain sockets gave off dim light that tended to distort more than it revealed. He wished he could use his flashlight, but the moving beam of light would only betray his presence.

The smell of frying plantains came to him, and he followed it like a bloodhound. Up ahead, near the far end of the basement, he saw light spilling out of an open doorway to yet another cubicle. Approaching with extreme care because of the increased illumination, he peered in. The cubicle had been set up as a one-room apartment. Along the right-hand wall was a narrow cot covered with a khaki surplus Army blanket and one of those small airline pillows. On the back wall, an old table, repaired many times, held a hotplate, some paper cups, plastic utensils, a couple of Mason jars of clear liquid. Clothes – including a plain denim jacket – hung from a pair of nails hammered into the concrete.

The right side of the cubicle was hidden from Christopher's vantage point, but he could see photos torn from glossy magazines taped to the walls. His breath seemed to freeze in his lungs. In among the ads was a Polaroid photo of the young girl – Christopher's doorway kid – her lifeless eyes staring blindly out at Christopher as if to reprove him for allowing this mortal affront to happen to her.

His attention was diverted by sudden movement inside the make-shift apartment. Someone emerged from the left side and stood with his back to Christopher, bent over the hotplate, stirring something in a blackened saucepan. Plantains sizzled. The figure wore jeans, a faded checked flannel shirt, a baseball cap with the brim turned backwards, and muddy work boots. A real Marlboro type, as the man had said.

Right, Christopher thought and, swinging the gun up, hurtled into the room. He reached out with his left hand, pulled off the baseball cap revealing hair as white as milk. He spun the figure around by the shoulder and swung the butt end of the gun. One blow and it would be over, the Pale Saint's nose and cheek shattered, his blood spilled onto the gritty concrete. The images of Bobby Austin and the runaway girl crossed his mind like the wraiths of passion and vengeance in a morality play.

In the instant when the face registered, Christopher had just enough time to jerk the gun butt away so that it smashed into the concrete wall by the side of the man's head. The man spun, terrified, and slammed into the wall, crumpling to the floor.

Standing over the squatter, this stranger who bore no facial resemblance to the Pale Saint, his chest heaving, his ears buzzing with excess adrenaline, Christopher thought: *Fuck me*. He went to the wall and ripped off the Polaroid. Squatting down beside the terrified man, he shoved it in his face.

The man shook his head and tears rolled down his cheeks. Christopher took some time to gather him onto his cot and to take a look at the side of his head. Some skin had been flailed off, but the worst of it was a deep bruise that was already starting to swell. Inside an hour it would be every color of the rainbow.

Christopher went over to the Mason jars and opened them. One contained cheap gin that made Christopher's eyes water. He took this and poured a good part of it over the man's wound while he winced and moaned.

The squatter, who said his name was 'Guy, just Guy' had no idea how that photo got on the wall, he'd never seen it or its subject before. He claimed he had been given these clothes by the same man who had dyed his hair – his scalp still itched from the Peroxide – a man with a deep tan and hair the same color white. It was play-acting for a prank, a practical joke, the man had told him, and Guy had believed him. Why wouldn't he? Besides, he needed the clothes as well as the twenty-dollar bill the man had shoved in his pocket. When Christopher showed him the mug shot of the Pale Saint, Guy said, 'He had a long, thick mustache like a rope and this little spade beard on his chin, but that's the guy.' Christopher told him who this man was, and Guy wept all over again in his terror. He put his hands to his head and rocked back and forth, making pathetic animal sounds, until Christopher asked him what was the matter.

'My head,' he whined, 'it's spinning an' I can't think, the pain's too much, whut did you do t'me?'

The way his weaselly gaze slipped up to watch Christopher, then darted away again led Christopher to believe that he was going to milk this incident for all it was worth. On the other hand, Christopher did not want to take a chance that Guy had a concussion, so he drew him up gingerly by the elbow. 'We'll get you X-rayed and looked at so the pain will go away,' he said.

Docilely, Guy took the denim jacket off the hook and Christopher shut off the hotplate and turned off the lights. The basement thrummed with electric life: boilers delivering heat, pumps delivering water, heaters delivering hot water. Up ahead, in a corner, hulked the incinerator, abandoned for years since the city had enacted its clean air laws. Still, the atmosphere down here was filled with dust and cement and disintegrating insulation particles.

'I didn't do nuthin' wrong,' Guy reiterated mournfully. 'Just doin' a dude a favor, just tryin' t'survive another day.'

'Nobody said you did anything wrong.'

'Acted like it, f'sure.' Guy was still holding his head.

'Pain any better?' Christopher inquired.

'Naw.' Guy began to laugh, then abruptly stopped because, he said, laughing made the pain even worse. 'My daddy was a farmer upstate 'round Rhinebeck. 'Spose city-boy like you don't know shit 'bout Rhinebeck.'

'I sure do,' Christopher said. 'I used to summer near there.'

'No kidding?' Guy moved slowly and gingerly through the ill-lighted basement, as if his legs had been damaged. 'Well, my daddy bein' a farmer an' all, he knew a little sumthing 'bout pain. I'll manage.'

'I can believe it,' Christopher said.

They were almost at the staircase that led up to street level when Guy said, 'Ah, hell, left my medication back at m'flop, city's givin' me asthma, need my inhaler.'

'I'll get it,' Christopher said. 'You stay right here and rest a bit.'

The metal inhaler was just where Guy had said it was, inside a paper cup on the old table. Christopher took one last look through the gloom at the wall papered with Guess and Calvin Klein ads of half-nude models, paper-thin, provocatively posed. In most, you couldn't tell what the ad was selling; all you saw was the model and what she represented. Christopher wondered at a culture in which manufacturers needed to eroticize children in order to sell their brand name.

He took the inhaler and went back to where he'd left Guy. A preternaturally large rat hunkered by the side of the incinerator, licking its whiskers. Its red eyes tracked him warily. The rat had the proprietary air of a commuter waiting for a seat on his morning train.

Guy was not where Christopher had left him. Christopher flicked on his small flashlight and turned slowly in a full circle. He called Guy's name. There was no answer.

Now he was concerned that Guy was indeed injured more seriously than he had thought. No doubt he had wandered away. Perhaps he had passed out, was bleeding internally. Christopher went to the base of the stairs, but there was no sign of the squatter. Then he retraced his steps.

He paused beside the bulk of the incinerator. Dragging the light beam over its face, he noticed that the fire door was slightly ajar. He was certain it had been closed when he and Guy had passed by moments before. He pulled the door open and played the flashlight's beam over the crusted interior. It wasn't empty.

Guy lay in the bed of old ash, his skin and clothes streaked with the primordial gray of a crocodile. His head was nearest the door and Christopher could see that some kind of sharp instrument or weapon had penetrated his left eye. There was no blood, but Guy was quite dead. His remaining eye, rolled up in the final trauma, seemed to stare through its film at Christopher with sullen recrimination.

With a resounding clang, he swung the incinerator's fire door all the way open and against regs pulled Guy out of there. It seemed intolerable to him that a man like that, a farmer's son born and bred beneath the open sky, with the hot beat of sunlight and the cool kiss of rain on his skin, should end up in a filthy, airless crypt in a disused city basement.

He was crouched beside Guy's corpse when he heard the soft scrape, as a shoe heel grating against the rough poured cement floor. Without moving, Christopher calculated where the sound had come from. Shadows behind and in front of him hung suspended as if waiting for a gust of breeze that would never come.

Slowly, carefully, Christopher backed up until he was completely hidden in the darkness. Then he uncoiled himself like an adder. His gun felt cool and comforting in his hand. In three swift, silent strides he rounded the far corner of the incinerator. He saw the partial outline of a figure before it disappeared into the recesses of the basement.

He retraced his steps, working his way around the other side of the incinerator, coming up from behind on the shadowy corner the figure was using to camouflage himself. He could hear the slight exhalation of breath, could feel another human's warmth. He stuck the muzzle of his gun into flesh, wrapped his left arm around the throat of the person in front of him.

He felt an elbow in his ribs; a heel struck his shin, and he tightened his grip.

'Shit!' he said under his breath.

'Loo?' Lewis said. 'Is that you?'

'Godammit, I almost broke your neck.' He let go, and the two cops faced each other.

'He was here,' Christopher said. 'He murdered a vagrant who was using this basement as a flop.'

'Well, he didn't get out,' Lewis said. 'That I know.'

'You're wrong.' Christopher shook his head. 'He's gone.'

'But how?'

They were joined by the rest of Lewis' team. Within minutes they discovered the old, rusted coal chute. Its access to a back alley was hidden by the bulk of a green metal Dumpster that had been pulled up against the rusted doors.

'That's how he got out,' Christopher said.

Lewis, kicking the Dumpster's side to no effect except a sharp pain that lanced up his leg, said, 'Shit! I blew it, Loo.'

'This perp outsmarted us today,' Christopher said, swallowing his disappointment. 'Let's make damn sure it doesn't happen again.'

In *Seven Pillars of Wisdom* T.E. Lawrence writes of his means to victory over the enemy: 'If we were patient and superhuman-skilled, we could . . . reach victory without battle, by pressing our advantages mathematical and psychological.' Of course, he used all the assets of the desert-bred Bedouins whom he commanded: their 'mobility, toughness, self-assurance, knowledge of the country, and intelligent courage' to psychologically soften up the enemy, to break his will, to, figuratively speaking, strip him naked before the final, decisive strike.

Having returned from his basement foray, the Pale Saint has cause to think about victory in the same terms T.E. Lawrence once did. He stands in the center of his one-room apartment and prepares for ingestion of the pineal he had so recently extracted from the squatter.

He is always alone. Always and forever. Even though Faith is with him, even though Mama is with him, even though the God of vengeance and blood is with him, still he is alone in the great lethal desert. Will it never end, he asks himself, this terrible aloneness?

Having ground his powders with mortar and pestle, having combined them with the proper liquids, he holds the viscous mixture in his throat while he pops the pineal between his lips. He chews, slowly and meditatively. His eyes are closed, and a vein in his temple pulses to a rising rhythm. Then he swallows, and his consciousness flows backward like a stream running uphill to its source.

Winters are particularly bitter for Faith, frostbite turning the ends of her long fingers and toes blue. Gloves are insufficient protection; neither are the high-topped boots Mama buys her. She has a delicate constitution, made the worse by her long sojourn in the hot Louisiana swamps where Mama sent her when she was two.

She returns immediately after Pappy's death, in a winter storm, and three years later in a winter storm she almost dies.

The crow, a skittish, distrustful creature, shows the Pale Saint where she lies, less than a mile from the house, but lost, blinded by snow, drained by the relentless cold. After wandering in a circle, she had collapsed into the side of a snowbank, lucky for her out of the prevailing wind, and he, made anxious by her absence, saddled up the roan and came after her with the woven Shawnee blanket Mama had given her across the pommel of his saddle. It being Christmastime, Mama is of course absent save for the blue light she emits like a satellite reflecting the sun, which is just as well for him. Had she been present, she would have pistol-whipped him for letting Faith out of his sight. The prospect would not have put fear into him; he knows well the coppery taste of blood in his mouth. He would have passed out rather than whimper, as Mama would have wanted.

He kneels beside Faith and turns her over. Her lips are blue, and an icy rime coats her face, but he can still faintly smell her scent, a mixture of glycerine soap and roses. Wrapping her in the Shawnee blanket, he lifts her onto his saddle and, taking the reins, trudges back through the snow and the wind to the dark and cavernous house from which he wishes only to escape.

Later, stretched by the fire, she calls his name. The effect on him is profound. He feels as if he has put his hand through a pane of glass, as if a vein has opened up and at last the pain, like blood, is flowing out of him.

Together, bound by silence and an intimacy he cannot understand, they share their usual bar of Hershey's chocolate, one half each, and for a moment there is no Pappy, no Mama, no God full of vengeance, fire and brimstone, no world at all save this tiny oasis in the vast and implacable desert.

It wasn't long before D'Alassandro showed up with her forensics team. The M.E.'s people arrived moments later and the basement took on the aspect of the aftermath of a war zone. After answering D'Alassandro's barrage of questions, Christopher reactivated his cell phone to call Esquival.

'Reuven, give me an update on the VCAP search,' Christopher said wearily.

'*Nada, niente*, nothing.'

'Shit, we've got two more bodies.'

'How charming; the press is already having a feeding frenzy. This will make them go ballistic. There are three daily cable TV shows devoted entirely to speculating on the case. Plus, D'Alassandro can tell you how many websites the Pale Saint now has. It's got to be more than a hundred. Seems like every looney's got a theory about him.'

'Great. Yesterday I fielded a call from *Vanity Fair*. Dominick Dunne's starting an ongoing story on the case. Plus, the department's fielding calls for me from the Hollywood studios.'

'I think you need an agent,' Esquival said.

'Right.' Christopher could imagine the smirk on his face. 'I can just see another press conference with Brockaw. After this, even I admit we need some serious spin control to keep the public from full-fledged panic.'

'By the way, I got an odd call from Dr Austin.'

'What d'you mean, odd?'

'It's just that – Hold on, lemme check the time of the call. Let's see. It came in during the time you were down in the basement. Here's the thing, though, Loo, she was kinda upset, almost like she knew there was trouble.'

'You didn't tell her anything.'

'You kidding? Not a chance. But still . . . I got the feeling she didn't believe me.'

Christopher wondered what was going on. 'Okay, I'll take care of it,' he said.

He filled Esquival in as quickly as he could about the encounter in the tenement basement. 'The Pale Saint's altered his appearance with a mustache and goatee. Considering the amount of time since we had him in custody it's probably false. Change the photos of him we're distributing, but don't stop there because he's sure to alter his appearance again. It's likely he's dyed his white hair; I would if I were him. Have the artist do ones with a full beard, long hair, dark hair, glasses, you know the drill.'

He disconnected. 'I'll be back at the lab if you need me,' he told D'Alassandro as he pocketed his phone.

'Hold on a sec.' She directed the forensic photographer, who had just shown up, to get the photos she wanted. She took him aside. 'Listen, Boss, are you okay? From what I can see, it was no picnic down here. Why don't you take an hour or so, let the sunlight kick out the jams.'

'I'm fine,' Christopher said automatically. 'Besides, I'm just going to pick up Cassandra. Sara's pitching in the citywide baseball championships today.'

'I know you must be thinking of Bobby.'

'He would've given an arm to see this game.'

'Yeah, I know.' D'Alassandro maneuvered so that she was between him and the forensics team poring over Guy's corpse. 'Listen, Boss, you know what I think?'

'Whatever I say, you're going to tell me anyway.'

'Right. I think this perp is messing with our heads. He set this thing up. He got you down here and he killed someone literally right behind your back. What the hell kind of sick, perverted game is that?'

'It's no game,' Christopher said. 'Not to him. I told you before: it's war.'

'Now I see you're right,' she said, glancing back over her shoulder. 'Only trouble is for us it's a war without rules, boundaries or even parameters.'

'Is it?' Christopher passed a hand across his eyes. 'I keep thinking the answer is right in front of me. If only I could see it.'

D'Alassandro put a hand briefly on his arm. 'Take that break, Boss. Watching the game will do you good. You look like –'

'If you tell me,' Christopher warned, 'you're fired.'

All the way over to the Vertex lab, Christopher thought about what D'Alassandro had said. He knew he was running almost totally on nervous energy now, knew from hard experience just how treacherous that could be, but he also knew that he could not stop now, could not even afford to rest. He was getting closer to the Pale Saint; he could feel it every time he came within the orbit of the clone. Their psychic bond was strengthening. It was just a matter of time – and how little time they all had! – before the clone pulled an image, clear as crystal, out of the Pale Saint's head that would lead them to the murderer.

Threaded through his thoughts, images of the runaway and Guy kept appearing, like images of death sewn into a homely quilt. Despite all his training, he felt diminished by their deaths, as if pieces of his own flesh had been plucked from him by carrion birds, and this both astonished and appalled him. For the first time since he'd been a rookie, he felt vulnerable. But when he got to the lab, he had other things to occupy his mind. Cassandra was wide-eyed and frantic.

'Jon, thank God you're all right.' She threw herself into his arms and her words came out in a rush. 'Lawrence had another vision. He said you were in that dark, dangerous place he'd seen. He painted his face and threw himself at the birth chamber door to try to go to you but Dillard had locked it so he couldn't get out. I tried to call you but there was no answer.'

Christopher pulled her away so he could look in her face. 'The clone *knew* where I was?'

'He said he saw you –'

Christopher felt a creepy sensation slide through him. 'Cass, I was in a tenement basement.'

'He said you weren't alone down there and he was right, wasn't he?'

Christopher nodded silently.

'What is it?' She searched his eyes, frightened now by what she saw there. 'Jon, please tell me. I know you too well. It won't do any good to keep it in.'

So he told her how the Pale Saint had set him up, how he had deliberately taken the runaway because he knew Christopher was helping her, had murdered her, performing his ghastly rituals, then carrying her into the pet cemetery in plain sight of the alcoholic busybody with the certain knowledge that Christopher would eventually interview her and discover the basement where he lay in wait to murder Guy.

'Dear God, no, two more people dead.' Cassandra raked her hand through her hair. 'But why would he do that? Why would he take the chance that you'd catch him?'

'That's a fair question,' Christopher said. 'The Pale Saint altered his signature slightly when he murdered William Cotton, the man in Tompkins Square Park. We thought that the "X" factor – the thing that had made the Pale Saint alter his signature – was Cotton; but every lead we got turned into a dead end. But now I'm beginning to see that everything leads back to me.'

Cassandra looked startled. 'You?'

He nodded. 'It's like a weird kind of battle plan that goes like this: he offs Cotton and gets nabbed. We think we got lucky, but no – turns out he wants to get captured. Why? So he can escape right from under our noses. Also, so he can come face to face with me. He gets out, in the process killing three of my men plus Bobby because I always call Bobby in for my high-profile cases.

'But none of that's enough for him, oh no. He stalks me, watches me go into the No-Name, sees me working with the runaway. Then he goes after her because he knows she's connected to me, that if she disappears I'll come after her. So he makes sure he's seen with her, makes sure the busybody at the tenement sees him, makes sure I'll be led right to the basement where he's hiding. Now he's established total control: he's escaped my custody, and killed someone in my presence.'

'But what kind of battle plan is that?' Cassandra asked.

Christopher turned and with a swipe of his powerful arm, sent beakers and test tubes flying in all directions. 'Damned if I know.'

'Jon.' Cassandra reached out to him, making contact, feeling how cold he was and wanting only to warm him, to take the pain away as he had done for her. 'Don't, no. Please don't.'

Christopher's face was filled with turbulent emotions. 'Jesus Christ, Cass, Bobby's murder was bad enough, but knowing that the Pale Saint stalked and deliberately chose a poor lost girl purely for her association with me is tough to take.' He slammed his fist down on the zinc-topped counter. 'God, I've got to get him before he kills again! The clone is my only chance, Cass.' Christopher looked around. 'I've got to talk to him. Now.'

'That's the terrible thing, Jon,' she said, leading him over to the birth chamber. 'I had gone out – no more than ten minutes, I swear – to get him some more chocolate bars and when I came back –' Her arm described an arc that took in the entirety of the chamber. 'Lawrence is gone. He's vanished into thin air.'

TEN

'Wuh-what's this?'

Sara shrugged off her teddy bear backpack as she moved over to where Lawrence was standing at the kitchen counter. 'That's a book by a man named T.E. Lawrence. You were given his name.'

'*Seven Pillars of Wuh-wisdom*,' Lawrence said. 'What does that mean?'

He had turned on the TV as soon as they had come into the loft, had stood watching an infomercial for the Abdominizer as if it were a fascinating human drama. He had completely ignored Sara, who circled him, watching the reflection from the electronic light turning his eyes a strange and translucent blue.

In order to engage him, perhaps even draw him out, she had shown him Cassandra's computer program, which converted phone messages to text and filed them in a single message center along with e-mail. A chime would sound each time a new message was received.

Lawrence had been interested, but not for long. The moment he had absorbed the concept and had played with several examples, he moved on, to T.E. Lawrence's book, sitting on the kitchen counter. 'My father says wisdom is a guh-good thing.' He closed his eyes for a moment. 'My father is safe,' he whispered as if to himself. 'Safe now.' He looked at Sara. 'Will you tell me about the pillars?'

She knew he was serious; in the lab he had exhibited an insatiable desire for knowledge. Plus, she'd never known him to ask an idle question. 'I don't know for sure because Lawrence was the kind of guy who never really explained anything he did or felt. He wrote in riddles, so I've kind of had to figure out a lot of it for myself.' She stood shoulder to shoulder with him as she found the place near the end of the book. '"To endure for another in simplicity gave a sense of

163

greatness," ' she read aloud. ' "There was nothing loftier than a cross, from which to contemplate the world." '

'Like Christ. He died on the cross, didn't he?'

She looked up.

'I read about it in the encyclopedia.' He frowned. 'It's good to have someone like that, who will look after you and protect you, right?'

'Right. Christ believed in redemption, and so did Lawrence,' Sara said, wondering how to talk theology with him.

She hesitated a moment. 'D'you know what redemption is?'

'I've seen it in the duh-dictionary. It's when you get buh-back something you've lost.'

'Right, but not like if I lost my baseball glove –' she picked it off the kitchen counter, '– which right now would be a great big fucking tragedy.' She thought a moment. 'Let's say you did something bad.'

'How buh-bad?'

'Really bad.'

'Like killing someone. Buh-but I wuh-wouldn't. Ever.'

She smiled. 'I know that. This is just pretend. If you killed someone it would be really bad, and you'd feel terrible, wouldn't you?'

'Yes.'

'Of course you would. You'd want to do something very good to atone – to make up for what you did that was really bad.'

'Like wuh-what?'

'Well, you tell me.'

Lawrence thought a minute. 'I'd duh-dedicate myself to catching people who killed.'

'Hey, that's very good.' Sara clapped him on the back. She realized that the more he spoke the less he stuttered. Maybe he was getting used to her. 'Now you would be redeemed. You would be clean inside and everyone would think of you as a good person instead of an evil one.'

'Like Dad?'

Sara shook her head. 'I don't know what you mean.'

'Sure you duh-do. Dad thinks he killed Andy.'

Sara drew a quick breath. 'How d'you know about Andy?'

'I overheard Mom and Dad talking about him,' Lawrence said in his forthright manner. 'He kuh-killed himself and Dad thinks it's his fault. I don't understand.'

'It's called guilt,' Sara said. 'It's like your conscience saying you've done something bad even though maybe it's not true. In Uncle Jon's case, he's sure he didn't do enough for Andy, that if he had Andy wouldn't have killed himself.'

'Is that true?'

'I don't think so and neither does Mom.'

Lawrence thought about this for some time. 'Either way it doesn't matter, does it?' he said. 'Dad nuh-needs to be redeemed. That's why he does what he does.'

Sara frowned in concentration. 'You know, I never thought about it that way, but maybe you're right.'

'Is that wuh-what happened to T.E. Lawrence?' he asked. 'He nuh-needed to be redeemed though he didn't do any bad thing – just like Dad.'

'Yeah, I think so. Lawrence helped the Arabs in their war to kick the Turks out of Arabia. He did this even though he wasn't an Arab.'

'Why?'

'Good question. Islam – the religion of the Arabs – is based on five principles, which they call pillars.'

'Wuh-what are they?'

'Okay, let me see if I can remember them.' She scrunched up her face. '*Shahada*, the witnessing of their faith which is sort of summed up by the phrase "There is no God but God and Mohammed is his prophet'; *salat*, which is prayer; *sanm*, which is the ritual fasting during the holy time of Ramadan; *zakat*, which is giving money to the poor; and *hajj*, which is making the pilgrimage to Mecca, the holy city.

'But Lawrence's pillars aren't about religion. See, Lawrence basically couldn't stand civilization – you know, cities and factories and crowds of business people.'

'Suits,' Lawrence said, remembering the slang word she'd taught him.

Sara smiled. 'Right. Suits and all that. I don't like them, either. Anyway, he saw himself as soft and white and squidgy –'

'Like Dr Dork.'

She had to laugh. 'Absolutely. See, being soft and white and squidgy – just like Dr Dork – was shameful to Lawrence. He needed to cleanse this shame, this sin from deep inside himself. The only way he could think of doing it was to sacrifice himself, to put himself on the line for people he didn't know.'

She pulled open the refrigerator door and took out fixings for sandwiches: packaged bread, Swiss cheese slices in deli paper, mustard, sweet pickles. She began to make the sandwiches as she continued.

'The Arabs were everything he wasn't: they were hard and brown and studly. They were deprived of like *everything* Lawrence was brought up with and took for granted. And they not only survived, they flourished in the midst of awesome hardships and deprivation. How he admired them! If he could only be like them, he thought. If he could only go back to the simple, primitive needs: food, clothing, shelter, redemption. Those were the first four of Lawrence's pillars of wisdom. Then, in the desert, during the war, he discovered the others: enlightenment of the mind, self-denial of the body, cleansing of the spirit.' She handed him a cheese sandwich. 'Seven pillars.'

'Wuh-when I think of pillars, I think of a house.'

'Well, that's natural, I guess. Mansions have lots of pillars.'

'Nuh-not a mansion.' Lawrence said with such utter conviction that Sara was brought up short. It was a peculiar thing, but his eyes seemed to have gone opaque, as if someone had thrown flour into them.

'What do you mean?'

'I see a house with pillars,' he said. 'All the way around it. Seven pillars.'

'Pillars like on a porch or something.'

'A porch, yes,' Lawrence said, taking an enormous bite of his sandwich. He always ate quickly, almost voraciously, like a predator in the forest crouching over its kill. 'The porch, like everything else, guh-goes up in flames. A fire that reaches all the wuh-way up to heaven.'

Then, just as abruptly as it had begun, it was over. His eyes returned to normal and he said: 'Tell me more about Lawrence. He wasn't luh-like the Arabs he loved so much.'

Sara, about to ask him what had happened, thought better of it. Instinctively, she knew he would have no idea how to answer her. 'Not at all. In fact, he wasn't like his own people, either. You could say he was an alien.'

'Like me.'

Sara chewed a bit, weighing his words. It occurred to her that she had absolutely no idea what was going on in his head. She doubted anyone did, even her mother or Uncle Jon. 'Like you,' she said as she poured them some cold milk. 'And like me.'

Someone else might have said: *You? What do you mean?* But Lawrence only drank his milk down in one swallow. The way he watched her scared her a little, because it was like the way an odds-maker sizes up a long-shot horse just before the race, like maybe there was a surprise waiting here for him.

It was odd, she thought, how it was *she* who was compelled to speak. 'It's been so hard since my father died, you know.'

Lawrence frowned. 'The evil man – the Skeleton in my duh-dreams – killed him. My father didn't tell me why, though.'

'Did he tell you that you look exactly like the Skeleton in your dreams?'

'He said I *am* him. But am I, Sara? I've been thinking. Could I kill your father? I could never find redemption then, the path to heaven.'

She had no wish to answer him. She understood that as much as she was drawn to this strange and unsettling creature, she must also secretly hate him because of where he came from and, therefore, who he was. It didn't seem to matter that it wasn't his fault, that he hadn't, in fact, done anything evil himself. The evil crouched inside him like a seed pod waiting to burst open. At least this is what Uncle Jon believed. She wondered whether she did, too.

Shaking herself free of these thoughts, she wiped her hands on a paper towel and ran her finger further down the page of the book. 'We haven't finished with T.E. Lawrence,' she said. 'You see, he writes here about a sense of greatness: "Honest redemption must have been free and child-minded." He had nothing to gain from what he did for the Arabs. It didn't make him rich or their head sheik or anything like that. He just did it free and clear.'

'He helped people. Like your father. Like mine.'

'Do you understand that Jon isn't really your father?' It was a cruel thing to say, and now, watching for an expression on his face, Sara suspected she had known that all along.

'You mean he wuh-won't take care of me? He won't protect me? That's wuh-what fathers do for their children, isn't it?'

'Yeah, it is. But I was speaking about where you came from. It wasn't from Uncle Jon and it wasn't from my mother.'

'They adopted me.'

'Can we just not have this discussion.' She put her hands up. 'It's starting to freak me out.'

'I'm sorry. You did such a good thing and now I've made you feel bad.'

'What d'you mean?'

'You got me out of the lab.'

'I promised you could come to the championship game, didn't I? And I wasn't going to go back on my word, especially when you told me Dr Dork had, like, permanently grounded you.'

167

'It's a good thing, what you did.'

'Uh huh. And then you said –'

'About the prison, yes.' His gaze slid away as if he was almost ashamed.

But perhaps, Sara thought, he was merely shy. She had to keep reminding herself that he had the most limited experience interacting with people.

'My mom's lab felt like a prison, that's what you said.'

He nodded. 'When I sleep, I duh-dream of being in the mountains. The air is fresh and cuh-clean and there's so muh-much space the trees march over the mountains, down to a valley and up again to the horizon. I cuh-can go anywhere I choose. And then I wake up to the cold, lifeless, sterile room with all the machines watching me, recording everything I do or say.'

Maybe it was at that moment that Sara realized he was no longer a child, or even an adolescent. It was hard to know what he was, anyway. One minute he was totally clueless, and the next he was offering some kind of amazing insight.

'When I'm on the baseball field,' Sara said, 'I feel like that. No constraints, no boundaries at all. It's just what's singing.'

'Singing?' When he cocked his head like this, Sara thought, he looked about eight years old.

'There's a singing inside myself,' she said. 'It comes from feeling free, doing what *you* want to do, not what grownups say you should do.'

'I luh-like to do what my father tells me to do.'

'I feel the same way about Uncle Jon. There's something special about him. I bet now that he and my mom are together, they won't fight the way my parents did.'

'Did they hurt each other?'

'Not the way you mean. They used words to hurt each other. See, they weren't meant for each other. I guess they loved each other, in a way, but it wasn't enough. They would say hurtful things, lies and accusations.'

Lawrence seemed to digest this for a long time. At last he said: 'It's bad to lie. My father told me so.'

'It's true,' Sara said. 'I mean, lately I've been thinking that it's best to tell the truth even though it might hurt the other person.' She sighed. 'See, about me and Mom. I've been awfully pissy to her, and now I think I know why. My dad is gone; all of a sudden I'm afraid she will be, too.'

'Wuh-where would she go?'

That made Sara smile. 'I mean go, as in die. Like my father died.' She snapped her fingers. 'Gone, just like that, in the blink of an eye.'

'That's buh-bad. I mean, he had to take care of you and protect you.'

All of a sudden, the floodgates opened and Sara began to cry.

Lawrence stood still, staring at her. 'Duh-don't cry, Sara.'

'See, the thing of it is, when your parents die, you're totally on your own,' she said. 'My dad's dying made me realize I'm not ready for that.'

'I'll be here,' he said. 'I'll take cuh-care of you and protect you.'

He said this with such feeling that she was momentarily taken aback. She was about to tell him how nice that was, but she stopped because it had just happened again. Maybe it was the light, or the angle of view, but half the time when she looked at Lawrence she saw the Pale Saint as he looked on TV and in the magazines. That awful mug shot had reduced him to a two-dimensional thing, an object of terror and loathing; a touchstone for her own fear and rage. And, then, Lawrence would move or the light would change and he would be Lawrence again, the odd, quirky character so out of tune with the world around him. Lawrence, who seemed so innocent, and yet was not. It seemed to her as if with every passing moment he was morphing like an image in a computer graphics program, maturing weeks, months in the space of minutes. And it was true. There was an intense excitement in this – for him and for her. But also a strange kind of melancholy. It was all about life rushing at you at the speed of light.

But that was what was happening to the physical shell. What went on inside him was what captivated her. Perhaps, in the end, it was the unnameable shame inside of him that drew her as it did with his namesake, T.E. Lawrence.

Lawrence fiddled with the book. Perhaps he felt how uncomfortable she had become. 'When she comes back, Mom is going to be very mad.'

'So will that asshole Dr Dork. But I tell you what. We'll both survive Mom being mad.' Sara threw him a Jonagold apple, biting into one herself as she tucked her glove under her arm and picked up her backpack. 'Okay, let's move it out. I promised you an up-close-and-personal look at the game, and that's just what you're gonna get.'

'Hot dog,' Lawrence said, just like Opie on *The Andy Griffith Show*, and Sara laughed. She tossed Lawrence her backpack as she snapped the leash onto Hound, and, together, they went out of the loft.

'Have you checked the video log of the chamber?' Christopher asked.

Cassandra nodded. 'That's the first thing I did after I checked out the entire lab.' At the flatscreen, she dialed up the log so he could see for himself. 'Someone unlocked the door for him and let him out. But when I came back to the lab, the bolt had been thrown.'

'So whoever let him out took the trouble to re-lock it.'

'They also knew enough not to speak. I could see Lawrence's expression, I heard him say, 'I thought you were Dr Dork coming for me.' I thought I heard a laugh, but no one else spoke. He moved out of the cameras' range when he left the chamber. There's nothing more on the video log.'

'That's enough,' Christopher said, as he took her hand and headed for the door. In his car, he said, 'Call the loft.'

'Why, do you think Sara has anything to do with this?'

'It seems the likeliest possibility,' Christopher said. 'Who has access to the lab? You, Dillard, me, Sara.'

Cassandra took out her cell phone and dialed. 'I got the machine,' she said.

'She must already be at the ballfield in Central Park,' Christopher said as he slapped the portable revolving light to the car's top and turned it on.

'Wait a minute, today's the championship game,' Cassandra said. 'No wonder she took Lawrence. She promised he could watch her pitch in the championships, then Dillard and I locked him away. Now Sara's alone with him on the outside. My God, Jon, what have I done?'

'Much as I hate to think of them together, let's hope it's Sara who's kidnapped him.'

'What do you mean?'

'The other possibility is far more dire,' Christopher said. 'Lawrence has demonstrated that the Pale Saint exists in his visions. What if the psychic connection works both ways? What if the Pale Saint knows as much about Lawrence as Lawrence knows about him?'

'Oh, God, no.' Cassandra put her head back against the seat. 'What if the Pale Saint has him?'

The ballfield was on the west side of the Ramble, between the Seventy-ninth Street Transverse and the Lake. On his right, Christopher could see the traffic – mostly taxis – on West Park Drive. The deep-green bleacher-type stands were full to bursting with exuberant families and friends of the two team members. The party atmosphere spilled over onto the walkways and grass lawns, where passersby from as far away as Bethesda Fountain stopped and rubbernecked as the crowd got more and more into a rooting frenzy.

To their immense relief, they spotted the clone right away. He was sitting at the end of the bench occupied by Sara's team. Holding Hound's leash, the Weimaraner's head on his knee, he looked like an All-American athlete. Shrewdly, Sara had given him a team cap to wear, and he'd pulled the bill down low, keeping the top half of his face in shadow. No one would recognize him. Cassandra made a move in his direction, but Christopher stopped her.

'They're both fine,' he told her. 'Leave him alone.'

'But, Jon, we can't just let him –'

'If you go get him now he's liable to make a fuss and bring attention to himself. Right now nobody knows he exists. Let's keep it that way.'

Reluctantly, Cassandra sat down in the bleachers beside him.

She looked nervously at the clone, as if at any moment he might burst into flames or explode. 'This is your doing, Jon.'

'Mine?'

'Yes. Look at him. You took him into the outside world. And when he left my closed little scientific orbit for the first time I see now that was the end. In the lab, he's become like an animal caged in the zoo, pacing impatiently back and forth, longing for his freedom.'

Christopher nodded. 'The bullet you created has slid home into its chamber. All it needs now is for the trigger to be pulled.'

'Too soon,' she whispered. 'Too soon. When he finally meets the Pale Saint he'll surely die.'

'He's going to die anyway,' Christopher said. 'It's just a matter of time.' He put his arm around her. 'Think of Sara now,' he urged. 'Enjoy the game and let him do the same. This is your only child's biggest day. Don't spoil it for her or for yourself.'

Sara had taken the mound and was beginning her warmup tosses. Christopher, who hadn't seen her pitch in a while, was suitably impressed. Bobby had taught her well. She rolled the hardball behind her back as she leaned in to take the catcher's sign. Kids of her age often gave away the kind of pitch they were going to throw by the way they held the ball – fingers across the ball's seams or along them – but she was already a master at keeping her intent hidden. But then, he thought, she had plenty of experience. How secretive the Austin women were, like the ancient Jesuits in the service of the Pope for whom they performed certain tasks as risky as they were undocumented. As the game began, Christopher noticed that Sara had spotted them. She smiled uncertainly and gave Christopher a pleading look, while pressing her palms together prayer-like.

He gave her a nod, and she seemed to relax.

Christopher quickly discovered that as well as the split-fingered forkball she was so well-known for Sara had a nasty slider that looked irresistible coming in, but fell down and away from the batter as it neared the plate. If Bobby had taught her to throw the spitter Christopher couldn't detect it. He felt inordinately proud of her. All the boy pitchers had in their arsenal was heat: they threw fastball after fastball with the kind of powerful whiplike motion only male body mass could generate. Sara had wisely chosen to go another route, mastering the finesse pitches that were the most difficult to throw.

She should have won the game; she certainly worked hard enough at it. But she got no support from her team, and without runs even the best pitchers eventually go down to defeat. In the eighth inning, she made a mistake – or perhaps she had simply tired. In any event, she hung a slider over the outside of the plate and the batter, a lug with shoulders like a football tackle, smacked the ball over the head of the center fielder, and that was that.

Christopher was gratified to see that Sara didn't hang her head while the lug pumped his fist as he rounded the bases. Christopher waited patiently, his capable hands at his side, while Sara was consoled by her teammates. Her coach clapped her on the back and beamed. Amid the whirl and confusion of the crowd, she came trotting up to them a short while after. She had hold of the clone's hand. Between them was Hound, his tail switching restlessly back and forth.

'Sorry, Mom,' Sara said. 'But when Lawrence told me he'd been seriously grounded by Dr Dork I –'

'That's no excuse for what you did, young lady. No excuse at all,' Cassandra said. 'Dammit, Sara, you can't just go off and do as you please without thinking of the consequences.'

'Don't be mad, Mom,' Lawrence said without a trace of his usual stutter. 'Sara did what she had to do. She was thinking of me. She'd promised to take me to see the game. She couldn't go back on her word. You wouldn't want that, would you?'

Before Cassandra had a chance to answer, Sara said, 'Look, Mom, I know what I did was wrong. But sometimes you've got to break a rule or two to make things right. It wasn't right that Lawrence should miss this game.'

'Do you have any idea what kind of danger you put yourself and Lawrence in? What if someone had recognized him and called the police? What if –'

She stopped as Christopher squeezed her hand, silently asking her to remember what he had said to her about not spoiling Sara's day. 'We'll talk about this later,' she said in her sternest tone.

'Great game,' Christopher said before Sara said something that would really tick Cassandra off.

'Thanks,' Sara said, 'but I wish that slider hadn't gotten away. Dad would have been mighty pissed.'

'Maybe not. He was a surprising man.'

'Not when it came to baseball,' she said. 'Trust me, he would've chewed my butt off. That kid's got a swing like Wade Boggs, and I knew it. I should've slipped him the spitter.'

'Why didn't you?'

''Cause you were watching and I didn't want you to catch me at it.'

Christopher found he was momentarily at a loss for words. There are times in life when you come face to face with the degree of influence you have on another person's life. It's not always a comfortable revelation; in a way, it's rather humbling, because it makes you reconsider even the things you might say off-handedly.

'You did the right thing,' Christopher said at last. 'It's cool to be able to throw a spitter, but the pitch isn't for real competition.'

Sara cocked her head. 'Funny,' she said, 'that's just what my father used to say to me.'

'Sara, I – It was wonderful to see you pitch in the championships,' Cassandra said.

'Thanks, Mom. I wanted to tell you –' Sara broke off as Hound began to bark hysterically. The Weimaraner strained at his leash with such determination he almost pulled Sara off her feet.

'What's going on?' Christopher asked.

'I don't know,' Sara said. 'I've never seen him act like this.' She was already being half-dragged away from them by the dog.

It was then that Christopher saw Lawrence hurrying toward the ballfield.

'Wait! Where are you going,' Christopher called, but Lawrence was already slipping away from him through the crowd.

As he crossed the first base line, Hound twisted his powerful shoulders, sending Sara stumbling off-balance. His leading shoulder slammed into the chest of the father of one of Sara's teammates, and the Weimaraner broke free. He loped toward Lawrence's side, his leash trailing behind him.

Cassandra raced after Christopher, who was hot on the clone's trail. Christopher, risking a quick glance behind him, knew there was no chance of telling her to go back. He did yell at Sara to stay where she was.

By the time he broke free and ran onto the baseball diamond, he caught sight of Lawrence nearing the far southwestern corner of the bleachers. Hound was at his side, its tongue lolling. Up ahead, Christopher could make out for just a split second the figure of a man who immediately disappeared behind the stands.

Close-cropped full beard, reddish brown hair, but unmistakable to Christopher nonetheless. *Christ*, he thought. *It's the Pale Saint!*

Lawrence feels the Skeleton in his mind. As in his dreams, there is a pull from an unseen force. Like a bass, he rises through the watery realm of his life to snatch the bright lure bobbing irresistibly just above his head.

There is a melody in his mind, and the phrase 'the times they are a'changin'' echoes like a rifle shot at the edge of a still and flawless lake. The bosom of the lake reflects the coming sun as Lawrence runs flat out after the Skeleton. He hears his father's shouts from behind him, mingled with Hound's panting as the Weimaraner races at his side. He feels the play of his own muscles, the pumping engine of his own body that for the first time seems to be fully alive. He rounds a corner of the bleachers, pushes through a knot of people and sees the structure of the boathouse. He cannot see the Skeleton now, but he knows where he is. The lure is spinning, reflecting the sunlight. He and Hound take off at the same time. He knows he is leaving his father farther and farther behind, but he cannot help himself. He is drawn onward as if following a predetermined path.

And there, on the other side of the boathouse, is the lake, glittering like a bright flat metal disk in the brittle autumnal afternoon sunlight. It is large. Lawrence has read about such bodies of water, has even on occasion seen them on his television monitor. But now that he is beside one it seems oddly frightening, not like dry land at all.

Abruptly, Lawrence stops. The Skeleton has reappeared from around the far side of the boathouse. They catch sight of each other. Lawrence's face beneath the lowered bill of his baseball cap, the Skeleton's face beneath the cosmetic changes of mustache and dark hair: identical bone structure and features reflected in their eyes. There is a disorienting flash, as if Lawrence is outside, looking back at himself. This disturbing feeling lasts for a very short time, nevertheless its effect is profound. He feels as if *he* is the Skeleton. In that instant, he sees like a string of bleached skulls all the moments of the Skeleton's deaths. He perceives that these deaths have their own life, that the Skeleton exists within them like a pearl within an oyster shell, and that this oyster shell somehow determines everything he thinks and does. Because the oyster shell has so completely enclosed him, sustaining him in a peculiar way, he can believe in nothing. He thinks and he acts; that's all he can do because he is damaged in the way someone with a grave illness is damaged. All this comes to Lawrence in the blink of an eye.

Hound, at Lawrence's side, is set to leap. The clone can tell by the bunching and trembling of his muscles. But with nothing more than a quick glance from the Skeleton, Hound sits back on its haunches. Its ears are flat to its skull as it crouches immobile.

'Hello,' the Skeleton says. He's eyeing Lawrence with the most peculiar expression. 'You look just like me when I was younger. What in the world have they done to you, son?'

'They created me. In a lab,' the clone says. 'I have been waiting for you.' And now he knows it's true.

The Skeleton licks his lips. 'So you're me and I'm you, is that it?'

'Is it? I don't know enough to say. Except that you're in my head. I dream about you.'

'Is that a fact?'

'Yes, and now you're here.'

'Now I understand. You're Cassandra's doing, aren't you?'

'She's my mother,' the clone says. 'Jon Christopher is my father.'

'Oho. I've underestimated no one, it seems.' The Skeleton gives Lawrence a long, admiring look. 'You see how it is, don't you?'

'What do you mean?'

'It's just us, son – us against the world.' He cocks his head. 'Don't you get it yet? Don't you see how *different* you are from everybody else? You're exactly like me.' He points to Hound. 'Even down to the Weimaraner that's connected to you.'

'How did you know that?'

'I know everything, and I'm willing to teach it all to you.' He reaches out and touches Lawrence. 'Isn't it wonderful? You and I are made from the same cloth.'

'Are we?'

'Just *look* at me. Who's inside your head?'

'You are.'

'And you're inside mine. You know what that means. We're not alone anymore.' He squeezes Lawrence's hand in his. 'Leave them; come with me. They don't care about you anyway. Not really. You're a trap they've sprung to get to me. Clever, yes, but that's all. You're a means to an end, a *thing*. I can take care of you, I can teach you. You belong with me.' The Skeleton takes a quick glance over Lawrence's shoulder, at Christopher sprinting toward them. 'Tell me, son, are you ready for the ride?'

'What ride?'

The Skeleton begins to whistle a tune, then to sing, 'A hard rain's a'gonna fall'. He winks at Lawrence. 'I don't know who they think you are, but I sure as hell intend to find out what you're made of.'

The Skeleton turns, and in a swift leap, plunges into the water. Lawrence, at the edge of the lake, hesitates only a split second. Then, as he sees Hound barking hysterically at the shoreline, he wades in after the Skeleton. Before he knows it, he's in over his head. He sees the Skeleton making rhythmic movements with his arms and legs. He tries to emulate those movements and immediately begins to sink. The water closes over his head and, still breathing normally, he begins to choke. His head rises above the surface. Dimly, he sees the Skeleton splashing onward, moving away from him at an astonishing speed. Hound, barking like a lunatic, is running back and forth along the lake.

Flailing his arms and legs, Lawrence goes under again. He tries to breathe, and chokes on the water. He sinks further and further beneath the surface until the fragile autumnal light dims to a green and distant glow.

Christopher, seeing the clone plunge headlong into the lake, shouted for him to stop. In his heart he knew it would do no good. The clone was tied to the Pale Saint as if by a leash. He had spotted the Pale Saint. Perhaps no one else would ever have, except for Hound. The Weimaraner had sensed him. Was that important? Christopher asked himself. As Christopher headed full tilt for the lake other, more pressing questions bombarded him: what was the Pale Saint doing here? Why had he risked being discovered?

Of course, the answer to both questions was the same: he had come because of the clone. Perhaps he had dreamed of the clone as the clone had dreamed of him. Clearly, they were drawn to each other.

Christopher, looking beyond the clone to where the Pale Saint was easily and swiftly swimming, began to run along the edge of the lake toward the point where he would come out of the water. As Christopher did so, he pulled out his cell phone and called for backup. *Now I have you*, he thought.

Then the clone, who had been struggling in the water, disappeared beneath it, and all other thoughts were wiped from Christopher's mind. He stopped and turned. He had no choice now; the clone was drowning. His innate antipathy for the creature aside, he was still a human being. More or less.

'Oh, hell,' Christopher said.

There was no time to rid himself of gun or shoes, items that would weigh him down. The water was so cold it took all the breath out of him, but he refused to slow down, plunging into the deep water and diving down toward the spot where the clone had disappeared.

His teeth rattled and his heart seemed to skip a beat. At this time of the year, the water was hardly at its most frigid, but it was cold enough. He'd been in the Hudson River during wintertime once or twice over the years, and he knew first-hand how quickly water could suck the heat from the human body.

The water was as murky and lightless as if it was already covered by a sheet of February ice. As Christopher dove deeper, it seemed to have the consistency of slush. The cold increased.

Darkness set in like the fall of night. The world above of light and heat became a dream, insubstantial as a puff of smoke. The only reality was here in this chill lock box, and as he continued his search, that reality became smaller and smaller, until only he and the clone existed together in the tiniest of spaces.

He was running out of breath, and abruptly, the possibility of failure entered his mind. It was so curious. The thought that he might not be able to find the clone, to bring him up for air, that he might drag him already dead from the depths of the lake was intolerable. He thought of Andy walking alone in the dark into the campus building housing the swimming pool. He must have smelled the new gunite. His feet would have crunched over the plastic tarps, the thick wires of the extruding machines. What was in his mind as he mounted the diving board, as he stared down into the black hole of the empty pool? How great was his anguish? He must have been so lost when he jumped.

And Christopher had not been there to catch his fall.

Now, beneath the lake, it seemed to him as if the past was overtaking the present, as if Andy, lost and isolated, was about to make that jump again. Cassandra had been right. There was a chance at redemption, to atone for how he had failed his son.

Breath burning in his lungs and throat, Christopher made one last desperate effort to move forward. And struck something solid with the back of his right hand. It went all the way up his elbow before he could react. His hands, stiff with cold, were slow to wrap around the leg, but he drew it in. Like a fish on a line, the clone appeared out of the murk and the gloom. The face was white, the eyes closed. Christopher could not tell whether he was alive or dead.

Christopher grabbed a handful of his shirt front and, with a tremendous effort, scissor-kicked upward.

He broke the surface with a gasp and a sob. How sweet New York air seemed to him. He kept his left arm around the clone's chest so that, though the head lay back in the water, the face would not go under. He struck out for the shore, but his legs were leaden, and he could no longer feel his feet at all. He tried to scissor-kick, but it took all his remaining energy just to move his legs. It occurred to him that he might not make it.

He must have blacked out for a moment because the next thing he knew he was choking on water. He'd gone under without knowing it. He pushed upward, but it was as if he had an anchor tied to his feet. He couldn't sustain it, and he went under again. The frigid water closed over his face, the darkness spreading upward as he and the clone sank deeper and deeper.

Then something – a current, an eddy of warmth – seemed to buoy him upward. His head broke the surface, he spit water out of his mouth, and gulped air. He became aware of a strong arm holding him securely, and a face close to his.

'Hello, Christopher,' the Pale Saint whispered in his ear. 'You were almost gone that time.'

Christopher, gulping in air, was too exhausted to answer. He felt the flat of a hand pressing down on the top of his head. He was held under until the fire in his lungs was almost too much to bear, and blackness swam at the edges of his vision. Then the Pale Saint hauled him upward again, gasping and retching, into the sunlight. With an animal grunt, he pushed Christopher's head back beneath the water, then as quickly drew him up again. 'I could drown you with one gesture.' He reached inside Christopher's jacket, jerked free the gun, and pressed the muzzle to Christopher's temple. 'Or I could blow your brains out. Death comes in many flavors. All it takes is imagination.' He threw the gun away. 'I could kill you now, Christopher. But what would be the point? I can't have you dying prematurely, can I? No, that won't do. It won't do at all. Not when we've just started to get *intimate*.' His lips trembled against Christopher's ear as he mouthed the last word.

Christopher could feel the water churning around them as the engine of the Pale Saint's legs kept them afloat. The Pale Saint's lips gently fluttered against Christopher's ear the way a lover's might. His breath smelled of chocolate, just like the clone's. Christopher was as much paralyzed by these small, abominable intimacies as he was by the chill and exhaustion.

The Pale Saint cradled the back of Christopher's head as Christopher's eyes began to go out of focus. 'Don't lose consciousness now.' He slapped Christopher smartly across the cheeks. 'I have so much more to tell you.' He kept up the stinging slaps until Christopher's eyes came back into focus. 'You see, I know all about you. Every little thing. I know how you feel about Cassandra, how Sara feels about you. I know all about Andy, as well: I know the guilt that gnaws at you like a starving rat. The questions inside your head about *what you did wrong*. I wonder what it's like to see the concrete coming up at terminal velocity, to know your skull is going to break open like a ripe melon. What were Andy's last thoughts, Christopher; how many times have you asked yourself that? Too many to count, I'll wager. Oh, yes, I know it all. You and I have a kind of, what would you call it, an *affaire de coeur*.' He nipped at Christopher's ear. 'Stay with me now. I'm a long way from being finished with you.' With an almost filial tenderness, he brushed the hair out of Christopher's eyes. 'I researched the Austins well; I knew Bobby better than you did, didn't I? I know the real reason he became a district attorney. But it didn't work.'

'I don't know what you're talking about.'

'Of course you don't. Not yet, anyway. The truth is we never really know anyone else. It's all an illusion. What goes on beneath the human facade – well, sometimes it's better not to know, right?' He slapped Christopher again, much harder this time. '*Wrong*.'

Something in his face seemed to relax. 'Time to let you go, Christopher.' He pushed on Christopher's shoulders, swinging him in the direction of the shore. 'For a little while, anyway.' Before he let them go, he put his hands on either side of the clone's face. Christopher could feel that peculiar warmth knifing through the chill that held him fast in its grip.

'Get away from him.'

'What a gift you've given me,' the Pale Saint said. He leaned over and pressed his lips to the center of Lawrence's forehead. 'After all, how often does a man get to see his own flesh reproduced.'

A last reserve of energy was slowly reforming. Christopher lunged as he tried to grab hold of the Pale Saint, but in doing so he lost his grip on the clone. Reversing course, he hauled the clone's head back up out of the water.

'Lord Jesus.' The Pale Saint was laughing as he turned away. 'Look at you.'

Christopher had no choice but to get the clone to shore as quickly as he could. His legs moved sluggishly, he paddled awkwardly with his free hand. He felt as if he were about to pass out again. Then, at the very edge of unconsciousness, instinct took over. He pressed his lips, as the Pale Saint had, to the clone's forehead. Warmth suffused him, and with it, feeling returned to his limbs. The twilight of semi-consciousness receded. He paddled on with renewed life.

After what seemed a long time – though it could not have been more than a minute or two – he felt solid ground beneath his feet. So numb and spent was he that this alone told him that he had gained the shore. He lay, panting, with the clone lying half over him.

He heard the wail of sirens, could dimly hear Cassandra calling, her voice coming quickly closer. She must be running at a helluva pace, he thought. He tried to locate her, saw that he had fetched up on the western bank of the lake, far from where he and the clone had entered. He heard an almost hysterical barking. Blinking watery scum out of his eyes, he could make out the Weimaraner as it raced around the lake due south of him. After having swum the entire north-south length of the roughly T-shaped lake, the Pale Saint was already on the grass past the lake bank. He headed toward the traffic along West Park Drive. The Weimaraner loped after him, its tongue lolling.

There are times, as in a dream, when one knows something terrible is going to happen: you see someone you know about to step off the roof of a building or someone you love is about to slip on a patch of ice and break his back. You call out but you have no voice; you try to run to them but you cannot move. You are utterly helpless.

This was Christopher's feeling now as he lay exhausted and breathless. He tried to roll the clone off him, watching as the Pale Saint zig-zagged through the traffic. Like a matador with a maddened bull, he snaked and squirmed his way through the blare of horns, the screech of brakes, the shouted multi-lingual epithets. And after him came Hound, running fast now because he had closed the gap. He was a city dog; Sara had taught him well about the dangers of motor vehicles. He dodged and leapt his way across the road. He was almost on the other side when the Pale Saint glanced back over his shoulder. Hound skidded to a halt, his head up, his neck arched, its ears flat as if listening to a silent command.

Hours later, Christopher would recall the perfect silver arch of Hound's neck, and the way his entire attention was focused on the Pale Saint in the instant before the taxi hit him. The dog, carried high in the air by the impact, cartwheeled over and over, his silver carcass already lifeless when he smacked into the trunk of an old elm tree and dropped to the ground.

Christopher would also have cause to remember how the Pale Saint paused, taking several steps back toward the animal. Something, perhaps an emotion, flickered across his face. Then, as if sensing that the Weimaraner was dead, he turned away, disappearing into the vast, gathering crowd.

Christopher was giving the clone mouth-to-mouth when Cassandra knelt down beside him.

'Jon! Jon, are you –?'

'I'm okay.'

'Thank God.'

'But I don't know about the clone.'

'Let me,' she said. She kissed him hard on the lips, then began to work on Lawrence, pounding his chest repeatedly.

'I did the best I could, but I'm just a little out of breath.' He watched her work, instinctively putting her body between the clone's head and the people running toward them. He was so glad to be out of the cold and the dark. He began to shiver. 'Where's Sara?'

'With her baseball coach. She hasn't seen what happened to Hound yet.'

Lawrence coughed and water spewed out of his open mouth. He took a long, shuddering inhalation and opened his eyes. He stared up into their faces.

'I'm alive,' he said.

Cassandra laughed with relief and kissed him on the cheek. He sat up. At that moment, Christopher seemed in worse shape than he did.

Lawrence looked into Christopher's eyes. 'He's gone,' he said.

'Who?' Christopher asked. 'The Skeleton?'

Lawrence got up. 'Where's Sara? I want to see her.' He spotted her. When she saw him, she broke away from the coach and ran to him. He took her hand and they went toward where Hound lay beneath the tree.

Sara gave a little cry and sprawled beside Hound, stroking his sleek head. Tears streamed down her face. Then she put her baseball jacket over the Weimaraner's twisted haunches.

Lawrence knelt down beside them. He held her briefly and she put her head back against his chest. He whispered something in her ear, and she nodded. Together, they touched Hound's sleek silver corpse.

Then, abruptly, Lawrence separated himself from her. He gave a harsh, inhuman cry, rocked back and forth on his haunches. 'Gone, gone, gone.'

It was the first time any of them had seen him cry as an adult.

Cassandra had been thinking on the fly, having gotten from the coach another cap, which she had put on him as before to make sure no one recognized him, and she had given him her own jacket to help hide his soaked clothes from the paramedics. Christopher watched the clone as the paramedics probed and poked; he seemed physically unaffected by his ordeal. As unaffected as the Pale Saint had been by his long swim across the lake?

It was uncanny how the Pale Saint was always several steps ahead of everyone else. It was as if he'd had all of this planned out from the start. Even the intervention of the clone had not fazed him; in fact, if Christopher was reading him right, he now felt as if he was no longer alone in the universe – he viewed the clone as a kindred spirit. Most disturbing of all, perhaps, was his allusion to Bobby having a hidden agenda for becoming an assistant D.A. If it was so, Bobby had never told Christopher. At the earliest opportunity he'd have to ask Cassandra if she knew anything about it.

Christopher began to lead them away from the scene. None of them, even Christopher himself, could afford to be interviewed right now. 'You're all right?' he asked Lawrence.

The clone nodded.

'Good.' Christopher saw Cassandra put her arm around Sara's shoulders. 'What did he say to you? I could see him talking.'

'He was . . . surprised. To see me. He asked me what you had done to me. To make me look like him, I guess. I said you made me. In a lab.'

Patrol cars came screaming over the lawn. Out of the corner of his eyes, Christopher saw more cops coming on foot. 'You mean you used Cassandra's name?'

'He already knew.'

A little shiver crawled down Christopher's spine. He was about to ask another question when he spotted Sgt Lewis sprinting across the grass toward him.

'I picked up the squeal and came as fast as I could,' Lewis said, slightly out of breath. 'You okay?'

Christopher nodded. 'Yes, but I need your help. I've got to get out of here now. Square it with the uniforms right behind you until I can phone Brockaw.'

'What happened?'

'The Pale Saint,' Christopher said. 'But we can't let the story get out, so make up something about a mugging. You know the routine.'

'No problem,' Lewis said.

'Thanks,' Christopher said as he hurried off with Lawrence in tow. 'I'll check back with you as soon as I can.'

Lewis nodded and turned back to face the onrushing horde of blue uniforms.

Christopher led the clone quickly away from the commotion, across West Park Drive and out of the park.

'I want you to think back to what the Skeleton told you,' he said. 'Who mentioned Cassandra's name first, the Skeleton or you?'

'He did.'

'You're sure.'

'Yes.'

'What did he say? Tell me *exactly*, word for word if you can.'

'He said, "You're Cassandra's doing, aren't you?" And I said she was my mom.' Lawrence glanced at her. 'Was that wrong? I told the truth.'

'What happened after that?' Christopher said without answering him.

'I told him that you were my father, and he said, "I've underestimated no one, it seems."'

'Anything else?'

Lawrence seemed unsure for a moment, then he nodded again. 'He said the two of us were no longer alone.'

Christopher saw cops coming. 'Do you know what he meant by that?'

Lawrence shook his head.

Ahead of them, Cassandra and Sara were waiting. Christopher, straining, could just hear the end of their conversation.

'I don't want Hound just left there.' Sara's eyes were large and liquid. Christopher thought she had never looked more like Bobby. 'I want to give him a proper burial.'

'Don't worry. I've already seen to that.' Cassandra squeezed her shoulders. 'Sara, I'm so sorry. I know how much Hound meant to you.'

Sara suddenly turned to her and burying her face in her breast, wrapped her arms around her. 'Mom, promise me you're not going anywhere.'

'Honey –'

'Promise me you won't let Uncle Jon get away.'

Cassandra tilted Sara's head up to her. 'Of course I'm not going anywhere. Where did you get an idea like that?'

Tears spilled over down Sara's cheeks. 'Dad is gone,' she whispered. 'Now so is Hound. And Lawrence is living life so fast . . . Who'll be next?'

'Oh, my darling.' Cassandra clasped her daughter to her. 'No one is leaving.' She kissed the top of her head. 'I promise you.' She smiled. 'I'll tell you a secret no one else knows. I'm not going to let Jon go.' She felt Sara clinging to her. 'See? You're safe now, darling. Look, here he is now. You're safe here with us.'

Tonight he tries to sleep but, like a sailor abandoning a ship on fire, sleep has given up on him. Outside his window midnight clouds as round and fleecy as sheep scroll by as if they were part of a carnival shooting gallery. Against a reflected background of the city's neon, the clouds move, pulled by a hidden engine.

Inside his dark, cramped, humid apartment, the Pale Saint knows the identity of that engine. He knows who's pulling the strings. Her image floats in his mind, brilliant with the phosphorus of electronic sparks. Blue. In his memory, she is always blue, because she rules the dusty Oklahoma night with her fiery eyes and even more fiery tongue. Strings of words fly from her mouth like lashes from a whip, rising and falling in cadence until a hypnotic rhythm is established. But the intensity never wavers. Unlike the cadence of her speech, the intensity rises and rises again, and keeps rising until it reaches a fever pitch, until the sweat breaks out and the palms turn clammy and the itch grows stronger, until the scent of sweet candle wax is all he smells, until the taste of soap is in his mouth, until rational thought is erased, and his need for release becomes overwhelming.

'Why weren't you ever home?' he whispers. 'Why didn't you ever speak to me?'

'I was in Service,' the image says with a welling of contempt. 'You knew that.'

'All the . . . terrible things that happened. If you had been home . . .'

His voice trails off at her withering look, and he feels defeated. Her power is a radiance, cold and blue and compelling. This is the way the Pale Saint sees his Mama. His secret heart is white with ash of pyres burned at the tombstone of memory. This is unacceptable. Memory requires him to feel; and he is certain that memory is false witness to the truth.

The truth is carefully folded inside the trunk that squats, bolted and locked, at the foot of Mama's bed, a tombstone itself, indelibly marking in that dark and cavernous house of his youth all that has gone before, all that has made the family what it has become. It is the past before it flared and flamed, turning to white ash in his secret heart.

He lies on the mattress no thicker than his forearm. His eyes are squeezed tight shut. His rituals have preserved his latest sacrifice, but he cannot see her now, not even in his mind's eye. In the land beyond his eyelids, the dark and cavernous house of his youth seems to thrust upward from the prairie like the roots of a gnarled ancient tree. That graveyard of his family blots out both the present and the future, leaving only the dangerous past.

He remembers the day he went out back to where Mama had buried Pappy. He had called out the dogs – three enormous black Dobermans he had raised after the albino was gone. He was fourteen, and the sky was as hard as colored glass. He gave them the scent from a scrap of Pappy's shirt. Barking and snuffling, their forepaws already scratched at the pale, chalky earth. He hid under the porch.

The dogs dug deeper and faster, snuffling with the sounds of men toiling at righteous labor. And Pappy appeared, white and black and wrinkled, like an old photograph, an arm, a shoulder, the side of the head. Everything was heavily wrinkled, as if the corpse was so old – ancient as Methuselah. But it was really only the dirt, which had grooved itself into the tiny folds of skin as the Pale Saint's Pappy slid toward oblivion – dust to dust.

The Dobermans' heavy gruntings brought Mama running toward them. She had these amazing eyes – so blue – a shade he has never seen anywhere else. And they were slightly pop eyes, which often seemed to bulge out alarmingly.

But lying in this dark place of sightless earthworms and indifferent insects, he was safe. Here he could hear his thoughts, traveling like lightning across the bowl of the Oklahoma heavens. Like the storm that appears in fury and is gone, these thoughts said nothing specific but meant everything. They expressed the chaos hidden deep inside him – the pain, loss and, yes, fear in which he had bundled like an insect inside a cocoon. He watched Mama toiling and sweating as she buried all over again the man she murdered while the dogs shook themselves, tongues lolling as they watched the dirt fly. They watched her in much the same way when she killed her husband, thinking their doggy thoughts. Now he imagines they watched her in much the same way when she opened the trunk at the foot of her bed and placed within it that which is most secret, that which is most sacred, that which must never be seen.

'This is your Pappy,' he whispers to Faith in a hushed voice. 'You never really knew him. Now you'll remember him this way, rotting, being torn apart by dogs. Which is all he deserves for what he did.'

A fitful New York City wind rattles the dusty Venetian blinds the Pale Saint uses to keep out the city light. It will be dawn soon. The nighttime is passing like a storm on its way across the plains. He thinks of the Weimaraner, its silver coat glowing in the autumnal light. He sees again the arc of its body, struck by the taxi, feels again the life wink out even before it strikes the hard, scaly bole of the tree. He is sure he would have gone back, would have risked Christopher coming too close had the Weimaraner been alive. But in a tiny ripple no more than an exhalation it had died. Abruptly, he is filled with thoughts of the end, and inevitably that brings him back to the night he came into the world.

That same night, a litter was born to the farm bitch, a peculiar mix of German shepherd and Weimaraner. Six pups died, until all that was left was the albino, the last-born, the largest of the lot, the one perhaps that had killed her. Hadn't been a dog born albino in that part of Oklahoma for as long as anyone could remember. To the Shawnee, albino animals are sacred. Among their people it is said that the birth of an albino is an omen that a circle of life is ending and another is beginning.

Staring at himself in the mirror, he is ashamed to admit that in those early days he wept bitterly whenever Mama left to go off to work. He never let on because that would have made Mama mad. When she was mad, which she often was at Pappy, blood flowed into her face the way it pumped out of other people's wounds. And with that, her face seemed to expand like one of those big, dry-skinned lizards whose throat sac blows up when they're angry or threatened. It was a terrifying sight, no question. So he watched her silently as she prepared to leave, even though he knew she would be gone for weeks at a time. Her work was a crusade with her; everything and everybody else fell away like the shed husk of a locust. Mostly, the young Pale Saint was left with Pappy. That wasn't good. When he wasn't ignoring his son completely, Pappy had a bad habit of flying into the most evil rages.

One time, he dislocated the Pale Saint's shoulder. After that, the Pale Saint took to sleeping in the barn with the albino. There, he felt closer to things: the smells of the changing weather, the small, vital sounds the land makes when one is really and truly listening; the constant stirring of life, and the freedom that brings.

What meant something to him was the albino dog's pain. There was a congenital defect in its stomach that made digestion painful. That was something the young Pale Saint could relate to. Nights he sat shivering, curled into a ball in the straw of the stall, he felt warmed by the constancy of the animal's presence. He sang a song he had heard, 'Stuck Inside of Mobile with the Memphis Blues Again', without really understanding the lyrics. And as the days passed something quite extraordinary began to happen. Gradually he realized that the pain was actually pleasurable. Because it was *his* pain, and because he could share it with the albino.

He once asked Mama if animals have souls. Mama said, No, not like people have souls that can be saved by embracing Jesus Christ. The Pale Saint knew she was wrong. The slow, stupid cows might not have souls, but the albino surely did. The albino was the only other creature that could feel the Pale Saint's pain. Mama couldn't, and Pappy, well, it was a sick joke even to think he might. The Pale Saint was sure the albino knew the mysterious process of how being stuck inside of Mobile brought on those Memphis blues.

The year he was ten the ides of March caught them in a freak snowstorm. They had been pushing hard through the east fork, and the albino had eaten nothing all day. In the gloaming of premature night, the dog came upon a coyote den, snatching from beneath the rocky overhang the smallest of the pups. The bitch coyote, half-starved by the weather, appeared upwind of them, so even the albino was unaware of her until she descended on them. The albino, standing its ground between the Pale Saint and the coyote, went down beneath the coyote's weight. It managed to kill the bitch, but not before being mortally wounded itself.

The Pale Saint tried to get it home, but he failed. He stared into the albino's sightless eyes and stroked its cooling fur. He tried to speak to it but he could no longer hear its echo in his mind. He felt a great darkness at the center of his being. This darkness opened up and, in the blink of an eye, swallowed him whole.

ELEVEN

Late that night, Cassandra and Christopher put Lawrence back in the birth chamber, making sure he cleaned himself up. While Cassandra was reconfiguring the numerous logs so that Dillard would never know that Lawrence had been once again out of the lab, Christopher stayed in the birth chamber with Lawrence.

'How are you doing?' he asked the clone.

'I wish I could be with Sara. She looked so sad, so alone when we dropped her off.'

'I do, too, but for the moment you have to be here when Dr Dork shows up. You understand that, don't you.'

'Uh huh.'

'There's something else on your mind, isn't there?' Christopher said, sitting on the bed next to him. He had just noticed that Lawrence had lost his stutter.

Lawrence peeled the wrapper and foil from a bar of Hershey's chocolate. 'Ever since you pulled me out of the lake I've been thinking, about what it means to be alive and what it means to be dead.'

'Don't bother. It'll just drive you nuts.'

'That's what you're thinking about, isn't it, Dad? I know it is.' He began to eat. Chocolate was the one food he did not wolf down. 'We're thinking about the same things. I like that.'

'When you're forced by circumstance to kill someone,' Christopher began, 'you learn how not to think about death. You wind up sealing off a part of you.'

'But it's an important part of you, isn't it?' Lawrence said with astonishing insight. 'I mean, death is one half of the equation. If there was no death, if everyone lived forever, then what would life

189

be? It would lose its meaning.'

Christopher shook his head. 'You're not even three weeks old and already you sound like you've been around for a hundred years.'

Lawrence's eyes stared levelly into his. 'When you grow a year older every day, each moment is so very important.' He spread his hands. 'It's like sprinting through a place you like very much. You know you can't slow down, so you've got to take in as much as you can in the short time you have.'

Christopher found that some arrow he did not even know existed had suddenly pierced his armor, penetrating all the way to his heart. There was a look in Lawrence's eyes that Christopher could not ignore. Perhaps he had seen it there all along, and had ignored it. But that was before he had dragged him from the lake bed. Christopher realized how successful he'd been at fighting down any feelings he might have had for this child – because no matter his accelerated age, to Christopher he was still in many ways a child. But now something had changed. In the nexus of events in the lake, a cord that had been wrapped tightly around Christopher's throat had been cut.

'I'm sorry this is so hard on you.'

'Don't be sorry, Dad. You and Mom gave me life. That's a gift that I . . .' Slowly and deliberately, he rewrapped half of the chocolate bar.

'What's the matter?'

'Dr Dork says I shouldn't call you Dad. He says you aren't my dad, not really, and that I'd better learn the truth. So did Sara. But I told her you are – my father, I mean. Because you'll take care of me, you'll protect me. And you did. I was going to die in the lake and you saved me. So you are my dad. Which means the Skeleton was wrong.'

Christopher watched the clone carefully. 'What do you mean?'

'The Skeleton said that you didn't care about me, that all you wanted was for me to find him. But now I know that he can be wrong. Even though he comes to me in visions.'

'Yes,' Christopher said. 'He's very, very wrong. Lawrence, if you understand anything I've taught you it should be that. The Skeleton is evil. He has to be stopped.'

'He's dead,' Lawrence said with an eerie kind of certainty. 'When we were touching in the lake I looked inside his mind. I saw him die. Over and over again. And I've been thinking. If he and I are the same, am I dead too?'

'No,' Christopher said, 'you're not dead.'

'That's good, because I love life too much.'

190

Christopher watched Cassandra hunched over the digital readouts. Unlike him, he was sure she would have been unsurprised to hear Lawrence say that. 'Tell me something,' he began. 'You said you looked inside the Skeleton's mind and saw that he had died many times. What did you mean by that?'

'You mean you don't know?'

'No.'

'Don't people – die over and over in their heads?'

'Tell me more about that.' Christopher leaned forward. 'I'd like to know.'

'But you already do. Like now. You're dead inside. Because of what happened to your son, Andy. You lost something – something very important – and you can't get it back, ever.'

'How did you know about Andy?'

'I heard you and Mom talking about him. But I also saw him. In the Skeleton's mind.'

Christopher felt a thread of fear run through him. 'Why would he be thinking of my son?'

'Maybe because the Skeleton lost someone close to him,' Lawrence said. 'Again and again.'

'Can you tell me who?'

'His family. Everyone.'

'Who? Mother? Father? Sister? Brother?'

'Never had a brother.'

'A sister, then?'

'Once.'

'Can you tell me anything about her?'

'Dead. They're all dead.' Lawrence licked chocolate off his lips. 'He's been alone a long time. I think he was happy to see me. Because of that.'

'Happy or eager for a convert? It must be tempting for you to feel sorry for him, seeing what you did in his mind.'

'I'm not sure.'

'Well, don't fall into that trap,' Christopher said firmly. 'He could also be very angry with you.'

'I don't understand.'

'Because he hates what he is – what all the deaths in his life have made him become. That's why he kills and keeps on killing. That's got to stop. See, it doesn't matter what the cause is. It doesn't matter that he's felt pain or that he may have died inside again and again. You don't willfully kill another human being. That's the bottom line; there is no exception.'

'But what about God's law?' Lawrence asked. 'I read in the Bible that God said: "Ye shall take no ransom for the life of a murderer, which is guilty of death; but he shall be surely put to death." Isn't there an idiom that says "Revenge is sweet"?'

'There is, but it's a lie,' Christopher said at once. 'What we're talking about here is morality, not animal revenge. What God knows is that the full scope of His morality is beyond even man's ability to understand. Society has its laws, just as it should, but mankind's version of morality isn't possible without outrage. And, to take Dean Koenig as just one example, the morally righteous are often the most disruptive elements of society.'

'Then are you the hand of God?'

'What on earth would make you say that?'

'You find evil men. Sometimes you kill them. What else could you be?'

'I'm just a man,' Christopher said. 'I make as many mistakes as the next guy. I made mistakes with Andy.' He reached into his pocket, drew out a ring of keys. Selecting one, he separated it from the others. 'This is the key to the swimming pool where Andy died. It was found in my son's pocket as he lay at the bottom of the dry pool. I've kept it because . . .' He rubbed his thumb across the flat of the dark bronze-colored metal. 'Because no one knew how he got this key. And I don't know why he jumped. There's a connection there and I don't want to lose it.' He pocketed the key ring and looked at Lawrence. 'If there is a hand of God, which I doubt, I would imagine He'd make no mistakes at all.'

'The Skeleton made a mistake,' Lawrence said. 'He let me see that he knows all about us. You, me, Mom, Sara, Andy. Everyone.'

'Why did he go to the trouble of learning all about us? What does he want?'

'I don't know. I –'

'*Think*, Lawrence.'

The clone screwed up his face. Christopher could see that he was struggling to put his thoughts into words. 'He wants to put things back the way they were before.'

'Before what?'

'Before he found his war. Before . . . the first bad thing happened. It was very, very bad.'

'What was it, Lawrence, do you know?'

'Someone died. But not right away. It took time. And in the meanwhile, bad things happened. Bad, bad things.'

'Like what?'

Rivulets of sweat rolled down Lawrence's face. The effort of extracting these images was titanic. 'I . . . don't know.'

'Can you tell me how he's going to make things like they were before the first bad thing happened?'

'A clean slate,' the clone said. 'A fire burning into the sky. A fire to cleanse all the bad things. Death and more death. And out of death, new life. Rebirth.'

'He thinks he can be reborn by killing over and over again.' Christopher considered this. 'That's the second time you mentioned a fire. Is that something that's already happened or something that's going to happen?'

'Both. Neither. I don't know. I see a house with seven pillars.'

'It's in the Rockies, right?'

'No.'

'Where then?'

Lawrence thought a moment. 'There were no mountains, just a flat and dusty place. Here and there a tree maybe, that's all.'

Christopher exhaled. 'A prairie. You know what a prairie is?'

'Yes. It's an extensive area of flat or rolling grassland with little or no trees, like in central North America,' he said, parroting the encyclopedia entry. 'The word is from the Old French, *praierie* and the Latin *prā ta*.'

'So it's in the prairie.'

'The house, yes. It's burning twice.'

'Twice? How can it burn twice?'

'Two houses,' Lawrence said.

'Where on the prairie is this house? Dammit, this is important.'

Sweat was rolling down Lawrence's face with the effort of concentration. 'Oklahoma?' he said at last.

'Oklahoma? Are you sure?'

'I don't –' Lawrence's eyes were pleading. 'It's a word in my head, that's all.'

'All right,' Christopher said, easing up. 'You did very well.'

'Thanks, Dad.' He wiped his face with his sleeve, heaved a sigh of relief.

'Lawrence, I can't say this too many times. There is something terribly wrong with the Skeleton. The pain he might feel – all the bad things that

193

happened to him – they might explain what he has become, but they can't excuse it. That's why I think he might want to hurt you, because he's hurting himself. I suspect that's why he went into the lake. You told him you were brought up in a lab. He would have known you couldn't swim. It's possible he wanted you to drown.'

'It is possible, if I don't act the way he wants,' he said. 'But if that's true, I know you'll protect me. You dove into the water to save me when you could have caught him. I know how much you want to catch him, Dad.'

Christopher was thoughtful. Even near the end his wife still had short periods of lucidity. During one of these she had said to him, *'Don't think when I'm gone I won't worry about you.'*

'What do you mean?' He had been startled. *'You never worry about me.'*

She had smiled. *'What makes you think that, my darling? I just never let you see it.'*

'Something happened in your mind just now,' Lawrence said. 'What was it?'

Christopher refocused on the present. 'I was remembering something my wife said to me just before she died.'

'Why did you think of it now?'

'I don't know,' Christopher said. 'Maybe it has something to do with you.'

'Is that good?'

'Yes. I guess it is.'

Lawrence took out the remaining half-bar of Hershey's chocolate. He peeled off the paper and foil wrappers and looked at it a moment. Then he handed it to Christopher. 'C'mon, Dad. You didn't eat any dinner. You must be hungry.'

'This is your favorite,' Christopher said. 'Don't you want it?'

'Yeah,' Lawrence said. 'But I want you to have it more.'

Christopher, feeling change all around him, found that he was hungry. 'How about we share it?' he said, breaking the chocolate in two.

'I'd like that.'

They both bit into the chocolate at once. Lawrence watched with pleasure as Christopher chewed. Christopher, enjoying the chocolate immensely, wondered whether they would be here like this if Andy had not made his ultimate choice. It was spooky, but in his heart, he knew the answer. He was stunned by what had begun to happen. Ever since Lawrence had been born, Christopher had seen him as the enemy; at every turn he'd belittled Cassandra's bond with him. But Lawrence wasn't the enemy; not really. All the arguments he had used with Cassandra as to why she should keep herself uninvolved with Lawrence now seemed to have lost their credibility. Lawrence might be genetically identical to the Pale Saint, but his continued contact with Cass and Sara and Christopher had allowed him to become his own person. In his first face-to-face contact with the Pale Saint he'd been able to sense that they weren't in fact identical. Christopher had connected with him in the way he'd so desperately wanted to with Andy. Beyond that, though, was the realization that Lawrence was responding to him the way Sara did. He recalled what she had said to him after the game. Christopher's actions and words had assumed the same import with Lawrence. The clone was now as much his responsibility as Andy had been. Christopher had at last grasped the essential truth that had come full force to Cassandra the moment Lawrence had been born: Lawrence was unique, individual, a separate human being with his own unknowable fate.

Through the thick glass of the chamber windows, Cassandra watched them sitting close together, eating in companionable silence. It was their first meal together, and she did not disturb them until they were finished.

'This is the last time I'm going to doctor the logs,' she said, when Christopher emerged from the chamber. 'It goes against everything I've been taught as a scientist.'

'What choice do we have?'

'I've made up my mind. I'm going to fire Dillard. After the last confrontation I have to admit I worry about Lawrence when I'm not here to keep them apart. Hutton actually threatened him. It's a damn good thing he isn't running this program. God knows how he'd treat Lawrence.'

Christopher looked at her. 'Won't he go crying to Gerry Costas? He's already threatened to do that once.'

'I've thought about that.' She tapped a fingernail against the counter top. 'I'm not going to fire him myself, Costas is. Hutton won't know what hit him.' She nodded. 'I have to meet with Gerry, anyway. He's been after me for a week to get him the lab's quarterly expense projections. I'll talk to him then.'

As soon as Cassandra got to the lab the next morning, she began to run again and again the computer log of Lawrence's strange 'serotonin spikes'. Jon was off at One Police Plaza, working on the aftermath of yesterday's incident in Central Park. The NYPD's spin doctors had already been at work downplaying the event as a simple mugging. The news that the Pale Saint had been in Central Park would undoubtedly cause a citywide panic. Christopher's presence alongside the Chief was needed for a first-hand account to the media to lend credibility to the cover story.

Cassandra opened a drawer. From a box she drew on a pair of disposable latex gloves as she always did and got to work. Several days ago, it became clear to her that serotonin wasn't the only substance being produced in unusually large quantities during these episodes, but it took her some time to decode the full range of activity. Each time the serotonin level shot up there was a corresponding imbalance of eicosanoids. Eicosanoids are hormones that are manufactured by the body as it breaks down essential fatty acids into glucagon and insulin. Eicosanoids that help build up the immune system are derived from glucagon, while those that weaken it come from insulin. Cassandra's study showed that when Lawrence had his serotonin spikes, the ratio of good to bad eicosanoids increased out of all proportion. She also noticed definite evidence that Lawrence's growth rate was accelerating beyond a year a day.

She showed her findings to a bleary-eyed Dillard. 'Look,' she said. 'It's almost as if the clone's body is preparing its natural defenses against oncoming danger, but of what sort I am at a loss to understand.' She snapped her fingers. 'Wait a minute. That's it!' she shouted.

'What's it?' he said with some annoyance.

She went to a small refrigerator within which was a row of test tubes containing samples of Lawrence's blood which they drew daily for analysis. She took out the test tube containing a specific sample and got to work.

'What are you doing? I've been over so many computer combinations I'm of a mind we'll never find the answer in time.'

'You're wrong. I'm extracting the eicosanoid from Lawrence's blood,' she said in a fever of excitement. 'I've never stopped believing that something in his altered blood chemistry is keeping the trans-gene from going berserk as it's done in Minnie.'

'This is useless, Cassandra. We've tried the serotonin therapy in the rat without any results.'

'Yes, but we used pure serotonin manufactured in the lab. If we'd used Lawrence's we might have gotten a different result because it would have contained this eicosanoid.'

'Cassandra, this is madness. I told you your personal involvement with the subject would lead to disaster. We have other work to do. The rat is terminal. At any moment, the rogue trans-gene will express itself in our human subject. In the short time allotted us we've got to summarize our findings and work on the wording of the presentation of our findings.'

Cassandra did not even pick up her head. 'I can't give up on this, Hutton, even if you have. To tell you the truth, Lawrence's life is far more important to me than a Nobel Prize.'

'Right. I can see I'm talking to the obsessed. I'm sorry we've come to this juncture, Cassandra.'

'What is that, Hutton? A threat?'

'I won't even dignify that with an answer.' He gathered up his coat. 'I'll be back.'

It took Cassandra more than an hour to extract the eicosanoid from Lawrence's blood. She injected it into Minnie, hooked her up, and switched on the readout and waited. Ten minutes, fifteen, twenty.

'Nothing,' she said, sitting down wearily on a stool. 'Another damned dead end.'

Esquival was listening to Robert Casadesus's sublime recording of Maurice Ravel's *Pavane pour une infante défunte*. This was not done idly but as an anodyne to the tedious process of on-line computer search. He had logged on for his daily perusal of the FBI's Violent Criminal Apprehension Program. He hated this kind of work, which he felt was more suited to D'Alassandro, who actually liked working on computers. He, on the other hand, would have given his right nut to have been in the tenement basement, or even better, at Central Park when Christopher had had his face-to-face with the Pale Saint. His was a dirty job, but he was the only one authorized to use the FBI's VCAP.

Casadesus's lovely cascading piano overrode the sounds of voices, phones ringing, all the clutter and junk of the Case Room at full throttle. Esquival was in a small back room, where he did all his major computer searches. He'd hooked up a cheap mini-component stereo, bringing in new tapes and CDs virtually every day to feed it.

Someone poked his head in and asked if he wanted a bite to eat, the only way Esquival knew that time had passed. He said No, and the head was withdrawn. The staff – even the uniforms on loan from various precincts – had been briefed to leave him on his own.

Up until now, he'd had no specific area on which to concentrate his search of the VCAP files. That all changed when Christopher had told him to hone in on the Rocky Mountain states. He said he had a hunch the spike was more important than they at first believed. And Esquival had had enough experience with Christopher to take his hunches very seriously.

Take, for instance, the Buried Child Case. It was how they had met.

Brooke, the daughter of Stewart Applewhite, the CEO and founder of Hubbart Aerospace, had been abducted from the family brownstone on the upper east side of Manhattan. The father was given an ultimatum: cough up five million bucks within thirty-six hours or Brooke, who was buried in a capsule with just enough oxygen, would die. Christopher caught the case, and Esquival had been foisted on him at the direct request of the senior senator from New York. Applewhite was a major contributor of the senator's re-election campaign and the senator played poker every Monday night with the assistant deputy director of the FBI.

The investigation team had been stumped until Christopher decided to take another look at one of Hubbart's best design engineers, a mousy little geek named Wilson with Coke-bottle glasses and a ninety-eight-pound-weakling body.

This guy had been cleared off their suspect list for a number of reasons: he was making a couple of hundred-thou a year. He had excellent benefit and options packages. Also, he'd been working at Hubbart for more than twenty years; Applewhite had recruited him right out of grad school.

Christopher's hunch had paid off. What they had missed the first, second and third times was that per Wilson's contract the patents for the stuff he invented were in Hubbart's name. The company was raking in millions on the poor schnook's genius. Esquival still remembered the first thing Wilson said when Christopher Mirandized him: 'I was a slave for years, and now I'm free.'

Well, it took all kinds, Esquival thought, and he didn't –

The warning chime on his computer cut through Ravel's liquid melody, and Esquival's attention snapped to the terminal display. The VCAP had found a match to the Pale Saint's kill signature. As the screen began to scroll, Esquival's eyes opened wide. Not just *a* match, but *four*! In a small town with the improbable name of Debenture, Montana.

In a fever of excitement, Esquival scanned the info: in 1983, four men were found dead in a space of five days. The former mayor, a current city councilman, a circuit court judge and a steel manufacturer. An odd thing, though. All the men were old, ranging from their mid-seventies to early eighties. They had been killed in an identical manner: with a single mortal puncture trauma that pierced the left eye. Esquival scrolled through the incomplete documents. There was no mention of whether the pineal gland was missing, but that meant nothing. Esquival knew from frustrating experience that these small towns sometimes didn't have a competent forensic pathologist to do a proper autopsy. These deaths occurred fifteen years ago. He checked the dates. As he suspected, the forms had been filled out and sent into the VCAP six months after the bodies had been found. Amazing incompetence, but then he was aware he should be grateful these entries appeared at all, considering the murders took place in the back of beyond.

He pressed the Print key, made a hard copy to present to Christopher. Then, he checked the number of the police station in Debenture, Montana and dialed. Chances were he'd hit a blank wall. After all, he was calling about a fifteen-year-old case. He didn't expect to be able to contact anyone who had personal memory of the case, but maybe he'd get lucky and the full file itself still existed.

'Lawrence!' There was so much excitement in Cassandra's voice, that the clone hurried over to where she sat monitoring Minnie's readouts.

'Take a look at this!'

'Minnie's rate of aging has slowed.'

Cassandra nodded. 'Dramatically. She's almost back to a normal rate of aging.' She pumped her fist into the air in elation. 'The eicosanoid in your blood is the answer.' She closed her eyes for a moment as a wave of profound relief swept over her. 'Thank God.'

'Was God involved?' Lawrence seemed puzzled. 'I thought he was invisible.'

'It's just a saying, God had nothing to do with it,' Cassandra told him. 'We just needed to increase the dosage fifteen percent above the level in your body for the hyper-aging to be brought under control.

'I'll make the necessary calculations, then call Hutton back here so he can prepare a series of eicosanoid subdermal patches so we can slow your aging back to normal.' *And as soon as I see Gerry in an hour,* she thought, *that will be his last official act in this laboratory.*

'I got your message,' Christopher said as he came into the Case Room. He'd been in the M.E.'s cold room with Stick and D'Alassandro, confirming what he'd known in his heart: that the pineal glands of both the runaway and the squatter had been neatly excised. He flung his coat across the back of his chair. 'What have you come up with?'

'This should make up some for what happened in the park yesterday.' Esquival, grinning, slung over a copy of the printout. 'VCAP came up with four murders that fit the signature, all within the space of five days.'

Christopher scanned the pages. 'Sounds like our boy.'

'Right. They were all found with their left eye excised. Haven't gotten records so I can't say about the pineal gland, but my guess –'

'Missing.'

'Bingo.'

'Which means our boy's signature didn't change with the murder of William Cotton,' Christopher said, 'it merely reverted back to the original.'

'Right. So something must have triggered the reversion. It wasn't Cotton himself, we've followed that route to its dead end.'

'Then what?'

'Dunno,' Esquival admitted. 'But that's the good news. The bad news is these murders happened fifteen years ago.'

'I see. Some backwater dump called Debenture.'

'That's in Montana.'

'Montana?' Christopher was surprised. 'Not Oklahoma?' He was thinking of the house with seven pillars, as Lawrence had described it, afire on the Great Oklahoma Prairie. Had he been mistaken about its location?

'Try to find it on a map,' Esquival said. 'It's in Montana, all right, but you might mistake it for a flyspeck.'

'Interesting.' Christopher reflectively tapped the printout. 'These towns that sprang up overnight as the tracks were laid were named on the whims of the railroad barons of the time. This sounds like one.'

'It is. I checked. The railroad went through Debenture.'

'There's our railroad spike link. Good work. You call?'

'You betcha. Nobody at the sheriff's office knew squat, and the records are toast. Seems the office burned down about ten years ago and all the files went up the flue. But they gave me the name of the sheriff who was there at the time. Harold Wilcox is his name. Retired now, of course, but he's still alive. Off elk hunting, it's the season. He won't be back until tomorrow.'

'For starters, I want background dossiers on those four victims,' Christopher said.

'Let me go, Loo. It's the least you can do after chaining me to this 200-megahertz anchor for weeks.'

Christopher nodded. 'I had the same thought. I know these back-woodsmen. They respond well to rumpled types like you.'

'Thanks for the vote of confidence,' Esquival said. 'I think.' He tapped a pencil on his desk. 'You know, Loo, now that we have confirmation this guy's murdered in at least two states, regs say I have an obligation to notify my bosses in Washington. This perp's the FBI's meat.'

'You're sick to death of this case,' Christopher said. 'Make the call.'

Esquival broke the pencil in half. 'Yeah, right. No way the guys back in D.C. are going to take this case away from us.' He grinned. 'Besides, call me nuts but I've grown kinda used to you as my boss.'

Out of the corner of his eye Christopher noticed Jerry Lewis was just picking a package off the portable X-ray unit that checked for letter bombs.

'This just came for you by messenger.' Lewis handed over a plain padded brown envelope. 'It had no return address, so we screened it. It's clean.'

'Right, I want you to call Chief Brockaw's office and get Reuven a round-trip ticket to –' he turned to Esquival '– do you know the closest airport to Debenture?'

'Kalispell, Montana.'

'Right.' Christopher swiveled back to Lewis. 'Also a rental car, a four-wheel drive.'

'Oh, goody,' Esquival said, rubbing his hands together, 'I'm gonna get out my wool checked shirts, and my shitkicker boots.'

'You'd better. And to complete the picture, why don't you bang out a couple of Willie Nelson songs on the piano?' Christopher threw the printout back at Esquival. 'When you have your cozy one-on-one with Sheriff Wilcox I want him to think of you as just one of the boys.'

'Not with *your* accent,' Lewis said.

'Now, son, ya'll don't know shit from shineola,' Esquival drawled in a pretty fair western accent. 'I got lots o' tricks up ma sleeve.'

'What the hell's shineola?' Lewis asked.

'You got me,' Esquival shot back. 'Mebbe they use it to clean their six-shooters, pard.'

'Shine-ola was a Southern shoe polish,' Christopher said.

'Never heard of it,' Lewis and Esquival said together.

'It's ancient,' Christopher said. 'Like Moxie.'

'Moxie?' they chorused.

'Never mind.' While they were bantering back and forth, Christopher had been examining the package. The envelope was the kind that could be found in any good-sized stationery store or post office. Christopher's name and address was hand-written on the front. There was no return address, but a receipt from the messenger service was taped to one end.

Christopher slit open the envelope with a letter opener, shook out a standard video cassette. It had no label.

Christopher tore off the receipt and, handing it to Lewis, told him to run it down. 'Reuven,' he said quietly after the uniform had left, 'take a look at this.'

Christopher was staring at the cassette much the same way he would a wasp trying to make its nest in the eave of his house.

Using the letter opener, Esquival slid the envelope into a large plastic evidence bag, and tagged it with date, time and place. 'I'll have one of the uniforms take it directly to forensics.'

'Tell them, 'Christopher said, 'I want a read on the fingerprints an hour ago.'

'Righto,' Esquival said as he beckoned another uniform over and gave him his instructions.

Christopher got up. 'Let's you and I go into Oz.' Oz was Christopher's term for the team's media room. It included a large-screen TV, two VCRs, a computer scanner, sound screeners, wave-form oscillators for isolating sections of the audio and video spectra and other even more sophisticated paraphernalia, chosen, super-charged, tweaked and otherwise coddled by Kenny. Christopher's snitch from the No-Name.

The two men sat in the darkness and watched the video. Christopher's spine crawled with icy dread as he watched himself enter the basement of the east side building, draw out his gun, and then make his way to Guy's cubicle apartment.

'Jesus,' Esquival breathed.

Christopher watched his own intemperate actions with the squatter. A man was dead and a document existed showing him striking that man minutes before his death.

They had reached the end of the video, across which had been written: 'This could have gone to Brockaw, to Minelli in Internal Affairs, the Mayor, the local media, the Networks, CNN. The choices were many, but it was sent to you.'

'Mother of God,' Esquival whispered. 'This monster must have compiled an entire dossier on you.'

So the Pale Saint hadn't been lying, Christopher thought. A trickle of cold sweat ran down his spine. After the screen went blank for three seconds, another caption appeared: 'Like a Sherarat you find me an enigma. Other men might have hopes or illusions. The Sherarat knows that nothing better than physical existence is willingly permitted him by mankind in this world or another.'

Another three seconds of blank tape was followed by a third caption: 'His desert was made a spiritual ice-house, in which was preserved intact but unimproved for all ages a vision of the unity of God.'

And a fourth and final one: 'Victory can be purchased only by blood. In general habit it leans to the clear-sighted, though I think you will agree, Christopher, that fortune and superior intelligence can make a sad muddle of nature's "inexorable" law.'

'Loo, you can see how it would look if Brockaw, IAD or the news media got hold of this,' Esquival said.

'Sure. It would be incriminating as hell.' Christopher shook his head. 'But this tape was never intended for Brockaw or IAD or the news media. It was meant only for me.'

'I agree. He's showing you the extent of his power.'

'I wonder if that's all it is.' Christopher partially rewound the tape, then replayed the captions in slo-mo as he jotted them down in his notebook. When he was finished, he took the video and placed it in the locked bottom drawer of his desk.

By that time, Lewis had discovered that the cassette had been delivered by a local messenger service, one of hundreds in the New York area. They had been paid in cash but no one at the service could accurately recall by whom. Christopher told him to pick up the new sketches of the Pale Saint, then show them to everyone at the service who'd been on duty in the last twenty-four hour period.

'Here's what concerns me,' Christopher said to Esquival when they were alone. 'He used two names: Brockaw and Minelli. The Chief of Police's name is common knowledge, but how many citizens know that Joe Minelli is head of IAD?'

'None,' Esquival said, 'unless they're recently retired cops, and even then not many would have had any contact with IAD.'

'Yet the Pale Saint obviously knows who Minelli is. That means one of two things: he has access to someone inside the Department or he has access to the Department's computer.'

'Either possibility gives me the willies,' Esquival said. 'He's using our own files against us. How do we fight this perp?'

Christopher knew, as he'd known from the moment Cassandra had floated her insane idea: Lawrence was their only hope.

'There's something else about the captions that interests me,' Esquival said, breaking into Christopher's thoughts. 'The first one is written in one style, while the others in another.'

'It's T.E. Lawrence. I remember some of those lines.' Christopher cracked open *Seven Pillars of Wisdom*.

'Something else intriguing,' Esquival said, taking a look at Christopher's notes. 'He speaks about God.'

'According to Lawrence, it's impossible to talk about the Arabs without talking about God.'

'No, this is no coincidence, Loo.' Esquival tapped the paper. 'Notice how he's chosen a quote that juxtaposes a "spiritual ice-house" with the "unity of God." This desolate place he inhabits, this "spiritual ice-house" has "preserved intact" but has "unimproved" this ancient notion of God.'

Christopher looked up from the text. 'And your point would be?'

Esquival hunched forward. 'My suspicion is that this man grew up with a clearly defined image of God. And not a turn-the-other-cheek God, either. No, I believe this was a vengeful God, an all-powerful deity, fearsome, without compassion, a sword blade to punish.'

'That sounds suitably sick.'

'You bet. But this is no joke, Loo. You get imprinted with this notion and it stays with you for life, believe me.' Esquival's eyes searched Christopher's. 'Where did it come from, this twisted image of God? If we knew that, I tell you we'd have the key that would unlock all this sick bastard's secrets.'

TWELVE

It was late in the afternoon. Minnie was continuing to improve and Dillard, bleary-eyed but back at the lab, was priming the subdermal patches for Lawrence when Cassandra left for her meeting with Gerry Costas, which she had pushed back so she could continue to monitor the eicosanoid dosage in Minnie until the last possible moment. When at last she emerged from her high-tech lair, she was thankful to drink in some real air, the last of the watery sunlight, to decompress from the events of the last several days. Increasingly, now it seemed to her as if they were all getting sucked into Lawrence's hyper-aging, as if the events of years were being compressed cruelly into a matter of hours, days.

Shadows had grown long in the street like the beards of old soldiers too tough yet to die as she bundled herself in her overcoat. She hailed a cab and cranked down the window as it sped uptown until the West Indian driver said, 'Hey, lady, d'you mind, I'm freezing up here.'

'Sorry,' Cassandra said, rolling the window back up. But she put her nose to the crack she'd left open.

Gerry Costas was waiting for her when she got out. 'Hello, Cass. My office is a madhouse today. Let's go for a walk.'

'Gerry, I'm sorry these are so late.' She handed him a folder with the quarterly projections

'Par for the course.' Costas put the file under his arm without bothering to open it. He was a short, blond, stoop-shouldered man with the perpetual projected bonhomie that devolved like an inherited trait onto those in the upper crust of society. Though he had degrees in pharmacology and molecular biology he did not look like a scientist, which was all to the good, considering the kinds of people he dealt with. With his family and school contacts he was the one who'd gotten seed money in the early days from venture capitalists, sailing buddies, indolent multi-millionaire friends of his family, and who now cajoled the big contracts out of the government. 'You know, Cassandra, you'll pardon me for saying this, but you look like crap warmed over.' He would never use the word 'shit'.

'You would, too, if you were working twenty-two-hour days.'

'Just my point. It's only been a matter of weeks since Bobby's passing. I've tried to be flexible in allowing you to get back to work so quickly, but now that I see you, it's clear you need some time off. Take it. As much as you want.'

Cassandra shook her head. Most of her concentration was on her strategy for getting Gerry to fire Hutton. She was just waiting for the right moment to begin. 'In a couple of months, maybe, but right now I'm at a critical junction in –'

'You're missing the point,' Costas said. 'This isn't a request.'

Cassandra's attention snapped back like a rubber band. 'Okay, Gerry, what's going on?'

Costas sighed. 'That little TV debate you missed with Dean Koenig is coming back to haunt us.'

'I know. That demonstration –'

'That's merely a part of it. Please understand I'm not blaming you. For all we know the debate could have turned into a PR disaster for us. Koenig is famous for that kind of thing. The point is, he's out to get us and unless we lower your profile he just might succeed.'

Cassandra was so shocked she felt all the breath go out of her. 'Jesus, Gerry,' she said at last, 'you've got to be kidding.'

'Actually, no.'

She was horrified. 'Come on, you can't just knuckle under to him. The man's nothing more than an extortionist masquerading as a preacher.'

Costas nodded. 'You and I know that, but there are millions of people out there who trust him, believe in him, and most important to us right now, will do what he tells them. And what he's told them is to institute a call-in campaign demanding that I fire you.'

Cassandra was starting to feel slightly disoriented, as if she was back on the Tilt-a-Whirl Christopher had taken her on one summer. 'Gerry, I don't – This is stone cold crazy.'

'Call it what you want, but Koenig attacked us – and you specifically – on the first night of his nationwide TV show, and he's showing no signs of letting up.'

'Gerry, if you buckle under to Koenig now, you're making the biggest mistake of your life. D'you see why? The next time I or someone like me makes a breakthrough we'll be having this same discussion, and the next time and the next, until we both realize that he's stifled all real research at Vertex. Without R&D any biosciences company – not just Vertex – is dead in the water.'

Costas suddenly looked tired and worn. 'It isn't just Koenig; God knows that's bad enough. The show's become some kind of media event. All the news wires picked up his diatribe. Now I've got senators asking hard questions about your work. For the moment I've been able to stall them, but you know that can't last. There's so much innate suspicion regarding gene manipulation, we've been fighting an uphill battle from the first. This media blowup has given Ken Reinisch at Helix Technologies just the kind of ammunition he's been looking for. He's after my ass in a major way. I'm going to have to pull all the files, all the computer records in order to prove you're not overstepping our guidelines on gene replication. But when I do that I'm going to shoot myself in the foot because this Minnie the rat project you cooked up is going to scare the living daylights out of some people. Important people.' He thrust into her hands the latest issue of *Time*, open to 'The Nation' section. 'Even the Vice-President's wife has gotten into it, and let me tell you she's not exactly on our side. So now the media's involved, which means all the vultures are circling right above my head, ready to take a crap.'

'So . . .' Cassandra felt as if she had lost the ability to breathe. All thoughts of getting him to fire Hutton had flown out of her head. 'What are you going to do?'

'I have to be practical. This attack could not have come at a worse time. In three weeks I have to go before the Senate Subcommittee on Aging for a refunding review.' Costas looked down then back up into her face. 'My board has given me no option. Cassandra, I'm sorry. I'm going to announce your indefinite leave of absence effective immediately tomorrow evening.'

'Just in time to make the six o'clock news, right, Gerry?'

'Dillard will be taking over your duties.'

Cassandra tried to swallow and couldn't. She forced down a rising panic. The thought of Dillard taking charge of Lawrence was intolerable. 'Gerry, there's got to be another way.'

'If there was, I'd take it.'

'At least give me a week to finish things up.'

'Uh uh, we're not going to get into that kind of negotiation.'

'A couple of days, then. I'll use the secret lab exclusively, go in and out through the entrance no one knows about. You can make a big show out of cleaning out my desk in the main lab. Okay?' She took a step toward him. 'Gerry, say it's okay. At least you owe me that.'

Costas said softly: 'I owe you a lot, Cassandra. More than I can say.'

'Then let me have this grace period. Please.'

He sighed. 'Twenty-four hours, and that's stretching it. But if anyone asks, I said no. If you get caught you're on your own. I'll have no choice but to act against you, is that clear?'

'Perfectly.'

'We'll get through this, Cassandra. You'll be back. I promise.' But even the master salesman could not at this moment summon the requisite amount of enthusiasm.

As she was turning to hail a cab, he said, 'There's one more thing. I've decided to run a few VIP tours through the lab next week.'

Cassandra, appalled, said: 'Do you think that's wise, Gerry?'

'At this point, I don't have the luxury of asking that question. I've got to go proactive in refuting Koenig's poisonous allegations. The best defense now is to be as open as possible when I go on the offense. Circling the wagons will only arouse further suspicion. I'm already rounding up as many members of the senate sub-committee as I can; if I'm real lucky, maybe I'll even get the veep's wife.'

'Now I get it,' Cassandra said. 'Dillard's just like you, upper crust family, a golden background at Harvard and Walter Reed. Having him help you shmooze the invitees won't hurt a bit.'

Costas sighed. 'Welcome to the big leagues, Cassandra. If I don't play it their way, Vertex gets left in the dust. There are always a dozen companies breathing down my neck, trying to get the contracts I fight for.'

Cassandra was indignant. 'I'm the one out of a job, am I supposed to feel sorry for you? You're not the only one who busts his ass for Vertex.'

'I was hoping you wouldn't take this personally.'

'I don't think you've given me a choice.'

'Godammit, Cassandra, you're making this harder than it needs to be.'

'Really? I didn't think being cut off from your life's work could be anything but hard.'

'If you could only see this from my point of view.'

'You rotten sonuvabitch,' Cassandra said as she walked away.

One thing Emma D'Alassandro was not was paranoid. A boyfriend in med school had called her a pragmatic realist. Since they had been making love at the time, it had not been meant as a compliment; nevertheless, it was accurate. But what D'Alassandro lacked in imagination she more than made up for in determination. Born into a poor, blue-collar family, she'd worked like a dog for every scholarship she'd earned. Even with that, she'd graduated in debt to NYU.

Her fantasies were limited to PC-rated idylls with John Kennedy, Jr and Lt Worf from *Star Trek*. Even as a child, it seemed she never daydreamed. Now, however, she couldn't shake the feeling that she was being followed. She'd moved from a green but dull Yonkers to Manhattan when she was a teenager; more than enough time to get used to handling herself amid the rough and tumble crowds of the big city. In those days, she had worked nights at Baskin-Robbins to pay her way. From time to time now, because she was uncomfortable walking down certain streets at night, she carried a vial of pepper spray in her purse, and she wisely avoided Alphabet City on her daily early-morning jogs.

But she'd never felt this antsy.

Something was up, and she knew it. As she trotted down the steps of the CME's office into the autumnal twilight she felt as if a clammy hand was pressed against the back of her neck. The feeling became more focused as she was crossing First Ave. to grab a bagel and tuna salad for dinner. She had this totally creepy feeling that she was being watched. Maybe it came from being on this grisly case for so many months, or the fact that she'd been at work for nearly thirty-six hours straight. But deep in her bones she didn't think so.

Frightened, she stopped in the middle of the street, looking around as the light turned against her. Consequently, she was almost run down by a cab whose driver bawled at her in some unidentifiable language. Gaining the west sidewalk, she considered calling Christopher, then thought, *Would Reuven go running to him? Dammit, don't be a girl.* Her heart was racing, and she'd lost her appetite. She hesitated again, but her very next thought was: *Screw it, I'll take care of it myself.*

When she got home, she felt compelled to turn on every light before she could put the bagel on a plate. She looked out the gated window past the fire escape into the almost lightless airshaft. Then, rather manically, she set about putting her third-floor studio apartment in order. She hadn't felt such unsettling compulsions since she was a child, listening at night to her parents' fights. Rolling over in bed, she would turn on her Wizard of Oz lamp. Shivering in the light, she promised herself that as long as it shone on her she would be all right and her parents would stay together. When her bladder was near to bursting, she would run as fast as she could to the bathroom, her heart beating like a triphammer, until she was again within the comforting pool of lamplight. 'Now I lay me down to sleep,' she would recite to calm herself because she had dared for a moment to be out of the light. 'I pray the Lord my soul to keep . . .' As she whispered to herself, the voices echoed eerily up the stairwell from the kitchen where the late-night fights inevitably erupted, so that she could sometimes trick herself into believing they were part of a dream. She envied Lisa, her older sister, who invariably slept through the night without so much as a twitch.

Hours later, awake as ever, when the stillness of the very early morning was broken by a nesting mockingbird's disorienting string of calls, she would creep down the stairs and into the kitchen. She would find in stoneware mugs the dregs of cold coffee, on mismatched plates the crumbs of cake or pie crust dissolving in puddles of ice cream. And always there would be a shattered plate or dish, bowl or mug that one of them – she never discovered which – had hurled at the crest of the fight. She'd clear the table, washing, drying and putting away each piece in its proper place, not looking at the spot on the floor where the broken vessel lay. After she was finished, all that remained was to sweep the shards of crockery into the trash. Removing every vestige of the fight became a very deliberate ritual by which she meant to mend the shattered lives of her parents. If she was perfect, if she could keep the house perfect for them, she reasoned, then surely they would not leave.

Her parents never did split up – what would her father have done without her mother; what would her mother have done on her own? – but their unhappiness had always weighed on D'Alassandro in a way that Lisa could never understand.

She brewed some tea, listening to the street noise filtering in from East 14th St, then ate her bagel standing up. It might have been good, but perhaps not; she couldn't tell. She burned her tongue on the tea, which she threw into the sink in disgust. There was nothing in the cupboards that interested her except for a box of Mallomars, which she began to eat on her way into the living room-bedroom.

Her tabby, Rigatoni, woke up when she powered up her computer. Typical. It blinked at the screen a couple of times before jumping down off the sleeper-sofa where it had been curled into a black-and-white ball. Stretching luxuriously, it padded over to her.

'How ya doing, kid?'

It rubbed its arched back against her calf, then jumped into her lap, where it promptly went back to sleep. 'What a life,' D'Alassandro said. It purred in its sleep as she scratched its neck. 'One of these days I'd like to find somebody to do that to me.'

She went on-line, searching for sites that supported collectors, and especially collectors of antique railroad spikes. It was odd the kind of crap you unearthed when you went surfing the Web. It was like turning over a rock and finding all sorts of disgusting but fascinating insect and invertebrate life

As she surfed, she kept a steady stream of Mallomars popping into her mouth. All too soon they were gone. She was having a lousy dinner, but she didn't care. A little salad, a little pasta with some of her own homemade tomato sauce would have been good, but tonight she was too on edge to taste anything but Mallomars.

She jumped at the sound of the phone ringing, and Rigatoni leaped to the floor to avoid being dumped. It mewed plaintively at her as she reached for the phone.

'Hello?'

Silence.

Gripping the phone, D'Alassandro listened hard. The line was open; someone was on the other end. Despite a certain knowledge that a quick hang-up was her best option, she heard herself say, 'Who's there? I can hear you, you sonuvabitch.'

Nothing.

Rattled, she jammed the phone back into its cradle. She wrapped her arms around herself and stood in her living room while Rigatoni stared at her as if she were mad. But she wasn't, she knew that. Someone had been on the other end of the line; just as she was certain someone had been watching her as she came out of the M.E.'s office. The same person? She shivered, without really knowing why.

She abandoned the computer and switched on the TV. She searched out AMC, finding an old film in luminous black-and-white. Fred MacMurray and Ava Gardner in an exotic Far East setting. *Singapore*. Just the ticket, she thought. She settled back on the sofa, pulling a cotton throw over her feet and legs as she watched the beautiful lighting play across principals and sets alike, giving them a vibrant three-dimensional quality. Manipulating light and shadow like that was a lost art, she thought.

The phone rang again, making her heart pound painfully in her chest. She sat immobile as it rang and rang. At last, she lunged for the receiver. Listening as hard as she could to the open line, she thought she could hear someone breathing. She made a mental note to sign up for Caller ID as soon as possible.

'Em?'

She started when she heard Lisa's booming voice.

'Hey, Em, are you there or what? You okay?'

'Sure.' D'Alassandro had to clear her throat. 'Sure. I'm fine. I was just watching *Singapore* on AMC.'

It was good to hear her sister's throaty laugh. 'You and your old movies. I thought you'd be hard at work cracking that Pale Saint case.'

D'Alassandro glanced at her computer screen, saw she had unread e-mail. It must have just come in. 'I'm taking a well-deserved break, Lise. I've been up to my elbows in dead bodies all week.'

'Why d'you think I called? To speak to my celebrity sis and find out all the dirt they aren't printing in the magazines.'

'C'mon, Lise. You know I can't talk about the case.'

'I know, I know, but I like to brag to my friends that we've talked about it. Now I don't have to lie.'

D'Alassandro got off the sofa and sat back down at her computer.

'Speaking of dead bodies,' Lisa said in her ear, 'd'you have any marriage prospects?'

'Mom says Hi. She wonders when you're going to bring the girls and come see her.'

'Touché. But, you know, California's a long way away.'

'It's only as long as a plane ride,' D'Alassandro said.

'Don't get pissed, Sis. I can't help asking about you. I'm your older sister – happily married with two kids. I want the same for you.'

'Maybe I don't.' D'Alassandro accessed her e-mail. 'I'm married to my career.'

'Oh, come off it. Everyone needs a little love and security. Why don't you snuggle up against that hunky boss of yours?'

'Christopher? Oh, man, wouldn't I just love to. I've got a crush on him the size of Manhattan. Unfortunately, he's –' Her blood froze.

Tried to speak to you,' she read off her screen, *'but the words wouldn't come. Anyway, what would I say? Only this: "Some of the evil in my tale may have been inherent in our circumstances."'* It was unsigned, which meant the e-mail had come from someone with an unregistered Internet address hacking into the system.

'He's what?' Lisa said in her ear.

'Taken.' D'Alassandro recognized the last line as a quote from T.E. Lawrence's *Seven Pillars of Wisdom*, the Pale Saint's Bible.

'Em? You sound weird.'

'Listen, Lise, I gotta go.'

'Hey, not so fast. Is everything all right?'

'Sure, just busy right now.'

'I thought you were watching *Singapore*?'

'Was. Something's come up. I'll call you tomorrow.'

'Okay, but –'

D'Alassandro hung up. She went onto the Web, on her own expeditionary mission. Since the address was unregistered, it was also most likely untraceable, but D'Alassandro knew a few tricks even the hackers didn't know about. It took her thirty-seven minutes of determined backtracking to find out who had sent her the ominous e-mail. She had to go through several firewalls – anti-hacking security programs – to do so. The last one belonged to the NYPD.

'Esquival!' His name escaped her lips in a burst of emotion. 'That sonuvabitch rat bastard, I'll kill him. No, I'll have Christopher kill him.' Rigatoni, no doubt concerned by her anger, leapt onto her lap and began to rub against her stomach. D'Alassandro looked down and stroked the cat's back. After a moment, a small smile gathered at the corner of her mouth.

She got up and, speaking to Rigatoni as if the animal could understand, said: 'No, I won't kill him. I'll get even.' One by one, she began to turn out the lights until only the metal floor lamp behind the sofa was on. 'How about it,' she asked the cat, 'want to go over to Esquival's apartment and help me exact a little revenge?'

Rigatoni meowed, then gave a great yawn as D'Alassandro said, 'Nah, didn't think so.'

She dropped the cat onto the couch, where it curled up on the throw, watching Fred fly away from an anguished Ava as it slowly and methodically licked its forepaws.

'Don't worry, kid,' she told Rigatoni as she grabbed her coat and headed for the door, 'he comes back to her every time.'

She opened the door and stepped out into the hallway. The building owners were remodeling. With the floor tiles stripped down to bare concrete sounds echoed eerily. Light from the overheads bounced off the chrome yellow ceiling and, with nothing to absorb it, the color had taken on a kind of unpleasant life of its own.

Just as she was about to close and lock her door, the elevator opened with a clang. D'Alassandro turned to look. The door was open but no one came out. A lozenge of light emanated from it, passing over the floor, rolling up the opposite wall. She stood there, vibrating ever so slightly with the spurts of adrenaline released in her body. Her heart was pumping like an engine.

'Hello?' she called. Stupidly.

Nothing but an echo to answer her. She started. Had there been a flicker in that lozenge of light, as if someone had moved inside the elevator cab?

Hurriedly, then, she turned and double-locked her door. She took one step toward the elevator, and found herself digging in her handbag for the pepper spray. Feeling spooked and slightly foolish all at once, she pulled open the door to the stairwell and rushed down the first flight of stairs, mindful of the clatter her heels were making on the hard, concrete steps.

When Esquival decided to live in Manhattan for a while, he knew he wanted to live somewhere cool, but also somewhere away from the madding crowds of SoHo and TriBeCa. He wouldn't live on the Lower East Side or where D'Alassandro had her apartment, considering both unacceptable ghettos. He at length settled on an area so new it was known only as WOC, West of Chelsea. Chelsea ran down the west side of Manhattan in the 20s, more or less from 6th Ave. to 9th Ave. He had bought a loft in a huge building that had been a warehouse ever since it had been built sometime before World War II.

Now the building was being slowly converted to ultra-large apartments. The first floor housed a pair of art galleries, which had been the first retail shops to move from high-rent districts downtown. Now, restaurants and movie theaters were popping up weekly. Esquival figured it wouldn't be long before the first Barnes & Nobles, Bed, Bath & Beyond, Armani A/X and Gap superstores followed.

For the time being, however, it was still sufficiently unbuilt-up to appeal to him. When you were used to the wide open boulevards and greenery of Washington, a city designed on the European model, the vertical canyons of Manhattan could feel mighty confining.

Esquival, wanting to throw a good scare into D'Alassandro, had followed her all the way from the M.E.'s office earlier that evening. He was angry and frustrated at the slow progress they were making with the case; he needed an outlet, someone on whom he could let loose a little impish fun. D'Alassandro fit the bill to a tee.

Now, as she approached his own apartment building, he smiled knowingly. Sometimes, it paid to be a behavioral psychologist. By following her into her building, he'd wanted to goad her into just this reaction, and it looked as if he'd succeeded. Excellent. He'd give her a bit of a surprise when she got up to his apartment.

Esquival was chuckling to himself as he crossed West 25th St. A cab, running the red light, hurtled toward him and he jumped back, cursing under his breath. Where was a traffic cop when you needed one?

He turned his attention back to D'Alassandro a block ahead of him, and his breath caught in his throat. Someone, other than himself, was following her.

Hurrying on, Esquival could make out through nighttime shadows a man with broad shoulders and long, dark hair. D'Alassandro went into Esquival's building and the man followed her. As he opened the outer door, Esquival got a good look at his large, square hands, and he thought, *Jesus!* All thought of practical-joke playing evaporated.

As he broke into a run, he pulled out his cell phone and punched in Christopher's number. He'd reached the front door by the time Christopher answered.

'I'm at my apartment, Jon,' he said breathlessly. 'I think I've spotted our perp. He's just gone inside.' Christopher barked something in his ear. No doubt it was an order of some kind. He swung the door open and said: 'I'm going after him.' He broke the connection before Christopher could say something else he'd have to ignore.

He stands amid the shadows of the building's dark and cavernous interior, loose-limbed and barely breathing. He feels like a pressure the cool air of the unheated interior. He can smell sawdust and tar, oft-heated metal and oil, turpentine and latex paint, human sweat and the remnants of Big Macs and fries. He hears the sound of footfalls. Two pairs. And, in the darkness, he smiles.

The one thing he has learned, the single most telling secret he has pried from the protesting arms of the ground upon which he walks is how to set a soul to flight. The death of a victim is meaningless without the reward of ingesting its soul. The soul, he has learned, must first be wrenched free of the conscious mind. This is done simply and effectively by engendering in the victim a severe reversal of emotion; in other words – shock. Either extreme fright or extreme anger in the victim will do, because in those moments of reverse polarity, the soul is ripped from its moorings and, with a single plunge of his railroad spike, he can incorporate it into himself.

Listening to the direction in which the footfalls are headed, he begins to move. The journey toward another's soul must be made in circular fashion, it must be approached in an ever-tightening spiral until the moment of shock appears like a lightning bolt out of a black sky. Then the swift, sweet plunge to the core, the heat of life running through him like a starburst.

Now, in this time and place, the sacrifice will be made all the sweeter because it will be made before a witness. *Even I,* he thinks somewhat in the words of T.E. Lawrence, *the stranger, the godless fraud inspiring an alien nationality, feel a certain relief from the hatred and eternal questioning of self at the moment of another's dissolution. And yet, unlike Lawrence, there is no true delivery from my torment. The light that enters me is fleeting, gone in the space of several heartbeats, leaving behind what I cannot shed: the nothingness of death.*

In his circling, he has come upon the woman and the man. He knows them well from the dossiers he pulled off the police archives, and yet he knows them not at all. As he moves ever closer to the flesh and the blood, to the quickness of life, he begins to know them in an entirely different way, as if his heartbeat, his breathing are synchronized with theirs. He has entered their world, as only he can. He sees them, hears them, smells them. Soon he will reach out and touch his victim. And snatch in the blink of an eye an entire lifetime, like a god holding it in his hand.

Esquival felt like a fool. Even a rookie right out of the FBI Academy wouldn't have lost his subject in his own apartment building. The trouble was this ground-level space was as large as a cathedral. Or an amphitheater. Worse, it was changing daily. He saw walls and open doorways where none had been yesterday. They were even installing an escalator, he saw, for access up to a mezzanine that would eventually house a boutique photography gallery. He saw posters for its opening. The owners had used one of Ansel Adams's stark black-and-white renderings of a moonrise over the Rocky Mountains. The photo possessed extraordinary power, at once oddly familiar and alien. Even if you'd never been out west, you knew you'd inhabited this particular piece of it in a dream.

At that moment, Esquival caught sight of D'Alassandro. She was standing beside the freight elevator, which was the only one currently working. Some idiot film maker had blown out one of the walls of the passenger elevator trying to get a vintage Harley-Davidson up to his loft. The building scuttlebutt was that his girlfriend was into chrome in a big way.

Esquival stood indecisively as she looked nervously around. He knew this exercise in blowing off steam had now gotten way out of control.

Having lost his fix on the male suspect he was sure was the Pale Saint, the sensible thing was to simply go up to D'Alassandro and get her the hell out of here. He had no idea why the Pale Saint – if the suspect *was* in fact the perp – would target her, but he had no intention of wasting time trying to make a positive ID. He glanced at his watch: only minutes since he'd phoned Christopher. God knew how far Jon was from here, but that couldn't be his concern right now. D'Alassandro was in danger and he had to warn her.

As he stepped out of the shadows, his heels struck the floor, echoing through the lobby. D'Alassandro's head whipped around and what she saw was a man with a drawn gun running toward her. She started and whipped into the elevator.

'Emma, wait!' Esquival shouted. 'It's me, Reuven! You've got to –!'

He hit the closed elevator door with the heel of his hand. 'Dammit!'

As luck would have it, D'Alassandro heard him and recognized his voice. Her icy insides began to relax as she leaned forward to press the open door button, but it was too late. The elevator rose to seven – Esquival's floor. The door opened onto a grayish nothingness – the hall lights had yet to be installed. D'Alassandro made a little sound in the back of her throat as she repeatedly stabbed at the Lobby button to take her back down to where Esquival was waiting.

She was going to hit him, she decided on the way down. Not just an open-hand slap, but a real honest-to-god punch on the jaw. Maybe she'd even break it. She hoped so, because this time he'd gone too far. Maybe he already knew that, she reflected. The anxious note of his voice certainly didn't sound like his usual breezy tone. But no, even if he was repentant for scaring the bejeesus out of her, she was damned if she'd let him get away with this.

She balled her right hand into a fist as the door opened. She saw him standing right there, almost in her face, and she swung from her pelvis, putting all her weight behind it as she had been taught in her class in interpersonal violence. The punch connected with a satisfying jolt she felt all the way up her arm.

His head snapped back at the same instant she felt the sharp pain in her knuckles.

'Okay, shit.' She shook her hand. 'I know that was a helluva reaction, but you deserved –' Her little speech ended in a short, sharp shriek as she saw the face she'd assumed was Esquival's come at her. Despite the dark hair and full beard she recognized those cold eyes, that aquiline nose.

'Oh, my God!'

It was the Pale Saint.

Instinctively, she kicked out at his torso, her shoe sole striking him full in the sternum. At almost the same instant, she jammed the heel of her hand into the '7' button, and the doors began to close.

With only eight inches left between the closing doors, he slid one forearm through, trying to get the other in, too. The automatic safety system began to open the doors back up.

'No!' D'Alassandro shouted. Keeping her palm firmly on the 'Door Close' button, she bit as hard as she could into the meat of the Pale Saint's hand. Any normal human being would have withdrawn his arm in pain, but not this man. He just kept coming on, slamming his body against the doors as they began to open, only to have them thump shut again as soon as the rubber bumpers released his arm. The elevator cab shuddered and an alarm began to go off.

'Oh, shit, oh, shit, oh, shit.' D'Alassandro repeated this epithet like a mantra that would somehow save her from the terror that threatened to overwhelm her. She could hear his rhythmic exhalations, the scent of his breath, little puffs of chocolate and cloves coming to her from the gap that widened and contracted like an iris.

It was at that moment that she remembered the pepper spray. Cursing herself for a fool, she dug with both hands in her bag. The doors began to open and she stopped her frantic search to slam the 'Door Close' button again.

That's when he caught her lapel and jerked her against the inside of the door. The breath rushed out of her, and she felt his bloody fingers dragging her forward against the doors. She was dizzied and shaken and her hold on the elevator button slipped. The doors began to open all the way, and she felt herself being dragged bodily out of the elevator cab.

The cool metal of the slim canister butted up against the palm of her hand and, drawing it out of her handbag, she depressed the firing stud. The pepper spray came spurting out into the widening gap. She heard a deep grunt, the grip on her disappeared and, gasping, she slammed the 'Door Close' button.

This time, the doors slid shut and the elevator began to ascend.

D'Alassandro leaned, panting, against the door. Her limbs shook and she was sure that if she had to move she'd fall over. When the doors opened, however, she stepped out into the seventh floor hallway without difficulty.

It took a sustained effort to stop herself from hyperventilating. Wide-eyed and shivering she made her way through the gloom to Esquival's door.

Swallowing hard, she searched her handbag for a bobby pin. She dropped it twice as she was trying to get it into the lock. *Dammit*, she thought, *where the hell is Esquival?* She penetrated the lock at last and moved the round tip through the narrow gap between the tumblers. She twisted the bobby pin forty-five degrees to the right and the lock popped. With a tiny sob of relief, she turned the knob, opened the door and rushed inside, slamming the door and locking it behind her.

The loft's huge space loomed at her. Esquival had moved in, had the place painted a pale aqua, but that was about all. There was a large-screen TV with VCR near the foot of the platform bed. A ludicrously large sofa of some slick material seemed to occupy the space where the movers had arbitrarily left it. There was a matching chair, but it was some distance away, facing the high, arched windows that looked out at the trucks rumbling by on 12th Ave. No rugs, carpets, tables, bookcases, or lamps. Just a jumble of cardboard boxes stacked up in the kitchen area. The space smelled of new paint, varnish and unwashed clothes.

Under normal circumstances D'Alassandro would surely have had a few choice words for Esquival's lack of decorating skills. Right now, however, she could care less. Where the hell was the phone?

She saw it lying on top of the bed, and she sprinted for it. She tried to call 911, but she couldn't get a line. She turned the unit over and cursed. The batteries were dead; the idiot had left it off the base for too long. She began to hunt all over for another phone.

'Come on, Esquival,' she said to herself, 'you've *got* to have a normal phone somewhere.' But he didn't, not even in the bathroom. And logically why would he when he could take the cordless anywhere in the loft. If it had been working, that is.

She was cursing him out for being a typical male, not caring what went on in his own apartment when someone leaned on the doorbell. She froze, her heart pumping. It rang and rang without letup. She had now expended so much adrenaline she was becoming sleepy in between spurts of hyper-energy. Now, over the ringing, she heard a voice. Was it Esquival's?

'D'Alassandro, c'mon. Open up.'

She took a step toward the door, then another. It sounded like him. But why did he need her to open the door? Why didn't he use his key?

'Esquival?' she said.

'Yeah, Emma, c'mon. I can't get at my keys.'

What the hell did that mean? She was now only a step away from the front door. She put a hand out to touch it. 'Esquival, there was someone else in the lobby. I think it was the Pale Saint. Didn't you see him?'

'You could say that. Emma, for God's sake, open up. I'm bleeding.'

'What?' She put her shoulder against the door. She was emotionally spent. 'What happened?'

'He used one of those damn railroad spikes on me, that's what. Look, I'll tell you everything, just open the damn door and let me in.'

'How do I know it's really you?'

She could hear him sigh on the other side of the door. 'Use your head, would you? Look through the peephole. I assume you remember what I look like.'

D'Alassandro, feeling belittled as she always did by his sarcasm, put her eye to the peephole and saw his face distorted by the fisheye lens. She closed her eyes in relief.

'Okay?' she heard him say.

'Okay.' She snapped open the locks. 'Oh, man, am I glad to see you.'

Esquival stumbled in. As he had told her, he was covered in blood.

D'Alassandro's eyes opened wide and she choked back a scream. 'Reuven what happened?'

'*I* happened.'

As Esquival fell headlong into her arms, D'Alassandro caught a glimpse of the Pale Saint standing just behind him. Then the dead weight of Esquival's body bore her down to the wood floor, pinning her beneath him.

She watched breathless, her life in her mouth, as the Pale Saint entered the loft. His face was puffy and blotched from the pepper spray, but his eyes were oddly clear. He knelt down beside her. He moved with an unhurried grace that held her spellbound. It was odd how benign his smile was, like a benefactor in a candle-lit doorway beckoning you to come out of a stormy night.

The Pale Saint bent over her. He was holding Esquival's service pistol. She trembled as his calloused hand passed over her face like a cloud across the sun. He pressed the muzzle into the center of her forehead and his finger tightened on the trigger.

Now I lay me down to sleep, D'Alassandro recited to herself. *I pray the Lord my soul to keep* . . . Her eyelids flickered as she stared into his eyes.

Abruptly, he pulled the gun away and, shoving the muzzle into his mouth, pulled the trigger. The sound of the hammer slamming seemed to reverberate in her ears like a thunderclap. He laughed, then, perhaps at her expression, and hurled the empty weapon across the room.

His fingers grasped Esquival's hair and lifted the head off D'Alassandro's neck. She gasped. Esquival was still alive. His eyes grew wide and clear as he focused on her.

'Em,' he mumbled, 'sorry about . . . everything.'

Then the Pale Saint spoke to her. 'Watch,' he said. But it was enough.

She could not tear her gaze away as he produced the railway spike and, as swiftly and expertly as a surgeon, inserted the tip into Esquival's left eye. Nothing came from Esquival's mouth, but the frenzied rolling of his right eye spoke to her more profoundly than words ever could.

She felt the bile rising in her throat as she watched the Pale Saint wield his spike, pushing it in, turning it forty-five degrees to the right just as she had done with the bobby pin to unlock Esquival's door.

Now he was withdrawing the spike. It glistened in the half-light, and D'Alassandro saw to her horror that on its tip rested a small, acorn-shaped organ.

Esquival's pineal had been extracted from the living body.

Slowly, lovingly, before her tortured gaze, the Pale Saint lifted the tiny organ upward. Then, he tilted his head toward the pale aqua ceiling, opened wide his mouth, and tilted the spike. In dropped the pineal.

He began to chew, slowly, methodically, languorously, and with a brief inarticulate moan D'Alassandro passed out.

Cassandra returned to the lab in a frenzy. The very first thing she did was to disable the video apparatus linked to the birth chamber. Then she gathered up all the cassettes – the entire record of their work with Lawrence – and incinerated them. Her heart felt heavy, as if part of herself were curling and melting in the acrid flames, but better that than the logs falling into the wrong hands. She shuddered at the thought of what Costas might do to Lawrence should he become aware of the experiment prematurely.

She looked briefly through the glass into the birth chamber, saw Lawrence's form wrapped in bedclothes, asleep in his bed. She glanced around the lab. It felt somehow dead, as if it were already buried beneath a ton of sand. She was numb, as if she were crawling around at the bottom of the sea where it was dark and cold. She went over to Minnie's cage and took her out. The rat ran onto her shoulder and curled up there, her tail draped down like a lock of hair. It was at this moment that Cassandra understood that the lab was no longer hers.

She picked up the half-filled test tube. Ever since Minnie's trans-gene expression, she had been checking Lawrence's blood twice a day for signs of the same problem. As of this morning he was okay. She put the test tube back in its rack. It would take her about ten minutes to thoroughly analyze the blood, and right now she didn't have the time. She had to get Lawrence out of there immediately.

'Hutton?' she called, but there was no answer.

Good, she thought. *He must be off in the bathroom.* She went about trying to find the eicosanoid subdermal patches Dillard had been making for Lawrence. She took out a plastic carry-case into which she would place the subdermal patches. But first she needed to line it with packs of dry-ice. She went out of the lab and down the hall into the small kitchen where she had had installed an ice machine and a second refrigerator she used for storage of blood and DNA samples and the clear plastic dry-ice packets. She turned on the lights as she went.

He was sitting on the kitchen floor facing her. His well-polished loafers were the color of ox blood. He did not blink when she turned on the overhead fluorescent light. His left eye stared blindly at her.

Cassandra gave a little cry, and she steadied herself against the wall so that she would not pass out. Then, she turned and ran back into the lab.

Christopher took the call from Cassandra as he was kneeling over the ritually disfigured body of Reuven Esquival. He felt sick in the pit of his stomach. He knew he had failed Reuven, but he didn't know how. The paramedics had already removed D'Alassandro to the ER of St

Vincent's Hospital, where he would go just as soon as the coroner's team arrived.

Jerry Lewis had snatched his cell phone from his overcoat pocket as soon as it began to ring. Christopher heard him speaking softly into it for a minute or so. Then he approached Christopher and said, softly, 'Loo, I think you'd better take this. It's Mrs Austin.'

Blindly, Christopher took the phone. He did not want to look away from Reuven's corpse, as if this was some form of punishment he must endure for failing to protect him and D'Alassandro from the insidious evil of the Pale Saint.

'Jon,' he heard her voice in his ear, 'Jon, something terrible has happened.' *Here, too*, he thought.

'What is it, Cass?' he said in a dead voice.

She was so distraught she did not hear the difference in his tone. 'Hutton's been murdered. There's no blood, but his left eye had been removed. You can guess the rest.'

'Oh, Christ.'

'It's a funny thing. He's got two fresh facial bruises, right where you'd expect punches to land if he had been in a fistfight.'

'Cass, are you okay?'

'Wait,' she said, not hearing him. 'There's more. Lawrence is gone. He deliberately made up the bed to make it appear as if he was asleep in it.'

'I showed him how to do that a week ago, when we were sneaking out of the lab. Was there any sign of a struggle in the birth chamber?'

'No. Nor anywhere else. Except for the bruises on Hutton's face.'

He thought a moment. 'Did you call Sara?'

'That was the first call I made. She swears she hasn't seen him. I believe her, Jon. She sounded frightened out of her wits.'

'Okay. Get out of there, Cass. Now. When the cops come the last thing we need is for you to be around. Now do as I say. I want you with Sara. Lawrence may want to come and get her.'

'He'd never hurt her.'

'You don't know that and neither do I. I'll meet you as soon as I can. Until then, keep an eye on Sara and don't let anyone in.'

'Jon –'

'Cass, I have to go. I have one helluva crisis here.'

'Jon, did he do it?' Her voice was trembling. 'Has the connection between Lawrence and the Pale Saint become so strong that he could actually commit murder?'

'Thirty seconds ago, I'd have said no. But now I don't know, Cass. I wish I did.' He stared down at Reuven's body and his heart sank. *I've got to get the M.E. to give me an accurate time of death for Dillard*, he thought. *Even the Pale Saint couldn't be two places at once.*

'Loo.' It was Jerry Lewis, shaking him. 'Loo, the forensic team is here.'

Christopher shrugged off his hand, refusing for the moment to leave Reuven's side. What was it Cass had said about Lawrence at the ballfield? *Too soon. When he finally meets the Pale Saint he'll surely die.* She could have been talking about Reuven.

The hole in Reuven's face seemed like a tunnel, sucking Christopher down into a whirlpool of sorrow and madness. The world was shrinking, distilled down to its purest essences. Good and evil; now nothing in between could exist. It was the world of the Pale Saint's making, the world in which Christopher now belonged – he and Lawrence and Cassandra. They were all players in the Pale Saint's play, marionettes dancing to his perverse tune.

All at once, into his head, popped the quote from T.E. Lawrence Sara had read to him: '*Our aim was to seek the enemy's weakest material link and bear only on that till time made their whole length fail.*' Sara had told him that T.E. Lawrence knew that the Arabs' resolute will was stronger than the Turks', that he knew in the end he could break them.

This is what he had been trying to see, what had been in front of him all along.

Taking in the totality of the carnage the Pale Saint had wreaked on him, Christopher could see the master plan. He had set out to bear on Christopher's weakest link until it broke. He'd murdered Bobby, then had methodically gone after Christopher's team. Reuven dead and D'Alassandro was down. What was next?

Lawrence.

Lawrence had disappeared. Either he'd murdered Dillard or he knew who had. But if he hadn't done it, why had he run? Christopher, on the verge of tears for the first time since Andy's death, felt as if he was hemorrhaging inside. His heart was torn to shreds. No sooner had the clone wormed his way through Christopher's defenses, his true nature was exposed. *It's my fault*, Christopher thought bitterly. *I taught him the con, and like a master he turned around and used it on me. He gained my trust, just as he needed to do. And then he did what his genes dictated he must.*

There was no point denying it. The clone had risen to his true calling. *God help us all,* Christopher thought. Lawrence was now another Pale Saint, at large in a city of ten million people.

Book Three

WAR

October 22 – October 24

The moment of change
is the only poem.
ADRIENNE RICH

THIRTEEN

He was sitting in precisely the position Cassandra had described, legs splayed out, hands in his lap as if he'd just dropped where he'd been standing. He was nattily dressed in a tweed jacket and worsted trousers, a white shirt and striped school tie. Hutton Dillard's right eye, already filming over, stared accusingly at Christopher.

When Christopher knelt down, the shadows shifted and he saw in a smear of dried blood a welt on Dillard's forehead, more blood on the ridge of one cheekbone. Both were swollen and livid. The cavity where his left eye had been was a tunnel straight to his pineal.

'He's just as I left him,' Cassandra said, coming up behind Christopher. The light from the fluorescent fixture seemed harsh and over-bright.

He stood to face her. 'I thought I told you to go home.'

'I couldn't.' She had her arms wrapped around her middle, as if she were deathly cold. 'I need to know what's happened here.'

'What about Sara?'

'I called her. She knows the seriousness of the situation. She's at a friend's for the night. Someone Lawrence doesn't know about.'

Christopher saw there was no use arguing with her. She was here now and they'd have to make the best of it. Squatting, he snapped on surgical gloves and got to work.

'You're right,' he said. 'He was struck at least twice with a great deal of force.'

'This isn't the Pale Saint's signature.'

He glanced at her. 'You're getting all too familiar with forensic terminology.' Then he returned to his scrutiny of Dillard's fingernails. 'He must have been hit very quickly with a great deal of force. There's nothing under his nails, no bits of skin or hair or anything to show he put up a fight.'

'So he must have known his assailant.'

Christopher dropped Dillard's hand. 'Not necessarily.' He turned the corpse's head to one side. 'Look here. He was struck a blow from behind.'

'Lawrence could have done that.'

'Cass, if I didn't know better I'd think you were making a case for Lawrence having killed Dillard.'

'Don't you think so? I mean, they despised each other. Dillard's dead and Lawrence is gone. What other conclusion –'

'Wait a minute. Aren't you the one who's been defending him all along? What's gotten into you?'

Her cool eyes looked haunted. 'Dear God, I never should have attempted this. You were right and I was wrong. Now he's become another Pale Saint and it can only end in disaster.'

Christopher got up, stripped off his gloves and led her out of the tiny kitchen which had become as cold as a mortuary. He took her in his arms. 'You should have gone home when I told you to.'

'So I could sit there and do nothing but stew in my own fear?' She shook her head. 'You know me better than that.' Her eyes searched his. 'Jon, I'm really and truly scared. What if Lawrence did kill Hutton –'

'What if he didn't?'

'But you're seeing the same evidence I am.'

'Yes, but what if the evidence is tainted? What if we're meant to believe Lawrence is guilty.'

'Why?'

'To turn us away from him. Look, Cass. You're already beginning to doubt him and so am I. But let's consider another angle. From day one, nothing in this case has been the way it at first seemed. We work like dogs to come to a conclusion based on the evidence only to find that conclusion is wrong or false. It's happened over and over again, and what I keep coming back to is the idea that we're being systematically fed evidence. This man – this Pale Saint – loves to manipulate us, he gets some kind of special kick watching us chase our own tails.'

'But how does Lawrence figure into this?'

'It doesn't make sense until you think of this as war. War means us versus them: whoever isn't on our side is the enemy. The Pale Saint wants Lawrence on his side. Esquival said this man is utterly alone, cut off from the rest of humanity. Now he comes face to face with himself – another creature identical to him. What does he think? He says to himself, I'm no longer alone in the world. Here is someone I can share *everything* with.' He turned her around. 'See, Cass, he tried to subvert Lawrence at Central Park, tried to get him to leave us and go with him, even told Lawrence we didn't care about him.'

'Did Lawrence believe him?'

Christopher took a breath. 'Well, now, that's the billion-dollar question, isn't it? Did Lawrence become another Pale Saint and kill Dillard? Or did something else happen here, something we don't yet know about that frightened Lawrence so much he felt compelled to run?'

Cass gripped him. 'Jon, do you really think –?'

'To be truthful, I don't know what to think,' Christopher told her. 'But, like you said, there's more to life than just DNA.'

'Jon, we've got to find out the truth. Where do we start?'

'Let's check the video log.' He strode down the hall. 'There'll be a record of how Lawrence left the chamber.'

'No, there won't,' she said as she followed him into the lab. 'Right after my meeting with Gerry I disabled the video log and burned all the tapes.'

'You did *what*?' He whirled on her. 'Cass, are you nuts?'

Abruptly exhausted, she sat on a stool and rested her arms on the zinc-topped counter. 'See, the thing of it is, Jon, I'm through here.'

'Without Lawrence we all are.'

She lifted her head. 'No, I mean here at Vertex. I didn't get a chance to tell you about my meeting with Costas. I went to see him about firing Hutton and he more or less canned me.'

'What?'

'He was going to put Hutton in charge of the lab here.'

'That makes even less sense than dismissing you.'

'Not from his point of view. Hutton had the academic and social credentials to shmooze the VIPs Costas needs to gather as allies.' She shook her head. 'All this is Dean Koenig's doing. Koenig's put so much pressure on Vertex, the board ordered Gerry to kick me out. Gerry says it's just temporary, but I don't believe him. The handwriting's on the wall for me at Vertex. My guess is even with Hutton dead Gerry won't be able to ask me back, assuming he wants to.'

Christopher held her. 'Cass, I'm so sorry. This is a helluva payback for everything you've done for them. Vertex wasn't only a job for you; it's been your life.'

'The big picture's even bleaker,' she said wearily. 'Right now Koenig holds all the power. With Gerry backpedaling so furiously who's left to stand up to Koenig and the others like him?' She looked at him. 'Don't you see, Jon? We were on the brink here of a bold new world, a leap forward so monumental it was sure to be analyzed for decades to come. Now look what's happened. Fundamentalism is about to throw science back into the Dark Ages where raw emotion and naked fear rule the day.'

Christopher took her hand, urged her gently off the stool. 'Do you have something – anything – to keep yourself busy for the next half-hour or so?'

Cassandra looked around and nodded. 'I never got a chance to test Lawrence's latest blood sample.'

'Okay,' he said. 'Work on that while I have a look around inside the chamber. Okay?' When she nodded without apparent enthusiasm, he gave her a squeeze and a kiss. 'Keep the faith, baby.'

'Jesus,' she said, shaking her head, 'you're going to have to get a set of gold neck chains if you keep talking like that.'

But he'd lightened her mood, at least temporarily. He watched her busy herself with her blood tests, then he went into the birth chamber. He went through everything: drawers filled with clothes Sara had picked out for Lawrence, shelves crammed with the toys of his childhood, the hobbies of his adolescence; the massive selection of his crayons and paints, all without finding anything. From another shelf he drew out the pile of Lawrence's drawings. Most of them he'd seen many times before – the jagged lines of the Rocky Mountains, the stepped green triangles of fir trees marching like an army across hillsides and valleys. It was interesting to see how these crude but powerful drawings of Lawrence's childhood had quickly gathered the richness of color, perspective, detail as Lawrence matured and grew skilled. There was no doubt he had talent as an artist.

A couple of the drawings in this latter category Christopher had never seen before. One was a portrait of Cassandra. It was in odd shades: blues and greens. No one could accuse Lawrence of being a realist. Nevertheless, he had caught a quality in Cassandra that Christopher instantly recognized and appreciated. There was also a pencil sketch of Sara in her baseball cap. Though it was much less finished than the portrait of Cassandra, it too, captured the subject's essential nature. The third was a sketch of a dark-red brick building. It was intricately, almost obsessively detailed. Christopher counted nine narrow steps on the stoop. Dark ironwork and patinaed bronze made up the handrails, the gridwork of an old-fashioned fire escape hung above a dark-blue awning. The doorway was arched with three carved stone faces peering down. On either side were stained stone columns. Set into the brick facade were a pair of bas-relief stone hunters in Roman dress, their long hair androgynously flowing down to their shoulders so that one of them could have been Diana, the goddess of the hunt. On the stoop, two people were playing catch. A crescent moon and many stars filled the sky. It seemed like the kind of drawing any kid would make, especially one who might long for a friend of the same age to play ball with. Then something curious caught Christopher's eye. In the lower left-hand corner, as if it were the artist's signature, were two numbers: a ten in black and, superimposed over it in red, a four. Christopher wondered what on earth that could mean.

Putting aside the drawings for the moment, he turned next to the stack of Lawrence's books. Picking up the top two, the ones Lawrence had been reading last, he discovered the Bible and Shakespeare's *Richard III*. An interesting combo, Christopher thought, since both deal mainly with divine justice. The play fell open to a scene in Act V. The Duke of Norfolk, King Richard's ally, had just been given a note that his master, Dickon, had turned traitor. Lawrence had underlined Richard's reply: 'A thing devised by the enemy. Go, gentlemen, every man unto his charge. Let not our babbling dreams affright our souls, Conscience is but a word that cowards use, devised at first to keep the strong in awe; Our strong arms be our conscience, swords our law! March on, join bravely, let us to it pell-mell, If not to heaven, then hand in hand to hell.'

Christopher struggled to remember the core of the play. Didn't Richard murder his brother in order to become king? Conscienceless, he killed everyone, in fact, who stood in his way. And he was able to do anything: woo women, gain allies, if only out of fear, realign the political landscape, conquer continents, in fact. He tried to remake the world in his image, and succeeded, too, if Christopher remembered right, but only for one solitary day. Through it all, he was alone, always alone. He was so very alive, a character whose lack of conscience made him fairly leap off the stage. But it was this poisonous aspect of his personality that made him inhuman.

A thing devised by the enemy. Christopher read the line over and over, hoping against hope that this was a message from Lawrence not to believe the evidence at hand.

Through the thick glass, he heard Cassandra calling him. He found her at her flatscreen. 'Look, it's happened.' Her voice was trembling. 'Jon, we've got to find Lawrence right away. His trans-gene has expressed itself in the same way Minnie the rat's did, except his levels are far higher. His hyper-aging is out of control; it's burning him up from the inside out. Unless I can implant the first of the eicosanoid transdermal patches Dillard and I prepared within forty-eight hours, he'll die.'

When Christopher saw D'Alassandro open her eyes he put Rigatoni on her stomach and said, 'Welcome back. Someone's been asking for you.'

'Boss,' she said dreamily, 'what're you doing in my bed?' Then full consciousness and, with it, memory, flooded through her. Gasping, she bolted up.

'Easy, Emma,' Christopher said, holding her as Rigatoni meowed in alarm.

'Esquival?'

'Reuven is dead.' Christopher waited as she gathered the cat into her arms and hugged him to her breast.

'So it wasn't a nightmare.' Tears formed in her eyes. As they spilled over, she said, 'Oh, no you don't,' and wiped them angrily away.

'Emma, what happened up there in Reuven's loft? Are you too –?'

She shook her head. 'No. I want –' She drew her legs up. 'I need to talk about it.' She looked around her apartment. 'What time is it?'

'Around midnight. I got you released from the hospital; I didn't think you'd want to wake up there. Are you hungry?'

She closed her eyes, shook her head, and shuddered. She told him what happened in precise, almost clinical detail: how she had felt she was being followed when she'd left the CME's office, the ominous phone call and threatening e-mail at home, her discovery that the e-mail was another of Esquival's twisted pranks, the eerie figure in her hallway, and her decision to give back to Esquival some of what he'd given her. Then she came to the terrifying encounter with the Pale Saint in Esquival's building lobby, how he'd almost got to her in the elevator, her subsequent flight up to Esquival's apartment, and Esquival's appearance at the front door. 'The Pale Saint was on top of me,' she said, nearing the end. 'His face was all puffy where the pepper spray had got him. He . . . Oh, God, he extracted Reuven's pineal and ate it while I watched.' Tears began to drop off her cheeks. 'I blame myself. I should've called you as soon as I got to my apartment. I tried at Reuven's loft, but he hadn't . . . The damn cordless was dead. It was ludicrous;

I was completely at the mercy of modern technology! I couldn't . . . I mean, there was nothing . . .'

'It's okay now.' Christopher put his arm around her. 'Reuven was idiot enough to keep playing with your head. Goddamn his warped sense of humor.' He got up and paced around D'Alassandro's sleeper-sofa. 'I got there too late. I –'

'No, you didn't. You saved me.'

Christopher turned to face her. 'When I got there he was already gone, Emma.'

She thought about this, worrying her lower lip. 'Why did he do it? Why did he murder Reuven and leave me alone?'

'But he didn't leave you alone. He killed Reuven in front of you. Mutilated him, cannibalized him, and made you watch it all.'

A slight tremor went through D'Alassandro and she ruffled the fur at the nape of Rigatoni's neck.

'Emma, I'm going to ask something of you.'

Her head snapped up. 'Anything, Boss.'

'I want to make sure you're up to it.'

'I'm not going to let him get to me, if that's what you're worried about.'

He smiled. 'You don't have to be so macho for me.'

'Right now, I need to be macho for *me*.' Her eyes held steady. 'You tell me what needs to be done and I'll do it.'

He nodded and sat back down on the bed. Rigatoni started to play with the cuff of his overcoat. 'I need you to take a trip. Right before he was killed Reuven pulled some vital information off the VCAP. Seems our perp was hard at work in a deadstop nowheresville named Debenture, Montana. Fifteen years ago he murdered four men in the span of a week. The records were destroyed in a fire, so I want you to fly out there and interview the sheriff who caught the cases, get as much detail as you can on the four victims.'

He scratched the cat's belly. 'The sheriff's name is Harold Wilcox. He's retired now and probably crusty as sin. These people don't much like phones or faxes, and they never heard of e-mail; they respond best to the personal touch. Besides, they seem to have an innate hostility toward big city honchos mucking up their patch of territory. I want Wilcox helpful, not suspicious. Just bat your eyes at him, but when you do make sure you're wearing jeans, a checked shirt and cowboy boots.'

She gave a brief laugh. Rigatoni, sensing that her emotional balance was on the mend, corkscrewed the top of his head against her palm.

'When d'you want me to go?'

He held out an oblong packet. 'Today at 10.35 too soon?'

She took it from him. 'The sooner the better, right?'

He nodded. 'Besides the ticket, there's a rental car voucher, a local map and directions on how to get to Wilcox's place. Don't bother packing much. You'll fly into Kalispell. There are a number of Western outfitters on Main Street.'

She grinned. 'I always wanted to be a cowgirl – until I saw just how big a horse really is.' She tapped the packet meditatively against the back of her hand and a cloud passed across her face. 'This trip's important, isn't it? I mean after all the effort I've put in I'd hate to be out of the action when you catch this perp.'

'It seems to me now that the key to catching the Pale Saint lies in his past.'

'What about *Seven Pillars of Wisdom*?'

'That book,' Christopher said, 'may be the blueprint for his war, as he would have us believe. But the T.E. Lawrence angle might be a diversion, nothing more than classic misdirection. He seems to revel in that.'

'Does this guy really have an objective?'

'Reuven believed he did, and I agree. Intuition tells me anything Sheriff Wilcox can give us is going to be important.' Christopher wasn't lying, but he wasn't telling her the whole truth, either. The fact was he wanted her out of harm's way. He was going to make damn sure that what happened to Esquival didn't happen to her.

D'Alassandro sighed and sat back against the pillows. 'Where are the remains?'

'At my request, Stick is doing the autopsy now. Reuven has an older brother in Oregon, and a twin sister back in Bethesda with his mother. Once Stick is finished, we'll fly the remains back to D.C.'

'God, I can't believe it, I knew next to nothing about him, and now he's gone. He could be a royal pain in the ass, but I'll miss him.'

'Reuven and I had been through a lot together,' Christopher said as he rose. 'I thought he'd always be there. Stupid, I guess.'

'No, it wasn't stupid at all.'

Christopher stroked Rigatoni's sleek back. 'Did you know that Reuven was a terrific piano player?'

'No.'

He smiled in remembrance. 'He loved honky-tonk, rag time . . . he was asked to sit in with Woody Allen's band one Monday night last spring, but he said he was too busy with the case.' He shook his head. 'The truth was he was flat-out terrified to perform.'

'Esquival? He was such a ham.'

'In the privacy of our own little family, but beyond . . . You never know with people. John Lennon was so scared of performing he'd throw up before going on stage.' Christopher smiled sadly. 'Man, could Reuven play the hell out of a piano.'

'You'll give me the addresses of his family. I want to write to them. Something personal.'

'They'll appreciate that.'

D'Alassandro gave him one of her clear, direct looks. 'Boss, are you okay?'

'Sure.' He knew what to say, what all good commanders must say when subordinates asked that question. But he also recognized that right here, right now, this woman needed something more from him than the standard stiff-upper-lip speech. 'Listen, Emma, there are times in every long investigation when it seems as if there's an evil cloud hanging over it, when it seems as if nothing's going right. But I'll tell you from experience in its own way it's a good sign.'

'It is?'

'Yeah.' He smiled. 'It means from now on we can only go one way.' He pointed to the ceiling. 'I've got another job for you. While you're on the road I'm going to give you Reuven's personal log-in codes to VCAP. On my advice he narrowed his search to the Rocky Mountains States. That's how he honed in on Debenture. But now I want you to check out Oklahoma.'

'What am I looking for?'

'I wish I knew,' Christopher said. 'Concentrate your search on rural areas surrounding small towns of under, oh, fifty-thousand population. Forget cities and metro areas altogether. Pull up anything unusual in the time frame of fifteen to twenty years ago.'

'I assume we're talking homicides here.'

Christopher thought a moment. 'Not necessarily. Like I said, anything unusual. But be on the lookout for residential fires. Specifically, a house with seven pillars. Also, go on-line. See if you can access local Oklahoma media archives using the same area and time criteria.'

'You got it, Boss.'

He got up. 'Before I leave, d'you still have the e-mail Reuven sent?'

'Sure.'

He took Rigatoni from her and she got up gingerly, padded over to the computer, booted it up. She went into her Internet software and accessed her most recent e-mail. 'There,' she said, moving back so Christopher could take a look.

'You sure Esquival sent this?' he asked. 'It doesn't sound like him.'

'That would be the point, wouldn't it? He wanted me to think it came from the Pale Saint.'

Christopher looked at her. 'What if it did?'

'What? Impossible. I went through a couple of pro-type firewalls to find that it was sent by someone inside the NYPD. Esquival.'

Christopher shook his head. 'Think a minute, Emma. You got through these firewalls, so could someone else.' He took a breath. 'All the detailed info the Pale Saint has on us could only come from one source: the Department computer bank.' He had no intention of telling her about the videotape which revealed the perp's inside knowledge of NYPD personnel. 'Either he's got an accomplice inside the Department –'

'Which, given his profile as an extreme loner, I would tend to doubt.'

Christopher nodded. 'I agree. Which leaves us with the other possibility. he's an expert computer hacker.'

D'Alassandro turned back to the computer terminal. 'Let's see just how expert he is.'

As her fingers flew over the keyboard, as the screens kept changing, Christopher said, 'Can you trace him back, find out where he is?'

'From a folder called Cookies that's in all computer software, any webmaster – that is, anyone who has a website – can not only tell how many "hits" a site has had each day – how many people have logged on – but also who has logged on. There.' She looked up at him and smiled. 'Someone *has* hacked onto the Departmental server. Whoever it was downloaded files.'

'That answers one question,' Christopher said. 'Can you tell which files he opened?'

'Even Bill Gates couldn't do that. But I can tell you his web name: Faith.'

The Pale Saint returns to his apartment alone thinking of Lawrence: his clone, his image, stamped out in a lab like so many of Mama's ginger cookies. His cheeks are still somewhat raw and swollen from the pepper spray D'Alassandro shot at him, but the pain is nothing more to him than an old friend he has lived with all his life. For him, pain has become a kind of pleasure because above all other things it has the power to lift him, at least temporarily, out of the abyss, the nowhere he inhabits.

But now maybe there is something else that possesses this same power. The thought that he is no longer alone in the universe fills him with a curious kind of frenzy. Not the kind of frenzy thoughts of Mama make him feel; not the kind of frenzy memories of the trunk at the foot of his parents' bed make him feel. No; this is something else entirely. The terrible black void inside him seemed to lurch and shift when he saw his twin standing there beside the lake in Central Park, just like it had at the beginning. Rage, fear, love, pity – all these emotions seething through him at once, making him change his strategy once again, just like the change he was forced to make when Dean Koenig took to the Evangelical Nations Network airwaves.

Speaking of which, the TV screen flickers with the image of the dangerous snake-oil salesman Dean Koenig. Today, in a repeat of last night's show, Koenig is turning the beautiful Book of Ecclesiastes into a rant that is typical of his kind.

'"Then I returned and saw vanity under the sun,"' Koenig quotes. '"There is one that is alone, and he hath not a second; yea, he hath neither son nor brother; yet is there no end of all his labor, neither are his eyes satisfied with riches. For whom then, saith he, do I labor, and deprive my soul of good? For this is vanity; yea, it is a sore travail."' He looks into the camera lens, directly at the Pale Saint. He has a tick on the upper lid of his left eye. It flickers ever so slightly as he rampages on. Tick-tock, tick-tock, an odd little out-of-kilter metronome, the wings of a dragonfly beating against a pane of poorly-made glass as Mama pinions it there. 'And the unspeakable vanity we confront tonight, my dear friends, is the unforgivable sin of man usurping that which belongs solely to God. The affront to God! The manipulation of human genes, the *creation* of human life should not, cannot, *will* not be carried out by Cassandra Austin, Gerry Costas and the immoral, unprincipled Vertex Institute. Not while I have a breath of life in my body; not while I can reach out to you, my dear friends – as I do tonight – for your help, your prayers, your unending support to maintain the glory of God's work. Please, my dear friends, be generous. I beg you, join me. Join God by contributing anything you can for our cause. Call our toll-free number now – 1–800-FAITH-4-U – and God will bless you for your good work on His behalf.'

The Pale Saint is no longer looking at Dean Koenig; he's looking *through* him to a universe only he can see. In it, Mama presses the body of the dragonfly against the windowpane, the upper lid of her left eye fluttering ever so slightly. It only does this when she speaks of God, when she explicates examples of his divine power. Proof positive of His existence, proof positive of the immorality of the world's many sinners, proof positive that any individual can be saved.

Today, Mama is using the dragonfly as an example. 'This is how God's hand manifests itself to us,' she says with that terrible, implacable conviction that turns his blood to ice. 'This is how easily God can make us, hold us, protect us from the evil all around us.'

He can see the freckles standing out starkly across the bridge of her nose. When she is home she never wears makeup, doesn't believe in it, she says, it's an implement of the harlot, she says. Yet when she is stretched across the desolate Oklahoman night, her mouth spewing endless exhortations, her lips are red, her eyelids are black, and there is not a single freckle to be seen.

'Sonny,' Mama says, 'let me tell you, the Devil, he can be a powerful presence; he can be mighty persuasive when he's a mind t'be, but I taught you to pray, to be an upright an' Godfearin' Christian. I told you how to recognize the Devil in sinful thoughts. I thought I taught you how to drive out the Devil if he made an appearance, but maybe I was wrong.' She peers at him as if he were a dog who had just wet her best carpet. 'Am I wrong, sonny? Because if I am I have just the remedy.' Mama's eyes look like chips of ice you hack from the back of the freezer, opaque and dark as the pelt of a wolf, ice that has been there since maybe the first day that old refrigerator replaced the wood and iron ice box.

'So assuming he *has* been 'round, puttin' nasty ideas in your head, this is what's going to happen to you. You see this big ol' insect that came 'round here after the rains? This's called a devil's darning needle. You know how it comes by that name? It flies at night to the beds of children like you, sonny, who harbor wicked thoughts, and do you know what it does, this devil's darning needle? It sews your lips together, that's what.'

She takes her finger away from the insect's thorax so that it spirals to the floor. 'This is how easily God can abandon us should we fall into sin and become unrepentant.'

Mama turns away from the stricken dragonfly, her eyelid twitching in an almost hypnogogic rhythm. She strikes a wooden match. The flame is repeated in her eyes, building heat. She quotes from the Book of Genesis using that special voice she has that makes it impossible not to listen: '"And he looked toward Sodom and Gomorrah, and toward all the land of the plain, and beheld, and lo, the smoke of the country went up as the smoke of a furnace."'

Turning back, she drops the flaming match onto the dragonfly's wings so that they curl and crisp until nothing remains but a curiously pungent coil of smoke, passing the pane of glass like a ghost.

FOURTEEN

The dark blue awning seems rough and shabby as Lawrence approaches the dark-red brick building. In white Old English lettering, the words: Jack the Ripper Pub are printed on the awning. Lawrence, feeling the familiar invisible hand clutch his throat, pauses while a gust of wind rattles litter along the gutter. A taxi cruises by, followed by two young men holding hands. Lawrence watches them as they turn the corner onto 10th St.

He has been drawn here as inexorably as a fallen leaf is whirled downstream. Ever since he passed this spot on his first night out with Christopher, when he was struck dumb with cold terror he knew that for him there could be no option, no other course: he had to return.

He closes his eyes, remembering a conversation he had yesterday with his mother, before the terrible thing in the lab:

'I think there are powers beyond your control here,' Cassandra had said. 'You were born . . . I created you from another man's DNA. The man is evil, he is powerful, and he is astonishingly clever. Worse, he comes to you in your dreams and in visions as a skeleton, and exerts some kind of base influence, insinuating his dreams, his memories, his desires into you. I'm afraid he's changing you, making you more like himself.'

'How can he?' Lawrence had said. 'You made sure I *am* him. You made me for a purpose. *Your* purpose. But sometimes I ask myself, what is it *I* want. Did it ever occur to you that I would want things for myself?'

'Of course, it −' Cassandra had stopped, as if abruptly changing her mind. She put a hand against his cheek. 'After you were born,' she said softly, 'when I held you in my arms, then it occurred to me that what I was cradling was an independent life. What could I – what could anyone – know of your potential – or of the imperatives lying dormant in your DNA?'

'So in that regard I am not so much different than you or Dad or Sara or any other human being.'

'But you are different,' Cassandra had said. 'So very different.' She sighed and ran her hand through his hair as she had done a week ago when he had been just a child. 'I made you – I gave you as much of the Pale Saint as I could. Inside you have his tendencies, yes. But it's also possible, we believe, for you to turn out *different* than he did. Jon and I are hoping that you will become your own person.'

'But you've raised me, Dad's trained me for one thing: tracking down the Skeleton.'

'That's true enough. Maybe we didn't give enough thought to your rights. That was morally wrong of us. But we've done the best we could.' She shook her head. 'You're a complete enigma, you see. When you were born, you were an empty well into which Jon and I poured sweet water. We filled you up. At least, that was our wish. But you're the first of your kind; we don't know the consequences of using another human being's fully developed DNA. How much of the Skeleton is really inside you? How much will emerge, and when? And what will it do to you if it does? These are questions none of us can answer.'

'Not even me?'

She gave him a weak smile. 'Right now, no. Not even you.'

Lawrence, looking up at the two stone hunters flanking the building's entrance, begins to climb the steep steps. Through the panes of glass set into the wooden doors he can see the darkness waiting for him like the open mouth of the Leviathan that swallowed Jonah. Truly now he is about to go into the belly of the Beast.

It is nothing to him to pick the lock on the inside door; Christopher has taught him well. The smells of curry and coriander hang in the air like veils through which he passes, silent as a wraith. He looks neither to the left nor the right as he ascends the staircase to the fourth and top floor. When he comes to the door at the far end of the hallway it opens before he has a chance to pick the lock.

'So you've come,' the Pale Saint says.

For long minutes, Lawrence stands looking into his own eyes, in his own face. 'It's done,' he says at last. 'Dillard's dead.'

'I know.'

'Now I have nowhere else to go.'

There is no emotion in the Pale Saint's face as he steps aside for Lawrence to enter. Somewhere in the building a TV is on, somewhere else a stereo is playing David Bowie.

'I am what they made me.'

The Pale Saint inclines his head ever so slightly. 'As am I.'

'I hate what I am. I hate that my life goes by so quickly.' He lifts his hands, open palms upward. 'I hate that they have left me nothing.'

'"In his life he had air and winds, sun and light, open spaces and a great emptiness,"' the Pale Saint says, quoting T.E. Lawrence. '"There was no human effort, no fecundity in Nature: just the heaven above and the unspotted earth beneath. There unconsciously he came near God."' He nods sagely. 'It is as inevitable as death. He who has spent his entire life in the desert of emptiness is inevitably thrust upon God as the only refuge and rhythm of being.'

As Lawrence steps over the threshold, the Pale Saint enfolds him in his arms.

'These bizarre rituals have to stop,' Stick said. 'Most assuredly they do.'

'Tell me something I don't know,' Christopher replied.

The CME was sipping a cup of Lapsong Souchong tea. He brewed the stuff so strong just a quarter cup would set Christopher's heart racing as if he'd sprinted 300 meters. 'The nature of them is changing, you see.' Stick moved around the bodies of Reuven Esquival and Hutton Dillard lying side by side in the underground cold room. Both had the long T-shaped incisions across their chests and down their abdomens typical of autopsies.

Stick set his teacup down. It was made of a delicate china so thin it was almost translucent. The vines and blooms of climbing roses wound around its circumference. 'Let me speak plainly, Jon. In the case of Bobby Austin there was an almost languid nature to the ritual. I believe I told you then that it took Austin some time to die.'

'That's right,' Christopher said. 'You did.'

'Neither William Cotton nor the young Jane Doe died right away.' He pointed. 'However, with these two, there is a marked and disturbing evolution. In the nature of the incisions, in the manner in which the pineal glands were extracted we can see a difference. There is a quickening, a certain rough determination that was not present in the previous victim.'

'Like a hunger or a craving?'

Stick gave him a little smile. 'It might be best to consult a criminal psychologist for that.' He glanced down at Esquival's corpse. 'I'm sorry, Jon. Considering the recent demise of your resident psych, that was thoughtless of me.' He raised his teacup. 'But if I had to make a guess, his ingestion of human organs notwithstanding, I'd say this man is not driven by a pathological hunger, at least in the sense you mean.' He drained his black tea. 'I think he is simply much nearer his ultimate goal, whatever that might be.'

'What about the times of deaths,' Christopher asked. 'Could the same man have committed both murders?'

'Hard to say.' Stick frowned. 'Times of death are difficult to pinpoint. That is to say, if it's a matter of a day or so, no problem. I can tell you that pretty much right off the bat. But if we're talking hours here, there's always a margin of error. Every human being is different.' He looked at Christopher. 'We all take a different amount of time to die.'

'So, bottom line?'

'Given what you've told me about the proximity of the two crime scenes, I'd have to say that, yes, it's possible that the same individual could have murdered both these men. But that's only an educated guess.'

'The signatures?'

'Ah, there I can be more precise. Save for the three contusions to Dr Dillard's skull, the signatures are identical.'

Christopher bent over the bodies. 'You're sure.'

'Quite sure.' Stick led Christopher over to a desk, where he took up a lined yellow pad and a pencil and began to sketch. 'Here's the human brain. In both cases, the incision took precisely the same route – puncturing the eyeball, proceeding through the orbital socket, through the *Thalamus opticus*, this oval here, to the back of the *corpus callosum*, which is this kind of long thing that more or less wraps around the top of the *Thalamus opticus*.' He smiled. 'Can you make heads or tails out of this? I'm no artist and reducing three dimensions to two is often confusing. That's why I've superimposed one over the other, to show where they intersect at the pineal.'

'Wait a minute.' Christopher's fingers stabbed out, circling the area where Stick had drawn the two parts of the brain one on top of the other. 'Did you say intersect?'

'Yes, but of course that was just a figure of speech to show you where – Jon?'

'Sorry,' Christopher said, racing to the door. 'I just remembered I have an appointment with an old friend.'

The dark-red brick building stood on the short block of 4th St just west of Sixth Ave., the block where, in one of the many illogical quirks typical of old Greenwich Village streets, West 4th St intersected West 10th St.

Christopher and Cassandra stood at the intersection. Christopher was holding the drawing Lawrence had made of the building. 'There was something about this drawing I couldn't get out of my mind,' he said. 'It was that blue awning.'

'For the Jack the Ripper Pub.'

'Right. He and I passed by here when I first took him out. I wanted him to be around kids his age. Now that I'm here again, I remember he had an odd reaction on this block. He said he felt as if he was suffocating.'

Christopher pointed to the lower left-hand corner of the drawing. 'And then there was this strange kind of signature on the drawing, this four superimposed over a ten. But see, it's a representation of the building's location, where 4th and 10th Sts intersect. This drawing's a kind of map he left for us.'

'But what's so special about this building?' Cassandra asked. 'Why did he come here?'

'Don't you see?' Christopher said, folding the drawing away. 'Lawrence has led us right to the Pale Saint's apartment.'

She gripped his arm. 'Jon. Call for backup now.' When Christopher made no move, she said: 'Jesus, you're not thinking of going in there alone, are you?'

'I had a ton of backup in the east side tenement basement, for all the good it did me.' He shook his head. 'Besides, if Lawrence is inside the last thing either of us needs is to have to explain his presence to the outside world.'

'Jon, it's too dangerous. It's –'

But Christopher was already running along the pavement, up the steps, pushing through the brownstone's outer door. The inner door was unlocked. In the square-tiled vestibule, he paused, waiting for his eyes to grow accustomed to the dimness. He could hear a dog barking, but it wasn't coming from behind him on the street; like most of these old buildings the rear gave out onto a series of vest-pocket back yards. He withdrew his gun.

On his right was a steep wooden staircase to the upper floors. If he were a fugitive hiding out here he'd want ready access should someone unwanted come in the front way. For that reason ground-floor apartments were too vulnerable, and those on the middle floors useless since their only egress was the staircase. That left the top floor apartments and their ready access to the roof.

Christopher went silently up the staircase. In this old building the landings were so narrow each one had an arched niche carved into the wall so that a coffin could make the turn as it was carried down after the old-time wake in the deceased's apartment. When Christopher reached the second-floor landing, he turned, aware that someone had followed him. A shadow crept up the stairs from the ground floor and he tensed.

'Cass.' He lowered the gun when he recognized her. 'Are you nuts? Get out of here. I don't want to have to worry about you and Lawrence.'

'Too late, I'm already in,' she said.

Christopher took a step toward her.

'You'll have to drag me out bodily, I promise you.'

'I could do that,' he said.

'I know.'

He searched her eyes as the realization dawned on him that the longer he knew her the less he knew about her. At last he let out a breath. 'Stay behind me, okay?'

'You're the boss.'

That got a tight-lipped smile out of him, anyway.

One behind the other, they gained the third floor, then the fourth. Each floor, Christopher had noted, had five apartments: two on either side of the hallway, one at the rear. He motioned to Cassandra to stay where she was, then he crept down the hallway toward the door at the far end. This was the obvious apartment for the Pale Saint to have rented: it would have quick and easy egress via a window to the back yard. In fact, glancing up, he could see a square soiled patch of painted plaster. Reaching up, he could just touch the ceiling. He felt carefully around the edge until he came upon a short length of grimy rope. Pulling down opened the access panel and a short, folding set of stairs.

Climbing up, he was gone from Cassandra's sight for several minutes. When he returned, she realized she had been holding her breath.

'Leads to the roof,' he whispered as he returned to where she was standing. 'This place gets better and better as a crib.' He gripped her hard. 'If he's here, he's inside the apartment so for God's sake stay put.'

He went back down the hall and crouched down, pressed himself against the wall so he wasn't directly in front of the door to the far apartment. Then he took out two slender picks. He was sweating by the time he heard the three tiny clicks, one right after the other. *Three blind mice*, he thought. *See how they run.*

He withdrew the picks, stood up, and gripped the door handle. He gave Cassandra one last glance, then, in one smooth motion, he turned the doorknob, shoved the door open, and disappeared inside.

Cassandra stood rooted at the other end of the hallway. But when she heard no sound, could discern no movement at all, she crept down the hall. Just inside the open doorway she saw Christopher standing. His gun was in its holster so she knew he'd searched the one-room apartment and found it empty. She was relieved and terrified all at once. Where was Lawrence?

As she moved she could see that Christopher had a peculiar look on his face. When she was growing up, she had discovered *The Aeneid* by Virgil. She had read and re-read the legend of Aeneas, from whom the ancient Romans believed they were descended. She had often wondered what expression Aeneas had when he was ferried across the mist-shrouded River Styx into sulphurous Hades, the land of the dead. Seeing Christopher's face now, she thought she knew.

'The place *stinks*,' Christopher said.

'Like under the ground.' She gave an involuntary gasp because she saw where Christopher was looking: a wall filled with Polaroids of all the dead people he had come to know more intimately than if they had been friends.

'My God,' Cassandra said in a hoarse whisper, 'so many people, so many *lives*.'

The air was choked with the mass of their stilled voices.

Christopher thought it odd the way the Pale Saint had grouped the victims. All the young girls inhabited one section, as if they were in a harem. The longer Christopher looked at the wall of photos the more it seemed to take on a life of its own, as if it were a piece of ornate, horrific architecture constructed of the flesh and bones of these victims, painted in their blood, adorned with their living hearts. It was a temple of evil, throbbing with its own dark pulse. 'No wonder it stinks in here. He's surrounded himself with death.'

Staring at this monstrous wall, Christopher could hear the Pale Saint's whispered words, as if he was trying to drown out the voices of those he'd already killed. Most disturbing of all, perhaps, was his allusion to

Bobby having a hidden agenda for becoming an assistant D.A. Was it just another of his clever lies, sowed to make Christopher's resolve falter?

'Cass, there's something I need to ask you. It's about Bobby.'

'What about him?'

Christopher took a breath before plunging onward. 'Did he ever give you any idea why he became a lawyer?'

She looked at him curiously. 'What d'you mean? You know as well as anybody he had this thing about the law and justice.'

'Right, but now I think about it he never actually told me where this *thing* came from.'

Cassandra shrugged. 'It's obvious it originated with his father. I mean, growing up with that sour old man would have had a major effect on any kid, let alone someone like Bobby.'

'What if it had nothing to do with the old man,' he said. 'What if something in Bobby's past made him so guilty he felt compelled to make amends.'

Cassandra shook her head. 'For once stop being a detective. He's dead. Let him rest. I couldn't bear to deconstruct him.'

Whatever Bobby's secret was – if there *was* a secret – it was clear she didn't know. Christopher turned his attention to a bookcase filled with dog-eared textbooks on anatomy, neurology, psychology, pathology, scholarly volumes on comparative religion, acupuncture, metaphysics and unexplained phenomena. Running his finger along their spines, he said: 'Reuven was only part right about him. He's very well educated, but I don't think he ever attended college, let alone grad school.'

Hershey's chocolate bars were stacked on a table beside the thin mattress.

'Look, Jon.' Cassandra picked one up. 'This is where Lawrence picked up his addiction to Hershey's.'

Their eyes met with the unspoken question: what else did the clone and his original share?

On a shelf otherwise bare Christopher saw the record collection. 'Hey, this guy's a Bob Dylan fanatic. He's got a complete set of albums, all on LPs, not CDs.'

'Maybe that's why he chose to live here,' Cassandra said. 'What album was "Positively 4th Street" on?'

'It wasn't on a regular album, just the *Greatest Hits* compilation,' he said. 'It was originally released in 1965 as a single.'

'No wonder you and Sara get along so well.'

He was busy searching the place for ID, anything that would tell him the Pale Saint's real name. It seemed impossible, but there was nothing. How did a human being exist in this day and age without a Social Security card, a driver's license, even a stolen credit card? Maybe he had all of that with him, but when Christopher had picked him up in Tompkins Square Park he'd had no ID on him whatsoever. Maybe he had evolved a way of life that was mobile and totally unencumbered. Except there were artifacts here that were clearly of a very personal nature.

Christopher was staring out the window at the plane tree. It was huge and scabrous in that way only Manhattan trees get from being pissed on so many times. He opened the window, stuck his head out and looked up. He had no doubt the tree would bear a man's weight up to the level where it over-arched the roof. Back inside, he noticed Cassandra staring at the thin mattress in one corner.

'How could anyone be comfortable on that?' she said. 'It's like sleeping in a barn.'

'Exactly,' Christopher said, coming over. 'I think that's just what he was used to before he came east.'

In the kitchenette, Christopher saw a line of clay jars where in most homes the herbs and spices might be kept. They had been painted black, and had obviously been hand-thrown. He opened one at random and pulled his nose away as quickly as he could. It and the others appeared to be the source of the smell.

'Cass,' he said, 'I want you to tell me what's in these jars. If you don't know, take samples.'

As she moved past him, he went to the desk and turned on the lamp. That's when he saw the dossiers on him, Esquival, D'Alassandro, and Bobby. All were dated at the top of the first page as to when they'd been illegally extracted from the NYPD computer records. *This clinches it*, he thought. *Now I know what he was looking for when he hacked into the Departmental server*. He carefully put back all the files.

Christopher began looking for the computer the Pale Saint had used to hack into the NYPD server, but there was none in the apartment. Maybe he had a notebook computer, but that would mean he'd have to carry it with him. Too risky. Then Christopher thought of all the missing ID. What if he had a stash somewhere else?

A thick stack of newspaper and magazine clippings – all on the Pale Saint – lay atop a TV-VCR. While leafing through them, Christopher noticed that there was a tape inside the VCR. He turned on the TV, hit the 'Play' button, and like the devil up popped the face of Dean

Koenig. The camera pulled back to a long shot of Koenig sitting like a spider in the center of that fake-homey set with its fake porch and fake pillars and golden light streaming through the fake windows behind him. The Pale Saint had taped the televangelist's late night show. Next to the TV were three other video tapes. Fast-forwarding through them, Christopher saw all of them were of Dean Koenig's show.

Now Christopher thought of what Reuven had said about the Pale Saint: *'My suspicion is that this man grew up with a clearly defined image of God. And not a turn-the-other-cheek God, either. No, I believe this was a vengeful God, an all-powerful deity, fearsome, without compassion, a sword blade to punish.'* Just like the God Koenig so gleefully invoked, Christopher thought. *'Where did it come from, this twisted image of God?'* Reuven had wondered. *'If we knew that, I tell you we'd have the key that would unlock all this sick bastard's secrets.'*

Turning off the TV, Christopher thought about his recent conversations with Lawrence about the nature of God. *Was the Pale Saint's notion of God imprinting itself on Lawrence?* he wondered. It was a frightening thought.

He returned to the narrow mattress. At the foot of it was a neatly folded blanket. It was woven in the tribal patterns of the American Plains Indians. Christopher, who had caught several cases involving American Indians, searched his brain.

'This is Shawnee,' he said to Cassandra.

'What would he be doing with an American Indian blanket?' Cassandra asked.

'Good question. Anyway, it's old. Maybe twenty years.'

There was a stain on one corner of the blanket, dark brown like blood. Christopher turned it over and saw that someone had printed a word in the wool in indelible ink: 'Faith.' The same word the Pale Saint had chosen as his on-line moniker.

'Jon,' Cassandra called, 'you'd better take a look at this.'

Christopher went back into the kitchenette. She had all the jars open, with little bits of their contents spread out on the tiny Formica counter.

Cassandra used the end of a paring knife to stir the dark piles of powder. 'My botany's pretty good. I can identify hemlock, blue toadflax and what appears to be senega snakeroot. That last stuff can be made into either an ecstatic drug or a rather nasty poison, depending on the concentration.'

'Why does he have all these things?'

'See this mortar and pestle? He makes a brew – a kind of tea; what has come to be known as a phyto-cocktail – that enhances his shamanistic powers. I went to a lecture on shamanistic herbal lore some years ago. A shaman needs to make a connection with his higher self. Only then can he resurrect the dead, help the sick and dying or bring messages back from those who have passed beyond the pale.'

'Odd. I've had some experience with mass murderers who felt they could do the same thing. They wanted nothing more than to have others join them in the kind of death-world they were inhabiting.' Christopher looked at her curiously. 'Didn't think you'd put much store in it, though.'

Cassandra shrugged. 'You're half-right. Because I'm a scientist I've been trained to look skeptically on paranormal activity. But privately, I know science doesn't have all the answers, and part of me believes it never will. You only need to look at Lawrence. You don't have to be a rocket scientist to figure out what my research colleagues would make of his psychic connection with the Pale Saint.' She pushed her fingertip through the powders. 'I do believe, though, that these natural substances can enhance his abilities.'

'Then take them,' Christopher said. 'I want to keep them out of his hands.'

Cassandra nodded. 'There's something else.' She picked up a small bottle of blue colored glass. It looked old, hand-made. It had been shattered and carefully – perhaps even lovingly – glued back together again. Cassandra pulled the stopper out the wide neck and up-ended it.

'What the hell is that?' Christopher asked as something rolled out. It was roughly the size and shape of a large marble.

'A human eyeball,' Cassandra said. 'It's the mate to this one.' She spilled out the other one.

'These must be the eyes he extracted from William Cotton or the runaway girl he murdered.'

'Impossible, Jon. Those people were killed recently. These two eyeballs – they came from the same person, incidentally – have been preserved. They're years old – perhaps a decade or more.'

'They must have some special significance for him to have kept them so long,' Christopher said.

'I agree.' She handed over the glass jar. 'It's the only one that's marked.'

A small slip of paper had been taped to the side. On it, in a felt-tip pen had been written one word: 'Faith.'

'Faith,' Christopher said thoughtfully. He went and got the Shawnee blanket, folded back the corner so Cassandra could see what had been written there. 'Faith.' The handwriting was the same. He looked at Cassandra. 'What do you think, a prayer or a name?'

'Two things about these eyes, Jon. They come from a female and she was young when she died, perhaps only in her teens.'

'Someone close to the Pale Saint,' Christopher said. 'So close he's kept a part of her with him for decades.'

'Jon, you have this strange look on your face,' Cassandra said as she put the eyeballs back in the jar. 'What are you thinking?'

'D'you remember what Lawrence made of the baseball Sara had given her?'

'Hollowing it out so he could put the desiccated mouse inside it?' she shuddered. 'How could I forget?'

'I think this is more or less the same thing.' He took the jar from her. 'The vessel is precious, too. Look at the care with which it's been repaired.' He ran his finger across the cracked glass as if its scars could speak to him of its history. 'Lawrence told me that the Pale Saint had a sister. So now I'm thinking that once upon a time the Pale Saint had a sister named Faith.' He turned the jar back and forth so it caught the light. 'And here's what's left of her: not merely her eyes, but in his mind her soul.'

The apartment. Positively *not* 4th Street. Not anymore. Piercing the newly-drawn darkness, the Pale Saint can see like fireflies stamped against inky foliage the images of Christopher's men in hiding, waiting in a cordon of military precision around the place where he used to live.

Singing the first few bars of 'All Along the Watchtower', he sees these things and more. That Christopher would find the apartment was a given. That he had done it so soon was another matter entirely.

The first thing the Pale Saint had done after he had embraced the clone in his apartment was to pat him down for weapons. The second thing he had done was to share a bar of Hershey's chocolate with him. These two acts were emblematic of the ambivalence he felt toward Lawrence. He might love him as he once loved his sister, Faith, but he could also despise him like Cain hated Abel.

'Why else would they have gone to the trouble to make you if not to track me down and find me?' he had said.

'I can't think of another reason,' Lawrence had answered truthfully. 'Nevertheless, I'm here and Christopher isn't.'

'That's because Christopher doesn't know what to think of you now that Dillard is dead. Have you become as dangerous as I am? he is asking himself right about now. Dillard has been murdered and the kid is gone. Gone where? Gone native?' He licked his lips as if in anticipation. 'Y'see, junior, it's unanswerable questions like these that bring confusion into a clear mind, that bring all thought to a standstill, that knock all strategy into a cocked hat.'

While he thinks these thoughts, the Pale Saint continues to sing softly. Once again, he has reinvented himself wholesale. He has shaved his head, as well as discarded his long, ropy mustache and goatee in favor of a real 'soul patch', a triangle of hair in the hollow just beneath his lower lip. He wears clothes bought in a gay boutique on Christopher St; three gold rings sprout from the edge of one ear. Gone is the rugged outdoors man swagger. In its stead are soft, vaguely effeminate mannerisms that blend in perfectly with his Village surroundings.

Lawrence waits until the Pale Saint is finished. Then, polite as ever, he says: 'What was that song you were singing?'

'You mean Christopher didn't introduce you to Bob Dylan?' The Pale Saint clucks his tongue against the roof of his mouth. 'Ba-a-ad daddy.' He proceeds to sing the song in its entirety in a soft, reedy voice.

The two men are hunkered down shoulder to shoulder in the evening on the tarred roof of a building fronting on Bleeker St. Take away the Pale Saint's clever surface alterations and they might as well have an umbilical cord linking them for all the difference there is between them. Lawrence, with his trans-gene in revolt, is nearing thirty-three, the Pale Saint's age.

'They think I can't see them,' the Pale Saint says, elbows on kneecaps, 'crawling like vermin all over the block.'

'Where? I don't see anyone.'

The Pale Saint oxygenates, drawing air in through his nostrils, letting it out through his mouth. 'You will. In time.'

'I doubt it,' Lawrence says with a sigh of resignation. 'It doesn't appear as if I have much time left.'

'Now that you mention it, junior, you're not looking so hot. What's up with you?'

'I believe I'm burning myself up from the inside. Something to do with how I was made in the lab.'

'Fucked by science, eh? Well, no surprise there. The march of civilization is most toxic; it poisons everything it touches.' The Pale Saint digs in his pocket. 'But there's an antidote to everything. Even death.'

254

He produces a tiny glass bottle with an eyedropper as a stopper. 'Maybe I can do something about that nasty fire inside you.'

Lawrence eyes the bottle. 'What is that?'

'Horn of rhino, eye of newt, gizzard of Komodo dragon.' The Pale Saint chuckles. 'Don't look so worried, I made it myself from all natural ingredients. This, my boy, is a cocktail for the Millennium.' He unscrews the stopper, squeezes the rubber top so the viscous fluid is drawn up into the eyedropper. 'Hold out your tongue.' He cocks his head. 'What's the matter, don't you trust me?'

'We don't trust each other,' Lawrence said in his direct way. 'Not quite yet.'

'You know, you're absolutely right. Unlike Christopher and Cassandra I have your best interests in mind. But these are only words, why should you believe them?' He puts the bottle away and leads them down off the roof. 'I'm going to show you something. Then you can make up your mind about me.'

He takes Lawrence northwest on Bleeker to Hudson St, north and then west again until they arrive at Little W. 12th St. They are in the meat packing district, a place alive only after midnight when pimps cruise, looking for new territory to conquer, and drug dealers are flushed from their daylight dens. On all sides, old turn-of-the-century warehouses rear up like Druidic pillars left over from another era. Streetlights spark and gutter like soggy fireworks. Trucks rumble over the cobbles carrying within their refrigerated innards mammoth sides of beef and veal, racks of butter-soft lamb, thick, marbled prime ribs glistening with fat.

They mount the metal stairs to an empty loading dock. An ancient, sun-faded sign says, 'Halloran & Sons, Fine Meats, All Cuts'. Below it has been affixed an official notice from the New York City Board of Health temporarily closing the place for third-time violations.

The Pale Saint produces a key, hand-filed from a legitimate one he must have stolen for an hour or so. Inside, it's dark and very cold. Their footsteps echo solemnly, as Lawrence imagines they might in a faraway Gothic cathedral like Notre-Dame.

The Pale Saint turns on a light, and says with a wicked flourish: 'Behold: the abattoir.'

They are standing before a line of butcher's tables stained the color of ebony. Though the air conditioners are wheezing mightily, there is a distinct smell of blood in the air. Above and behind the tables are three tiers of wooden racks holding a stadium of stainless-steel knives. All kinds, all sizes, all shapes: carving knives, de-boning knives, paring knives, serrated knives, as well as compact hatchets to chop through joints, hammers with large, square, ugly heads to tenderize veal fillets. Galvanized slop buckets everywhere to catch the offal. On the floor, in the cracks, like a new form of grout, rivulets of dried blood. And just above, water spigots to sluice away the leavings.

Reaching up behind the top tier of knives, the Pale Saint withdraws a package wrapped in brown paper, tied with brown cord.

He hands it to Lawrence. 'Here, open it.'

Lawrence pulls the cord and like a piece of origami the paper unfolds in his palm. Inside, he sees a dozen long metal implements.

'These are my railroad spikes.' The Pale Saint plucks one up and turns it slowly between his fingers. 'This is what I use.' He lowers the pointed end until it rests against the center of Lawrence's forehead. 'I insert it through the left eye and remove the pineal gland.' He spins it, making a mark. But the clone does not flinch.

Abruptly, he takes it away, drops it onto the pile and rewraps the package. 'No one else has ever seen this. No one but you.'

He replaces the package, then takes a long-bladed knife out of the rack. Holding it out to Lawrence handle first, he says, 'If you're going to do it, now is the time.'

He looks into Lawrence's eyes, into his very heart, or so it seems.

'No? Didn't Christopher give you instructions to kill me? Sure you don't want to give it a stab?'

'No mention was ever made of killing you,' Lawrence says. 'Besides which, whatever I was made for, I am more than that. I am, therefore I think. Thinking, I make my own decisions. I follow my own path.'

The Pale Saint presses the knife into Lawrence's hand. 'Then you won't kill me?'

'I won't kill anyone. Killing is wrong.'

'Christopher kills.'

'So do you.'

The Pale Saint takes back the knife. 'In that case, I applaud your logical mind.' He kneels down and puts the blade to his throat. 'You have only to say the word, and I will do the deed myself.'

'Is this a test?' Lawrence asks. 'Is it that you don't believe my convictions?'

'What are words but pretty pictures painted by artists?' the Pale Saint snarls. 'Liars all!' He offers up his neck. 'What convictions could you have? You are just twenty-something days old!' His eyes burn with a cold, calculating fire. 'The question before us is this: are you Christopher's creature or are you mine? Choose!'

'You are trying to twist me.' Lawrence appears agitated.

'Not a bit of it.' The Pale Saint rises; the knife hangs idle at his side. 'As I say, I am trying to get at the truth.'

'As to the truth,' Lawrence says, 'why did you murder Bobby Austin?'

The Pale Saint purses his lips. 'You know there's a reason, then.'

'Yes.'

'Tell me, junior, would you kill me to find out?'

'I have told you. It is not for me to kill anyone.'

'Well, then, that's settled.' The Pale Saint chuckles as he replaces the knife. 'I killed him because . . .' As he pauses, Lawrence who knows him intimately, yet does not know him at all, can see him hold his deliberation on his tongue like the last precious square of chocolate. Something is coming to fruition, and Lawrence holds his breath.

'Henry Miller once wrote something that resonates for both of us,' the Pale Saint says. 'He wrote it in the spring of 1932 but, by God, I swear it was meant for this moment. "Nobody, so far as I can see, is making use of the elements in the air which give direction and motivation to our lives," he wrote. "Only the killers seem to be extracting from life some satisfactory measure of what they are putting into it. The age demands violence, but we are getting only abortive explosions. Revolutions are nipped in the bud, or else succeed too quickly. Passion is quickly exhausted. Men fall back on ideas, *comme d'habitude*. Nothing is proposed that can last twenty-four hours. We are living a million lives in the space of a generation."' He gives Lawrence a look that makes his eyes burn like lamps. 'I killed Bobby Austin because I had to; because it was the penultimate step in completing the circle.'

'I don't understand.'

'That is only because you are still mostly Christopher's creature.'

They retrace their steps. On the loading dock, they sit on the edge, swinging their feet just like Tom Sawyer and Huck Finn on the banks of the Mississippi.

The Pale Saint takes out the bottle of liquid and opens his mouth. Seven drops spill out onto his tongue, his jaws snap shut, and he swallows convulsively. He moves the eyedropper toward Lawrence. 'Now open and say "Ah!"'

Lawrence feels the cold-hot sensation of the liquid rolling backward on his tongue toward his taste buds.

'Only two more doses left,' the Pale Saint says ruefully. 'Your daddy has gone and confiscated the rest of my stash. Damn inconvenient timing. Still, it can't be helped. In war, the situation is always fluid.'

Another truck rumbles past, a cow's stupid bovine face stenciled on its side.

'How curious it is just to be with someone. To speak of simple, mundane things; things I'd never tell anyone else. I feel like I could talk to you till midnight, then fall into a dreamless sleep until dawn. What a relief that would be.'

'Don't you sleep?'

'With the world on fire, how can I? I haven't slept in years.'

'When I sleep, I dream of you.'

'I know, junior. Having you around is like having a weasel lock his jaws onto the back of my neck. You're not fuckin' gonna let go, are you?' The Pale Saint laughs, as if he's making a joke, but in his current state Lawrence feels a cool assurance that the Pale Saint has told him the truth – or, at least, some form of it.

'Tell me about Andy,' the Pale Saint says. 'Christopher must have spoken to you about his son.'

Lawrence feels a ribbon of cold inside him as the definition of the word *betrayal* slinks through his mind. 'He has never spoken of him to me.'

The Pale Saint cocks his head. 'Don't lie to me, junior. Big Brother can tell when you're lying.'

'Does it really surprise you that Christopher doesn't confide in me? I think, to him, I am a temporary thing, passing through his world in a blur of motion.'

The Pale Saint nods. 'Where you came from, where you will go afterward doesn't enter his mind. Well, you're more to me than that. *Much* more.' He puts his arm around Lawrence's shoulders. 'Feel anything when I do this? Not yet? Give it time; the cocktail requires some to work. And if you begin to sweat heavily, don't give it any mind, hear? Just part of the process.'

'What process?' There is an odd taste in Lawrence's mouth, and such a thickness to his tongue he's sure his words are slurred. The streetlights have gone smeary, like pastel chalk marks on water.

'I am continuing your true education, junior. Now listen . . . and learn. There is a ceremony among the Altaic shamans. It occurs on the night of the first battle, when revenge is uppermost in everyone's mind. The shamans are ritually purified with water. Then they drink a certain liquid. This liquid opens the Channel. The Channel leads back to where the First Power resides inside them. The power used by the ancients. It is very dangerous, this First Power, even though to some extent it lives inside everyone. It can eat a man alive, gobble him up like a ghoul, leave him wasted, a gibbering idiot. I know what you're thinking, but there's little danger, really. As long as I'm your guide, your guru, your avatar. We'll pass through the fire together.'

The Pale Saint grins. 'What I like, I don't have to put on an act with you. I can just be me. Haven't felt that since before Faith left the farm. Good long time ago.' He peers at Lawrence. 'Hey, your eyes are glazing over.' He strikes him gently on the cheek.

'Okay, now, I'm going to tell you a story. Or at least the pertinent part. About Faith. You'll need to know about her if you're going to help me. Now concentrate on my voice and you'll be okay. With everything speeded up inside you it's possible you're metabolizing my cocktail too fast. But you're strong. I can feel your First Power rising.' He takes Lawrence's hand. 'Anyway, not to worry. I'm here to make sure you come to no harm.'

He wipes the sweat off Lawrence's face with the sleeve of his jacket. 'After the fire, after I cleansed the past as best I could, I traveled west – to the place where all the storms that sweep across the vast dusty plains begin – to find Faith. A year before, when she was seventeen, she'd lost all patience with Mama. She stole the food money out of the cookie tin Mama left for me and headed west. Before she went, she begged me to come with her, but I couldn't just abandon the family; could I? I couldn't leave Mama. Not then, anyway. She told me where she was headed. I watched her leave without saying a word. I couldn't have stopped her without hurting her, and I'd never do that. Never. Faith's the only human being I know worth dying for. And I will if I have to.'

He rolls his head on his neck so that he is staring up at the sky, where past the hard radiation of city lights, stars shine and a moon glows like a cherry on a sundae.

'By the time I had reached the foothills of the Rockies I had grown the first mustache of adulthood. Just over the Montana state line I bought a cowboy hat and a checkered bandanna I tied around my neck. I let my mustache grow long and ropy, adding a neat goatee, thinking of the photo I'd once seen of an old-time cowboy.

'I caught up with Faith in a small town named Debenture, Montana. She was lying face down on the floor of her mean and filthy room in a flea-bitten boarding house. She had been robbed and raped and beaten to death in a particularly savage manner. There were ligature marks on her wrists, thighs, ankles, and across her breasts. The sheriff, when he arrived, was unsympathetic. In his eyes, Faith was a drifter and a whore, contributing nothing to the welfare of Debenture. People like her are nothing but trouble, anyway, he told me. I should have bitten his nose off on the spot. I knew he was dissembling. He wore his complicity right next to his tin star. He evinced no surprise at the horrific nature of Faith's demise.

'All that was left of her possessions was a blue glass bottle she had bought in Grand Junction. Angry as sin, I threw it against the wall. And what d'you know? Inside, I discovered a small piece of paper that she had hidden there. A list of five names, men who lived in town or near it, important men, even now in their semi-retirement – politicians, a county circuit judge, businessmen.

'I knew these were the men who had murdered Faith. What kind of relationship had she had with them? I didn't know, didn't want to know. Hell, what did it matter, anyway? They had used her, then killed her; they had basely taken a girl most precious, rare and beautiful and had driven a stake right through her heart.'

The Pale Saint pauses to wipe more sweat, which is oozing freely out of Lawrence's wide-open pores. 'Slowly and methodically, I picked up every piece of blue glass. Then I found a hardware store and glued all the pieces back together. But, of course, that wasn't enough. Can you understand what it's like to be entwined with another person so deeply their very soul is sunk inside you? No, how could you? But you'll come to know, I promise you.' The Pale Saint waits while a fleet of trucks turns the corner, the exhausts echoing ominously like a grizzly's call across a saw-toothed mountain ridge.

'Just before dawn, I began with the name at the top of Faith's list. When I was finished, I proceeded to the next one, and so on. I killed them one a day. I slept during the days, a miraculous deep and dreamless sleep from which I woke refreshed and ready to go. When, at the end of five days, I was finished, I left Debenture forever.

'To be honest, I was profoundly disappointed because I had come to realize that my body was an empty container and would remain so no matter how fast I tried to fill it up. The ecstatic feeling of life as it exited each of the five sacrificial bodies was so fleeting I barely remembered it.

'Empty I had come to Debenture, and empty I left. Only Faith remained.'

The Pale Saint holds Lawrence tight as he begins to shiver as if with a terrible ague. 'You still with me, junior?' He swabs the back of the clone's neck, but Lawrence's eyes are opaque and unfocused. He was in the midst of a vision.

Night in Debenture as it had been fifteen years ago, after the last of the murders. By the light of a copper Harvest moon, he watches the Pale Saint crouched over his sister's unmarked grave. Above him, the immediate skyline is dominated by a huge wooden water tower, which looms beside the railroad tracks. Not too far beyond, the outskirts of town are swallowed whole by the wild land. From the train bed the Pale Saint takes a handful of railroad spikes.

Now he sees what is in the Pale Saint's mind. He becomes the Pale Saint as he purifies his hunting knife in his own blood. He is in another time, another place as he parboils the corpse of a small girl, stripping it of all flesh. That done, he removes her skull, carves out the top. Reaching in, he wraps his hands around the brain. He explores with his fingertips the tiny convolutions, while repeating like a chant the questions that plague him: *What is life? What is death? Where is that place where the two meet?* Lawrence can feel this too, as if he is there, as if he himself is the Pale Saint. He can feel in the Pale Saint's mind another presence moving, insinuating itself like a serpent. His mother, spewing the holy words into the ether of the Oklahoma darkness, the television microphone transmitting her voice to the four corners of the state. At the same time, the precious brain grows heavy between his palms, as if its wisdom is flowing into him from some unseen and unknown place. The ritual completed, he wraps the skull in swaths of cloth and plastic, for he will take it with him on his long, arduous, bloody journey.

Lawrence opens his eyes. He licks his lips; his mouth is very dry. He feels weak, as if he is profoundly, bone-achingly ill. He feels like the young man with too much drink inside him who has appeared across the street with his girlfriend. The young man staggers against a raised metal grate and, almost falling over, vomits. Lawrence, his gorge rising, turns away. But it doesn't help; he continues to feel ill. When he mentions this, the Pale Saint says, 'It's the cocktail. You have to be cleansed before the Channel opens and ushers in the First Power. The sweat contains all the toxins in your system. When you're purged, it will be time. You'll feel the universe opening, and then as naturally as breathing or thinking you'll step inside.'

In truth, Lawrence feels as if a great chasm is sucking him down into its maw. The sense of himself is rapidly receding, as if he is looking up as he falls, watching someone who looks very much like himself standing on the lip of the chasm, observing himself falling.

Who are you? Lawrence whispers to himself. *Who are you?*

Not unexpected that he should ask this question. The Pale Saint has asked in the same circumstances: *What is life? What is death? Where is that place where the two meet?* because these are the questions to which he must have answers before consciousness is extinguished for the final time. For Lawrence, life has flown by far too swiftly for him to have a sense of who he is.

He feels the drug lifting. He knows he has to think fast, that now he will have his chance to prove his loyalty to the Pale Saint. What is there for him now but to build trust, to cement the confidence the Pale Saint has shown him by recounting the history of Faith's awful demise?

'You shared your drug with me,' he says. 'Now I'll do something for you.'

'Really?' The Pale Saint looks uninterested. 'And what do you suppose you can do for me, junior?'

'Faith's eyes are back in your apartment. I know how much they mean to you,' Lawrence says. 'You can't get them without being captured. But I can.'

'Is that so? But Christopher has found Dillard by now. He's already begun to suspect you.'

'Yes, but he doesn't know for sure. And, in any case, I am who I am. A secret creature, skulking in the shadows. He'll see me coming and get everyone else out of there.'

'In that event, I'll go,' the Pale Saint says. 'We look exactly alike now. With a little cosmetic doctoring on my part, he won't be able to tell us apart.'

'Not by sight,' Lawrence replies, 'but he'll ask questions. Within a minute, he'll know the difference. Believe me, you won't be able to deceive him.'

The Pale Saint considers this for a moment. 'It's fatal to underestimate the enemy, isn't it, junior.'

'From everything I've read about war, yes.'

The Pale Saint stands, and Lawrence with him. 'So, bottom line, I'm faced with testing you by letting you go back to Daddy. What happens if you don't come back?'

'I'll come back,' Lawrence says.

'Yes, you will. And this is going to guarantee it.' He saunters across the street to where the girl is still trying to rouse her boyfriend.

Lawrence can hear him speaking softly, gently to the girl, and he thinks, *No!*, a shout in his mind, that's all, the frail, impotent whimper one makes in a dream. All too soon, the Pale Saint is back with the girl in tow.

'Lawrence,' he says, smiling, 'this is Marcy.'

'Hi.' She holds out her hand and in a daze Lawrence takes it. 'Am I glad we met you guys.' A tow-headed girl with the feverish eyes and semi-detached air of people who have been newly released from panic. 'We're from Jersey. My boyfriend Frank got a little too loaded at a party over on Jane St so I thought we ought to walk it off.' She glances back across the street with a little grimace. 'Guess it wasn't such a hot idea. Suddenly, he pitched over and I didn't know where we were or who to turn to.'

'Not to worry,' the Pale Saint says genially. Some eerie transformation has come over him. He is radiating charm like a klieg light throws off heat. 'Lawrence, I'm going to help these nice people while you run your errand, okay?'

It's most decidedly not okay, but Lawrence knows there is nothing he can do about it. He can see in the girl's beady, grateful eyes that she has already given something of herself to the Pale Saint. It is irrevocable, this thing, Lawrence knows, like Sara's pitch the batter hit over the center fielder's head. Marcy was only too happy to give the Pale Saint her confidence.

'I know that look. Don't worry,' the Pale Saint says in a soothing tone. He turns to the girl. 'He worries about me, the dear boy. I'm always picking up strangers in need and he's forever lecturing me on how dangerous the city can be.' Then, with impeccable timing, back to Lawrence. 'I'll be safe enough with these people until you get back, won't I, Marcy? Please try to convince him you're not going to suddenly sprout fangs and claws the moment his back is turned.'

'Oh, God, no,' the girl says, giggling. 'We wouldn't hurt a fly. Honest.' With fear gone, the trust she has placed in the Pale Saint has turned her somewhat giddy. She has the air of someone already composing the punch line to a story she will tell her friends tomorrow. 'We'll all take care of each other. Promise.'

'That's the spirit.' The Pale Saint is grinning like the Cheshire Cat, a creature for whom until now Lawrence has had a particular fondness.

'I'll be back,' Lawrence says, hoping it will sound like a warning.

'But of course you will,' the Pale Saint replies in the sunniest of voices. 'Now hurry off, Lawrence, and do that voodoo that you do so well.'

FIFTEEN

'I've seen a lot of bad news in my day, but this . . .' Chief of Police Anthony Brockaw stared at the Pale Saint's grisly gallery of photos. 'This is the worst.' His blue-jowled face looked haggard and worn. Keeping the voracious press at bay was beginning to wear him down. He turned to face Christopher, the mass of his eyebrows beetling like storm clouds. 'Jon, I'm afraid I have bad news. The FBI has taken Reuven Esquival's death quite personally. The Deputy Director is flying in tomorrow at noon with an elite task force to take charge of the case.'

Christopher felt his stomach clench. 'You know what kind of a mess they'll make, Chief, because they've done it before. Remember Joey Big Eyes? Remember John Sheen, the "Riverdale Rapist"? How could you –?'

Brockaw spread his hands in a gesture of helplessness. 'It was Hizzhonor himself who made the decision. I was merely notified.'

'He ordered in the Federales without even consulting you?'

'It's his prerogative.'

'No. I won't let it happen. I've worked too hard, too long. Too many of my team have been sacrificed. Look where we're standing. This is his home base, for God's sake. I'm so *close*, Chief. I'm not going to lose control of this case to a team of federal nitwits. He'll fuck them like cheap whores, and then he'll really get nasty.'

'The Deputy Director is bringing in his best profilers.'

'Screw those statisticians; this sonuvabitch doesn't fit any profile. He ran rings around Reuven, and take it from me Reuven was the best.' Christopher squared his shoulders. 'You've got to buy me the time to –'

'Impossible.'

Christopher looked out the back window of the Pale Saint's apartment. Down in the postage-stamp-sized garden someone had lit a votive candle. The tiny flame flickered, throwing shadows fifty times its size into the corners beneath the plane trees. 'With all due respect, sir, I wasn't aware that word was in your vocabulary. Remember the Buried Child Case? You brokered a deal with the FBI that brought Reuven Esquival here and kept the case under my command. Remember when I told you I needed Grand Central Terminal cleared on a Friday at rush hour in order to trap that serial rapist? I've never heard the word "impossible" from you.'

Brockaw turned and went slowly to the window. His hands were clasped behind his back, the thick fingers clenching and unclenching. 'That candle down there reminds me I need to go to church and say my prayers for my brother. It's been five years since he died and already I'm beginning to forget what he looked like. Sometimes I catch myself staring at his face in photos and wondering who that guy was standing next to me.' He turned to Christopher. 'Is it the same for you with Mercedes and Andy?'

'No, it isn't.'

Brockaw nodded. 'How I envy you, Jon. Your job is all substance; mine is pure, unadulterated bullshit. D'you know how many times I've wiped the Mayor's ass? How many times I've made him look like a prince among mere mortals? So at the end of the day this is how he rewards me. I imagine he thinks it's in my job description to be fucked royally.'

'Chief, we still have seventeen hours before the Feds land. All I need is your blessing.'

'Give me one reason, Jon.' Brockaw's face was sheened with a thin film of sweat. This was not a good sign from a man inured to the constant hectoring of the city's voracious press corps.

'You just have to trust me, Chief. I've got an edge on this one.'

'Hizzhonor would have my nuts in a sling.'

'Go out to a long, leisurely dinner. Then go to sleep. By the time you wake up it'll be all over.'

'How can you possibly deliver on that promise?'

'I can.'

Brockaw shook his head. 'In the end, that's the difference between us. You still believe. I've spent too much time with the big boys. These New York politicians squeeze every last ounce of juice out of you.'

Christopher gripped Brockaw's shoulder. 'Not every last ounce. Not yet.'

The chief glanced back at the candle throwing its light around the garden. 'Such a tiny thing.' His gaze lifted and he scanned the skyline as if searching for something he had lost. 'I remember, even if the Mayor doesn't, all the cases you've made, all the impossible odds you've overcome. See, the way I look at it, Jon, in all this gigantic slimepit of a city you're my only friend. The only one when the shit hits the fan that I can count on.'

He settled his shoulders, as if throwing off a weight. 'Understand, even if I give you the time you need, it's strictly unofficial.'

Christopher smiled. 'Don't worry. I know all about plausible deniability.'

'I wish to Christ I didn't. That's not why I joined the Department.' There was a wry twist to Brockaw's mouth. 'Don't fail me, Jon.'

'Hell, no.' Christopher gave him a clap on the back. 'What are friends for?'

Approaching the Pale Saint's apartment on W. 4th St, Lawrence expected to see at least a couple of the policemen Christopher had earlier deployed in a cordon around the block. Instead, he found Sara.

'What are you doing here?' he said with a quick stab of pain in his gut.

'Are you all right?'

'Of course I'm all right.' He hustled her into a doorway across from the Jack the Ripper Pub. 'But you've got to tell me what you're doing here. Mom –'

'Mom came over to . . . well, where I'm staying to check up on me. She said she could only stay a minute but she was so hyper she got me freaked. So I followed her here. If she knew what I've done she'd bite my head off, and I don't even want to think of what Uncle Jon would say.'

'But they're both right,' Lawrence told her. 'It's far too dangerous. Promise me you'll go right back where you were.'

'It's boring there.' She grinned at him. 'Besides, I'll be damned if I miss any of this.' Her smile broke apart almost immediately and she put a hand against his cheek. 'Lawrence, you feel like you're burning up, what's happening to you? Are you sick?'

'Not sick the way you mean, but I guess the result's the same. I'm hot all the time, I see things rushing at me or away from me in the corners of my vision. My mind is going a million miles a second.' He gave her a thin smile. 'I'm afraid I'm like a comet entering a planet's atmosphere. I'm burning to a crisp.'

Sara gasped. 'But we've got to get you to Mom. She'll help you, I know She can –'

He shook his head as he took her hand away from his cheek. 'Listen, Sara, I have a job to do.'

'The hell with that,' she cried as she threw herself against his chest. 'I don't want you to die.'

Slowly, as if some kind of understanding was breaking inside him, Lawrence enfolded her in his arms. 'Sara,' he said, and stopped, unable for a moment to go on. He kissed the top of her head, inhaled her fresh, citrus scent. 'This is an important job, and only I can do it.' He pushed her away from him, peered into her tear-streaked face. 'There's more at stake here than just my life. So many people have died, so many more will die unless I do what has to be done.'

She shook her head. 'I don't care what they say, I don't believe you did it.'

'Did what?' But something inside him froze, because he knew what she meant.

'Mom and Uncle Jon suspect you murdered Dr Dillard. But you couldn't have, I know it. That's why I ignored Mom when she warned me to stay away from you.'

'Sara, remember when we spoke about redemption?' And when she nodded, he said, 'The thing is, right now I feel as if I need to be redeemed. I don't have much time now. No, no –' He shook her gently. 'No crying, okay? But with the time left me I have to do this. I've got to get back this thing I've lost. Do you understand?'

Sara's eyes were swollen with tears. 'Have you done something that bad?'

He gathered her into his arms and held her tight. 'Will you promise me something?' he whispered into her ear.

With her face buried in his shoulder, she nodded.

'Think of me as I was that day you sprung me from the lab, when we spoke about redemption and prayer and doing things free and clear.'

He felt her shaking against him, and he tasted with wonder the salt of her tears. 'Go on now. With what I have to do I need to know you're safe.'

She shook her head. 'Nothing you can say will make me go back to Beth's. Not doing anything, it's like a little death. Don't ask me –'

'It's just not safe –'

'I don't care about being safe when it feels like I'm entombed. I've got to *do* something or I'll go out of my mind. I'm going with you.'

'Absolutely not.' But he could feel the streak of stubbornness she'd inherited from her mother and he knew she simply would not listen if he ordered her to leave. How could he stop her from following him? 'Listen, we'll make a pact. I'll meet you at Beth's when it's safe.'

'You'll come?'

There was a pleading in her eyes that caught in his throat like a sob. 'I promise,' he said when she told him the address on Greene St, not far from the loft. His heart shredded as he pushed her away. He remembered the Pale Saint saying to him: *Can you understand what it's like to be entwined with another person so deeply their very soul is sunk inside you.* He understood that what he wanted now more than anything was to cling to her as she wanted to cling to him, but he shut that part of him down and locked it away as he turned his back on her and hurried across the street to the building that waited for him like a demented lover or a ship with billowing black sails.

His death.

'Let's go inside,' the Pale Saint says to Marcy as they stand outside Halloran & Sons. He's got her boyfriend draped over his shoulder in a classic fireman's lift. 'We'll get Frank washed up and feeling nice and comfy in no time.'

'I know it's stupid,' she says, peering into the vast, echoey interior, 'but I'm afraid of the dark.'

'Hey, no problem, so's Lawrence.' He turns on the lights as they walk through the meat market. 'I used to work here,' he says breezily. 'I suppose it's an odd thing to do, but my daddy did the same. I just followed in his footsteps.'

'If I followed in my father's footsteps,' Marcy says, 'I'd have to learn how to put those dumb little plastic thingies on the ends of shoe laces.'

'Aglets.'

Marcy screws up her face unprettily. 'What?'

'Aglets,' he repeats, with an insidious grin. 'The plastic ends of shoe laces are called aglets.'

'Whatever.' She seems totally uninterested. 'Is Frank gonna be okay?'

'Oh, yeah.' Another stupid cow, the Pale Saint thinks, as he swings the boy onto the butcher's table. He turns on the tap and water begins sluicing down. In one motion he draws a knife from its rack and slits the boy's throat from ear to ear. The body jerks and kicks in galvanic response, and blood fountains like a fireworks display. Like the sound of thunder following a lightning flash, the Pale Saint grabs hold of Marcy.

She is utterly paralyzed by his hideous transformation from protector to devil. Because she has given him her trust, his evil, so abruptly revealed, seems unreal to her. She cannot get her mind around this rupture of the reality he so artfully presented to her.

With one hand wrapped around her windpipe, he smears himself with the boy's warm blood. He anoints Marcy's face with it, drawing crosses on each cheek, in the center of her forehead. She is already weak, gasping for air. Her beady eyes are big around as marbles. Gibberish pours from her mouth like foam. She watches, spellbound, as he slips his bloody hand into the waistband of his trousers and pulls out a long railroad spike.

The spike pierces her left eye. It happens so quickly that she doesn't have time to draw another breath. As she does a little dance, the Pale Saint hums as if to a tune only the two of them, so intimately linked now, can hear.

What is life? What is death? Where is that place where the two meet?

Quite unexpectedly, she becomes a fighter, this girl. She will not go quietly into the long dark. This makes him happy. That there's always a surprise or two left in the human race is to him a sign of hope. Soon enough, though, she is stilled, and it is time to excise her pineal, to hold the still warm gland in the palm of his hand, to drink of her, a grisly toast to her last moments, to that place where life and death collide like two oppositely charged atoms.

Every last fiber of him has been excited to its utmost. And yet, the hollowness, the vast black void remains. As always. Because she is not the one.

At last, sadly, he is finished. For some time, he stands looking at what he has wrought. Into his mind comes a passage from the Word of the Lord unto Joel he's heard his mother roar out many times. Yet today it has acquired another meaning: *A fire devoureth before them; And behind them a flame burneth: The land is as the garden of Eden before them, And behind them a desolate wilderness; Yea, and nothing shall escape them . . .*

He goes into the refrigerated locker room and returns with his notebook computer and his cell phone. Then he hurries out of the abattoir.

*   *   *

'Cass, I'm going to say this one more time and that's it.' Christopher was watching as Chief Brockaw with a two-man escort of uniforms in riot gear hurried across the tiny back yard below the Pale Saint's window. He was using the circuitous route by which he had come to see Christopher. 'The Pale Saint knows too much about you. You're too much of a liability to stay here. You should be with Sara.'

'Jon, Lawrence is my son, and he's dying. If there's any chance I can get to him I'm going to take it, period. There isn't anything you can say that will –'

Christopher whirled on her. Taking her by the arms, he shook her hard so that the small black satchel she was carrying swung back and forth like a demented pendulum. 'Don't you get it? I couldn't bear it if something happened to you.'

'Something's already happened to me. Enough to know where I belong.'

'Cass, this isn't the time or place to have one of those semantic arguments you always win.'

'This isn't semantics! This is my life!' Her eyes blazed. 'Dammit, Jon, stop treating me this way. I'm not going to scream "Eek!" at the sight of a New York-sized rat. I can run as fast as you can.' She drew out a gun from her black satchel, careful to point it at the floor. 'I can even shoot this if I have to.'

'Where did you get that?'

'It's Bobby's. Naturally, he had a permit to carry.'

'Put that away,' Christopher ordered. 'You're not going to shoot anyone.'

Cassandra did as he asked. 'Besides,' she said in a softer tone, 'I know you don't want to be the one to sign Lawrence's death sentence.' She showed him one of the patches with the eicosanoid serum Dillard had prepared. 'I won't let him die, Jon. I just won't.'

'Even if it turns out he murdered Dillard in cold blood?'

'You know the answer to that. No matter what he's done, I won't be his judge and executioner.'

'Good,' he said. 'I wanted to hear you say that. Now give me the patch. I'll put it on him myself.'

'Unless you've miraculously turned into a surgeon, you can't. It's subdermal. I have to do it.'

At that moment, the walkie-talkie squealed and he grabbed at it. 'What's up?'

'Loo, we've got a sighting,' Jerry Lewis's voice said in his ear.

'The Pale Saint?'

'Right. The sharpshooter I'm with has got him square in his sights.'

'Where is he?' Christopher asked.

'Walking east on Fourth St, heading right this way, calm as you please.'

That didn't sound like the Pale Saint; that sounded plain stupid. Unless . . . 'Gimme a full description.'

'He's got light brown hair, this time. Crew-cut. No facial hair.'

Christopher was gripping the receiver with white knuckles. 'What's he wearing?'

Lewis described the outfit Lawrence was wearing when he disappeared from the lab. 'Lewis, get everyone out of there.'

'But Loo –'

'Now!' Christopher thundered.

'What is it?' Cassandra asked.

'They've sighted someone coming this way. It looks like Lawrence.'

'But what if it's not,' she said. 'What if it's the Pale Saint pretending to be –?'

'Yeah,' Christopher said, double-checking the ammo in his gun, 'just my thought.' The walkie-talkie crackled again, and Lewis said: 'Everyone's pulled back to the perimeter. The sharps are standing down.'

'Good,' Christopher said. 'Keep them that way.'

'He's entering the building, Loo.'

'Now you go,' Christopher barked into the receiver. 'You're in charge of the perimeter, Lewis. I don't want anyone with an itchy trigger finger to do something precipitous. Read me? The Chief wants this one alive and kicking.'

'Roger, Loo.' Christopher could tell he was unhappy. He was a good soldier, nonetheless; he'd follow orders. 'God be with you.'

The absence of God is God enough, Christopher thought as Lawrence entered the apartment. Or was it the Pale Saint? He'd find out soon enough.

'Lawrence,' Christopher said as he emerged from the shadows, 'you've come back.'

Lawrence was still framed by the wan hallway light. 'Hello, Dad.'

'Are you all right?'

'There isn't any way for me to answer that. How's Mom?'

Mom is in the bathroom with her heart in her throat, Christopher thought. 'She's worried about you,' he said. 'We both are.'

272

'I'm sorry about that. I –'

He'd begun to move into the room, but Christopher's upraised hand halted him.

'I need to ask you some questions.'

'I know,' Lawrence said. 'If I were you, I'd do the same.'

'Remember when I asked you to tell me how the Skeleton was going to make things like they were before the first bad thing happened?'

'Of course,' Lawrence said.

'What did you say to me?'

'"A clean slate. A fire burning into the sky. A fire to cleanse all the bad things. And blood running. Death and more death."'

'What was the first thing you said after I pulled you from the lake?'

'"I'm alive."'

'And after that?'

'"He's gone."'

'Who did you mean?'

'Hound. Sara's Weimaraner.'

Christopher relaxed. He holstered the gun he'd been holding at his side. He called Cassandra's name and she emerged from the bathroom. She stopped as she came face to face with the clone. She gave Christopher a questioning glance, and when he nodded, she went to him.

'Hi, Mom,' he said awkwardly, as if unsure or afraid of her response.

'Lawrence, you –' Relief had washed through her, leaving like the wrack of the outgoing tide a residue of anger. 'You shouldn't have run away.' Then she gave a little cry as he faltered, staggering in her arms. 'What is it?'

Christopher dragged over a chair, and sat Lawrence down. He slumped for a moment against the back. 'He gave me something . . . some liquid we shared. It comes in waves, this dizziness.'

Cassandra gave Christopher a quick look. 'The phyto-cocktail,' she mouthed.

Christopher's heart began to pound. 'You were with the Pale Saint?'

Lawrence nodded.

'All right, from the beginning. Why did you run off?' Christopher asked. 'Who killed Dillard?'

'I know you think I did. The Skeleton told me.'

'Did he kill Dillard?'

'First things first,' Cassandra cut in. 'Lawrence, take off your shirt,' she

273

commanded. She opened her small black satchel, took out anaesthetic, scalpel and gauze, all the paraphernalia she had brought along, and began the procedure for implanting the subdermal patch.

While she worked, Christopher snapped off questions. 'Okay. What happened?'

'I don't know.'

'What d'you mean, you don't know? Cass came into the lab, found Dillard dead and you gone.'

'I realize that.'

'So?'

Lawrence seemed unconcerned that Cassandra was peeling back the skin on his shoulder. 'It's all a blur. One minute I was lying down on my bed, the next I was standing over Dillard.'

'He was dead?'

'Yes. I was breathing hard, my pulse was pounding, and I was very, very angry. I had blood on my hands.'

'Hold them out,' Christopher commanded.

'I washed off the blood,' Lawrence said as Cassandra slid in the patch, positioned it, and began to suture him up.

'The blood would have told me nothing.' Christopher scrutinized Lawrence's knuckles. 'But this does.' He touched two spots. 'The skin is bruised and abraded, and here you have a small cut.'

'Like I hit someone several times,' Lawrence said. 'Hard.'

Christopher stood up. 'You're sure you remember nothing until you were standing over the body?'

'I beat him, I just know I did.'

'How do you know? Do you remember?'

'No, but –'

'Then how?'

'Jon, stop badgering him,' Cassandra said.

'I'm not badgering him. I just want to get to the truth.'

Lawrence closed his eyes. 'The truth is I was angry. Very angry. I –' His eyes snapped open.

Cassandra brushed her hand across his forehead, sweeping back his damp hair. 'What is it, Lawrence? Tell us?'

'He said I shouldn't tell. He said that you'd think I was bad if I told, that you'd hate me.'

'Who said that?' Cassandra asked. 'The Pale Saint?'

'No,' Lawrence said in a whisper. 'Dr Dillard.'

Silence rushed into the void. Christopher could hear his quickened pulse like the roaring of a rapids. 'What happened between you and Dillard, Lawrence?'

The clone licked his lips. 'It happened when he'd give me tests. He'd pinch me, gouge me, hurt me.'

'When did this start?' Christopher could see that Cassandra was in shock.

'I don't remember,' Lawrence said slowly, 'it not happening.'

'Oh, God.' Cassandra wrapped her arms around him. 'Dear, sweet God. How could I have been so blind?'

'That's why you think you beat him?' Christopher said.

'Yes.'

'That's why you think you killed him?'

'Yes.'

Christopher watched as Cassandra rocked him gently back and forth.

'It's all right now,' Christopher said. 'Do you understand that?'

There were tears in Lawrence's eyes.

Christopher knelt down beside him. 'Tell me what you remember before you found yourself standing over the body.'

Lawrence put a hand briefly to his head. 'I must have been asleep because there are images, jumbled, feverish . . . a dream.'

'Tell me about the images,' Christopher said. Cassandra had returned to wrapping the wound. He could tell she was forcing herself to be calm.

Lawrence licked his lips. 'I could smell horses, and hear them whinnying, as if from a small distance. I was crawling up a ladder, going straight up. I saw her.'

'Who?'

'Faith, my sister.'

'You mean the Skeleton's sister.'

'That's what I said.' Lawrence looked from Christopher to Cassandra and back again. 'Someone was with her. He was on top of her, or she was on top of him. I saw her thighs, so white against the straw. It's all blurred. I was moving. I felt a rage, deep in my belly. I was moving. It's all a blur, breathing heavy and the rage and using my fists . . .'

Lawrence stared down at his knuckles. 'And then I was standing over him and he was dead.'

'Jon –'

Christopher put his finger against his lips to silence her. 'Who were you standing over, Lawrence? The boy who was with Faith?'

Lawrence shook his head. 'He was gone. They were all gone, a dream. I was standing over Dillard and he was dead.'

'What about the pineal?'

Lawrence lifted his head up. 'What?'

'His pineal gland was taken out through his left eye socket,' Cassandra said. She was not, as she had promised Christopher, going to scream 'Eek!' no matter how big the rat was.

'I saw that.' Lawrence shook his head. 'It was the first thing . . .' He spread his hands in a gesture of helplessness.

'None of this proves you killed Dillard,' Christopher said.

'It doesn't prove I didn't.'

Christopher knelt beside him. 'Listen to me, Lawrence. I don't think you killed Dillard. You very well may have hit him, but even that wasn't your own doing. I think the Skeleton forced you to re-live something that happened to him. He somehow transferred to you his rage at this boy who was having sex with his sister, Faith.'

'How can you know that?'

'You told me. You said "my sister" when you mentioned Faith. But she's not your sister, Lawrence, is she?'

'No.'

Christopher nodded. 'I think the Pale Saint got you so angry you went for Dillard, knocked him unconscious. Then he killed him, just like he's killed all the others.'

'Then why wouldn't I have seen him?'

'By your own admission, you remember nothing.'

'Not knowing,' Lawrence said, 'that's the hardest part, isn't it?'

'Yes.' Christopher went to the window. 'It's the hardest part with my son, Andy. The not knowing. He killed himself, but why?' He took a breath. 'Brockaw told me he's already begun to forget what his dead brother looked like. If that ever happened to me with Andy I couldn't bear it.'

'But it won't.' Cassandra went to him, stroked the back of his neck. 'It's time for you to let go, time for you to stop torturing yourself by asking a question that can never be answered.'

Christopher shook his head. He wondered how it was he could understand the truth of what Cassandra was saying, yet still fight against it.

'Dad, if you had been there with Andy I know you wouldn't have let it happen. But the difference with me is even if I didn't murder Dr Dillard, I was there when he was killed.'

'You couldn't have stopped it, Lawrence.'

'But see, I didn't even have a chance to try.' The clone looked down at the floor, then at Cassandra. 'Mom, you told me that I'm a complete enigma because I'm the first of my kind. But maybe that's not quite right. Something T.E. Lawrence wrote, I think, defines me. He was struggling to describe his friend Feisal, but it's me nonetheless: "a brave, weak, ignorant spirit, trying to do work for which only a genius, a prophet or a great criminal, is fitted".'

'My God, what have we done to you?' Cassandra whispered as she embraced him.

'We've given him an impossible assignment,' Christopher said. 'And, Lawrence, believe when I tell you I'm sorry about that.'

'I do, Dad.'

He checked the window, staring down into the inky darkness. The candle had at last guttered out, but electric lights burned through window curtains in precise and unflickering squares to shed upon the plane trees a kind of whiteness that hovered somewhere between holy and ghostly. Shadows hung still and unmoving in the last of the dry, yellow leaves. These shadows, like his past, seemed more serene now, as if they were almost home. Christopher pulled himself away from his thoughts, and nodded. 'Tell me about your work, then.'

'I was drawn here, to the Skeleton, the Pale Saint.' He told them what had happened. When he got to the part about the Pale Saint putting the knife in his hand, Christopher interrupted him.

'You didn't try to kill him.'

'No. I couldn't. It would have been like trying to kill a part of myself,' Lawrence said. 'Besides, I think it was a test. If I had tried I'm certain he would have slaughtered me on the spot.'

'Considering where you were, that's an apt image.' Christopher gestured. 'Go on.'

'We shared the drug. He told me the story of how he had found Faith murdered.' He recounted the story as the Pale Saint had told it to him. 'It was terrible, what those men did to her.'

'This story, it made you feel sorry for him, didn't it?' Christopher said.

Lawrence nodded. 'It's such a sad story.'

'He's a master at psychological manipulation, Lawrence. He told you a lie so you would empathize with him, more easily bond with him, so you would feel what he wants you to feel. He's trying to confuse you.'

277

Lawrence nodded again. 'Yes, I can see that. But maybe that's okay. I wanted to make him trust me –'

'He'll never trust anyone but himself,' Christopher said.

'But I *am* himself. In a way.'

'He must love that,' Cassandra said.

'Yes and no. He wants to love me but he can't help despising me. That's who he is.'

Lawrence said this with an odd kind of sadness. Christopher could understand why the clone couldn't find it in himself to kill the Pale Saint. Besides, he knew from experience just how hard it was to take another human life. Unless they were in immediate mortal danger, most people simply couldn't do it.

'Here's the thing,' Lawrence went on. 'I know he needs those eyes back. They're Faith's eyes and they're important to him.'

'So he sent you back to fetch them?' Cassandra was shaking with anger. 'He's got a pair of brass balls.'

'Cass –' Christopher warned.

'Actually, it was my idea,' Lawrence said. 'I thought this would prove my loyalty to him. I know if he begins to trust me, he'll let his guard down and you'll be able to capture him.' He looked from Cassandra to Christopher. 'I mean that's the idea, isn't it?'

'Yes,' Christopher said.

'Because he was sure you'd sent me to kill him.'

'That would be how he thinks. Justice is the only thing I've ever looked for,' Christopher said. He was silent for a minute. 'The question is, why did he let you come back?'

'He doesn't trust me at all, does he?' Lawrence said.

Christopher shook his head. 'You were right when you said this was a test. If you came back with the eyes, well and good. But if not, if instead you led me to where he is now –'

'No, no, you don't understand. If I don't come back, he's going to kill this girl.'

'What girl?'

Lawrence told them about Marcy and her drunken boyfriend.

'Oh, Jesus,' Christopher said as he grabbed Lawrence's arm and propelled him out of the apartment. 'We've got to get to Halloran & Sons. He's going to kill this girl whether you come back or not.'

'But why would he?'

'To use your own phrase, it's in his nature. It's what he is.'

Behind them, at the other end of the hallway, the access door to the

278

roof crashed open and a figure dropped down. 'Now at last the face of the enemy,' the Pale Saint cried as he hurtled toward them.

As Christopher drew his gun, the Pale Saint smashed the heel of his hand full into Lawrence's nose. In almost the same motion, he jammed his elbow into the side of Christopher's neck, pinning him back against the wall. His hand chopped down onto Christopher's wrist, and the gun clattered to the floor.

Christopher barely managed to block the edge of the Pale Saint's hand as it flew toward his windpipe. He got his knee into the Pale Saint's ribs, then drove his fist into the side of his head. The Pale Saint staggered back, and Christopher came after him. That was a mistake. The Pale Saint waited until the last possible second, then slammed Christopher over the heart.

Christopher blinked heavily, tumbling backward against the wall. He reached out even before he hit the floor, but the Pale Saint had ripped open his coat. Finding the jar with Faith's eyes, he lit out for the ladder up to the access panel.

Lawrence, blood streaming from his nose, pulled himself upright and staggered toward the ladder as the Pale Saint disappeared into the square hole in the ceiling. Christopher, coughing heavily, saw the Pale Saint affix a thin metallic filament to the top rung of the ladder, and he shouted: 'Lawrence, no! Keep away from there!'

As Lawrence hesitated, Christopher threw his keys over the clone's head. They hit the side of the ladder, sending a shower of sparks into the hallway.

'He's booby-trapped the ladder,' Christopher said as he retrieved his gun and pushed his way past Lawrence. 'Stay here. Let Cass take care of your nose.' Then he was racing through the apartment. He threw open the back window and leapt across the short space to the welcoming arms of the scabrous plane tree. He grabbed the slick bark, felt his shoes skittering down the trunk as he began to fall, then got a purchase with his heel in a crotch, and reaching up, began his climb through the branches to the rooftop.

The highest crotch on the tree was still more than three feet below the roofline. At the point where the tree paralleled the rooftop, Christopher estimated that a gap of about his body length separated the branch from the roof. A moment later, he was standing in the highest crotch. Without hesitation, he stretched out along the overarching branch and began to shinny his way up. Now, out on the limb, he was faced with a choice: he could try to gather himself for a blind leap across almost six feet or he could lift himself to the next higher branch that actually overarched the rooftop.

Wrapping his thighs around the branch he was on, he sat up and, balancing himself, reached upward and grabbed onto the branch over his head. It was somewhat thinner than the one he was already on but, testing it, he felt confident it would hold his weight. He took a quick glance below him at the dizzying sight of the tiny back yard. From this height it looked as small as the palm of his hand.

He took several deep breaths, then lifted himself by his biceps until he was standing on the lower branch. He walked three steps forward. At this point, the branch above diverged. Flexing his arms, he went hand over hand, his body dangling in space. Sweat broke out on his face and the back of his neck. It dribbled down the small of his back. He tried not to think of how long a fall it was to the ground below. At length, he crossed over the edge of the rooftop. He let go of the branch, fell perhaps four feet to the tarred roof.

He took in everything at once: the door leading down to the access panel up which the Pale Saint climbed, the two old-fashioned air vent housings with their revolving onion-shaped fans. He checked these first. One was too small for a man to hide in, the other held nothing but the fan and its rheumy motor.

He surveyed the roof's perimeter: the opposite side offered a similar drop to W. 4th St. The buildings on either side rose higher than this one. There was no way to get to the one to the east, but there was a metal ladder running up the grimy brown brick side of the building to the west.

Christopher gained the parapet on that side and leapt onto the ladder. He began to climb. As he did so, he saw that areas of the rungs were shiny, the grit of the city wiped off as if by someone recently grabbing hold: the Pale Saint.

On the rooftop of the neighboring building, he ran to the door leading down into the building. It was padlocked. He checked the air shaft and the small water tower. Nothing. There was a small shedlike structure which he approached with caution, his gun drawn. On the front, two hinged panels could be swung open for access. He put his ear against one of them, heard a soft, lulling cooing. This was a coop. Someone in the building had homing pigeons.

Christopher turned away. This building was on the end of the block, literally at the intersection of W. 4th and W. 10th Sts. Where could the Pale Saint have gone from here?

The doors to the coop flew open with a rattle and bang like a rifle shot, and a horde of clattering, wing-flapping pigeons flew raucously out. Christopher, in the midst of them, jolted back, his hands instinctively covering his face. Which was when the Pale Saint leapt at him from out of the coop.

He took Christopher by the shoulders and flung him across the rooftop. Down on his knees, Christopher received a vicious kick to his ribs. As he toppled over, he kicked out, tripping the Pale Saint as he flung himself headlong toward Christopher.

Christopher butted him in the head so hard that the Pale Saint's teeth clacked together. He reached for his gun, but the Pale Saint clubbed him with both hands. They rolled toward the far parapet, fetching up against it with bone-jarring suddenness.

Using the heel of his hand, the Pale Saint slammed the back of Christopher's head against the brick and cement. He did it again, then dragged Christopher to his feet. He buried his fist in Christopher's stomach, then hauled him upright as he began to retch. He bent him backward over the parapet. As he did so, he put his mouth against Christopher's ear and said:

'When Daniel was brought by the assassin Arioch before Nebuchadnezzar, the king of Babylon, this is what he told the king: "The secret which the king hath demanded cannot the wise men, the astrologers, the magicians, the soothsayers, show unto the king; but there is a God in heaven that revealeth secrets."' He grinned fiercely. 'You want to know my secrets, Christopher, you grubby little garbage man? I'll see you all in hell first.'

'Never,' Christopher said through bloody lips.

The Pale Saint hit him again. 'You don't have a say in this, Christopher. This is my show. I am the Almighty, the only one who can deliver up the secrets, not any of your modern-day, computer-toting astrologers, soothsayers, or magicians. You're all at my mercy.'

Christopher closed his eyes, appeared on the verge of passing out.

'Oh no, you don't,' the Pale Saint said as he hauled him up. Then all the breath went out of him as Christopher drove his knee between his legs. Christopher swung from the shoulder, connecting with a satisfying jab, snapping the Pale Saint's head back.

Christopher didn't hesitate; he hit him again, a short, sharp jab. But the Pale Saint jammed the sole of his shoe behind Christopher's knee, and Christopher went down. The Pale Saint pounded on the back of his neck, threw Christopher back against the parapet.

'Now you'll take the plunge,' he said. 'Just like your son took his fatal dive. Why did he go to the pool that day, Christopher? Hmm? Was it on a dare or was it a deliberate act? If it was deliberate he had a lot of anger inside him. Was he cursing your name when he went off the diving board?'

He rolled Christopher's body up onto the parapet's edge. Christopher's heart constricted as he scrabbled for a hold, but the Pale Saint chopped down. He tried to keep his attention on saving himself, but the Pale Saint's words pierced deep into the core of him like a quiver full of arrows. 'You couldn't help him, Christopher, not even when he needed you most, when he walked out onto that diving board, in the last pathetic moments of his sad life.' The sorrow was welling up inside Christopher as the Pale Saint tapped into the well of grief-stricken guilt. 'Isn't it ironic? And somehow fitting, don't you think? You and Andy will both break your necks on concrete.'

Christopher, tears streaming down his face, felt himself losing purchase. Already his legs were dangling in space. He reached back, but the Pale Saint hammered him repeatedly. 'Time to let go, Christopher. Time to join your son in oblivion.'

Weeping, Christopher felt himself slipping over the edge. He was falling.

'Goodbye, Christo –'

The Pale Saint's words were drowned out by a gunshot. He jerked back, and Christopher saw a spurt of blood coming from his shoulder. Another shot, and Christopher grabbed onto the rough concrete top of the parapet, swung his legs back from the abyss as he saw the Pale Saint toppling over him, over the top of the parapet, plunging down five stories.

He was coughing and hacking up blood as he gained the rooftop. His legs still felt shaky and his gorge rose dangerously into his throat, his temples throbbing wildly as he leaned over the parapet and looked down.

A heavy canvas canopy had come down and an outdoor stand full of fruit and vegetables was in disarray. A young Korean greengrocer was screaming at the Pale Saint, who was racing away through the gathering throng of people. Christopher could see cops in riot gear trying to move through the crowd, but it was hopeless. They were hemmed in on all sides, unable to follow the Pale Saint's flight.

'Goddammit,' Christopher said as he turned around. 'He's gone.'

He saw Cassandra coming toward him. She had Bobby's gun down at her side. As soon as she got a good look at him, she broke into a run.

'Jon, how badly are you hurt?'

'I don't think anything's broken,' he said, 'but I'm beginning to feel a bit like Wile E. Coyote.' He tried to smile at her, but he broke down instead, the tears squeezed out of his eyes.

'Jon,' she whispered.

'This bastard knows how to get to me, Cass. He knows how Andy died, he reached down inside me and pulled up the pain and grief and guilt and rubbed it all in my face.'

She put a hand to his cheek and he flinched. 'Don't let him do this to you, Jon.'

'Easy to say.'

As he sank to his haunches she knelt beside him, holding him close. They stayed that way for a long time. It had begun to rain, and he lifted his face. It felt so good to let the water sluice away the blood and sweat while he caught his breath. He could not stop thinking about Andy, about the last lonely moments of his life. How he longed to turn back time so he could run into the poolhouse and pull Andy off that diving board, put his arms around him, hold him close and tell him how much he loved him.

He thought of how close he had come to capturing the Pale Saint, and still had failed. At every turn, the Pale Saint knew how to get to him. No vulnerable point had been overlooked. But that's what you did in war, exploit the enemy's weaknesses.

'Jon,' Cassandra whispered, 'what are you thinking?'

He caressed her cheek. 'That you're right about many things, not the least of which is you can run and shoot with the best of them. Thanks.'

She kissed him tenderly.

'Was it difficult?'

'Pulling the trigger? I suppose it would have been if I'd thought about it. I didn't. I just reacted like Bobby told me to do.'

'That's good.'

She laced her fingers in his and squeezed. 'I just wish I had killed him, but I had to make sure I didn't hit you.'

'You did good, Cass.' He rose with her help. The rain was coming down harder, drumming against the tarred roof, turning it into a sheened black surface. 'Let's go see how the kid is holding up.'

SIXTEEN

Water dripped dolefully, echoing through cavernous rooms. The air felt dank and heavy. Halloran & Sons would never be the same. The owners had been notified that in addition to being closed down by the city their premises was the scene of a multiple homicide.

'Jesus.' Jerry Lewis stared at the bodies of the young couple. 'This guy had a field day.'

'Yeah, he definitely enjoyed himself.' Christopher bent down to study the young girl's face. 'Lawrence,' he said, 'this is Marcy?'

'Yes.' Lawrence's face seemed as white as that of Marcy's boyfriend. But some of that came from shock. He was all but unrecognizable behind his swollen and heavily bandaged nose. 'He lied to me.'

'Try not to take it too personally,' Christopher said, patting the clone on the back, 'it's par for the course.'

'What?'

Christopher often forgot about the gaps in Lawrence's knowledge. 'It's an idiom. Par for the course is taken from a golf term. It means this is the normal way a person operates. In other words, the Pale Saint is a born liar.'

'"I am, therefore I think," I told him.' Lawrence's hands were curled in tight fists. '"Thinking, I make my own decisions. I follow my own path," I said.' He shook his head ruefully. 'I should have killed him here or died trying.'

'No,' Christopher told him. 'You followed your instincts and your instincts were right.'

'If I killed him these people would still be alive.'

'Perhaps. On the other hand, he might have killed you *and* them, and I'd be no closer to finding him.'

Lawrence went to the top rack of knives and, reaching behind it, took out the package. 'It's still here.'

'What is it?' Christopher asked.

'You'll see.' Lawrence unfolded the wrapping.

'Oh, mama,' Jerry Lewis said, staring avidly at the pile of long, wicked-looking railroad spikes. 'The motherlode.' He looked from Lawrence to Christopher. 'This, I take it, is your secret source on this case, am I right, Loo?'

'Secret as sin,' Christopher confirmed as he snapped on rubber gloves and called for a large plastic evidence bag. As Lewis held it open, he took the package from Lawrence and placed it inside.

'I ask no questions.' Lewis sealed the bag, marked it with date, place, and time, and hurried out to hand deliver it to the forensics lab.

Christopher was taking Lawrence out of the meat packing plant when his cell phone rang.

'Boss?' It was D'Alassandro.

'Yeah. Where are you?'

'Just got into the hotel at Kalispell. Boss, there are handmade quilts on the bed and spruce rocking chairs on the porch, for God's sake!'

'Take a breath of clean air for me,' he said. 'What's up?'

'Plenty.' The excitement in her voice crackled down the line. 'I don't know what frequency you're tuned into but so far it's right on the money. About sixteen years ago there was this televangelist out of a nowheresville called Tangent, Oklahoma. Smack dab in the middle of the Oklahoma Dust Bowl, just like you said. Anyway, this televangelist – her name was Myra Woods – was real big time locally and regionally. She was even on her way to making a national name for herself when – hold onto your petticoats – she was arrested, tried and convicted for torturing and killing her husband. Seems she hog-tied him to the bed for months before slitting his throat and burying him out back.'

At that moment, by an eerie coincidence, Christopher was staring down at the slit throat of Marcy's boyfriend spread out before him like an exhibit in a very private, very dreadful museum. Then again maybe it was no coincidence at all.

'Yeah, this Myra Woods was a real nasty piece of work, Boss. When she was apprehended, she swore up and down that the murder had been committed by a traveling salesman. Ruined him, poor bastard, by denouncing him on her TV show. But the forensics were conclusive. She did it, all right, and they threw the book at her, made an example of her, I guess.'

Christopher gripped the phone tightly. 'What does that mean?'

'She got the death penalty. They fried her, Boss, nine years ago. Thing is – and this is how I got onto the whole thing – the night the mother was arrested, her farm burned down, the whole shebang. I saw a photo of the main house in the Oklahoma City newspaper on-line archives. Apparently, it was some kind of historical building. Anyway, it had seven pillars, just like you said. And, get this, old fire-and-brimstone Myra's son up and disappeared that same night. Just vanished into thin air.'

'Did the authorities determine the origin of the fire?'

'Arson, Boss. There was clear evidence of an accelerant. Kerosene. It was deliberately set. By the son, I'll bet a year's salary.'

'I won't bet against you. About the son, anything yet?'

'A little.' She gave him the birth date. 'That puts him at the same age we approximated for our perp. His name is Neelon Woods.'

'Good work, Emma. Is there any way for you to see Sheriff Wilcox tonight?'

'Sure thing. In fact, he wants to burn the midnight oil, if you can believe it. According to him, old buzzards don't need much sleep.' She hesitated. 'Funny thing, he seemed real eager to speak to me, like he was relieved or something.'

'I hope it's just a case of a guilty conscience,' Christopher said. 'Be careful, okay?'

'Got my six-shooters strapped on, Boss,' she said in a bad imitation of Gary Cooper's Western drawl.

'Jesus, Emma,' he said, 'don't quit your day job.'

The Pale Saint is hunkered down inside his temporary quarters. It is a makeshift flop of old, rotting plywood sheets and sodden squares of corrugated cardboard. It sits over those large metal grates through which the subway system vents. Outside, it has begun to rain hard enough to shift some of the cardboard squares. The gutters of Houston St are flooded. Water trickles in, rolling through the grate, down into the subway tunnels. Tick-tock, tick-tock.

Having made a make-shift window so that he has a clear view south down the block, the Pale Saint takes out a Hershey bar and snaps off half of it, devouring it in two enormous bites. He listens to the hiss of the traffic passing on the street, and watches the homeless man as he surveys the aches, bruises and wounds his enemies have inflicted on him. He can feel the bullet in his shoulder as if it's a burrowing mole gnawing away at his flesh from the inside out. It's an interesting sensation, like an itch he cannot scratch. He's oh so familiar with that sensation. *Die, Mama, die!* he shouts in his mind. But she just won't die, will she? *Live, Faith, live!* he silently shouts, but it's taking so long to bring her back from the dead.

Soon, though, those itches will be scratched. The end is nigh.

He douses his shoulder with alcohol from a bottle the homeless man has been drinking from. Then he sets about removing the bullet. With his knowledge of anatomy and medical procedures, it does not take him long. He uses more of the alcohol on the raw, bleeding wound, and it feels as if he has set himself on fire. A brief whistling emanates from between his gritted teeth, and he rocks back and forth until the searing flames subside. He rips off strips of his sodden shirt and bandages his shoulder, tying the ends tight.

The grate on which he sits is uncomfortable but warm. The filthy, unquiet bowels of Manhattan manifest themselves to him in many ways. Steam is venting, the smells of urban decay rising like a flock of blackbirds, filthy water, old oil and other lubricants ooze from pipe joints like vital fluids seeping from a dying body. In one corner is the homeless man he displaced when he invaded the flop. The homeless man is trussed up like a chicken ready for the spit. A bunched up dirty sock fills his mouth over which the Pale Saint has criss-crossed two strips of silver duct tape. He has placed the homeless man so that he can see his black eyes, which carry silent messages he does not have to guess at. In the beginning, these messages seemed to hold a degree of interest for him; now, however, he has grown bored with the narrowness of their range. Unlike fear, which can blossom, terror remains static; after the initial surge it drops off his internal radar screen.

The homeless man, with his pinhead and beady crow eyes, reminds him of the Oklahoma county sheriff.

Mama had been taken into custody by the time the sheriff came for him. The sheriff's liver-colored bloodhounds discovered the plot of earth beneath the old white oak where she had buried Pappy. The police had been searching for a teenage boy last seen in the fields near their property, who had been reported missing. The same boy who had taken Faith up to the hayloft; the boy the Pale Saint had in a rage killed and, subsequently, burned to a crisp to get rid of the body. Pappy wasn't a pretty sight when they dug him up, not having had the benefit of the undertaker's chemicals and makeup and all. For a fact Mama had had no cause to make him ready; she had been too busy sweating and cursing his sorry ass as she had hauled him from the house to the pit she had dug beneath the tree.

At first, she claimed a felon fleeing from the law and passing himself as a feed salesman done Pappy in, and for a while she was believed. That was natural, of course, her being a celebrity and all, and supposedly having God on her side. But Mama was a born liar, and she didn't know when to shut up. She kept yammering on, thereby simultaneously drumming up sympathy, larger audiences, and greater celebrity for herself. So the sheriff re-interviewed her. That was when she told him that her son had done his pappy in.

'Now, listen up, son,' the sheriff said to the Pale Saint when he had got the boy into his office, 'I gotta feeling you know what happened to your pappy. Take it from me, now's the time to tell me.'

So the Pale Saint told him: about his sister, about Pappy, and what Mama did to Pappy in return. The sheriff looked like he'd got a fishhook caught in his throat. It seems now to the Pale Saint remembering that day after all these years, that the sheriff could not wait to get him out of his office, as if he were a piece of meat that had unexpectedly begun to stink.

Back at the farm, there was a big hole beneath the old white oak. The sheriff took the Pale Saint inside the house. The faucet was dripping in the dusty soapstone kitchen sink. Already there was an air of disuse that would be difficult to dispel. Upstairs, the sheriff wanted the Pale Saint to show him where it happened with Pappy. In Mama's bedroom, there were the two beds – the one she had strapped Pappy into, and the other, newer one, she had slept in afterward. Then the sheriff noticed the locked trunk, sitting at the foot of Mama's bed, and asked the Pale Saint if he knew what was in there.

He shook his head. 'It was always locked. It belonged to Mama.'

'Your Mama ain't here now,' the sheriff said. 'What say we open it and find out what's inside.'

'It's forbidden.'

The sheriff took the butt-end of his gun and smashed the lock. He lifted the lid and peered inside. He made a tiny strangled sound as, white-faced, he staggered backward. Then he vomited all over Mama's beautiful imported rug.

The Pale Saint peers out the make-shift window he had made in the homeless man's lean-to. He picks up the thermos and drinks the last of the tea while he observes a peculiar emotion crawling around the homeless man's face. 'Finished.' He turns the empty thermos upside down. He grins suddenly. 'Don't worry.' He taps the side of the thermos with his nail. 'Such an expensive item. I'll remember to give it back to Bobby Austin's wife.'

Christopher was back in the Case Room, poring over the obits of the four men the Pale Saint had murdered in Debenture, Montana fifteen years ago. Per Esquival's request, they had been faxed over from the newspaper morgue of *The Debenture Picayune*. The county circuit judge, the Debenture mayor, the city councilman, and the steel manufacturer appeared to have little in common except that they lived in the same town and played poker together every Friday night. Christopher, disgusted, was praying for D'Alassandro to call when the phone rang. It was Cassandra.

'Jon, there's a problem with Lawrence.'

'Tell me.' She had taken the clone back to the loft to work on his broken nose. Bringing him to a hospital ER was out of the question; too many people would see him, too many forms would need to be filled out.

'While I was waiting for his nose to drain I did a blood test. The patch isn't working. He's continuing to age at too rapid a rate.'

Christopher put aside the obits. 'I thought you said the eicosanoid was effective in turning off the trans-gene.'

'It is. The problem is with the patch itself.' She took a breath. 'It looks as though Dillard sabotaged it.'

'Goddamn his pompous ass. I'm telling you, Cass, he had it in for Lawrence from the beginning.'

'But why? The experiment's success would have made his career.'

'Maybe so. But there was something even more important to him. You. He saw Lawrence as a threat to him. You lavished on the clone all the love and attention Dillard craved from you but never got.'

'And he never would have.'

'Bingo. Who better to take his frustration out on than the child.'

'Jesus.'

'It's simple human dynamics, Cass. The question now is how are we going to help Lawrence.'

'We've got to get him back to the lab. I can start direct eicosanoid treatment there.'

'Will it work?'

'Using a protocol of massive doses is completely untested, so I don't know. To be honest, it could kill him. Unfortunately, it's his only chance.'

'The lab is still considered a crime scene,' Christopher said, 'but I think I can get you in. I'll be right over. When I get there I want to collect Sara. You said she's staying with a friend up the street. Until this is all over, I don't want her anywhere near the loft. I'll order up some police protection for her.'

'Do you really think that's necessary, Jon? She's already pretty frightened.'

'I understand, Cass, but it's got to be done.'

'All right,' she said. 'You should get some X-rays done.'

'No time. Look, finish up with him. I'll just swing by my apartment to get some rain gear and be over quick as I can.'

But when he got to his building and dug in his pockets, he realized he'd never picked up his keys after he'd thrown them at the booby-trapped ladder in the hallway outside the Pale Saint's apartment.

Lawrence, holding Christopher's keys in his hand, put down the extension phone as soon as he heard Christopher tell Cassandra that they had to move Sara. Where would they take her? He'd never know. Stealing out of the loft, he tore at his shoulder where Cassandra had implanted the eicosanoid patch. If he could, he would have bitten through skin and flesh to get it out.

Within seconds, he was drenched. The cold rain hammered down on him, but he was oblivious. As he ran, he was on the verge of tears. Just hours ago he was okay with his difference, with the speed of his life. But that was before he had been betrayed, before he had seen Marcy and her boyfriend spread out like slaughtered carcasses. That was before he had held Sara in his arms, had allowed something inside him that had been caged and muzzled to be set free. Somehow, these two moments hung in the theater of his mind apart yet, curiously, fused. Hidden away, protected, coddled, it was as if he had been a somnambulist, only half alive. Now he had suddenly awoken into the real world of horror and ecstasy. Now the taste of life was too sweet for him to be content to let it go. There were so many things he hadn't done, so many places he had read about but had never seen except on video. The feast of life had been set. Everything was here before him yet he could experience none of it.

And the worst of it was that he was alone; always alone. He wanted to be with Sara. His need to see her again, to keep her safe from harm was overwhelming. He knew he would die for her, if need be.

He found the address of Sara's friend Beth on Greene St where she was staying, and leaned on the apartment buzzer in the doorway until the heavy door swung open. Too impatient to wait for the elevator, he vaulted up the stairs. She must have watched him coming down the hall through the peephole because the door opened as he approached, and she was there, framed in the doorway, waiting for him.

'Oh, my God,' she said as she saw his bandaged face. 'It's over, isn't it? You've come to take me home.'

For Sara, it was eerie being back at the site of Andy's death. She remembered being here two years ago, staring at the perfectly innocuous brick facade of this building, and thinking, *They must have made a mistake. It can't have happened. Nothing sinister could go on inside that building.* But what were all the cops and paramedics doing here then? Slippery as an eel, she'd slithered her way between the adults, up the gritty concrete steps, and into the building before anyone could stop her.

She'd seen Uncle Jon. He was standing at the edge of the huge pool, apart from the other people who were milling around. The air was chill with grief and disbelief. Flashes of bright light coming from the bottom of the pool threw sharply-etched shadows against the vaulted ceiling, making it seem as if the place were populated by barely-seen giants.

As she neared the pool, Sara could see that the bursts of light were coming from a photographer. He stood on the gray Gunite surface of the pool's dry bottom, pointing his camera at a broken bloody thing that lay in front of him. People all around the rim of the pool were staring down at this same object, especially Uncle Jon.

With a jolt, Sara realized it was Andy they were all looking at. Andy with his broken neck and the blood spilling out of the back of his head. Andy, who was gone forever.

'Are you okay?' Lawrence was looking at her as she stood in the building's doorway as if rooted to the spot. They were illuminated by the tall sodium security lights that lit up the entire block.

'Yeah,' she said hoarsely. 'I was just remembering that day when Andy died.'

'It's important to get inside,' Lawrence said. 'So we're not seen out here.'

Lawrence put his arm around her, guiding her inside. The door closed behind them, the deep clang echoing in the huge space. The air smelled of chlorine and rubber. Light from the sodium lamps filtered in from the series of windows high up in the walls. A skeletal black metal staircase along one wall rose to the running track that encircled the huge space above the pool. It was renovations on this that had necessitated the draining of the pool.

Sara stood by the edge of the pool. 'Why did you pick this place?'

'Dad said you needed to be moved away from the loft area. Because the Pale Saint killed your father, I think Dad's concerned he might show up at the loft.'

She was staring at the Olympic height diving board that hung over the empty pool like an old-time gallows. 'No, I mean why *here*?'

'It occurred to me because I picked up Dad's keys. He told me he had kept the key to this place. There aren't too many spots in New York I could think of.'

'It's dry, just like it was two years ago.' She turned to him. 'That's not the only reason, is it?'

He shook his head. 'Life is so precious to me. I'm trying to understand why someone would throw his away.'

'I've spent a lot of time wondering the same thing.' Sara worried her lower lip. 'In the summers, when I was younger, Andy and I would go to the beach out in Coney Island. That's in Brooklyn. Before our time it was such a cool place, with huge roller-coaster rides and cotton candy to eat. Anyway, we'd wade out into the water and dive under the waves. It was cool and green and peaceful there. Like a temporary oblivion. We'd have contests to see who could hold their breath longer. But, you know, no matter how long we held our breaths we'd have to surface, and then all the things that had been overwhelming came rushing back at us.' She took a breath and slowly let it go. 'I guess this one time Andy wanted to go down and never come up.'

She turned away from the pool, as if she'd had enough of her memories of Andy's death. 'This *really* reminds me of a prison. How long do I have to stay here?'

'Not long, I hope.'

'At least you saw Mom. She fixed you up, like I said.'

'She tried. Dillard did something to the patch so it won't transmit the chemical I need.'

Sara turned to him, a look of disbelief on her face. 'There's got to be something she can do.'

'She says so, but there's no telling whether it will work.'

She flung herself into his arms, holding him tight. 'I wish I could reach inside you and make things right.'

He could feel her love for him like a palpable thing. Perhaps it was a residue of the Pale Saint's phyto-cocktail, perhaps it was a function of the rogue trans-gene that was flaming inside him. He could hold her trust in the palm of his hand, close his fingers around it, feel its particular warmth that was unlike anything else. He had never known something could be so precious.

'What would you find there, I wonder.' He stroked her hair. 'I dream of him so much, I see his past, I sometimes don't know where I end and he begins.'

'Don't say that. He's only trying to confuse you, and you're scaring me.'

'Please don't be frightened,' he said.

'You're not him, Lawrence, and you never will be. I know that, even if you don't.'

'I'm okay as long as I have you to remind me.'

'I think about Thanksgiving and Christmas,' she said in a small voice. 'I don't want to celebrate them without you.'

He couldn't bear to hear the anguish in her voice. His mind cast about for a way to distract her. '"Tell the clock there,"' he said, quoting Shakespeare's King Richard. '"Give me a calendar. Who saw the sun today?"'

'"Not I, my lord."' Sara smiled as she took for the moment the part of the King's ally, Sir Richard Ratcliffe.

'"Then he disdains to shine; for by the book he should have braved the east an hour ago. A black day it will be to somebody."'

It was their old game of playing Shakespeare together. From the old English lines that seemed a part of another world was manufactured a moment, suspended, insulated from the chaos and danger that lay beyond these four brick and lathe walls. The words, weaving their eternal spell, lifted them up, transporting them, bringing them together in the manner only actors, who have shed their identities for other, grander ones, can accomplish.

'"Ratcliffe!"' he cried.

'"My lord?"'

'"The sun will not be seen today; the sky doth frown and lour upon our army. I would these dewy tears were from the ground. Not shine today! Why, what is that to me more than to Richmond? For the selfsame heaven that frowns on me looks sadly upon him."'

Sara, speaking the Duke of Norfolk's lines, answered: '"Arm, arm, my lord! The foe vaunts in the field."'

She started at a tiny sound, its echo scampering after it along the walls toward them.

'What was that?' she whispered, drawing near to Lawrence's sheltering shoulder.

'Nothing,' he said. 'Just the building settling.' He moved toward the open doorway to the locker rooms beyond. 'Or a rodent the exterminators missed.' He looked back at her. 'But just to be sure, I'll take a look, okay?'

She nodded. 'I'll tell you one thing. I'm not going to stay here by myself.'

'Yes, you are.' He took her hand, took her down into the pool. The far wall of the deep end was lined with sacks of cement and marble dust. 'Stay here,' he said to her. 'I'll be right back.'

She watched wordlessly as he jumped up onto one of the aluminum ladders and climbed out. Too soon he was lost from view. She shivered as she hunkered down between the sacks, waiting for him to come back and tell her they were all alone in the building.

Beyond the open doorway, Lawrence found himself in a small entryway. Directly ahead was a short service corridor leading to the door down to the basement. On either side of where he stood, the locker rooms were divided into two symmetrical wings, one for the boys and one for the girls. Each contained locker facilities, lines of sinks, toilet stalls, and showers.

He stood in the center, listening for anything out of the ordinary. All he heard was a soft background noise he assumed was the heating and cooling system. Choosing at random, he went to the right. As he did so, the background noise diminished. He stopped, turned, retraced his steps into the left wing. Halfway down the twin lines of lockers the sound began to distinguish itself: somewhere nearby water was running.

He moved past the sinks, seeing himself reflected over and over again in the mirrors that covered the walls. Past the toilet stalls he could hear it clearly now: a shower was on full force.

He stood at the entrance to the tiled shower room. All the stalls were open, except one at the far end which had its white plastic curtain closed. Steam rose from behind it as the water poured down. In front of the stall was a wooden stool, painted white. On it was a neatly folded towel. Beneath the towel lay underwear, a blue Oxford dress shirt, striped tie, slim leather belt. A pair of polished loafers were lined up on the floor below an expensive-looking dark-gray pinstripe suit a lawyer or a banker would wear, which hung from the curtain rod of the adjoining stall.

Lawrence walked across the tiled floor, down the rows of stalls until he was standing in front of the last stall. Steam billowed up, and the smell of scented soap was in the air. He moved the stool to one side, reached up and quickly drew back the shower curtain.

'Greetings, junior,' the Pale Saint said as he grabbed Lawrence's shirtfront, jerked him into the shower, and butted him hard in the head.

'Well, I'm done.' As the Pale Saint stepped over Lawrence's unconscious form he drew off the shower nozzle the roll of silver duct tape he'd taken from the homeless man. Ripping off strips, he tied Lawrence's hands behind his back, then wrapped his ankles together. Without turning off the water, he stepped out of the stall and toweled off. He re-bandaged his shoulder. As he climbed into his clothes, Lawrence's eyes opened.

'Now don't you look foolish.' He neither rushed his words nor looked directly at Lawrence.

Lawrence opened his mouth, but it filled with water, which he was obliged to spit out.

Lawrence struggled to sit up. He could see this much, that the Pale Saint had once again transformed himself. 'I can't breathe.' The water beating on his bandaged nose sent bright sparks of pain through him.

The Pale Saint, adjusting his tie, glanced at him. 'Would you rather I tape your mouth shut?' He swung the stool around and sat, spread-legged.

'I want you to tell me,' Lawrence whispered, 'whether I killed Dillard.'

'What's the matter?' His tone was mocking. 'Can't remember?'

'You know I can't. Is that your doing, as well?'

'You did what you had to do, junior. You got your hands bloody. It's all a part of growing up.'

Lawrence shook his head. 'All I remember is something that happened to Faith up in the hayloft. Dad says you transferred your anger to me to get me to attack Dillard.'

'Christopher.' The Pale Saint snorted. 'Gosh, junior, you certainly are a major disappointment. I so much wanted to think of you as an ally, someone I could count on in the upcoming finale. It would have been fun, I admit, to have you at my side when I brought Faith back from the dead. Would have opened your eyes, that's for sure.' He pursed his lips. 'But it's not to be, I see. Pity.' He cocked his head. 'No matter. In a different sense, you've done me a great service.'

'I did you a service?' Lawrence managed. Pain had spread throughout his skull to his injured nose, which throbbed incessantly.

'You mean you haven't gotten it yet?' The Pale Saint stood, hands on hips, looking down at his clone. 'It's Sara I want. It's Sara I need. That's why I was in Central Park the other day. Did you think it was a coincidence? No, I was after her. I thought I could snatch her in all the confusion after the game.' He frowned. 'But that damn dog gave me away.' He shrugged. 'Not his fault, really. And I was damned sorry he was killed. Ever since I was a kid, I've had this ability – a connection to animals; they're drawn to me. Like dragonflies to a flame.' For an instant, his eyes went opaque, as if he was staring right through Lawrence, through even the wall of the shower stall to some other place known only to him. 'It's a bond,' he said as his eyes refocused on Lawrence. He leaned in, his face becoming beaded with spray. 'Like the bond I thought you and I had.'

'That was no bond,' Lawrence struggled to say. 'That was manipulation. You tried to make me into you.'

'You poor fool. Don't you get it yet? You *are* me. You can struggle all you want but we're of one mind, you and me. Eventually you *will* understand. If you don't die first. I must say, junior, you look less peaked since some of my potion.'

'Never mind me. I want to know what you're going to do with Sara.'

'She's piqued your interest, I see. But I wonder why I should tell you anything, you who've betrayed me to Christopher.'

'There's no reason I can think of.'

'But I can.' The Pale Saint smiled unkindly. 'I want to see the look on your face when I tell you. See, junior, when the time is right she and I are going to take the potion. I'm going to open the Channel. Not only in me, but in her. She's going to be the vessel.'

Lawrence's eyes opened wide. 'Ah, no!'

A slow smile spread across the Pale Saint's face. 'Ooh, yeah, baby. She will die – or at least her soul will. With the Channel wide open I'll summon Faith from out of the limbo in which she has been patiently waiting.'

'You can't.'

He laughed. 'Who's to stop me? You?'

'My father.'

'Oh, yes. Christopher will certainly try. But he'll fail. I'll see to it.' The Pale Saint hitched the stool closer. 'See, junior. I have no other choice. Only when Faith is resurrected in Sara's body will the circle finally close.'

'What circle?'

'Death. Life. And every insignificant thing in between.'

Lawrence shouted a warning to Sara, but this only made the Pale Saint laugh. 'Go on, scream yourself hoarse. She can't hear you. Not over the water, not through these old thick walls.'

Lawrence paid him no mind, but kept shouting at the top of his lungs.

The Pale Saint took his suit jacket off the hanger. 'Be seeing you, junior.'

As soon as he left, Lawrence shut his mouth. He squirmed back against the slick wall, and struggled to his feet. A wave of dizziness momentarily overcame him, forcing him to slump against the showerhead. Launching himself like a missile, he half-fell, half-stumbled out of the stall. Lying on the tile floor, he began to shiver as his soaked clothes clung to him.

He looked around. There was no implement lying conveniently around like in the movies he'd seen, nothing he could use to cut through the duct tape. He inched his way down the length of the room to the doorway, then over to the corner of the far wall. He had to push hard, banging his shoulder repeatedly against the tiles in order to even attempt to stand up. He almost made it on the third try, but slipped on the slick tile and fell clumsily against the wall. A welter of old, dried-out grout fell with him.

He tried to stand again. As he did so, his gaze fell upon an area where the grout had shaken free. At about knee height, a sharp upper corner of the tile was now exposed. He turned around and jammed his wrists back against the corner. He felt the edge of the tape catch on the rough lip and he began an almost maniacal sawing motion. One section of the tape gave way, then another and another until he was through. He reached down, frantically ripped the tape off his ankles, then went quickly past the sinks, the lockers and out to the pool, where he had left Sara.

Christopher could see trouble coming a block off. Cassandra was in front of the loft entrance, pacing back and forth like a caged cat.

'Dammit to hell, Jon, Lawrence is gone,' she said when he pulled up.

'Why would he –?'

'I found one of the phones in the loft off the hook,' she said. 'He apparently overheard our conversation.'

'About how Dillard fucked him over with those damn patches.'

'Who knows what's on his mind now that what Dillard did to him is out in the open? For all we know he could hate us for allowing it to happen.'

'Try to think clearly, Cass. He doesn't hate us.'

'How can you be sure?'

'We're his only family. Unlike the Pale Saint he's desperate for family. He wants to fit in; he's anything but a loner.'

'Then why did he run out of the loft?'

'He's confused, frightened. You said the eicosanoid protocol might kill him, remember?'

'Oh, God.'

'Not to worry. I have a good idea where he went.' Christopher gestured her into the car. He got behind the wheel and took off. 'I couldn't get into my apartment because I didn't have my keys. I threw them at the ladder outside the Pale Saint's apartment, remember?'

'Yes, the sparks . . . the ladder was booby-trapped. You forgot to pick them up when we went back to fetch Lawrence.'

'They weren't there,' he said, hitting the horn as he ran a red light. 'I checked with Lewis. The apartment building's been secured. No one saw the keys. I figure Lawrence must have picked them up and forgot to give them to me.' He took a corner with alarming speed, ran another red light as horns blared to either side of them. 'The thing is, I showed him the key I kept to the pool where Andy killed himself. It's the only place he'd think of.'

'It still seems like a long shot,' Cassandra said.

Christopher's cell phone rang and he answered it, expecting D'Alassandro's voice.

'Recovered yet, Christopher?' the Pale Saint said.

Christopher felt the tension ripple through him.

'You'd better have, because your little clone isn't up to the job you assigned him.'

'Meaning?'

'He's trussed and tied like a hog to the slaughter,' the Pale Saint said. 'He'll be of no use trying to get Sara back.'

'What did you say?'

'I have her, Christopher. Now I want you to imagine her spread out on a slab at the morgue. Drained of blood. White as milk. What a pretty sight! Not that I have any illusions you'd think so. In which case, you'd better hightail it over here.'

Christopher was making a supreme effort to stay calm. This is war, he kept telling himself. War. 'Where's here?'

'You mean you're clueless? Okay, I'll give you one. In a couple of minutes your little clone is going to go out the same ghastly way Andy did.'

'I know where you are.'

'There you go, soldier, you only needed a bit of help. One more thing. Any hint you've brought the SWAT team you ordered up in the Village, and I'll snuff them both. Got me?'

'Read you loud and clear, Neelon.'

There was a peculiar silence.

'That is your name, Neelon Woods, right?' More silence. 'Your Mama was some nasty piece of work, there, Neelon, she surely was. Strapped your father to the bed and tortured him for how long –?' More silence. 'Well, a good long time, anyway. Then she slit his throat. Tell me, Neelon, you see all that? Did your sister Faith see it? Must have been blood flowing like a fountain that day.'

He was gone; the light winked out. The connection was broken.

'My God, Jon, that was him, wasn't it?'

'I'm afraid so,' he said, as he floored the accelerator. 'He's got Lawrence.'

'Shit.' She stared out the window. 'I shot him, he fell five storeys, and still he's alive and well.' She turned back to Christopher. 'Jon, if I get another chance I *will* shoot to kill.'

'I have no doubt you want to, Cass. But my mandate is to bring him in – alive.'

'And if there's no other choice?'

Christopher shook his head. 'I can't believe I'm hearing you talk like this. What's going on?'

She sighed and put her head back against the car seat. 'Oh, God, Jon. I thought I was handling this thing with Vertex. I thought, okay, so my life's work has been wrapped up in this place and now it's all gone. Vertex has been my support system since I was at NYU Medical. Gerry took me away from all that. He backed me, believed in me, gave me free rein. But now I see that it was no blessing that he protected me from the hypocrisy and the lies and the political bullshit that people like him represent. It was all going on around me, like an invisible world I thought would never touch me.' She stared out into the night, her eyes welling with tears. 'The truth is, it's hit me like a hammer. I feel like it's the end of everything. Gerry's taken away everything I've worked so hard for, everything I care about.'

'You've given him the best years of your life, that what you're thinking?'

'Something very much like that, yes.' She gave him a brief smile through her tears. 'Gerry betrayed me. I trusted him; he was a mentor to me. But I've still got my technology. I've got a notion to march over to Ken Reinisch's office at Helix Technologies and cut myself a deal.'

'Didn't you tell me that Reinisch was a slimeball?'

'So's Gerry. As it turns out, the only difference between them is their background. Gerry was born to privilege, Ken worked his way up to success like Bobby.'

'You're disillusioned.'

'You bet I am.'

'And pissed as hell.'

'Furious.'

He shot her a pointed look. 'Now you want to kill the Pale Saint yourself.'

'Now I want to kill the Pale Saint myself,' she said. 'But I take your point.'

'I hope to Christ you do.'

His cell phone rang. *If it's him again* . . . he thought.

'Boss?' It was D'Alassandro. 'I got the skinny on the Pale Saint's four victims. That's been Debenture's secret, you see. It looks like an innocent flyspeck backwater, but fifteen years ago it was as rotten as Shakespeare's Denmark. This small group of millionaire robber-baron pigs ran the whole works. Without conscience, they did what they pleased when they pleased out of the glare of the big city spotlight. Anyway, they did more than play poker once a week, let me tell you. For one thing, they were involved in a lot of business dealings together, not all of them strictly legit. For another, they had a kind of club.'

'What kind of club?'

'A sex club. Real kinky stuff. S&M, bondage, humiliation. Pain was their pleasure, as the saying goes. But here's the kicker: their victims were real young – teens, mostly.'

'Girls?'

'These lovelies chose from column A *and* column B.'

'Delightful. I noticed you used the word victims.'

'It fits. When they tired of their disgusting games they got rid of the victims. Mostly sent 'em away with a bit of money and a railroad ticket. But occasionally not. Sometimes their victims rebelled, sometimes things got out of hand during their sexual Olympics. Sometimes both. Sheriff Wilcox said that was the way it happened with Faith Woods. She didn't like what they were doing to her.'

'They raped her, beat her, and to shut her up they killed her.'

'That's about the size of it.'

'Wilcox give it up freely?'

'Like a gusher. As you suspected, his guilty conscience has been eating at him for years.'

'Still, all this time he did nothing.'

'Why should he? They paid the bastard well enough. He ran interference for them, made sure they were protected from any prying eyes they hadn't already paid off, sent packing or had killed.'

Christopher thought a moment. 'How many people Wilcox say died that week?'

'Four. Just like it says on the VCAP.'

Christopher had remembered Lawrence telling him that the Pale Saint claimed he'd murdered five people in the same span of days. The Pale Saint was a born liar but why would he lie about something like that? 'Emma, listen to me carefully. I have a hunch there was someone else killed following Faith's murder, someone who for some reason Wilcox still won't roll over on. Maybe he was a member of this club, maybe not. But for sure he was involved with Faith Woods. Find out for me, will you?'

'Permission to break this sonuvabitch's kneecaps, Boss?' she cracked.

'Only as a last resort.' He ran another light; even with her seatbelt on Cassandra was holding onto the door panel for dear life. 'Seriously, be gentle but firm, Emma. From what we know Wilcox wants to spill it all. He just needs your help is all.'

'Gotcha, Boss. *Then* I'll punch his lights out. He's the kind of pig that gives law enforcement a bad name.'

'I hear you,' he said. 'Listen, things have gone white hot back here. We're closing in on the perp.'

'I'll give you a shout ASAP. Good luck.'

'Roger that. You too.' He wasn't taking any more chances. He called Lewis, ordered him to tighten the perimeter check at all bridges and tunnels leading out of Manhattan. But even when he'd hung up he was still thinking about his lie of omission to Cassandra. In her current state of mind, how on earth could he tell her that the Pale Saint had both Lawrence and Sara?

Lawrence was waiting for some movement. He crouched in the shadows of the doorway, looking out at the vast expanse surrounding the pool. No movement. No sound. Nothing but the imagined hum in his ears of his metabolism eating him alive. Rain rolled down the windowpanes high above his head. He tried to imagine Sara crouched where he had left her, safe from the Pale Saint. Was she still there at the deep end of the pool? Where was the Pale Saint? His mind cast about for answers to these questions but all he heard was an echo inside his head of the Pale Saint's mocking voice: *You can struggle all you want but we're of one mind, you and me.*

One mind.

With a harsh cry of despair, he understood what was required of him now. He had to forget Christopher and his training, he had to forget his love for Sara. He had to forget everything that was *his*, let go of everything he had struggled to acquire that made him different from the Pale Saint.

One mind.

It wasn't shamanism, or mysticism, but simple cell biology. If he was a prisoner of his own DNA, so was the Pale Saint. In order to beat him, he had to become him.

Lawrence was openly weeping now. The surrender to what was bred in the bone was a brutal torture, far worse than the anguish Dillard had caused him. In order to save Sara he had to lose himself, perhaps forever.

He wiped his eyes with the heels of his hand as he tried to pull himself together. The Pale Saint was counting on his weakness, he knew that much. Then he realized that the Pale Saint was counting on many things. He had made basic assumptions about his enemies based on the psychological profiles provided by the NYPD files and, in the case of Lawrence and Christopher, speaking to them in person. That was a weakness that could be exploited.

Still no movement in the pool room. Lawrence got down on his belly and crawled to the edge of the pool. He had a direct line of sight to the deep end. Sara was no longer there. Had she somehow, miraculously escaped or did the Pale Saint have her?

Lawrence went back into the locker room, tried the door to the basement. It was unlocked. A single light shone at the bottom of the stairs. He went down to it.

The place stank of chlorine and mildew. The rough concrete walls and ceiling were lined with pipes and ducts for heating, water, air conditioning, as well as for the pool itself. The air was warm and thick with the insistent cough and hum of machinery. A miniature city rose all around him, composed of oil burners, massive air-conditioners, pool filters, compressors, hot water heaters, water tanks and the like. He moved through these as silently as he could.

He saw Sara, curled like a salamander. She was bound and gagged as he had been with silver duct tape, wedged between two circular fiberglass pool filters. Lawrence had to resist the urge to rush to her. He knew this was a trap; if the Pale Saint had only wanted to take her they would have been gone by now.

The basement stretched away from him, huge and unknowable as if it were a living being.

He's here, Lawrence thought, *waiting. No matter which route I take, he's going to see me.*

Reaching up, he touched the pipes briefly. Too hot to hold onto. Quickly, he stripped off his sopping shirt and, tearing it in two, wrapped the strips around his hands and forearms. Grasping the pipes, he hoisted himself up until he could cross his sneakers around them. Steam rose from the points where the wet cloth of his shirt touched the hot metal. The pipes hung perhaps a foot from the ceiling, which gave him just enough room to maneuver. Hand over hand, he inched his way along the maze of pipes. Once, at a turn, his shoulder brushed against an adjacent pipe and he winced with the pain as it seared his skin. He bit his lip and kept going.

He concentrated on areas that had a direct line of sight to where Sara lay huddled; the Pale Saint would need to see her from where he lay in wait. Lawrence found him in the spot he himself would have chosen. This frightened him because minute by minute he found himself merging with the Pale Saint's orbit, but he pushed the fear down, and kept going. This was no different from learning to walk, he told himself. Just put one foot in front of the other and *don't think of the consequences.*

He moved more slowly, now with great deliberation, though as his makeshift protection dried he could feel the heat penetrating the cloth. He'd begun to sweat, the beads rolling into his eyes, making him blink and shake his head. Half-blinded, he shook his head again to clear his vision.

This was a mistake. The Pale Saint, feeling the wetness, looked up a moment before Lawrence released his grip on the pipe overhead and dropped on him.

He ducked away from Lawrence's attack, grabbed him by the back of the neck and, swinging him in a short arc, slammed him against the wall. Lawrence grabbed a length of pipe, swung it viciously at the Pale Saint. Blood was in his heart, death clogged his mind, paralyzing all other thought. He wept inside as he swung again, made contact, and raised the pipe again for the killing blow.

At that instant, the Pale Saint drove a two-handed punch into Lawrence's naked side and all the breath went out of him. Then the Pale Saint kicked him in the side of the head.

As Lawrence fell to the floor, the Pale Saint said, 'Give it up, junior. You're really no good at this.'

Christopher screeched to a stop outside the all too familiar brick building. His stomach felt hollow as he got out. Cassandra, right beside him, said: 'It seems spooky being back here.'

'Too spooky for words,' Christopher agreed. He took her hand. 'Look, Cass –'

'Jon, just don't tell me to stay in the car. I couldn't bear it.' Her gray eyes searched his. 'I know I've been acting like a bitch with a battle-ax, but I haven't exactly been a liability, have I?'

Christopher shook his head. 'Just keep your finger off the trigger, okay?'

She nodded wordlessly as they hurried through the rain. He noted the 'Caution' sign posted beside the entrance. As he suspected, the door was unlocked. Lawrence had used the key.

'Aren't we going in?' Cassandra asked.

'Not this way.'

He led her around to the side of the building. 'The Pale Saint called to bait me, daring me to come to get him. Which means he's laid some kind of trap for me. As he said, it's his game. I've got to find some way to beat him at it.'

'How are you going to do that?' she asked.

He shot her a tense smile. 'When I figure it out I'll let you know.'

Reaching up, he pulled down a metal ladder that led to the fire escape. He began to climb, Cassandra right behind him. They gained the roof, went across it to the banks of windows. All were fixed in place save one, which was used for maintenance access. Christopher broke the small lock, twisted the lever. The window swung up.

Cassandra peered over his shoulder. 'It must be a twenty foot drop to the pool.'

'More.'

'Then would you kindly tell me how the hell we're going to get in this way?'

Christopher pointed down as he went through the opening. He dropped down onto the running track, found a rolling scaffold and moved it under the window so Cassandra could clamber down without having to jump.

Together, they crept around the track.

The cold, purplish illumination from the sodium lamps outside turned the interior into a kind of underwater maze.

Suddenly, Cassandra froze. 'Jon –' she whispered.

Down below them, amid the gloom, Christopher could see something hanging from the edge of the diving board. He scrambled around to get a better look. It was Lawrence. His fingers had been taped to the end of the board with silver duct tape. The same tape had been used as a blindfold. Christopher could see the muscles of his arms bulging as they bore the weight of his entire body.

He went and got a length of rope off the scaffolding, then moved to the inner edge of the running track, crawling past the guardrail. 'I'm going down to get him,' he said as Cassandra crouched beside him.

'You said this was a trap. Isn't that just what the Pale Saint wants?'

He was tying off the rope to one of the vertical stanchions of the guardrail. 'Cass, look at him. How long d'you think he can hold on like that? In a few minutes he's going to dislocate both shoulders. I have no choice.'

Cassandra took out her gun. 'All right, but the moment the Pale Saint shows his face I swear I'm going to blow it off.'

Christopher pulled on the rope, rechecking the knots. 'Listen, since you're in such a bloodthirsty mood, if you do shoot make damn sure you hit him, because you're my ace in the hole. If you miss, he'll know you're here and exactly where you are. I don't want that, understand?'

She nodded. 'Jon, I –' With her gun in one hand, she leaned over and kissed him hard on the lips. 'Come back with him.'

He nodded wordlessly as he began playing out the rope. It hung down approximately ten feet from where Lawrence hung, which meant he would have to gain some momentum and swing over in order to grab the clone.

As he went slowly down the rope, he could see the bottom of the pool and, for an instant, it seemed to him as if he was back two years ago, the flashbulbs popping, the forensic team scuttling like huge beetles around the broken body of his son. He could still hear Stick saying to him, 'God in heaven, you have my sympathies. No parent should see his child come to such an end.'

Such an end . . .

It was an end without any finality. If only he knew what was in Andy's mind when he stood on that diving board. In the last instants of life what rage and despair had driven him to end his life. *If only he had talked to me*, Christopher thought for the ten thousandth time. *If only I had talked to him.*

Reality broke through his black thoughts. He was now far enough down the rope so that he was on a level with Lawrence's stretched-out body. He kicked out with one leg, beginning to build the momentum he would need to bridge the ten-foot gulf between them. With each swing, the arc increased. Closer and closer he came to Lawrence, until he was able to open his legs and wrap them around the clone's waist.

He could feel Lawrence flinch and he said, 'It's me.'

'Dad!'

Christopher felt a peculiar thrill go through him. 'I can't let go of the rope,' he said. 'You'll have to work your hands free yourself.'

'Okay, Dad. I can do it.'

It was the same thing Andy had said years ago when Christopher had begun teaching him how to dive. Christopher's heart broke with a combination of grief and love.

Lawrence moved his hands back and forth until he had a bit of play beneath the tape. Then he curled his fingers, using them to push upward. He pulled one hand free, then the other.

'Very good,' Christopher said. 'We're suspended over the pool. We're going to swing back and forth. You just concentrate on holding onto me, okay?'

'Dad, I have to tell you –'

'Just do as I say.'

The clone nodded and, as they began to swing, he groped blindly, finding purchase as he wrapped his arms around Christopher's back. Christopher tightened his grip with his legs.

'Now listen to me, Lawrence. We're still a long way from safety. There's too much weight for me to take us both back up and the rope isn't long enough to get us all the way down. We're going to go down almost to the end, then we'll get the rope swinging again so we can jump to the floor. Don't worry about not being able to see, I'll protect you when we fall. You listen to me and I'll guide you every step of the way, okay?'

'Yes, Dad.'

'All right, we're going down the rope.'

Slowly, painfully, Christopher inched them down. The bunched muscles in his shoulders and thighs ached and there was a savage throbbing in every place he'd taken a drubbing. His fingers were almost completely numb from gripping the rope and holding on with Lawrence's added weight.

Lower and lower they went until, with his feet, he could feel the end of the rope.

'Okay, we're there,' he said. 'Ready?'

Lawrence nodded, shifted his weight to help Christopher gain the momentum they would need to bring them out over the floor that ran around the sides of the pool.

'Christopher. I see you, Christopher.'

'It's him!' Lawrence said. 'Where is he?'

'Somewhere in the shadows. I can't see him.'

'This is some rescue job you're pulling,' the Pale Saint said. 'D'you think the little twerp's worth it? After all, he's only a tubie, a clone, a cipher, a zero, a nullity.'

'Let's talk about you for a minute, Neelon. You had one sister, Faith. She died fifteen years ago. She was found murdered in Debenture, wasn't she? But not before she'd been raped, beaten and hog-tied. Not a pretty end.'

'Don't want to talk about her.'

'No, I don't blame you.' Christopher wondered if Cassandra could see him. 'But then your sister was used to being raped.'

'What d'you mean?'

'The hayloft, Neelon, that's what I mean. Some boy took her up there. He was raping her when you happened upon them. What happened then? Did you beat him to death? Was that the real beginning to all this?'

'Just because your resident shrink is nothing but a memory don't try out your dimestore psychology on me.' His voice became a derisive whine: 'Oh, please, Mr Detective, take me into custody before I do any more harm. Yes, I want to be beaten by cops, felt up by prison guards, and corn-holed by my cell mates. I just can't wait until you put the cuffs on me!'

Christopher ignored his histrionics. 'Murder just runs in your family, doesn't it?' He calculated he had built up almost enough momentum to swing them over the edge of the pool. 'John Woods, your father, was murdered by your mother; she was put to death nine years ago in Oklahoma State Penitentiary.'

'Shows how much you know, Christopher. My mother's still alive, not that it's any of your business.'

Just a little more: one swing, two. 'But it is my business, Neelon. She's a criminal. You've taken after her.' They were moving over the lip of the pool; there was no time to warn Lawrence. Christopher readied himself to let go.

'Not me!' the Pale Saint shouted. 'I'm nothing like her!' And, emerging from the shadows, he kicked Christopher in the stomach just as he let go of the arcing rope.

Christopher, his momentum stymied, plummeted straight down, Lawrence with him, to the bottom of the pool. In mid-air, Christopher curled his body around Lawrence's, in order to protect him. The two of them hit one of the piles of cement sacks, Christopher on the bottom. They rolled heavily off, then down to the floor of the pool. Just before Christopher's head hit the side of a sack, he heard a gunshot. Then he blacked out.

The Pale Saint looked up, found Cassandra crouching at the inner edge of the running track, ducked away as she squeezed off another shot. Deep in the shadows, he turned on the four massive spigots and water began to gush into the pool.

'You're over-ambitious, Cass,' he called to her as he sprinted up the staircase to the track. 'Now it's going to be the death of you.'

She fired twice more while he was on the staircase, but her angle was poor and she should have waited. But he'd unnerved her, and she was in a panic, not knowing what had happened to Christopher and Lawrence. As the Pale Saint gained the track, she ran. She could hear him gaining on her and she turned, planted herself. No time to aim, she simply fired.

The Pale Saint, running full tilt, plowed into her. She'd run out of time.

Below them, at the bottom of the pool, Lawrence struggled off Christopher's inert form. Where they lay, the water was already ankle deep and rising fast. When Lawrence ripped off his blindfold, he saw that Christopher's head was half underwater. He hauled him to the side of the pool, propped him up into a sitting position.

'Dad,' he said. Then more forcefully: 'Dad!'

He slapped Christopher's cheeks and Christopher's eyes fluttered open.

'Are you okay?'

Christopher stared at him groggily.

'I've got to go get him.'

Christopher started to shake his head, but Lawrence was already on the aluminum ladder. He turned, reached back, and grabbed a fistful of Christopher's shirt. With his help, Christopher stood, leaning heavily against the side of the pool. He grasped the ladder, swung up behind Lawrence. He looked up, saw Lawrence running toward the stairs. 'That's not the way,' he shouted, but he was drowned out by the roar of the water.

Cassandra had gotten the gun up as she struggled with the Pale Saint.

'If you shoot me,' he said, 'you'll never know what happened to Sara.'

'What?'

'Your daughter.' His lips pursed. 'Ooh, don't tell me Christopher failed to mention that I have her?'

Cassandra felt paralyzed with terror. The Pale Saint hit her hard on the jaw, ripped the gun out of her hand and, turning, pressed it to her temple.

Lawrence was walking toward him. He'd caught a glimpse of the clone skulking up the staircase. 'It seems the longer you live the better you do in water.' He cocked the hammer on the gun. 'Don't come any closer, junior, otherwise mommy will get another hole in her head.'

'Why do you bother threatening me?' Lawrence asked. 'You said we're both the same. If we are, I won't care whether or not you shoot her. If I'm just like you I won't care about anything or anyone.'

'But that isn't true, junior. I do care. Not about her, and certainly not about Christopher.'

'Liar! It isn't Faith you care about. She betrayed you; she went up into the loft with that boy. I felt it. You made me live it. But I also know what really happened up there.' Lawrence took a cautious step in the Pale Saint's direction. 'He didn't rape her; she took him up there. She pulled off his pants and begged for it. And it wasn't the first time, was it? No, I saw everything that you remembered. I saw how you ripped him off her, how you beat him senseless while Faith screamed and clawed at you to stop. I saw how you took a shovel and stove in his head. I saw how you burned the body to ash, and I saw how Faith lit out of there the next morning. She left you all alone with your mama, didn't she? So don't tell me you care for her because I know better.'

'It's you I care about, junior.' The smile painted on the Pale Saint's face was taut, as if he had manufactured it out of rage. 'You who are a part of me. How could I ever harm you? How could you ever harm me? We're closer than flesh-and-blood. You can't sever that kind of tie.'

Lawrence kept his gaze fully on the Pale Saint. 'Before I met you, before you gave me the drug I would have agreed with you. But you've done nothing but deceive me and manipulate me.'

'Have you treated me any differently?' the Pale Saint howled. 'No! So let's not let a few lies get in the way. We have something, junior. God knows, it's something unique.'

'Too late for that,' Christopher said as he let go of the rope he'd painfully shimmied up and vaulted over the track railing. The moment Lawrence had glimpsed his head out of the corner of his eyes as it came abreast of the surface of the track, he knew he had to keep the Pale Saint distracted.

Christopher slammed his elbow hard into the Pale Saint's chest, bowling him head over heels backward so that the gun flew out of his grip. Lawrence darted toward Cassandra, gathering her up in his arms.

Christopher went for his gun, but he'd somehow lost it when he and Lawrence had fallen into the pool. He spied Cassandra's gun and dove for it. So did the Pale Saint. Christopher tromped on his hand, and the Pale Saint screamed. He kicked out, catching Christopher's knee. Christopher went down, and the Pale Saint reached for the gun. Just as his fingers curled around it, Christopher chopped down with the edge of his hand. The Pale Saint grunted, turned, struck Christopher a glancing blow as Christopher used his elbow again, burying it in the Pale Saint's solar plexus.

As the Pale Saint doubled over, Christopher scooped up the gun and as the Pale Saint rushed him, he pulled the trigger. The hammer fell, but there was no discharge. The gun was out of ammo.

The Pale Saint vaulted over the guardrail, grabbing the rope. Christopher recovered just in time to see the Pale Saint swinging far out over the pool. At the apex of the arc, he let go, flying through space. He struck the floor on the opposite side of the pool, rolled into a ball, tumbling along the concrete. Then he was up and running, disappearing through the doorway to the locker rooms.

'Take care of her,' Christopher instructed Lawrence, as he half-ran, half-slid down the stairs. He tried to find his gun, but the swirling water was black as pitch. He gave it up, went through the open doorway, saw immediately the stairs down to the basement. To be certain, he made quick forays into both locker rooms. Finding them empty, he followed the Pale Saint down into the basement.

'You've trapped yourself, Neelon,' he called as he moved down the narrow aisles between the machines. 'There's nowhere to run. You're out of real estate.'

The Pale Saint stepped out from behind a boiler. He held Sara tight against his body. 'This basement connects with the others in the adjacent buildings. I have miles to go.' Sara's arms were bound behind her back, and her mouth was taped shut. But her eyes, staring wide open, implored Christopher for help. 'Not that it matters to you. Back off, Christopher.' He began to walk backwards, pulling the terrified girl with him.

Christopher held his hands up, palms toward the Pale Saint. 'Let her go, Neelon, she means nothing to you. If you want a hostage, take me.'

'Hostage?' The Pale Saint laughed. 'My God, even after all this time you're clueless. You started off with a good deal of promise, I admit. But in the end you're like all the rest,' he sneered. 'No, the girl's no hostage. Want me to prove it to you?' He took out one of his long, wicked railroad spikes, and pushed its tip against Sara's left eyelid. She tried to scream, squirming futilely, but he held her fast. 'This is your only warning, Christopher. Believe me when I say ten seconds from now if you aren't out of here I will kill her.'

'Neelon, let's talk –'

'Nine . . .'

'This isn't going to get you what you want.'

'You haven't a clue what I want. Eight . . .'

'Then tell me. Maybe we can work –'

'Don't be absurd, Christopher. Seven . . .' He pressed the spike in further, and Sara tried again to scream, weeping uncontrollably with terror. He shot Christopher a concerned look. 'Just look what you're doing to her. Six . . .'

'There's something you want. Whatever it is, I'm prepared to give it to you if you let the girl go.'

'Right out of the hostage negotiation manual. Only pathological criminals and morons listen to bullshit like that. Five . . .'

'Sterngold, Matthews, Braddock, Peterson.' Christopher recited the names D'Alassandro had given him. 'I know about them all, what they did to Faith. But they're all dead, Neelon.'

'They are now. Four . . .'

Christopher stopped in his tracks. 'What more do you want? I know there's something. Why the girl?'

'"Why the girl?"' he mimicked in his derisive whine. 'How I despise weakness, Christopher. Take my advice and get out of here, now.' The spike moved a millimeter further. 'Three . . .'

'Okay, okay. I'm going,' Christopher said as he began to back off.

'Faster. Two . . .'

Christopher turned back toward the staircase.

'Run, Christopher, run. One . . .'

Christopher went up the stairs, back to where Cassandra and Lawrence were waiting, the Pale Saint's mocking laughter following him all the way.

SEVENTEEN

Cassandra was sitting inside the car, Lawrence kneeling by the open door when Christopher emerged from the building. The rain had lashed the city clean, at least for the time being.

He gathered her into his arms. 'Cass, how are you?'

'My jaw hurts like hell,' she said, touching it gingerly. Her eyes were wide and staring. 'Jon, where –?'

'Gone. He has Sara with him.'

'Oh, God.' Cassandra slumped back against the seat.

'This is my fault,' Lawrence said. 'Sara told me where to find her. The Pale Saint followed us here.' Tears spilled down his cheeks. 'I tried to protect her but I couldn't.'

Christopher put a hand on his shoulder. 'Don't blame yourself. You saved my life back there. Thanks.'

The clone looked at Christopher. 'It's Sara he wanted all along. That's what I tried to tell you before,' he said. 'It's why he came to Central Park. To kidnap her.'

Cassandra looked stunned. 'What could he possibly want with her?' she asked.

'He claims he wants Faith back. He thinks he can resurrect her. Her soul, her essence is still alive inside her skull. He's going to take more of the drug, open up the Channel and transfer her into Sara.'

Cassandra shook her head and winced with the pain. 'But that's nonsense, Lawrence, and you know it.'

'I know what's in here.' He pulled out the baseball he had hollowed out. 'I know there's something living in there.'

'But it's dead. Look.' Cassandra turned the baseball around so they could all see. 'The body is nothing more than a dry and shriveled shell.'

'It's not the body I'm talking about. There's something alive in there,' Lawrence insisted. 'I can feel it.'

'Lawrence, do you know where he's headed?' Christopher asked.

The clone screwed up his face. 'He's going to the place with seven pillars.'

'The house you saw being set on fire?'

Lawrence put his head against the seat back and closed his eyes. 'I was wrong. It's not a house.'

'What else would have seven pillars?' Cassandra said anxiously.

'The pillars aren't real.' Lawrence's eyes snapped open. 'I don't understand so I don't expect you to. The pillars are flat, made of plywood, and behind them there are cut-outs.'

'Cut-outs? You mean like windows?'

'Uh-huh.'

A tremor of recognition began to snake up Christopher's spine. 'Where are you, Lawrence? Can you tell me?'

'I don't know. I only saw it for an instant in his mind.'

'Close your eyes,' Christopher instructed, 'and picture it.'

Lawrence did as he was told. For a moment, nothing happened. Then, abruptly, he said: 'Inside a building.'

'The house with the seven pillars?'

'It's not a house, and the pillars are *inside*. I see bright lights, and snakes as thick as my arm.'

'Snakes?' Cassandra exclaimed. 'There are no snakes that big anywhere in New York State.'

Christopher hushed her. 'What else, Lawrence?'

'The snakes are alive with energy, but they're not moving. There's light coming from behind, through the cut-out windows.' Lawrence opened his eyes. 'I'm on a porch.'

'Not really,' Christopher said. 'You're on a make-believe porch.'

'Jon, you're not making any sense,' Cassandra said.

'Oh, but I am. Remember the videos of Dean Koenig's show we found at the Pale Saint's apartment?'

'So he's a fan of Koenig's? So are a lot of other misguided people.'

'Listen to me, Cass. The snakes Lawrence saw are TV cables, the cut-outs are fake windows in the fake house that's the facade of Koenig's set. He sits on a fake porch – a porch with pillars!'

'That's ridiculous,' Cassandra scoffed. 'What would he want with Koenig?'

'I'm not quite sure yet,' Christopher said thoughtfully. 'But I'm

314

beginning to see the light of day.' He went around to the driver's side. 'Everybody in.' He got behind the wheel, waited for Lawrence to climb into the back seat, then fired the ignition and pulled out into the street. 'Listen, Koenig's a televangelist just like the Pale Saint's mother. There's a connection there, I know it.'

'If there is,' Cassandra said, 'it seems pretty remote to me.'

'No, Dad is right,' Lawrence said. 'He definitely hit a nerve when he told the Pale Saint he was like his mother. He hates his mother.'

'That's the part I don't get,' Cassandra said. 'His mother was killed nine years ago, yet he seems to think she's still alive.'

'What if she is,' Christopher said, 'in his mind?'

'There's something else,' Lawrence said. 'He lied when he said that Faith was raped. She brought that boy up to the loft, and it wasn't the first time.'

'With him?' Christopher said.

'With him, with others,' Lawrence said. 'After he beat the boy to death, he and Faith had a furious screaming match, and though he begged her to stay she finally left. It seems somehow wrong to me that this is the person he wants to bring back.'

'And yet the skull you've seen is Faith's.'

'That's what's in his mind,' the clone acknowledged.

'But how does his sister's resurrection tie in with Koenig?' Cassandra said. 'I just don't see it.'

'Neither do I,' Christopher said, 'but I think I know a way to find out.'

'Where are we going?' Cassandra said, glancing out the window.

'Downtown. I need a little help. And there's someone I know who can provide it.'

'We're near the loft,' Cassandra said. 'Stop by there so we can drop Lawrence off.'

'What?'

'Jon, I've come to a decision. Lawrence has done enough. I want him out of this.'

'You've got to be kidding. I've got just over twelve hours left before the Feds come in and I get booted off this case. If we take the time to bring Lawrence back to the loft, we'll have less of a chance of finding the Pale Saint – or saving Sara.'

'Unless we start the eicosanoid protocol now, he might not have any chance at all. Besides, you know where the Pale Saint is headed. What more can Lawrence do now?'

'I need his insights. Cass, this is war. We're coming to the crunch. I can use all the allies I can get.'

'Allies – or cannon fodder?'

'Who said she was going to blow the Pale Saint's face off if she got the chance?'

'Men and their wars.' Cassandra shook her head. 'This isn't a war, no matter what the Pale Saint says. Wars kill people, destroy entire families. Is that what you're aiming for?' She looked at him while he drove headlong through the nearly deserted city streets. 'Remember when I said I thought I'd made a mistake in going ahead with the experiment? Well, I was wrong. It wasn't Lawrence that was the mistake; it was our plans for him. Don't you see that he's become a slave to our revenge. We've taken a human being and diminished him. You once referred to him as a bullet in a gun. We have no right to think of him that way.'

Christopher ran a yellow light, then came to a halt at a red light a block further south. 'You've seen first-hand what the Pale Saint is capable of. Are you going to let him go on murdering people?'

'This isn't so simple. It isn't what's moral versus what isn't.' Cassandra shook her head. 'Jon, we're talking about sacrificing a human being, we're talking about justifying the means by the end. You know as well as I do the spurious morality of that defense.'

'Goddammit, Cass, this isn't the Nuremberg Trials, for Christ's sake.' He hit the accelerator the moment the light went green.

She was trembling. 'Jon, don't you understand what you're asking of me? One of my children is in mortal danger, and now you want to commit another to the same fate. It's too much. I can't. I –'

'Stop, both of you,' Lawrence said so forcefully they both looked at him. He leaned forward so his head and shoulders were between them. 'I can't stand these arguments. It's like I don't exist. Don't I have any say in what happens to me? After all, it's my life. I should be the one to choose, don't you think?'

'Oh, Lawrence, yes.' Cassandra turned part way around. 'In a perfect world, of course you would. But you're so young. How could you possibly know what to do?'

'I know what's in here.' He put his hand over his heart. 'I can't let anything happen to Sara.'

She took his hand. 'Lawrence, you've been exposed to so many terrible things.'

'Polluted is what you mean, isn't it, by the Skeleton's evil.'

'Yes,' she whispered. 'Oh, I don't believe you'd deliberately do anything bad, but Dillard's dead and we don't even know –'

'We don't even know who killed him,' Lawrence finished for her. 'Yes, I know. Does this mean you don't trust me? Do you think I'm lying when I tell you I'd do anything to keep Sara safe?'

'No.' Christopher spoke from his heart. 'I've taught you what's right and what's wrong. I know that you've found the rightness in the world and that you hold it dear.'

Cassandra's face was flushed with anguish. 'But, Lawrence, if you go you may die.'

'Then that is my choice. If you take that away from me, then what am I? I'm nothing.' He looked from her to Christopher and back again. 'Anyway, from the beginning that was the point, wasn't it?'

There was a small silence. In the distance, the crimson neon sign for The A List lit up the steel-shuttered shops along Avenue A. A line of people waiting to get into the late-night dance club snaked past a Puerto Rican church that had, years ago, been a Ukrainian funeral home. On the corner of Second St, black-clad kids drifted in and out of a sofa-strewn cafe called V.I. Lenin.

'In the beginning, maybe,' Cassandra said at length. 'Then you were only a concept, an experiment, a means to get to the Pale Saint. A bullet in a gun. Now you've become something more, something neither of us could have predicted or anticipated. Every moment you're alive, it becomes clearer to us what you have become. That's why it's so difficult to continue our original plans for you.'

'Mom, you and Dad gave me life,' Lawrence said. 'Now it's up to me to live it.'

'He's right, Cass.' As he pulled into the curb in front of the club, Christopher held his hand up for Lawrence to take. 'You've become part of the family. In all the ways that matter, you're our child now.'

'Cass, try to get some rest,' Christopher said softly. 'There's nothing more you can do for now. The minute we get to the lab I'll wake you.'

She nodded and closed her eyes, resting her head against the window. She'd moved to the back seat when Christopher had emerged with Kenny, his snitch who had been doing his usual midnight to five DJ stint at the club.

As soon as Kenny was on board, Christopher made two calls. The first was to Jerry Lewis, who said he'd have a police helicopter standing by within fifteen minutes; Christopher had few illusions that the dragnet around Manhattan would hold the Pale Saint. By the time Christopher arrived, Lewis promised, the pilot would have the exact location of the Evangelical Nations Network studio outside Kingston, the place from which Dean Koenig's show was broadcast every night. He told Lewis to get the studio's e-mail address. The second call was to D'Alassandro. She was still chewing the fat with Sheriff Wilcox. Christopher told her what he wanted her to do, and she said if she had to contact every damn radio station in Oklahoma she'd get him what he needed.

Ten minutes later, Christopher pulled into the curb outside the Vertex lab. He shook Cassandra awake and, together, they ran to the entrance to the back lab. Christopher used his shield to get them through the police guards.

'I'll give him one eicosanoid injection now,' Cassandra said as she rummaged around the lab. 'And then another in an hour.'

'Will that do it?' Christopher asked.

'God alone knows,' she said tightly. 'But right now it's our only chance.'

Christopher who, with his usual detective's eye, was automatically checking out the lab, said, 'Cass, d'you know you've got a dead rat here?'

'What?' She turned. 'What are you talking about? All my lab animals are –' Her gaze fell upon the creature he was talking about. 'Oh, my God.' She ran to the cage, opened it, took out the lifeless animal. She examined it carefully, then, white as milk, looked at Christopher.

'Jon, this is Minnie.'

'The rat on the eicosanoid protocol?'

She nodded wordlessly.

He looked down at the rat. 'What does this mean?'

'The eicosanoid injections won't work.' There were tears standing in her eyes. 'No matter what we do Lawrence is going to die.'

Christopher felt his heart beating slowly, heavily, painfully. 'How long?'

She shrugged helplessly. 'There's no way to know. A week, a day. Hours.' She put Minnie down. 'How can it end like this? How?'

He put his arm around her. 'How can anything end?'

She turned to him. 'Jon, we won't tell him. No one deserves to live the last of their life without hope.'

Christopher nodded. There was a great welling in his chest, as if he had been set on fire. He was thinking of Andy poised at the edge of the high diving board, stepping out and falling, falling . . .

Lewis was as good as his word; he was standing by the 'copter at the helipad at 33rd St and the East River. Its rotors turned lazily as the pilot idled the engine. Lewis's obvious excitement was overlaid by worry when he saw his beat-up boss.

'Loo, what the hell happened to you?'

'Buzz-saw,' Christopher said. 'You got what I asked for?'

'Right here.' Lewis handed him a gun, extra ammo, and a folded slip of paper. 'Listen, Loo, how about I ride shotgun on this mission?'

Christopher saw how badly Lewis wanted in on the finish; he'd certainly earned it. But Christopher needed someone he could trust manning the fort back here. If he had to have anything ASAP he knew he could count on Lewis to get it for him.

'Sorry, but I need you here,' he said, clapping him on the shoulder. 'Next time.'

Christopher watched Cassandra; she was holding Lawrence's hand. She had administered the eicosanoid injection as soon as they had returned to the car from the lab. Even though the situation was hopeless, she would not give up hope. That was Cass through and through. She was tight-lipped now, her expression grim. Christopher smiled at her, as if to say, *Don't give the kid a hint that there's anything wrong*, and she nodded.

As soon as they were airborne, he briefed Kenny on his role.

'No fucking sweat,' Kenny shouted over the din. He was grinning fiercely. 'Now all you need is a month in the Caribbean, sipping piña coladas and taking in the sun. You look like refried drek, amigo.

'Feel like it, too.' Christopher had introduced Lawrence by his first name only. Kenny had taken one look at the bandage smothering his broken nose and kept his mouth shut. He produced an arm-load of snack food he'd grabbed from the club before he'd left. 'Food of the gods,' he announced, handing around packets of Oreos, Reese's Peanut Butter Cups, and Goober's. 'Never leave home without 'em.'

An hour later, the pilot set them down on a huge expanse of lawn that fronted the ENN studio building. A two-story concrete edifice with small square windows, it looked like a corporate structure.

Christopher wondered whether God knew what His minions were up to inside.

'There's something I want to tell you,' Lawrence said as they hurried across the lawn.

He steered Lawrence further away from Cassandra and Kenny. Huge elms, sycamores and oaks stood guard at the edge of a dense forested area just to the west. Lawrence pulled at his lip. 'When I asked the Pale Saint why he had killed Bobby Austin, he told me it was the penultimate step in closing the circle.'

The short hairs at the base of Christopher's neck stirred. 'What circle?'

'I don't know for sure. But I think he meant the circle of death that began when Faith was murdered.'

'I don't understand.'

'Neither do I.' Lawrence glanced at Cassandra. 'But somehow Sara is the key. She's the last step. Whatever he does with her will close the circle for good.'

'Christ, why are Sara and Koenig so important to him?'

He had no answer, and neither did the clone. In the shadow of the big trees, they watched the 'copter take off. Christopher did not want it around when the Pale Saint showed up. Hurriedly, they ate the last of Kenny's sweets. All but Cassandra, who refused the last Oreo Christopher offered; she'd seemed unable to get anything down. 'Jon, what are we doing standing here when we should be searching for Sara? I mean, where are the state troopers? Why don't you just flood the area with cops?'

'Because we'd never find her in time. The moment the Pale Saint got a whiff of a dragnet he'd kill her.'

'But how would he know? If they were careful –'

'Listen, Cass, he knew I'd thrown a cordon around his apartment. How he knew I can't imagine because my men were concealed. They were *very* careful. Believe me, I'd like nothing better than to call in a couple of hundred troopers as backup. I can't.'

Despair was burned into Cassandra's face. 'Then how on earth are we going to find her?'

'I'm counting on the Pale Saint to lead us to her.'

Cassandra looked alarmed. 'What do you mean? Why would he –?'

His cell phone rang. He started and cursed, on edge with the possibility that the Pale Saint was calling again. He separated himself from the group.

It was D'Alassandro. 'Listen, Boss, how you making out?'

'I'll tell you tomorrow,' he said wearily.

'I've got news for you; it *is* tomorrow.'

'That's heartening.' He glanced at his watch: 3.30 a.m., eight-and-a-half hours before the Feds landed. He stretched, arching his back, and almost groaned aloud. It felt as if every muscle, joint and bone in his body was going to give out.

'Boss, it looks like this sonuvabitch has taken quite a shine to me, as they say hereabouts, like I'm his salvation or something. You were right, I only had to nudge him a little and he fell.'

'How far?'

'Farther than you or I could have guessed. Listen, there *was* a fifth man. The sex club was his idea. He was so powerful that he was protected from everything, even the VCAP posting. He was one of the partners in the Hutchinson, Fargo Railway that went through here. The trains that came and went transshipped all the contraband that made these guys megabucks. Packed in his very own private car, no less.'

'Cosy.' Christopher dug the pads of his thumbs into his eyelids. He was dizzy with pain and exhaustion. This chase had to end soon, he knew, or he'd be done.

'But this isn't what makes him of special interest to us,' D'Alassandro said. 'Boss, his name is Joseph Winthrop Austin.'

'Wait a minute.' Christopher felt as if he'd been punched in the stomach, and for an instant he lost the power to speak. His mind was racing a mile a minute. 'Bobby's grandfather was named Joseph Winthrop Austin.'

'They're one and the same. I checked.'

I researched the Austins well; I knew Bobby better than you did, didn't I? the Pale Saint had said to him. *I know the real reason he became a district attorney. But it didn't work.* Christopher was thinking of the circle closing with Bobby's death and, if he didn't stop it, with Sara's. *The truth is we never really know anyone else*, the Pale Saint had told him. *It's all an illusion. What goes on beneath the human facade – well, sometimes it's better not to know.*

'Boss? You still there?'

'Yeah. Things are starting to fall into place.' *So it was Bobby who was the starting point. He was the 'X' factor, the one who caused the Pale Saint to alter his signature*, he thought. 'We're at our destination. How'd you make out?'

'Had to rattle a few cages, but I got everything you wanted. I packed 'em into a zip file. You just tell me where to send it and as soon as I'm on-line it'll be there in two seconds.'

'Great,' Christopher said, 'but what the hell is a zip file?'

'It's a computer file with lots of info that's been electronically compacted so it can be sent instantaneously over the Internet. The people at your end will know how to unzip it so you'll be able to play what's in 'em.'

'Great job, Emma,' he said. 'Haul your ass on back here.'

'Yes*sir*,' she said excitedly. 'But, hell, it looks like I'm going to miss all the fireworks.'

Hell just about fits it, Christopher thought.

Stopping to put gas in the car he has stolen, the Pale Saint cups the skull. The rain has stopped. Overhead, a procession of black crows, like old soldiers wordlessly questioning their fate, maunder through the gray, blank, airless sky of the small hours of the night.

In order to avoid the dragnet Christopher has undoubtedly thrown up around the city, he has driven a battered Ford he has stolen north into Spanish Harlem. Sara, bound and gagged, lies in the Ford's trunk beneath a brace of filthy blankets. He has gotten rid of the corporate drone's suit, opting for dirty overalls, denim shirt and work boots. From his kit bag he has produced a cream that has darkened his skin. He has placed between his gums and cheeks a pair of small hard lozenges he has fashioned himself out of silicone. Dark-colored contact lenses complete his transformation. Walking into a bodega on 135th St he speaks only Spanish as he buys food and a carton of orange juice.

Sure enough, on the approach to the Willis Ave. Bridge, he joins a long queue of vehicles. At the end of it are four squad cars, their lights flashing. He peels a banana, eats that and one of the apples he bought. By that time, he's at the roadblock. He smiles at the cop who bends in, shining his long flashlight into the interior.

'Can I see some identification, sir?'

'Righto.' He flips open his wallet, shows the uniform the ID he downloaded from the NYPD server that says he's Patrolman Alfredo Molina out of the 21st Precinct.

'Hey, you should've said,' the uniform says, waving him through.

'What's the roadblock all about?'

'Can't say. You know how it is.' The uniform's attention is already on the car behind. 'You have a good one, buddy.'

'Sure thing.' The Pale Saint is laughing silently as he pulls away.

Now, at the filling station near Beacon, he fixes his gaze on the skull lying carefully wrapped on the seat beside him. Next to it is his trusty notebook computer and his kit bag. In all, they form the axis of whatever it is he calls his world. The skull is inside two plastic bags sealed with twist ties. Clots of dirt still cling to the moist outside of the plastic bag. Just before leaving the city, he'd dug up the bag from a spot beneath a leprous plane tree in Tompkins Square Park. Hidden within a clump of scraggly, overgrown junipers, he was able to dig them up unobserved.

'Eighteen bucks even,' the attendant says, and the Pale Saint hands him the money. The faraway look in the attendant's eyes reminds the Pale Saint of the look in Mama's eyes the day they took her away. He had asked to see her before she was to be bound over for trial. It was a shock like raw electricity to the skin to see her shackled, draped in chains. Mama had that nasty look on her face that never failed to cow Pappy. On the sheriff it had no effect at all. Two beefy police deputies sat in the front seat of the squad car that brought her. Neither of them moved or said a word. They were just there, like the Sphinxes guarding pharaoh's tomb.

The sheriff beckoned toward the Pale Saint, then moved out of earshot.

Mama looked sloppy and unkempt, two things she could not normally abide. Still, underneath, there were the same qualities that made her mysterious, luminous, compelling. It was how she had hooked so many thousands of people all across the state. Mama might have been a born liar, but she surely was no charlatan. She had the power, all right, even beaten, bowed, and shackled. He called to her over and over as he neared her. Still she did not acknowledge him. She continued to stare out over the dustbowl she had called home for all of her life, thinking thoughts of what? He could not imagine. She was such an enigma to him that he did not know what was real to her, what was important, and what was already in her eyes dead.

'MAMA!' he shrieked as he fell upon her in a rage of jack hammering arms and windmilling legs.

The two police deputies never moved. Only their eyes, synchronized as metronomes, flicked to the rear-view mirror, and sharp as knives flicked away again.

It is the Pale Saint's impression even now that the sheriff took his own sweet time hauling him off Mama. Certainly not before the Pale

Saint had made her cry out, once, her scream echoing like a turkey buzzard's harsh cry over the prairie.

'Attaboy, son!' the sheriff said as he spat into the blood-brown muck beside her head. 'Kiss your Mama goodbye.'

EIGHTEEN

'What is the meaning of this?' Paul Layton said in his crisp, officious manner. 'Who are you people? Jesus wept, you can't just –'

'I'm an officer of the NYPD,' Christopher said, holding up his shield.

Still he blocked their way. 'I don't care if you're the New York City Chief of Police, you have no jurisdiction here.'

'Dean Koenig is in imminent mortal danger. We can protect him.'

'Thank you very much, but you see Mr Koenig has his own private protection,' Layton said. 'We're used to lunatic threats. We're more than capable of taking care of anything –'

'How about the Pale Saint?' Christopher said, pushing Layton aside. 'You think you're up to dealing with him?'

'The Pale Saint?' Layton, just three weeks into being station manager, felt his knees go suddenly weak. Then he recovered. 'Just a minute!' He called for station security, and three beefy men came running. 'If there's a problem, we'll call the local sheriff's office.'

'No offense to the local sheriff,' Christopher said, 'but he won't cut it.'

The security team had moved to block Christopher's path. Behind him, Cassandra held Lawrence's hand. Kenny stood a little to one side, his arms folded across his chest.

'Nevertheless,' Layton said obstinately, 'he'll have to make the determination. He gets into the office at nine.'

'We have no time for that. Is Mr Koenig here?'

'Yes, he is,' Dean Koenig said as he came striding toward them. His bright blue eyes were dancing. 'What's all the ruckus, Paul?'

'This New York City policeman is making outrageous claims. He says you're in danger, Mr Koenig.'

'Liberals are always trying to silence me or bury me.' Koenig smiled warmly. 'No matter. I'm still here.' He extended a hand. 'My goodness, this isn't just a New York City police officer, Paul. It's Jonathan Christopher, the vaunted Pale Saint Hunter.' He cocked his head. 'Isn't that what they call you, Lieutenant?' Not waiting for an answer, he slipped his hand free of Christopher's grip and went past him. 'However, here's the person I'm most anxious to meet. Paul, say hello to Dr Cassandra Austin.'

Layton's jaw dropped open. '*The* Dr Austin?'

'None other,' Koenig said, as genial as Santa Claus. He took Cassandra's hand. 'I must say, this is an unexpected pleasure, Doctor. I've been wanting you on my show for weeks.' Before a stunned Cassandra could reply, he turned back to Layton. 'These illustrious people are my personal guests, Paul. Please give them whatever they want, even if it's the run of the studios.'

'Mr Koenig, please listen to what I have to say,' Christopher began. 'The Pale Saint is on his way here. We found tapes of your show in his apartment. His mother was a televangelist just like you, which is why we think he's fixated on you.'

'Since you're here, Lieutenant, I must assume you have a plan.'

'That I do,' Christopher said.

'Then by all means implement it.'

'I'm going to have to take over your control room. Plus, I'll need full access to your show's video archives.'

Koenig seemed distracted. 'Whatever you need, Lieutenant.' He drew Cassandra away from the others. 'At the moment, however, I'm most interested in talking with Dr Austin.' He took her down the hall to his dressing room.

Christopher saw there was no point in arguing the point; Koenig was like a force of nature. Instead, he asked Layton to guide them to the studio's control rooms. On the way, he asked Layton for a list of all entrances and exits. In the control room, he told one of the engineers to see if there was a zip file waiting in the e-mail program.

The engineer looked questioningly at Layton, who shrugged. 'Mr Koenig okayed it.'

The zip file was just where D'Alassandro said it would be. Christopher blessed her ten thousand times. When the engineer opened it up, Christopher could see the audio files D'Alassandro had acquired from the local TV station in Oklahoma City.

'Right, Kenny,' he said. 'It's all yours.'

Kenny, who had been talking to the chief engineer about their equipment, got behind the computer. When the engineer had put a tape on the huge commercial tape recorder, Kenny transferred the audio files to the tape. Then he had the engineer play back the tape.

'I know that voice,' Lawrence said.

'Who the hell is she?' Layton asked. When no one answered, he said almost to himself. 'Whoever she is she can have a show right here any time she wants.'

Midway through the playback, Kenny turned to Christopher, gave him the thumbs up sign. 'Plenty here to work with. Now what exactly do you want her to say?'

'So,' Dean Koenig said, 'in the middle of the long night up pops the devil.'

'I'm not the devil, Mr Koenig. But he's on his way.'

Koenig laughed good-naturedly. 'But of course you are, my dear.' Cassandra hadn't seen such big, white, even teeth since the last time she'd seen Bert Parks on TV. 'If only because I say you are.' He shrugged. 'It's simple power of the media.'

'Simple manipulation, you mean.'

The room was warmly furnished in homey pine furniture. A sideboard held a platter with fresh fruit and the fixings for coffee. There was a very masculine leather sofa against the far wall. Closer, a pair of plush upholstered chairs faced one another; a side table held a phone and an alarm clock. In the corner opposite the sofa a TV was playing without the sound. It showed a closed-circuit frame of Koenig's set.

'Do sit down, Cassandra. Please.' He gestured to one of the chairs. 'You don't mind if I call you by your Christian name, do you? It's exceedingly lovely.' His voice was as plummy as twenty-year-old port.

Cassandra stood with her arms folded across her breasts. 'What do you want of me, Mr Koenig?' She stressed the formality of his name.

'You know, being a TV show host, seeing guests come and go, has made me something of an amateur psychologist. I'd say your stance is more than a little hostile.'

'Can you blame me? You've attacked me verbally, hounded me, humiliated me publicly, demonized me, and cost me my job. Not that you would care.'

'Ah, yes, your job.' Koenig went to the pine sideboard, poured two mugs of coffee from a glass coffee-pot on a single electric burner. 'Cream or sugar?'

Cassandra, struck almost dumb by his demeanor, could barely manage a mumbled 'Both.'

He nodded, stirred milk and sugar into both mugs. 'Like you, I cannot abide artificial sweeteners.' He turned and handed her a mug. 'I hope I've put in the right amounts of each.' There was an expectant look on his face. 'Go ahead, try it. I choose the beans and grind them myself.'

Cassandra took a sip. It was delicious but she was damned if she was going to tell him that.

Koenig shrugged. 'That's quite all right. I know it's first-rate coffee.' He took a sip himself. 'I truly hope, Cassandra, that you haven't taken any of my actions personally.'

Cassandra felt her gorge rise. This was too much. She felt like strangling him and his perfect paterfamilias smile. Instead, she slapped him hard across the cheek. 'You sonuvabitch.'

Koenig stood very still. 'I suppose I should have seen that coming.'

'You're damned straight.'

'All right.' He put down his mug of coffee. 'Now that you've vented, d'you think we could sit down and talk like adults.'

'What do you think this is, some kind of a business discussion?'

He pursed his lips. 'In a very real sense, that's precisely what it is.' He gestured again to the chair. 'Would you allow me to explain?'

'There's nothing you could say that would –'

'Please.'

Reluctantly, she lowered herself into the chair. He sat in a matching chair opposite.

'You know, God moves in mysterious ways, Cassandra, he surely does.' He lifted his hands. 'Case in point, you coming here tonight. Quite astonishing, really, when you consider that I've been racking by brain in an effort to find some way for us to meet in a non-stressful situation.'

'Given your monstrous actions, I don't believe that's possible.'

'Monstrous? Is that how you view me? Well, my goodness, I –'

'Don't try that "sakes alive, Mary," crap with me, Mr Koenig,' Cassandra snapped. 'It's as false as that set you broadcast from.'

'My dear Cassandra, let's try to get our perspectives clear, shall we? That Pale Saint person your friend Christopher is pursuing, *he's* monstrous. I'm merely a businessman trying to make a living.'

Cassandra jumped up. 'Businessman, my butt. You're a religious fanatic. Too much exposure, too much power, and an overinflated ego have made you a menace to society at large. You're petty, small-minded, obstructionist, and just plain vindictive. Everyone seems scared of you, but trust me, I am not. I find it highly ironic, not to mention somewhat pathetic that Jon is here risking his life to save yours.'

'In God's eyes, all lives are worthy of salvation.' Koenig eyed her from the chair in which he still sat. 'But, in fact, I am a businessman. It just so happens that my business is religion.' He set his fingers in a steeple in front of him. 'And, whether you choose to believe me or not, I was perfectly serious when I said that my attacks were nothing personal. The fact is I do care that you've lost your job. I care very much.'

He picked up the phone that sat on the side table and dialed a number. 'Hello. Sorry for the late-night call, but something quite extraordinary has happened. Cassandra Austin is here . . . Yes, that's right, she's here with me right now . . . I thought so.' He handed her the receiver. 'It's for you.'

Cassandra stared at him wide-eyed for a moment.

'Go ahead. I assure you it won't bite.'

Cassandra grasped the phone, put it to her ear. 'Hello?'

'Dr Austin, that you?' boomed a deep masculine voice.

'Who is this?'

'Ken Reinisch.'

'Who?' Cassandra's brain just wasn't prepared to process this kind of information.

'Ken Reinisch. The CEO of Helix Technologies.'

Cassandra looked at Koenig, who was grinning at her from ear to ear.

'Listen, Dr Austin, I know what happened to you over at Vertex,' Reinisch continued. 'Gerry's a damn fool for letting you go.'

'He didn't have a choice. Dean Koenig pressured the Vertex board.'

'Well, sure he had a choice,' Reinisch shouted. 'He could have stuck with you, but he chose the line of least resistance, and he bailed.'

'The pressure he was under.' She wondered what the hell she was doing defending Costas.

'Yeah, the pressure,' Reinisch was thundering. 'I mean that was kinda the point, wasn't it?'

'What?' Cassandra felt like a straight man in an Abbott and Costello routine. Everyone was making jokes at her expense. 'I don't quite follow.'

'Which part?' Reinisch bellowed. 'Me snookering Jerry or you coming over to work for me?'

'The part where Mr Koenig fits in.'

'Oh, that. Dean and I do favors for each other. It's a kind of – what d'you call it again – a de facto partnership. Listen, Dr Austin. You come around the office tomorrow and we'll cut a deal. I'm prepared to give you whatever you want within reason so do me a favor and try not to break my balls too much, 'kay?'

Cassandra stared at Koenig. 'He hung up.'

Koenig took the receiver from her. 'Offered you the moon, didn't he?'

'And the stars.' She shook her head. 'You and Reinisch? He's in the same business I'm in. It doesn't compute.'

'Now that all depends on your point of view. I told you I was a businessman, didn't I? Now Ken and I go way back. Fact is, we were frat brothers in college; raised some kind of ruckus together, let me tell you.' He chuckled. 'Before that, though, our families knew each other. We come from the same place.'

'Geographically?'

'Well, yes, that too. But I was speaking about up here.' He tapped the side of his head. 'Can't stand these blue bloods who've never toiled to honest sweat a day in their lives. They have a way of looking down on you like you were a lower form of life, am I right, Cassandra? I imagine, from time to time, you've felt the same thing, haven't you?' He spread his hands. 'So now you see I was telling the truth. It was nothing personal, what I did. Ken called, said he wanted you to work for him but he knew you would never leave Costas. Not unless you were pushed. So I pushed.' He stood. 'I know you had a sweet deal at Vertex, but Vertex is finished. And believe me, I know Ken. Now you'll have an even sweeter deal. I'll go on to pillorying someone else. There are new headlines to be made. In that regard, you're already yesterday's news; everyone will forget I ever said a word against you.'

'My God, this is something,' Cassandra said. 'A couple of minutes ago I thought you were monstrous, but I thought you at least had the courage of your convictions. Now I see you don't have any convictions. You have nothing at all.' She took her coffee and threw it full into his face. 'The next time you see your pal, Ken Reinisch you can tell him this is my answer.'

At that moment, Christopher opened the door. 'We're good to go.' Then he looked from Cassandra to Koenig. 'Well, hell, Cass.'

'Fucking men,' she said as she brushed past him. 'He's all yours,

Jon. See how long you can stand to be with him before he makes you puke.'

There was a small, awkward silence into which Koenig injected a deprecating shrug, as if to say, *Women, who can understand them?*

'What can I do for you, Lieutenant?'

'You and your people need to vacate the building. Now.'

Koenig shook his head. 'I won't abandon ship, let's get that straight from the get-go. If I let every threat or stalker cow me, I'd be a virtual prisoner, and that, sir, I refuse to be.'

'This is no mere stalker,' Christopher said. 'This is the Pale Saint.'

'I don't care whether it's Lucifer himself, Lieutenant. I won't run and hide like some lily-livered coward.' A genial smile spread across his face. 'Besides, I've got the best protection money can buy.'

'I don't have time to argue with you,' Christopher growled. 'Just stay out of the obvious places. Here and the studio. Can I count on you to do that much?'

'Consider it done.' He slapped Christopher on the back. 'Now go get him, Lieutenant.'

'Remember, sonny, the Lord knows, in this life you only get whut you deserve.'

But not everyone, certainly not Faith. All at once, the Pale Saint is thrown back in time. He is staring into the trunk the sheriff has opened. That day, he didn't need look to know what Mama had stashed inside the trunk for so many years. It was no surprise at all that she had kept the corpse of her first child, swaddled in the musty sateen and lace of her baptismal dress. A pitifully small body, shriveled into itself so that the leathery skin curled around the tinder-stick bones like crepe paper at a funeral. This is Faith, who had been sexually assaulted by Pappy over and over until she had died. Faith, who had suffered the First Bad Thing, whose skull he has carried around with him all this time. The daughter Mama had given birth to before either he or the daughter who would bear the same name was born. Faith, the reason Mama had sent her second daughter away until Pappy could no longer get his hands on her. Faith, the reason Mama finally did in Pappy. There she was, staring at him from the depths of the trunk with sightless, desiccated eyes.

It has begun to rain again, a hard, black rain on the verge of becoming hail. Deep within the forested area just west of the ENN studios he settles his shoulders and hips more deeply into the hollowed-out bole of a rotten oak tree. He shares this cozy place with a family of maggots, a colony of ants, and a lone racoon caught away from its den in the downpour. He feels the rise and fall of its pelt, the rapid flutter of its heartbeat. Its forepaws are crossed over its chest, bright black eyes glare at the foul weather as if in anger. The maggots are, as always, feeding. The ants scurry about their tasks; the precipitation, like the darkness, has no meaning for them.

Being among these small creatures makes the Pale Saint feel at home.

A single discordant element disturbs the tranquility. A short distance away, Sara whimpers through her gag in her disorientation and her terror.

Two deer – young bucks who have recently rubbed the velvet from their antlers – regard him with curiosity. They are not afraid, as they would be with any other human. He is not like other humans. He calls to them softly, a low, ululating sound that causes them to snort and paw the black earth. They do not come closer but they do not back away. They have the demeanor of sentinels, patiently waiting for the war to catch up to them.

The Pale Saint now prepares himself. A fire is not possible; he will have to do without. He crawls on all fours to where he has placed Sara. In the deepest part of a dell he has scooped out and enlarged an old, abandoned fox den. His shoulder is a fiery mass of pain; he knows he needs antibiotics, but his herbs will protect him; they will heal him.

He makes a small cut on the inside of Sara's arm. As the blood oozes out, he captures seven drops on the lip of the vial in which he carries the last two doses of the herbal mixture. They roll down the inside, mixing with the herbal cocktail. He will take his dose now. When he returns from his last errand, he will force her to drink hers. The Channel will be open. Her blood will have distilled inside him. Through his hands, Faith's soul will rise from the place where it has slumbered for so long. It will enter the host at the precise moment he presses down on Sara's windpipe. Faith's essence, rather than oxygen will fill her up. And, at last, Faith will be reborn. Too quickly dead, she will live again.

He throws back his head, feels the viscous liquid rolling back on his tongue. He swallows convulsively, recaps the vial, and grasping two metal cans, takes off into the night, heading unerringly toward the two-story concrete building to the northeast.

He arrives by stealth. No one has seen him. He enters through the gardener's cast-metal doors to the basement. Closing the doors behind him, he is in utter darkness. He strikes a match, finds the light switch. Also a pile of rags. He uses several to wipe himself down. He is especially careful to dry the soles of his shoes so that when he gets upstairs he will leave no footprints. Then he makes a circuit of the basement. At a large, square metal box painted red he snaps open a lock with a pair of wire cutters and disables the basement's fire sensors and alarm.

By the light of a bare bulb he opens the blueprints for the ENN studios he has stolen from the Kingston Municipal Building. He has studied them before, sitting in the stolen car. He has the layout memorized. But now is not the time to make a fatal mistake; he wants to be certain he hasn't overlooked anything. His forefinger traces a line from the stairs up to the main floor, down the service corridor to the studio where Dean Koenig broadcasts his nightly show, to Koenig's dressing room. He will leave no stone unturned.

Counting off paces from the west wall, he goes to a certain section of the basement. Dragging several cardboard shipping containers over to the spot, he douses them with the contents of the first metal can. The harsh stench of kerosene fills his nostrils, instantly reminding him of another night long ago when the flames burned bright, lashing upward toward the starless Oklahoma night.

On a small maintenance ladder, he strips the fire-retardant material from the ceiling directly above the doused containers. He paints the bare ceiling with pitch from the second metal can. Climbing down, he surveys his work, inhaling the rich chemical odor. He lights a match and throws it onto the soaked cardboard. A whoosh as blue-gold flames rush upward like the tongue of a ravenous serpent, licking at the pitch. The heat is intense. He know the materials used in the construction of this building, just as he knows the nature of this virulent accelerant-generated fire. He has ten minutes, he calculates.

He refolds the blueprint, turns off the light, and heads for the stairs. He finds the studio's service corridor deserted, but not for long. As he waits and watches a maintenance man emerges from an office, pushing a cleaning wagon. Stealing up behind him, he rabbit-punches him on the back of the neck. As he collapses, the Pale Saint catches him under the arms, drags him into the empty office he has just finished cleaning. Propping him against a wall, he studies his face.

Back in the corridor, he pushes the cleaning wagon outside the men's room, goes in. It is empty. He locks the door from the inside and proceeds to sluice away the temporary pigment he had put on when he was in Spanish Harlem. He removes the silicone lozenges from his cheeks, changes contact lenses, uses powders, makeup pencils and brushes to gain the desired effect. Observing his face in the mirror one last time, he unlocks the door, checks the corridor, then pushes the cleaning wagon he has appropriated down to Dean Koenig's dressing room.

He knocks politely on the door. Hearing no answer, he pushes the wagon inside. Koenig is nowhere to be seen. But now he knows where to find him. On the closed-circuit monitor in the far corner of the room he can see Koenig on the set of his show. He is sitting in his chair on the porch with the seven pillars. He appears to be reading and editing a script. Perhaps the opening monolog for tonight's show.

In his mind Mama is sitting on the porch of their house outside Tangent, Oklahoma. Though it is early afternoon, the sky is dark as a starless night. A wicked wind is rising. Already dust streaks line her face like Indian war paint. She holds him in her arms even though he whimpers in fear of the darkness, the rising wind, the plummeting air pressure, which he experiences as a clammy hand pressing painfully against his forehead.

'It's coming, sonny, the avenging right hand of God.' She holds him out in front of her as if he were some kind of sacrifice.

The twister appears over the horizon. It is coming fast, moving with a terrifying speed improbable for such a vast phenomenon.

' "Wherefore dost thou forget us forever, And forsake us so long time?" ' Mama croons, quoting from Lamentations. ' "Turn thou us unto thee, O Lord, and we shall be turned; Renew our days as of old. But thou hast utterly rejected us; thou art very wroth against us." ' By the end of this incantation, her voice has risen to the righteous war cry she uses on her television show.

The Pale Saint watches Mama reading on the porch. Then he blinks and sees Dean Koenig. The two of them seem to merge, flowing into one another like two fish circling, like two peas in the pod, like two atoms that, together, form a single molecule. With an effort, he tears himself away from the monitor. Five minutes remain before the hungry fire eats through the basement ceiling.

Back out in the corridor, he pauses to clear his mind. The herbal potion flows through him like rocket fuel. He feels his First Power rising; soon the Channel will be open. Concentrate! There are two routes to the main studio. He chooses the one that goes past the control room. It's more risky, therefore the more unexpected.

On his way, he passes three people. All of them are distracted, in a hurry. None of them gives him even a second look. As far as they are concerned, he is part of the background hum of the place.

He enters the studio. It is larger than he imagined, though the set is small, almost intimate. It seems dwarfed by the gargantuan space in which it has been erected. Above the set, like a bank of devil's darning needles, are suspended seven huge television monitors. They are dark now, dark as the vengeful right hand of God. Once again into his mind swims the image of that dark and cavernous house, squatting like a poisonous toad beneath the high, windswept sky of the prairie. The house of his youth. The house of violence. Mama's house. Burned by him to the ground for the sins it contained. Three minutes remain. His nostrils flare, detecting the faint scent of smoke.

Now here it is again, resurrected. And into his head rises like the dark wind of the twister a verse from Lamentations:

The crown has fallen from our head: Woe unto us, that we have sinned!
For this our heart is faint: for these things our eyes are dim.

A figure sits in his chair upon the porch so painfully remembered. Though he is unaware that he is observed, having turned toward the house, still the Pale Saint knows him. The Pale Saint walks through the studio toward the porch. The warm lights streaming through the windows beckon him on. There is only death in his heart.

At that moment, the bank of monitors wink on. He pauses, seeing replicated in all seven of them the face of Dean Koenig smiling down at him. Koenig opens his mouth and speaks.

'Let us learn from Jeremiah. Let us feel his pain and his anguish as he cries out: *"O Lord, thou hast deceived me. Let not the day wherein my mother bore me be blessed."* '

The Pale Saint started, shivering. It was Mama's voice, amplified to almost painful loudness, echoing around the cavernous space.

' *"Cursed be the man who brought tidings to my father, Saying, 'A man child is born unto thee'; Making him very glad."* '

Mama's voice reverberating through the suddenly dark and starless night sky. Only the blue remains. The flickering blue light of the image of Mama replicated seven times in the monitors. Mama shouting out her sermon:

' *"And let that man be as the cities which the Lord overthrew, and repented not: And let him hear the cry in the morning, and the shouting at noontide; Because he slew me not from the womb; Or that my mother might have been my grave."* '

Mama alive again, as he knew she was. They couldn't kill her, though they naively claimed they had. They didn't know Mama; had no idea of her power. Mama deceived them, just as God deceived Jeremiah.

'Now Jeremiah thought his hand was the will of God,' Mama shouted in that voice that reached deep down inside you and grabbed hold of something you never even knew was there. And that voice shook that thing inside you, drawing it out, even as it drew you in close to her you were sure you could hear her throbbing heart. 'But God's will is revealed by His hand alone. Man cannot stand before the will of God; neither can he wield the will of God. Man can be only what God made him to be: the instrument of His divine will. Man is as a reed before the whirlwind that is the will of God, bending, bowing to the greater force, a force he cannot understand yet still must obey. For man is in the service of God, and in that service only obedience will bear the fruit of understanding.'

Dimly, he is aware of the heat building beneath his feet. Forced by the incandescence of the white-hot flames, smoke is curling like blind, gray worms through tiny fissures in the floorboards.

It is too much hearing her voice again, unbearable to suffer her declaiming again, to see her grinning at him in all her righteous glory from out of the blue electronic flame of the monitors. With a harsh cry, he hurtles up the porch steps one last time. He makes a grab for her, spinning the chair around so he can grab her up.

And sees, instead, his own face, patched and bandaged and beaten, but his face nonetheless.

He recoils into the poisonous bosom of Mama's spewed words: '"Then said the Lord unto me, 'What seest thou, Jeremiah?' And I said, 'Figs; the good figs, very good; and the evil, very evil that cannot be eaten, they are so evil.'" What are we to make of this parable? All the figs looked the same. What, then, did Jeremiah see that we cannot?'

The Pale Saint turns away from his own beaten and battered face, turns away from Mama's speechifying, and sees Christopher coming toward him. There is a gun in his hand, and it is pointed at the Pale Saint.

'He saw nothing; but he had the will of God in his heart. His obedience to God showed him the good figs from the evil figs.'

The Pale Saint hurls himself at Christopher, and Christopher pulls the trigger.

Christopher wanted so much to shoot to kill. Despite what he had told Lawrence and Chief Brockaw there was vengeance in his heart, vengeance for Bobby and the runaway girl and Guy and all the others the Pale Saint had murdered. But it was Bobby's voice rising inside him that made him alter his aim at the last possible instant. He shot at the Pale Saint's hip.

The Pale Saint went down for an instant, and Christopher, assuming he was incapacitated, made the mistake of coming toward him. The Pale Saint used a two-handed blow to knock Christopher's gun to the floor, where it went skittering under one of the camera dollies.

That was when Christopher became aware of the intense heat emanating from the studio floor. Where were the alarms?

'Fire in the basement!' he bellowed as he made a grab for the Pale Saint, but his antagonist was already loping for the door. Two of the studio's security team were running toward him. The Pale Saint headed the other way.

Flames had begun to eat their way into the studio, and the fire sensors at last triggered the alarms and the automatic sprinklers. But already Christopher could see that they would be inadequate. So did the studio personnel.

Lawrence had already retrieved Christopher's gun. Now he handed it to him as they took off after the Pale Saint. They could see people running toward the studio. Christopher recognized Layton, some of the control room engineers, and a couple of Koenig's bodyguards toting hand-held fire extinguishers.

'He's used accelerants,' he told them as they ran by.

Then he took off, Lawrence at his side. Up ahead, the security team was already stymied, having lost him in the maze of corridors.

Mama, still alive, was taunting him to track her down. By a supreme act of will, she refused to die. Ten thousand volts of electricity weren't enough to slay her; incarceration was useless. She was here, now, and she had to be dealt with.

Running with the fire in his nostrils, the cleansing fire by which he had leveled that dark and cavernous house that had squatted like a malignant tumor on the wide prairie, the house which had sprouted anew here. He could smell Mama; he knew just where she was. She wouldn't hide; that was not Mama's way. She had courage, give her that. She would not be found cowering in the toilets; he would not have to haul her down from behind as she ran in fear.

Mama knew no fear.

But he could sense Christopher and that wretched beast close behind him. They would not be fooled like the others. He was running out of time.

And then he saw her.

Mama!

'Howdy, son,' Dean Koenig said with a smile as he stepped out of the shadows beside the front door. He had leveled a .38 caliber gun at the Pale Saint's head. 'I hear you want a piece of me, son. Everyone does. Well, here I am.'

He fired as the Pale Saint leapt toward him, but he'd never shot at a moving target before and he missed badly.

'Shut up, Mama!' the Pale Saint screamed. 'Shut up!' Howling wildly, he swung from his hip, driving the heel of his hand into Koenig's throat. Cartilage cracked and imploded like a sun-baked hose. Koenig's eyes opened wide with surprise, shock and disbelief. A weird, horrible gasping emanated from him as he tried to breathe.

'You're not gonna die, Mama,' the Pale Saint said through gritted teeth. 'Not until you see Faith reborn.'

He hauled Koenig by the shirtfront toward the front door, his nails scraping skin like talons. At that instant, Christopher and Lawrence rounded the far corner of the corridor. The Pale Saint screamed, threw Koenig at them, and disappeared out the door.

Christopher and Lawrence bolted down the corridor, through the front lobby, and out the front door. Hail, hard as nails, pelted them. They ran around the front of the building, turned the corner in time to see a figure loping awkwardly across the lawn toward the first stands of oaks and sycamores that led to the forested tract to the west.

They ran after him, into the dense, dripping gloom of the trees.

'Stay here,' Christopher said,

'But, Dad –'

'No, listen, Lawrence, Cassandra was right. You've done enough. I don't want to jeopardize your life again.'

He plunged into the forest, following a trail of broken twigs. He looked for drops of fresh blood, but could find none. The trail wound around for some hundred yards, then abruptly stopped. Christopher, panting, stood very still. There was no point in trying to peer through the darkness. Instead, he listened: to the hail pattering through the red and gold leaves, to the wind's melancholy song as it stirred the branches high overhead, to the mournful hoot of an owl, to the insects' tiny tread through the deadfall leaf carpet of the forest floor.

Then again, maybe the tread did not come from tiny insects.

He moved off at a slow, deliberate pace, pausing every so often to orient himself to the sound of the tread. Through the gap between two oaks, he saw the deer. He might have missed it save for the lumpen human shape sprawled across its back.

As Christopher watched, spellbound, the Pale Saint urged the deer forward by a gentle movement of his knees against its flanks. Christopher followed. As he did so, he recalled how Hound, Sara's Weimaraner had alerted them to the Pale Saint's presence in Central Park, how it had lit out after him, how it had appeared that in some mysterious way he had been communicating with it when it had been hit by the taxi.

It was difficult going. What with the darkness and the extreme density of the underbrush Christopher lost sight of the deer several times. He always found it again by moving west with a slight southerly tack. There came a time, however, when he lost sight of the deer and could not find him again for another fifty yards. Just when he was certain he had lost him for good, he spotted the animal in a small glade just past a huge sycamore. He moved toward him until he was beneath the tree, in the shadows where the Pale Saint could not see him even if he was looking in the right direction.

The deer shook his head, the sharp tines of his antlers whistling a little as he moved through the clearing. Christopher shifted, following him. But now he could see that there was no one on the deer's back.

He grunted heavily. The taste of dead leaves was in his mouth as the Pale Saint, dropping from a low branch above him, pressed him into the ground. Christopher struck out and up, felt the weight come partially off him, and flipped over onto his back. He tried to sit up, but the Pale Saint was arched over him, his arms high over his head. Then they dropped swiftly, decisively, irrevocably like the blade of a guillotine. Christopher caught an instant's glimpse of a long, thin object as he tried to twist out of harm's way. The railroad spike pierced the skin of his side, penetrating through the flesh. Pain seared into him, through him, consumed him entirely. He struggled against the rising tide of blackness, but then it, too, consumed him.

NINETEEN

'Dad,' Lawrence said softly, urgently. 'Dad, don't move, you're bleeding all over me.'

'Where am I?' He looked up at the clone; his lips were pulled slightly back from his teeth.

'In the forest. You're pinned to the ground with one of the Pale Saint's railroad spikes.'

'Christ almighty.'

'That was a very clever thing you did, using the Pale Saint's mother's voice. It really unnerved him.'

'Yeah, it did.' Christopher grinned through the pain. 'All I did was what he's been doing to us: exploit the enemy's weakness.' He grunted as he moved. 'Get me up.'

Lawrence stared down at the wound. 'I don't know if I can.'

'Yes, you can,' Christopher commanded. 'You just have to do it.'

Lawrence nodded. His hands gripped the railroad spike. 'Okay, now,' he whispered. 'Here it comes.'

Christopher gritted his teeth. Even so, the white-hot flash of pain seemed to go on forever. He was sweating and trembling when Lawrence held the bloody spike so he could see it.

Christopher took it from him, gripping it hard while Lawrence examined the wound.

'I watched Mom while she patched both of us up,' he said. 'Also, I think I know more about anatomy than she does.'

'So,' Christopher wheezed through the pain, 'what's the prognosis, Doctor?'

'Lucky, I think. It looks like a simple flesh wound through muscle and adipose tissue.'

'I have no adipose tissue. I'm in better shape than that.'

Lawrence gave him a grim smile as he began to work on the wound. 'On the other hand, you've lost a good deal of blood.'

The breath rattled through Christopher's clenched teeth. 'Keep talking,' he said. 'It helps me not to think of the pain.'

'Back at the pool, I asked the Pale Saint to tell me whether I had killed Dr Dillard.' Lawrence was using a mat of wet leaves to try as best he could to clean out the wound. 'He said I did what I had to do, that I got my hands bloody, that it was all part of growing up.'

'That's bullshit,' Christopher said in a rush of agony.

'This is not good,' Lawrence said. 'There's too much bleeding.' He went off for a minute, returning with a handful of mushrooms. 'These are part of the ergot family,' he said as he crushed them underfoot and pressed them against another mat of wet leaves. 'They're full of alkaloids that will constrict the blood vessels in the area.'

'I'm gratified your time with the encyclopedia was put to good use,' Christopher said.

'There's a lot more knowledge in there I thought was useless.' Lawrence gently centered the poultice against Christopher's wound. 'So the upshot is I still don't know whether or not I murdered Dillard. Just like you don't know what made Andy jump.'

Christopher went very still.

'You think you need to find out what made Andy do it.'

'Yes, I do,' Christopher said hoarsely. 'I've searched and searched for what made Andy dive into that empty pool, but the answers never come.'

Lawrence prepared another poultice for the exit wound in Christopher's back. 'Some questions we ask have no answers. And some . . . some that we do ask, when we find the answers, they're no longer relevant. This is what I saw when he gave me that liquid, when things opened up inside me. Life moves.' He arranged the poultice on Christopher's back, then tied the two together with strips ripped from his shirt, binding them around Christopher's waist. 'I'm so aware of it because my own life is racing by so fast. And I see this: human beings spend so much time trying to slow life down, but they can't. Because that movement is the nature of things, and it can't be changed. So we've got to, you know, move along, too. I know how much you value the truth, Dad. I know it's sacred to you. Well, this is the Truth.'

Christopher licked his lips. 'The past has consequences. It always does.'

'It seems to me the past is what we make of it,' Lawrence said as he checked the makeshift bandage. He adjusted one of the poultices. 'What is the Pale Saint but a product of his past? He has no present, and he certainly has no future. He's stuck in time, in the moment when the first bad thing happened. Time to move along, Dad.'

He said it in such a simple, pure and unselfconscious way, that Christopher felt something inside him melt, and that melting flooded him with a sudden warmth.

'Get me up,' he said. He gripped Lawrence's offered hand, but he could not lever himself up without Lawrence's help. Sitting up, he became so dizzy he thought for a moment he was going to pass out again. 'Gotta keep going, otherwise he'll get to Sara without us knowing where she is.'

'Look at you, Dad. You'll never make it.'

'No, Lawrence.' Christopher knew what he was thinking. 'Absolutely not.'

'What choice do any of us have? Sara's life hangs in the balance.' Lawrence stood up. 'Let me do what I was born to do.'

Christopher tried to follow him, but couldn't make it.

'Maybe it's fate,' Lawrence said, 'for one of us to kill the other.'

Christopher shifted uneasily, painfully. 'Don't be ridiculous. There's no such thing as fate. Not the way you mean, anyway.'

'Then maybe it's God's will. See, Dad, from the beginning there was one thing we never spoke about: – how this would all end for me. Surely you and Mom knew there would be violence – quite possibly lethal violence – when I finally met the Pale Saint. It's only logical. We're like oil and water – too much alike and too much opposed. Don't you see, there can be no middle ground for us.'

'It's because of that we'll go together,' Christopher said. 'Now help me up.'

Stooping, Lawrence grabbed him under the arms. Christopher pushed back against the bole of a sycamore, using it to help him slide upward, onto his feet. His legs felt like Jell-O, and there was a fire in his side that seemed to rip the breath from his lungs. He stood for a moment, shakily leaning back, Lawrence's shoulder pressed into his sternum for support.

'What is that?'

They paused, smelling ozone and a curious, pungent resinous substance.

A weird light seemed to emanate from between the trees, hovering as if in midair. The light had an ethereal purity, marred only in its center by the outline of a figure. The figure was bent over, almost hunched, almost shaggy, like nineteenth-century illustrations of werewolves. And when it turned so that its face was visible, because of the eerie glow, they could tell it was the Pale Saint. Surely his face was covered in blood.

'Is it a ghost?' Christopher said in a hoarse, reedy whisper. 'An illusion? An apparition?' At the sound of his voice, the figure dissolved, but the odd bobbing light, now disembodied, persevered for several moments still. Then it, too, vanished, leaving them plunged in a heavy, vertiginous gloom.

'He's taken the herbs,' Lawrence said. 'What we just saw . . . That's the manifestation of the shamanistic process. The worst has happened. He's opened the Channel.'

'Sara,' Christopher groaned in despair.

Lawrence nodded. 'Dad, whether you like it or not I have to go.'

Christopher took a step away from the tree, almost fell on his face. 'Oh, hell.' He grabbed the tree bole with one arm. 'Then take this.' He handed Lawrence his gun. 'And, dammit, don't take any chances. Be sure. Get close before you pull the trigger.'

Lawrence nodded. 'I will. Goodbye, Dad.'

Christopher looked at him in anguish. 'God go with you, son.'

Lawrence disappeared almost immediately into the forest. Christopher, for the moment not wanting to think about what was to come, peered into the glade. The deer was still there, serene as moonlight. From the corner of its eye, it seemed to be watching him.

Christopher took a couple of breaths. It felt as if there was a fire in his belly. Clumsily, painfully, he put one foot in front of another. In this halting, agonizing fashion, he went from tree to tree until he moved out into the clearing.

The deer did not budge. It eyed him calmly as he approached. Now Christopher could see the dark patches of the Pale Saint's blood that speckled its back and haunches. He could feel himself falling; his knees began to buckle. He reached out and grabbed hold of a tree limb, and hung there swaying slightly until the deer moved off. It was heading southwest.

Calling on the last of his reserves, Christopher followed. He staggered, fell, got up, kept on going.

'What mischief are you making, little miss?' The Pale Saint kneels over Sara, checking her bonds. 'Trying to weasel your way free?' He observes the cool curve of her cheek, the shadowed eyes, the sensual line of her neck, the steady pulse in the mysterious silver-dollar hollow of her throat, and thinks of Faith. 'Too late.'

He digs up the skull, removing it from its protective coverings, lays it gently, reverently on the wet earth beside him.

Soon, he thinks. *Soon.*

He turns Sara over in the modified fox den and, taking out the vial, uncaps it. 'I had wanted to do this another way, Faith, with Mama watching as you returned to the land of the living. So I could kill her once and for all. Christopher stopped me from bringing Mama here but he won't stop you from being born, Faith.'

He pinches Sara's nose so that she cannot breathe. She writhes and kicks and flops like a landed fish. When all the fight is out of her, he rips off her gag. While she gasps in air through her open mouth, he tips the edge of the vial against her lips. 'Drink,' he intones, 'drink so the Channel between us can be opened.'

She immediately clamps her mouth shut.

'You'll only pass out that way,' he warns. Her eyes stare at him in defiance. 'All right.' Laying a heavy hand on her windpipe, he begins to exert pressure. Sara's eyes open wide. She makes a pain-filled noise deep in her throat. The Pale Saint is about to press harder when his senses, heightened by the herbal mixture he has ingested, pick up a foreign sound.

In one smooth movement, he is up and moving away from her. His gait is hampered by the wound in his thigh, but he has managed to stanch the flow of blood. He moves through the trees, his eyes searching for Christopher. He knows he is there, knows, as well, that it is only a matter of time before he spots him.

'Don't move,' Lawrence says from behind him.

The Pale Saint tries to turn around, but feels the cold steel of a gun muzzle pressed against the base of his skull.

'"Let God arise,"' Lawrence says, quoting from Psalm Sixty-eight, '"let his enemies be scattered; Let them also that hate him flee before him. As smoke is driven away, so drive them away; As wax melteth before the fire, So let the wicked perish at the presence of God."'

The Pale Saint feels the muzzle's pressure like the toe of his mother's boot. He imagines himself a dragonfly whose wings she is about to set on fire. 'Okay, junior. I have to admit, you have me.'

He doubles over, slams his elbow flush into Lawrence's stomach. The gun goes off, he feels a streak of heat as if he had been standing next to a bolt of lightning, and he falls to the forest floor.

Lawrence is on top of him. He pushes the heel of his hand into Lawrence's broken nose and Lawrence reels backward. He kicks the gun, and it disappears into the darkness. Then he regains his feet, begins to stagger back to the fox den and Sara. He takes out the vial.

Lawrence tackles him from behind, and he pitches forward. He's hit on the back of the head, and he loses his grip on the vial.

'No!'

He sees Lawrence gather it up and, in one motion, uncap it and drink down the last of the potion. He punches the clone hard on the jaw, then sits astride him, choking him, hoping the potion won't go down.

But it has; he can feel it. The clone's First Power is rising. Blood covers his face, and the bandage over his nose hangs wet and useless. He strikes the Pale Saint just over the bridge of his nose, dazing him. The Pale Saint is hit again and again, and the world tilts over on its side. He can feel everything slipping away from him. It's over, he knows.

But not yet. He will not give up, he will not go quietly, not unless he takes everyone around him down with him. He deflects Lawrence's next attack and, bulling his way inside the clone's defenses, hits him hard in the kidneys.

Lawrence gives a strangled little cry and falls back into the bloody bed of leaves. Now the Pale Saint has his advantage and he makes the most of it. He puts one arm behind the clone's neck, turns his head to the side, and places the heel of his other hand against the clone's jaw. One swift motion is all it will take, the neck will snap like a tree limb, and it will all be over.

The hate burns in him like a furious engine on overload. He looks down at his own face and like a flock of blackbirds ten thousand thoughts rush by in a welter of sight and sound. He sees again the moment when the trunk at the foot of Mama's bed was opened. He sees the broken lock, the sheriff's hand is lifting up the top as he peers into the depths of Mama's soul.

The Pale Saint, remembering, hesitates for just an instant. Then the fury comes rushing back and he puts all his effort into one final motion.

In that moment of hesitation everything changed. It was no more than the span of time it took for a wing to beat, an eyelid to blink. Time enough for Christopher who, silent as death, had come up behind the two, to drive the Pale Saint's own railroad spike through his back.

With the herbal mixture fueling him, the Pale Saint struck out with fists and legs, trying to get to his antagonist. He gnashed his teeth, snapping his jaws like a crocodile, and fought with an almost superhuman strength. Christopher felt his grip slipping, the last dregs of ferocious energy fueled by rage and fear ebbing. If they were not enough to hold him, the beast would be loosed. The Pale Saint would turn and, even in his death throes, within seconds throttle the life out of him.

The Pale Saint was gaining the upper hand, and now Christopher knew he needed something more than brute strength or animal stamina. They had passed beyond these easily recognizable stages, had entered the sacred inner domain of war where only the heart remained, open and vulnerable to the right form of attack.

'Can you see him on top of Faith in the hayloft?' Christopher whispered as the Pale Saint thrashed and spun beneath him in a frightening adrenaline frenzy. 'Can you see Faith gripping his hips with her legs? Neelon, I can see it, too. I can see him thrusting into her, I can see her thrusting back. Jesus, she's enjoying it . . .'

The Pale Saint's howl rose upward as if to dismember the trees. An owl gave flight on silent wings, its great shadow passing over them. The Pale Saint struck a feverish blow, nearly gouging out Christopher's eye, but Christopher would not let up. And when at last he gained the right position, he leaned his full weight behind the long spike. With a rush and the snapping as if of a massive tree limb, it broke a rib and pierced clear through to the Pale Saint's heart.

The Pale Saint arched up, making one last vain attempt to pull the weapon out of his back. He looked up at the night sky through the canopy of trees, tried to howl again, failed, and toppled backward in a welter of leathery leaves and last leavings of the long dead summer.

Christopher, on his knees, crawled to where Lawrence lay. He cradled the clone in his arms. 'How are you doing?' he said.

'I took the herbs,' he said in a voice as hoarse as a croak. 'I had to to save Sara.'

'It's okay now,' Christopher said. 'It's okay.'

Lawrence struggled to sit up. 'He's still alive.'

Christopher turned, his hands balled into fists.

'No,' Lawrence said. The Pale Saint lay on his back. The spike had

346

gone clear through him, but there was no blood. The force of his will augmented by the herbs was keeping it bound inside him.

'*Princes are hanged up by their hand: the faces of elders were not honored,*' he whispered as soon as he saw the clone. '*They took the young men to grind, and the children fell under the wood.*'

Lawrence recognized the verses from Lamentations. His blood was dripping onto the tip of the railroad spike, onto the ruined chest in which it was buried.

The Pale Saint's voice was very faint, like a wisp of cloud on a clear summer's day. 'Now you know what was in the trunk.' His eyes began to cloud over and now the blood came in a river, a veritable torrent that rose and spread in a darkening pool that threatened to encompass them all.

Before that could happen, Lawrence dragged Christopher away from the bloody corpse, propping him against the bole of a towering cedar. Then he staggered some distance away. Christopher squinted into the gloom. He could hear Lawrence as if he were a large foraging animal. Moments later, Lawrence returned carrying Sara. He had cut her bonds, stripped off her gag. She had her arms clasped tightly around him, her head resting against his chest.

Halfway to where Christopher sat, Lawrence stumbled and fell. Sara gave a little cry as she hit the ground.

Christopher heaved himself painfully away from the support of the tree, crawled to where Lawrence lay. Sara threw herself into his arms.

'Uncle Jon,' she whispered. 'Uncle Jon.'

'It's all right,' he said as he smoothed back her hair. 'It's all over now.'

'But Lawrence . . .' She swung away from him, touched Lawrence's forehead. 'Oh, look what's happened to him. Where's Mom?' She looked around wildly as if they were in the Vertex lab. 'Mom will know how to –'

'Mom tried.' Lawrence's gaze moved from her to Christopher. 'Didn't she, Dad?'

Christopher nodded. 'She tried everything.' Suddenly, he could not breathe. He was thinking of Andy, alone in the chill gloom of the pool, toppling into dead air, into the void.

Sara was crying as she held Lawrence's cheeks. 'Get up,' she whispered. 'Oh, please, Lawrence, get up.'

A shudder, as profound as the ripple of an ocean's tide, passed through him.

347

Christopher dragged himself over, laid Lawrence on his lap.

'Lawrence –'

'Dad, do you smell it?'

Christopher shook his head.

'The forest: the cedars and the sycamores and the elms. The oaks, too. Especially the oaks. They're old, Dad. They'll be here for a long time. Longer than any of us. Gosh, they smell good, don't they?'

'Yes,' Christopher said, 'they do.' Sara was gripping his hand tightly. Tears were streaming down her cheeks.

Seeing her weep, Lawrence said, '"The day is ours; the bloody dog is dead,"' quoting *Richard III* again.

'"Courageous Richmond, well hast thou acquit thee,"' she replied, and placed a handful of golden oak leaves on his forehead. '"Lo, here this long usurpèd royalty From the dead temples of this bloody wretch, Have I plucked off, to grace thy brows withal. Wear it, enjoy it, and make much of it."'

'Ah, Sara.' He smiled, and looked at Christopher. 'Is she right? Did I do good, Dad?'

Christopher, his heart breaking, said, 'You did great.'

He could feel Lawrence's life pulsing in his hands, perhaps just as strongly as Cassandra had felt it at the moment of Lawrence's birth. Had he ever felt the enormity of life from Andy? Had he ever held his son in this loving way, feeling the blood rush through his veins, the air beating like wings in and out of his lungs, his heart pumping to its own distinct rhythm? He could not remember.

'I accomplished something,' Lawrence said. 'Now I will be redeemed.' He closed his eyes for a moment. 'It's good I'm here now. In the forest. It's so peaceful, isn't it? Not like the city, a hive of bees too busy making honey to see anything important.' He opened his eyes. 'I'm so lucky, Dad.'

'To know all of that.' Christopher nodded. 'Yes. Very lucky.' He was rocking Lawrence a little. 'Don't worry, I'm here,' he said. 'I'll catch you when you fall.'

Lawrence smiled. 'And I will fall so very far, won't I?'

'No one knows.'

'I know.' He sighed, a long, shuddering rale that made it sound as if all the bones in his body were clashing together.

'Lawrence –'

'It's okay, Dad. Really. See, it's right that this should happen. Living at light speed, it's not right. It shouldn't happen again. I know it and

348

you know it. Nature has its own laws that cannot be broken or even bent a little.' He smiled again. 'For all she provides, that's fair enough, don't you think?'

He was going. Christopher, so close to him now that it seemed as if their very molecules had meshed, could feel it. Like the tide ebbing back out to sea. Lawrence's life was draining away into that mysterious place where no living being could follow.

'Lawrence!' Still, Christopher could not let him go. He waited until the clone's eyes focused on him. 'Lawrence, I want you to know . . . I'm proud of you.' His tears fell as he wept unashamedly.

'"Now civil wounds are stopped, peace lives again . . ."' he began, then faltered.

'"That she may long live here, God say amen!"' Sara finished for him.

A monumental spasm seized him. 'Catch me, Dad.' His whispered voice stole through the forest. 'Catch me, I'm falling.'

EPILOGUE

Seven weeks later, Christopher and Cassandra were again upstate. It was close to Christmas, and it was snowing, whiteness filtering down from heaven out of the white sky. The air was cold and crisp and, mixed with woodsmoke and fir resin, it sure smelled like the holidays. Kenny had loaned them his cottage for as long as they wanted it.

A week after Lawrence's death, while Christopher was still in the hospital following surgery to clean and repair the puncture wound in his side, Cassandra took Sara to the Animal Rescue League where she picked out a muscular Boxer named Butch. It was Cassandra, as well, who told Christopher that as a result of Koenig's injury his career as a televangelist was at an end. The artificial larynx which had been surgically installed had withered his voice to the brittle rattle of blown desert sand.

Sara had come daily during Christopher's convalescence. He had learned from Cassandra that she had gone into crisis therapy to help her deal with her kidnapping. She read Shakespeare to him and brought him his favorite mint chocolate-chip ice cream to go with the cookies she'd baked. They spoke of music and baseball, but really what she wanted to talk about was Lawrence and the Pale Saint. When it came to these subjects Christopher was content to let her tell him what was on her mind. As she spoke, he was reminded of Myra Woods' reading of the Parable of the Two Figs. Good and Evil, Evil and Good. They might appear the same, but that was as far as it went. Still, because most people couldn't be bothered to look beneath the surface it wasn't always so easy to tell one from the other. Sara wasn't one of them. When she recounted to him her long talks with Lawrence about God, sin, and the nature of redemption, he had said: 'Lawrence was lucky to have you as a friend.'

'And I'm lucky as well,' she said. 'He helped me understand how important my family is to me. I spent much too much time being pissed off at my folks. Now I can't even tell Dad how I felt about him. I'm not gonna make that mistake with Mom.'

Later, he remarked on these changes to Cassandra.

'She's no longer isolated and alone,' Cassandra had said. 'She feels part of a family.' She stroked his cheek. 'She and I are spending more time together, and it's all because of Lawrence. They bonded in a unique way. In a sense, he was precisely what she needed. He grounded her, allowed her to see her place in the world.'

'I agree,' Christopher had said. 'At last she's finding out who she is.'

But as for Cassandra herself, what was she thinking? There wasn't a day that went by that Christopher didn't try to get her to talk about her feelings for Lawrence. Steadfastly, she refused to say a word, so at last he stopped asking her.

Almost from the moment he'd recovered sufficiently, Chief Brockaw put him on the high-profile media circuit. After appearances on the *Today Show*, *Larry King Live*, the *Charles Grodin Show*, *Rivera Live*, where he shared opinions with the psychic who had first named the Pale Saint, and the *Charlie Rose Show*, he felt he had to draw the line somewhere. He refused to take Sara on *Oprah*, he turned down an offer from the producers of *America's Most Wanted* to host a new program they had designed around his expertise in serial killers, and had declined to consult on a quickie TV Movie-of-the-Week hideously titled, *The Saint that Killed*. But he'd agreed to write a book, his memoirs of the case, even though he reckoned it would take a fiction writer's skills to bring it off. Predictably, HBO and a couple of the major movie studios were nosing around for an advance look.

Christopher was grateful to leave all that behind.

In a few days, on Christmas Eve, Sara would come up to join them. But for the moment, he and Cassandra were blissfully alone. In the first week of January, they were to be wed in a small ceremony just for the family and a few friends. Absurdly, because of Christopher's new-found celebrity, their plans had to be laid out with the secrecy of the D-Day invasion.

They went out together daily. Sometimes they took the car to go shopping for presents for each other and Sara, other times they just walked. Christopher's surgery had gone well, and he was insistent on exercising each day. Sometimes, however, Cassandra made sure it was of a distinctly indoor nature. During those bouts in the bed, on the bathroom floor, in the kitchen, it was up to her to see that he didn't re-injure himself.

Even so, he was happiest simply being outdoors. The fresh, clean air exhilarated him, and gradually the stress, intensity, publicity attention, the job myopia that others might term obsession – all the detritus engendered like oily soot by the city – fell away from him, leaving underneath a happier, freer man.

Gradually, they increased the length of their walks. They moved from well-known roads clogged with traffic, to narrow country lanes frequented only by locals, to hard-packed paths where barely a car or truck passed them by. At last, there came a day when they abandoned the last vestiges of civilization for the pathless woods itself.

Amid the trees, the foraging gray squirrels, the querulous winter grackles massing overhead, they felt most comfortable, most alone, most themselves.

Christopher hardly felt any pain, and they pushed onward, confident in their ability to find their way home. Just past noon, they stopped to drink some water out of their plastic bottles, and eat a Spartan lunch of bread and cheese. Afterward, they crunched contentedly into apples. They pushed on and, after about a half a mile, they broke through a high bramble and found themselves looking at a pond, frozen over. Christopher took Cassandra out on it. They knelt on the ice, bending over so that they could peer through it, into the depths where the dark shadows of sleeping fish hung suspended like preserved apricots in honey.

Cassandra was thinking of Bobby, sorrow mingling with a kind of wonder. It astonished her how different they had been from one another. This admission somehow made her feel closer to him, just as it helped to cauterize the hurt. Christopher was thinking of Andy. In his mind, he spoke to him as a father does to his son. It felt good, because he didn't ask Andy the question he had always asked him from the moment he had learned of Andy's dive into the dry pool: *Why?* That was one mystery he would never solve. As he spoke to Andy in his mind, he had a sense the bitter edge of guilt would in time fade if not disappear altogether.

He squeezed her hand. 'Do you remember what you said to me, that Lawrence was born to seek out the Pale Saint and to confront him. In the end, whatever happened was between them.'

'Oh, God, Jon, I hope to Christ Lawrence was born for more than just that.'

'Born, no,' Christopher said as he climbed over a gnarled root that had risen up out of the ground like a restless spirit. 'But he grew into something more, didn't he?'

She turned away, silent as the snow drifting down.

'Cass,' he said, coming after her, 'you've got to talk about it sometime.'

She nodded. 'I know, but . . .' She shuddered and he held her close. At length, she put her head on his shoulder. 'Why couldn't I have saved him? Even in my dreams, I keep asking myself that one question. Why?'

'Because you're not God.'

'Oh, Jon, cut the crap.'

'No, I mean it.' He turned her toward him. 'Listen, I can't count the number of times since Andy's suicide that I asked myself: why did he do it? Why wasn't I there to save him? Why did it have to happen? *Why?*' He looked deep into her eyes. 'It was Lawrence who taught me to stop asking a question that has no answer. It's not our purview to know the answer. Just like it's not yet in our purview to make a creature like Lawrence. Oh, we know we can; the theory's been there for years, and you proved it. But the fact remains we aren't ready to face the complex questions his existence demands of us.'

Her eyes closed. 'I feel like I failed him.' But the bitterness was already leaching out of her voice.

'You know that's not true. Just like I know I didn't fail Andy. We both did the best we could. We failed to keep them alive; we didn't fail them.' He tipped her head up to him and her eyes opened, beautiful and luminous in the winter's pearly dusk. 'There's a world of difference between the two.'

Slowly, they walked hand in hand back toward the cottage. For a long time, Cassandra appeared lost in thought. At last, she said, 'Jon, this is difficult and painful for me to say, but I've come to realize that all my professional life I've been dependent on men. My first theoretical papers were published because they were championed by Digger McKay, my mentor at school, my career leapt ahead because the chief gerontologist at NYU Medical hired me and fought for my programs during budget cuts. Then Gerry Costas made me an offer I couldn't refuse, and now Ken Reinisch wants to be my sugar daddy.'

They crossed over a small, wooden bridge. The snow here had been turned to slick slush by the vehicular traffic, and they had to pick their way with extreme care.

'And d'you know, last year or even six months ago I would have jumped at Reinisch's offer. Even knowing it was the result of the squeeze he put on Gerry, because Gerry's turned out to be such a shit. But not now. This is what Lawrence has taught me. Even though it must have been so very hard for him, in every step of his life he had the courage to abide by the moral laws you taught him.'

She took his hand again as they came off the bridge into deep snow. 'All these years I've had it soft. It will be much harder for me to go out on my own. I'll have to learn how to fund-raise –' she laughed '– and schmooze a little as I try to convince the money people I'm a good investment. I worked for years for Gerry and what do I have to show for it? Nothing. At least now, whatever I do will be for myself.'

'Sounds like you'll be back working night and day.'

'Oh, no. Not on your life. Bringing up Lawrence made me see how Bobby and I shortchanged Sara. But, see, I never thought I could do anything else but run a lab. I didn't think I had it in me to be a mother; well, I see I was wrong. Whatever I decide to do, however I decide to do it will be balanced with time for my family.'

Christopher, who had gotten a little winded, called a temporary halt. They were surrounded by snow-laden oaks and sycamores. 'You should tell all this to Sara,' he said. 'I think she'll be excited to be part of the process.' He laughed. 'You know how she likes change.'

Cassandra laughed, too, and kissed him hard. 'Jon, us being together out here in the woods, it seems like a dream.'

That was when they came upon the deer. Later, Cassandra would claim that it was the same one that had led Christopher to the Pale Saint that night. Last year or even six months ago, Christopher would have dismissed that notion as pure fantasy, but not now. It was, indeed, a young buck with velveteen antlers. And for a fact it was searching for something. Its large, soft, dark eyes scanned the whiteness, its nostrils trembling as if it were on the verge of a truth long hidden and since forgotten. Snow fell on its back and melted into dew. Breath emerged from it as it did from a child, pure and sweet, unsullied by anger, envy or resentment.

Keeping upwind, they spent the better part of the early afternoon following it. But it never found what it was looking for, and they never discovered what it might be. In the waning light of late afternoon, they headed back. Even so, they'd left it too long, and the sudden, complete darkness of a winter evening overtook them. They found the highway and thumbed a lift from an old farmer coming back from doing his

Christmas shopping. While they were grateful for the lift, the moment they spied his headlights coming at them out of the snow, they both felt a small sadness, and wished him gone. His truck smelled of manure and caramel. When he dropped them off a hundred yards from Kenny's place, he wished them happy holidays and they wished him the same.

As Christopher and Cassandra walked slowly back down the snow-covered path to Kenny's cottage, she said, 'What d'you think that deer was searching for?'

Christopher turned and looked back up the path for a moment. 'We'll never know what was in the deer's heart.'

They had the presents laid out under the tree by the time they arrived at the cottage from the bus depot with Sara. But they had waited to trim the tree. Now everyone chipped in, hanging lights and baubles, stringing dried cranberries and plump yellow popcorn, dropping tinsel everywhere, and trying with a laugh to keep Butch from knocking over the tree. Cassandra had heated hot local cider, spiced with cinnamon and nutmeg and all manner of things, and Sara set about baking Toll House cookies with red and green M&Ms embedded alongside the chocolate chips. Butch gnawed deliriously and noisily on a T-bone Christopher had saved for him from a previous dinner. The cottage was warm and bright and smelled delicious.

'It's time,' Sara said.

They all trooped out into the blue winter twilight. Rimes of ice glowed like diadems at the bottom of the sea. Sara helped Christopher clear snow away from the spot where they had buried Lawrence. The only marker was inside their heads.

Christopher delivered his armload of dry wood to the spot and Sara lighted the fire. It cracked and sparked, reflecting itself on all their faces.

When it was well established, Sara dug in the pocket of her parka and drew out the baseball she had given Lawrence. Christopher looked at Sara, and she nodded, as if they had previously arranged this part of the ritual. He threw it into the fire. For an instant, the flames licked up as if eager to devour whatever was inside the baseball.

Then the baseball itself was gone.

For a time, Cassandra stood at the foot of the grave. The tall trees sighed in a brief gust of wind. A shower of snow fell upon them. Cassandra knelt down and, tugging off her gloves, warmed her hands on the last remaining flames.

'I can feel him,' she said as Christopher and Sara, standing behind her, put their hands on her shoulders.

Christopher turned his face upward to the star-strewn night sky and breathed deeply of the scent of snow-laden cedars. 'We all can,' he said.